AFTERPARTY

Daryl Gregory

AFTERPARTY

A Tom Doherty Associates Book  New York

AFTERPARTY

Copyright © 2014 by Daryl Gregory

A Tor Book
Published by Tom Doherty Associates, LLC
175 Fifth Avenue
New York, NY 10010

www.tor-forge.com

Tor® is a registered trademark of Tom Doherty Associates, LLC.

Library of Congress Cataloging-in-Publication Data

Gregory, Daryl.
  Afterparty / Daryl Gregory.
      p. cm.
  ISBN 978-0-7653-3692-7 (hardcover)
  ISBN 978-1-4668-2928-2 (e-book)
  1. Drug abuse—Fiction.   2. Science fiction.   I. Title.
  PS3607.R48836A69   2014
  813'.6—dc23

                        2013025194

Tor books may be purchased for educational, business, or promotional use. For information on bulk purchases, please contact Macmillan Corporate and Premium Sales Department at 1-800-221-7945, extension 5442, or write specialmarkets@macmillan.com.

First Edition: April 2014

Printed in the United States of America

0 9 8 7 6 5 4 3 2 1

For Jack

If some great Power would agree to make me always think what is true and do what is right, on condition of being turned into a sort of clock and wound up every morning before I got out of bed, I should instantly close with the offer.

—T. H. Huxley

And he said unto them, Unto you it is given to know the mystery of the kingdom of God: but unto them that are without, all these things are done in parables.

—Mark 4:11

AFTERPARTY

THE PARABLE OF

the Girl Who Died and Went to Hell,
Not Necessarily in That Order

There was a girl who lived on the streets in a northern city. She was sixteen years old when she found God, and had just turned seventeen when God abandoned her.

She didn't understand why He would turn His back on her now, after He had saved her life. She'd been living rough for two years. At night she navigated by bunk-finder apps, competing for space in the shelters with the thousands of other teenagers roaming the city. She did bad things to get by. She worked the crowded sidewalks, beaming her profile pic to the dashboards of the trolling cars, climbing into front seats and climbing out again fifteen minutes later. She stole, and she beat other teenagers who tried to steal from her, and once she did something terrible, something unforgivable.

When she thought of what she'd done, even glancingly, a black tunnel seemed to open up behind her eyes. Anything might trigger the memory: a word, the sight of an old woman, the smell of soup burning on a stove. On those days she thought the black would swallow her whole.

Then one night, at the end of a week of black days, she found herself in the Spadina station looking over the edge of the platform, measuring the short distance to the rails. She could feel the train coming, growling to her, pushing its hot breath down the tracks. The concrete rumbled encouragement to her feet. She moved up to the yellow line, and the toes of her sneakers touched air. The only way out of the black tunnel, she realized, was through it.

She felt a hand on her arm. "Hey there." It was a friend, one of her first on the street, a tall black boy older than her by a few years who maintained a crazy rectangular beard. He said, "You doing anything?"

She didn't know how to answer that.

She followed him up out of the station. A while later, an older man with hardcore prison tattoos picked them up in a rusting SUV and drove them a few miles to a strip mall. Most of the stores were empty. The man, who said he was a pastor, opened one of the doors and said, "Welcome to our little church."

People began to filter in and take seats in the circle of folding chairs. The service began with singing, songs she didn't know but that sounded familiar. And then the pastor stood in the middle of the circle for the sermon. He turned as he talked, making eye contact with the people, making eye contact with *her*, which made her uncomfortable. She couldn't remember now what he'd spoken about.

At the end of the service, everyone stood up and formed a line in front of the pastor, their hands out, mouths open like birds. Her friend looked at her questioningly; it was her decision. She stood up with the others, and when it was her turn the pastor held up a piece of paper with a single word printed on it: *Logos*. "This is the word made flesh," he said.

She wasn't stupid. She'd eaten paper before, and knew that the ink could contain almost anything. She opened her mouth, and he placed it on her tongue. The paper dissolved like cotton candy.

She felt nothing. If there was anything mixed into the ink or the paper, it was too mild to affect her.

That night, as she lay on a bed in a shelter that the pastor had lined up for her, the black tunnel was still there. But there was something else, too: a feeling, as if she were being watched.

No: watched over.

She made her way back to the church the next day, and the day after that. The feeling of a loving presence grew like sun rising over her shoulder. The pastor called it the Numinous. "It's knowledge," he said. Proof that we are all loved, all connected.

Her problems weren't solved. She still slept in restaurant bathrooms, and lifted snacks from gas stations, and gave blow jobs to men in cars. Still struggled with the black tunnel. But she could not shake that secret knowledge that she was loved. She could not yet forgive herself, but she began to think that someone else might.

One night, a month after that first church service, just a few days before her birthday, the cops swept through the park, and she was arrested for solicitation. Because she was underage, they would not release her until they found her parents. She wouldn't help the police; the last thing she wanted was to let her parents know where she was. God, she thought, would provide a way out of this.

But as the days passed in the detention center, something was changing. God's presence faded, as if He was moving away from her, turning His back on her. She began to panic. She prayed, and wept, and prayed some more. Then a female guard caught her creating her own sacrament, swallowing scraps of toilet paper, and thought she had smuggled in smart drugs. They took her blood and swabbed her tongue and made her pee in a cup. Two days later they transferred her to a hospital west of the city, and locked her up with crazy people.

On her second night in the hospital, a red-haired woman appeared in her room. She seemed familiar, and then suddenly the girl remembered her. "You let me sleep on your couch once."

The woman stepped into the room. Her red hair, the girl saw now, was shot with threads of gray. "Wasn't my idea," the woman said. "But yeah."

It had been ten below, and the red-haired woman had found her shivering outside a gas station. The girl had thought the woman wanted sex, but no; she'd fed her pizza and let her spend the night, and the girl had slipped out of the apartment before morning. It was the kindest thing a stranger had ever done for her, until she met the pastor.

"What are you doing here?" the woman asked. Her voice was soft. "What did you take?"

How could she explain that she'd taken nothing? That they'd locked her up because she'd finally realized that God was real?

"I've lost it," the girl said. "I've lost the Numinous."

The woman seemed shocked at the word, as if she recognized it. Perhaps she was part of the church? The girl told her her story, and the woman seemed to understand. But then the woman asked questions that proved she didn't understand at all: "This pastor—did he tell you the name of the drug? Where he got it? How long have you been in withdrawal?"

The black tunnel seemed to throw itself open, and the girl refused to say any more. After a time the red-haired woman went away, and the nurses came to her with pills that they said would help her with her depression, her anxiety. A psychologist brought her to his office—"just to talk."

But she did not need antidepressants, or soothing conversation. She understood, finally, why God had withdrawn from her. What He was trying to tell her.

When she was full of God's love, she couldn't do what she needed to do. God *had* to step back so that she'd have the strength to do what she should have done months ago. So she could make the required sacrifice.

At her next meeting with the psychologist, she stole a ceramic mug from his desk. He never noticed; she was practiced at lifting merchandise. An hour after that, before she could lose her nerve, she went to the bathroom and smashed the mug against the edge of the stainless steel sink. She chose the largest shard, then sawed apart the veins in her left arm.

God, she knew, helps those who help themselves.

—G.I.E.D.

CHAPTER ONE

"So you want to leave us, Lyda?" Counselor Todd asked.

"It's been eight months," I said. "I think it's about time, don't you?"

Dr. Gloria shook her head, then made a note on her clipboard.

The three of us—Todd, Dr. Gloria, and I—sat in Todd's closet-sized office in the NAT ward. Three chairs, a pressed wood coffee table, and no windows. Todd leaned back in his chair, flicking his smart pen: *snick* and the screen opened like a fan; *clack* and it rolled up again. The file on the screen appeared and disappeared too fast to read, but I could guess what document it was.

Todd liked to portray himself as a man of the people. A white man who favored work shirts that had never seen a day of work and work boots that had never touched mud. This in contrast to Dr. Gloria, who occupied the seat to his right. She believed in the traditional uniform of doctors: white coat, charcoal pencil skirt, femme heels that weren't so high as to be impractical. Her nondigital clipboard and Hot Librarian glasses were signature props. I did not want her in this meeting, but neither Todd nor I had the power to keep her out.

"Lyda," Todd said in a knowing tone. "Does your desire to leave now have anything to do with Francine's death?"

Francine was the girl who had killed herself with Todd's mug. I presented my I'm-not-quite-following-you frown.

"The transfer request was placed two weeks ago, on the day after she died," Todd said. "You seemed upset by her death."

"I barely knew her."

"You broke *furniture*," he said.

"It was a plastic chair," I said. "It already had a crack in it."

"Don't quibble," Dr. Gloria said. "It's the display of anger he's worried about."

"I was mad at you doctors," I said. "I told you to put her on antidepressants—"

"Which we did," Todd said.

"Too Goddamn late. Jesus, her symptoms were obvious. I couldn't believe no one had taken steps. Her parents should be suing the hospital's ass off right now."

"We haven't been able to find them," he said.

"Perfect. Homeless orphans can't sue either."

Dr. Gloria put down her clipboard. "Insulting everyone who works here isn't going to help you."

"I'm sorry," I said. "It's just—she was so young."

"I know," Counselor Todd said. He sounded suddenly tired. "I tried to talk to her."

Todd could be an idiot, but he did care about the patients. And as the only full-time counselor on the ward, he worked essentially alone. The neuro-atypical ward was a lab for the hardcore cog-sci docs, the neuro-psych researchers. They didn't much care for talk therapy, or for talking therapists like Todd.

So as Todd became more isolated, he couldn't help but grow attached to the people he spent the most time with: The patients had become, without him realizing it, his cohort, his troop. I knew that my degrees intimidated him. He suspected that because of my résumé I was more aligned with the neuropsych folks—which was true. But my highfalutin background also made him secretly desire my approval. Sometimes I used my power to get the lab to do the right thing for the patients, but I wasn't above using it to get myself out of here.

Todd did his best to pull himself back to counselor mode. "Were you disturbed by Francine's symptoms?"

"How so?"

"They were so similar to your own. The religious nature of her hallucinations—"

"A lot of schizos have religious delusions."

"She wasn't schizophrenic, at least not naturally. We believe she'd been taking a designer drug."

"Which one?"

"We haven't figured that out yet. But I was struck by the way she talked about God as a physical presence. That was how you used to speak about your angel."

Dr. Gloria looked at me over her glasses. This was her favorite topic. I stopped myself from glaring at her.

"I've been symptom free for months," I said to Todd. "No angels. No voices in my head. I didn't think the antipsychotics you prescribed would work, honestly. My hallucination's been so persistent, so long, that . . ." I shrugged. "But you were right, and I was wrong. I'm not too proud to admit that."

"I thought they were worth a try," he said. "When you showed up here, you were in a pretty bad place. Not just your injuries."

"Oh no," I said, agreeing with him. "It was everything. I was fucked up." I'd been sentenced to the NAT after creating my own drive-thru at a convenience store. I swerved off the road at 60 KPH and plowed through the wall at three in the afternoon. My front bumper crushed a woman's leg and sent another man flying, but nobody was killed. The owner told a reporter that "somebody up there was watching out for them."

God gets the easiest performance reviews.

I said, "I feel like I've finally gotten a handle on my problems."

I glanced up. I'd delivered this statement with all the sincerity I could muster. Todd seemed to be taking it in. Then he said, "Have you been thinking about your wife?"

A question as subtle as a crowbar. Counselor Todd trying to pop me open.

Dr. G said, "He noticed that you're touching your ring."

I glanced down. The wedding band was polished brass, six-sided on the outside. A friend of ours had forged a matching pair for us.

I placed my hands on the arms of my chair. "I think of her every day," I said. "But not obsessively. She's my wife. I miss her."

Perhaps this struck him as an odd thing to say about a woman who had tried to kill me. Instead he said, "It's interesting that you use the present tense."

"She *has* been dead almost ten years," Dr. Gloria said.

"I don't believe that there's a time limit on love or grief," I said. A paraphrase of something Counselor Todd had told me very earnestly in my first month on the ward. I was detoxing then, vulnerable and wide open, sucking in Todd's bromides as if they were profound truths. When you can't get the heroin, take the methadone.

"And your child?" he asked.

I sat back, my heart suddenly beating hard. "Are you working through a checklist there?"

"You're sounding angry again," Dr. Gloria said.

Todd said, "You mentioned her only once in our therapy sessions, but according to your file . . ."

If he flicked open that damn pen I was going to leap across the table at him.

"I don't have a child," I said.

Dr. Gloria looked over her glasses at me, the Medical Professional version of an eye roll.

"Anymore," I said.

Todd pursed his lips, signaling disappointment. "I'm sorry, Lyda, I just can't sign off on this. I think you're trying to get out of here so you can score, and you still haven't addressed some key issues in—"

"I'll take the chip."

He looked up at me, surprised.

"The terms of my sentence give me the option," I said. "All you have to do is sign. You know I've been a model patient."

"But you're almost done here. Two more months and you're out. If you go on the chip, that's a mandatory year of tracking. You won't be able to leave the province without permission."

"I understand that."

He gave me a long look. "You know they can't be spoofed, yes? Not like the old chips. Your blood alcohol levels will be sent to us every ten seconds. Anything stronger than aspirin throws up a red flag. And any use of a controlled substance, other than those prescribed to you, gets immediately reported to the police."

"Any drug can and will be used against me," I said. "Got it."

"Good. Because the last time I brought up the chip, you told me I could shove it up my ass."

"Well, it *is* very small."

He suppressed a smile. Todd enjoyed being joked with. Made him feel part of the troop. And as the least insane person on the floor (if I said so myself), I was the person he could most easily talk to. The only question was, would he be insecure enough to keep me here, just so we didn't have to—sob—break up?

Time to seal the deal. I looked at my feet, feigning embarrassment. "I know this may not be technically allowed after I leave, but . . ."

"This room is a safe place to say anything," Todd said.

I looked up. "I'd like to keep in touch with you. If that's all right."

"I'm sure that would be fine," Todd said. "If I sign on for this." But of course he had already made up his mind.

. . .

The NAT ward was small, a population of twenty-five to forty, depending on the season. News traveled the floor with telepathic speed. Two of the residents believed they *were* telepathic, so who knows.

I was packing when Ollie appeared in my room. Five foot two, hair falling across her face. Quiet as a closed door. And like everyone on the ward, Severely Fucked in the Head.

She stared into the room, eyes pointed in my direction. Trying to work out the puzzle. That stack of shapes probably belonged to one thing, those horizontal shapes to something else. Once sorted, labels could be applied: bed, wall, duffel bag, human being.

To help her out I said, "Hi, Ollie."

Her face changed—that slight shift of recognition as she assigned the label "Lyda" to an arrangement of red hair and dark clothes—then went still again. She was angry. I'd made a mistake by not telling her I was leaving. Not as big a mistake as sleeping with her, but enough.

At last she said, "Can I see it?"

"Sure," I said. Ollie concentrated on the changes in the scene: The object that swung toward her in her visual field must be, logically, my arm. From there she found my wrist, and slid a finger along my forearm. Tactile information integrated more easily than the visual. She peeled back the Band-Aid, pressed the tiny pink bump. She was as unself-conscious with my body as with her own.

"So small," she said.

"My new portable conscience," I said. "Like I needed another one."

Her fingers lingered on my skin, then fell away. "You're going to look for that dead girl's dealer."

I didn't try to deny it. Even on meds Ollie was the smartest person I'd ever met, after Mikala.

She closed her eyes, cutting out the visual distraction. She looked like a little girl. Told me once that her Filipino mother was 4'10", her white Minnesota father over six feet, and she was still waiting for those Norwegian genes to kick in.

"You can't know that it's the same drug that hit you," she said without opening her eyes. "There are thousands of countertop tweakers out there. Somebody just happened to whip up something with the same symptoms."

The glories of the DIY smart drug revolution. Any high school student with a chemjet and an internet connection could download recipes and print small-batch drugs. The creative types liked to fuck with the recipes, try them out on their friends. People swallowed paper all the time without knowing what they were chewing. Half the residents of the NAT ward weren't addicts; they were beta testers.

"You're right," I said flatly. "It's probably not the same drug at all."

She opened her eyes. Now seeing right through me. "I can help you," she said.

There was a certainty in her voice. Ollie used to do things for the US government, and the US government used to do things to Ollie.

"I don't think they're going to let you walk out of here," I said. Ollie was not one of the voluntary patients. Like me, she'd been convicted of a crime, then sent here because the docs thought she was an interesting case. "Just stay here," I said. "And heal."

Heal. That was a NAT joke.

She said, "I can be out of here in two—"

"Nurse," I said in a low voice, warning her. We residents did this a lot on the ward, like kids playing in the street calling "car."

"Seconds," Ollie finished.

Dr. Gloria and one of the day-shift nurses walked toward the room. "Ready?" the nurse asked me.

Dr. G looked at Ollie, then back toward me, a knowing smile on her face. "If you're all done here," she said.

I picked up my bag. "I've got to go," I said to Ollie. I touched her shoulder on the way out. This is me, the touch told her. This is me moving away from you.

· · ·

"She's in love with you, you know," Dr. G said.

"Hospital infatuation," I said.

We stood on the sidewalk outside the hospital, waiting for my ride under a gray sky leaking sunlight. Dirty snow banked the sidewalk, peppered with black deicer pellets. Behind us, staff and visitors passed in and out of the revolving doors like ions through a membrane.

I folded up the plastic bag that contained my prescription and jammed my hands into the pockets of my thin jacket. It had been early fall when I went in, and my street clothes had failed to evolve while in storage. But I was not about to go back inside that building, even to stay warm. I was a free woman—tethered only by the plastic snitch attached to my vein, broadcasting each taste of my bloodstream to the ether.

Dr. G had followed me out. "You'd be better off staying with her and finishing your sentence inside," she said. "Less temptation. You were staying clean, Lyda."

"Edo's making NME One-Ten."

"You don't know that."

"All Francine could talk about was 'the Numinous.' That is no fucking coincidence. Edo broke his promise."

"He never made that promise," she said.

"Yeah, well, I made a promise to *him*."

"Listen to yourself," Dr. Gloria said. "You're pissed off. Have you considered that you're overreacting to the girl's death? You have a blind spot for little lost girls."

"Fuck off."

"Lyda—"

"I'm responsible for the drug that killed her."

"Even if the substance *is* the One-Ten, which is doubtful, that doesn't mean that it's Edo Vik."

"Then I guess I have to find out who *is* making it."

A car pulled up to the curb, a decrepit Nissan hybrid. The cost of the gas had to be enormous. The driver jumped out of the car, ran to me with arms out. "Lyda!"

Bobby was a could-have-been-handsome white boy, twenty-three years old, with stiff black hair and almond eyes, so maybe a little Asian in the mix. A former ward-mate, and batshit crazy. But a good kid. More importantly, he lived in Toronto, and he owned a car.

I let him hug me. The price to pay for the ride.

"You look all healthy," he said. Hanging from a leather thong around his neck was a small plastic treasure chest, one of those aquarium accessories with *Real Working Hinge*. He never went anywhere without it.

"Where are we going?" he asked me.

"Take me to my dealer."

He blinked in surprise. "Uh, are you sure?"

"Relax. I just want to talk to him."

"You just got out of the ward. Don't you want to go home?"

"I don't have a home. That apartment is long gone."

"Oh, then maybe a hotel?"

"I'm getting cold out here, Bobby."

He opened the passenger door for me, then hustled around to the other side.

Dr. Gloria said, "I can't protect you if you don't listen to me."

"Then stay here."

"Oh, you don't get away that easy." Dr. Gloria's wings unfurled from her back with a snap, and the world vanished in a blaze of heavenly radiance. I winced and looked away.

"Lo, I am with you always," she said. I opened one eye. She pulsed like a migraine aura, throwing off megawatts of holy glow. Then her wings convulsed, and she was airborne.

CHAPTER TWO

We rode into Toronto on the 401 with Dr. Gloria flying point: a star to guide us. Bobby couldn't see her, of course. The doctor was *my* permanent hallucination, a standing wave thrown up by my temporal lobe and supported by various other members of my mental parliament. My supernatural companion was a fake, but unlike Francine, I knew it.

We left the highway and dropped south toward the lake. I rolled down the window, and cold wind filled the car.

"What are you doing?" Bobby asked.

I tossed out the bag containing my prescription bottles. "Ballast," I said.

"What?"

"Eyes on the road, kid." He slowed as we entered the university campus. It was a Wednesday, the start of the college weekend, so Brandy, my old dealer, would be working the frats. We cruised past Victorian houses lit up and vibrating with heavy bass. College boys in shorts stood outside, ankle deep in the snow. Girls in microdresses teetered on high heels across the icy sidewalks. Bobby drove slow, one hand on the treasure chest and the other on the wheel, while I kept an eye out for Brandy's vehicle, a beat-up VW delivery van. Twice we jerked to a stop as drunken kids lurched into the street.

"Jesus Christ, pull over," I said.

"Why are you mad?"

"You're distracted. You keep playing with yourself."

He let go of the treasure chest. "No I'm not."

His first week on the NAT ward, Bobby shyly explained to me that he used to live *up here*—he poked a finger at the spot between his eyes—but now he lived *in there*—the plastic chest. Most of us have the illusion that our consciousness sits behind our eyes like a little woman at the controls—very handy for steering a body, or a car. Bobby, however, thought he lived inside an aquarium toy. Who the hell knew what that did to your reflexes?

I climbed out of the car. A few feet away, Dr. Gloria descended in a nimbus of righteousness. She folded her wings, adjusted her glasses. "Of course," she said. "If you want to find a drug dealer, go to a college."

"Higher education," I said. We were in front of a row of rundown frat houses that I assumed looked more glamorous through the alcohol-blurred eyes of the young. I walked up to a group of boys, all holding red plastic cups. "I'm looking for a guy named Brandy," I said.

They ignored me. I smacked the nearest one in the shoulder, and he jerked away from me, sending a fan of piss-colored beer across the snow. The other boys fell out laughing.

I pointed to the next closest kid. "Where's Brandy?"

"Are you her mom?"

"It's a guy," I said. "Brandy. Deals specialty stuff."

"Narc!" one of them said. Another of them took it up, quacking like a duck. "Narc! Narc!"

"Yes, very good. You've penetrated my disguise. Now where the fuck is he?"

The guy I'd whacked said, "Sigma Tau maybe?"

"Yeah! The GFD party."

Most of them pointed in the same direction.

"Thanks, boys."

I waved Bobby over to me, and the three of us walked the street, reading the giant Greek letters on the fronts of the buildings. Every house was rocking, the parties spilling outside. Scent trails of marijuana etched the cold air.

A boy burst out the front door of the Sigma Tau house, threw up his hands, and screamed a war cry. He was skinny and naked but for a pair of flip-flops, grinning madly, with an erection like a wall sconce. He jumped down the steps, and half a dozen naked boys charged after him, hooting, beer sloshing from red cups. They ran straight at us, hard-ons first, like a herd of rhinos.

"Oh geez," Bobby said. The stampede broke around us. The lead boy ran for the corner, white ass shining, with the frat brothers in pursuit.

"GFD," Dr. Gloria said, getting it now. "Gay for a Day."

"Maybe we could come back later," Bobby said nervously.

I marched up the steps. The party was going full tilt. The crowd was all boys, many of them naked, others in boxers and tighty-whities and terrycloth kilts. I started asking for Brandy, and followed a chain of nods and maybes through the house. Doors hung open, every room part of the party. In some of them the brothers had thrown down mattresses and set up display tables stacked with condoms and lube. The kegs were decorated with rainbow bumper stickers. A male blow-up doll dressed in vinyl bondage gear lay sprawled across a foosball table. Nobody did gay kitsch like straight boys. And they were enjoying themselves. A pile of white bodies writhed in a kids' wading pool, slathered and shining in Crisco. I stepped over two kids going at it on the stairs, the one on the bottom trying to hold onto his Natural Lite can.

"Watch where you put your feet," Dr. G said.

In the basement, a dozen boys in various states of undress played beer pong, shouting over music that was half a beat behind the bass thumping from upstairs. I spotted our guy sitting on the couch. He was the only male in the house over twenty-five, and the only one wearing all his clothes. Chubby, grinning like a Baptist preacher, with tufts of gray hair sprouting from the neck of his sport shirt.

He'd made the couch into his office. A shaggy-headed kid in Valentine-heart bicycle shorts held out a HashCash card, and Brandy tapped it with his smart pen—presto, crypto, anonymous monies transferred. He gestured for the boy to hold out his hand, then dropped four blue-and-green pills, one at a time, into his palm.

"How you doing, Brandy?" I said.

He looked up, then smiled wide. "Lyda Rose! My home-again rose!"

I was afraid he was going to start singing. My mother liked musicals, and had named me after a number in *The Music Man*. This was not the

worst gift she ever gave me—that would be her tote bag of genetic predis-
positions I inherited—but it was one of the most annoying.

"I thought you left town!" Brandy said.

"I'm back now."

"Wrong night for you!" I could never place his accent. Something Eastern European. "No action from these boys."

"I bet," I said. "May I?"

"I can't see how they will do you much good." He laughed, then handed
me one of the capsules.

I rolled it between two fingers. Blue with a band of green, a smudged
"50mg" on the side. The drug had several street names—Flip, Velveeta,
Vertical—but its brand name was Aroveta. Made by Landon-Rousse to treat
hypothermia, it massively increased the production of vasopressin, a busy
little peptide with a hand in vascular constriction (which is where the
hypothermia application came in), but also kidney function, circadian
rhythms, and sexual attraction. Aroveta had a few side effects, including
water retention and wakefulness at night. Oh, and if you owned a dick,
other dicks suddenly looked a lot more attractive. Not something that
most fishermen pulled out of the chilly ocean were likely to appreciate.

The party culture had turned all these bugs into features. Stay up late,
stay hydrated, fuck your buddies . . . what's not to like?

Flip couldn't turn you gay—sexual orientation was too deeply wired for
that—but the drug did let the brothers get down for a night of uninhibited
man-love, with a chemical third party to blame for any morning-after
regrets. That wasn't me, bro! It was the Flip!

"The colors are wrong," Dr. G said.

She was right. The casing was too thick, opaque where it should have
been translucent, and the blue was the wrong shade. The capsules definitely didn't come out of a Landon-Rousse factory. Probably the product
of a small-batch gel-cap press in somebody's basement.

I said to Brandy, "Do these kids know they're knockoffs?"

I didn't raise my voice, and maybe he didn't hear the whole sentence
above the music. But I'm pretty sure he made out that last word. "Hey!"
Brandy said angrily. "Enough of your crazy talk!"

Bobby took offense at this. "She's not crazy! She saved my life from a
werewolf!"

Brandy raised his eyebrows. "You don't say?"

"Were-hyena, actually," I said.

"Okay then," Brandy said.

"I'm looking for something," I said. "Got a minute?"

"Amphetamines? Oxy? I think I have all your favorite ingredients."

"Something special," I said. "Can we talk somewhere without all these . . ."

"Genitalia?" Dr. G asked.

". . . distractions?" I said.

· · ·

Brandy had parked his van around the corner. I told Bobby I'd ride with Brandy, which may have been a mistake: The inside of the van smelled exactly like what it was, a rolling drug lab. I climbed in the front passenger seat, then pushed aside the curtain that separated the compartments. Steel racks lined each side, bending under the weight of beige chemjet printers and car batteries. Foil precursor packs were scattered over the floor. The c-packs were technically legal for someone with the right papers (and Brandy had all the right papers), but break open those silver packages, and some major toxic shit would hit the air.

"Jesus, Brandy," I said. "You're a movable cancer cluster."

We drove to a diner on Bloor Street. Brandy knew the waitress, who seated us in the back. I made Bobby sit next to the dealer, because Dr. Gloria wanted to sit down with us. God knows why.

"I'm looking for something designer," I said. "I think it's new."

He opened his hands: Yes?

"Some people call it Numinous," I said. "Ever hear of it?"

"Nope. What else does it go by?"

I doubted anyone was calling the substance by its birth name of NME 110. "I don't know. Maybe Logos. This one makes you see God."

"Like LSD?"

"This is different, it operates on the temporal lobe, makes you—"

"Because I can print LSD out in the parking lot," Brandy said.

"Please shut the fuck up and listen to me," I said. Bobby winced. He didn't like conflict.

Brandy chuckled and raised his hands in mock surrender. The waitress arrived with water glasses and a plate of french fries and gravy, which she placed in front of Brandy. He thanked her with enthusiasm.

"She walked away without taking our order," Dr. G said, miffed.

"The drug makes you feel like you're in touch with a higher power," I said to Brandy. "The supernatural being is there in the room with you. You can see it, integrated in the visual field. Sometimes it talks to you."

"It's very convincing," Dr. G said.

"And it's very annoying," I said. "The drug makes you *believe* in the higher power. Depending on the dosage, the effect can last for hours or days. And if you OD . . ."

Then it doesn't go away. For the rest of your life, you have to expend a tremendous amount of energy, every day, reminding yourself that it's a delusion.

"Well, it's exhausting," I said. "Have you seen something like that?"

"Nope," Brandy said, chewing. Didn't even pretend to think about it. Bobby eyed the plate of fries.

"There was a homeless girl named Francine Selwig," I said. "Cute chick, colored streaks in her hair. Her friends were getting it from some guy who ran a church."

"Does this preacher have a name?" Brandy asked.

"I don't have that, either."

"You're wasting my time, Dr. Lyda." He shoved several more goop-laden fries in his mouth, but chose, unfortunately, to continue talking. "I have horny college boys waiting for my product."

"You mean your placebo."

"My customers are happy. Did you not see how happy?" He lifted his forearm and made a fist. "Grrr."

"How much did you cut it?"

"I'm offended." He looked anything but offended. "Okay, maybe twenty-five percent dextrose. But it doesn't matter, because what I give them is better than Aroveta. I add a secret ingredient." His eyebrows levitated. "Sildenafil."

Everybody's a cook, I thought. "That would work."

Bobby looked at Brandy, then back to me. "Wait, *what* would work?"

"Sildenafil is what Viagra's made out of," I said.

"Oh."

"These boys are so easy," Brandy said. He wiped his mouth with a napkin, then took out his smart pen and waggled it at me. "When the mast is high, it's any port in a storm."

"I don't think he knows how metaphors work," Dr. G said.

Brandy gripped the pen with two hands, snapped it in half, and dropped the two pieces onto his plate. It was a practiced gesture, like stubbing out a cigarette. Drug dealers, I thought, went through a lot of phones.

He stood to leave, and I put out a hand.

"Here's what I'm buying," I said. "Pass the word to your suppliers. Your other customers."

"You *don't* want to talk to my suppliers, Doctor."

"Have them call Bobby. I don't have a phone yet. I'll pay good money to whoever tells me where to find Numinous."

"Oh, the *good* money?" Brandy said. "Not the bad money?" He fished a new smart pen from a plastic-wrapped six-pack of the devices.

"Fine upstanding money," I said. "Goes to church on Sunday."

Brandy grinned. "You look like a person who used to know money, but he left you for another woman."

"Back to metaphors," Dr. G said.

"I'll look around," he said. "But are you sure you don't want me to print up one of your old favorites?"

I thought of the little daub of plastic fastened to the inside of my forearm. "Maybe later," I said.

. . .

My apartment was long gone, and all my belongings had been left behind in a storage locker. I didn't have the energy to find out if the locker had been emptied and my stuff auctioned off because of lack of payment. Bobby seemed a little too happy that this meant that I was going to spend the night at his apartment. Not anything sexual to it; he just liked sleepovers.

He waved his key fob at the door, but it refused to unlock. He fiddled with the lock, waved the fob again. Finally he got it to open.

"No pillow fights," I said.

"Ha!" A bark like a Tourette's outburst, direct from his body and unmediated by the consciousness in the treasure chest.

His apartment was a single-bedroom place over a Turkish takeout, and the smell of fried onions had risen up to bake into the carpet and paint every surface. The furniture looked like it had been collected from a variety of garage sales: a brown-and-orange couch; a blue swivel chair with a broken strut, tilted at an angle; a white wicker table from a lawn set. The kitchen was just big enough for one person to stand in and spin. No room for an oven, just a fold-down cooktop and a hanging microwave.

So. This is where Bobby lived. We'd spent three months together on the ward, and in that time I learned what he was most afraid of, and the kind of person he wanted to be, and how he felt about me. I understood, for lack of a better word, his heart. But I didn't know what his job was now, if he had a job at all, or who his friends were, where his parents lived, or what he liked on his pizza. That was the nature of bubble relationships. Prison, army, hospital, reality show—they were all pocket universes with their own physics. Bobby and I were close friends who hardly knew each other.

He smiled, embarrassed. He gestured toward the bedroom door. "My roommate lives in there," he said. "He never comes out. Well, hardly ever. I sleep on the couch." He quickly added, "But not tonight! That's for you. I'm going to sleep on the floor."

Dr. G said, "We can't let him do that."

I thought, Sure we can. I'm a forty-two-year-old woman. He's a twenty-something kid with a good back. "I'll need clean sheets," I said.

His eyes shifted up and right. Trying to picture where, in this tiny apartment, there might be undiscovered clean linens. "I'll be right back," he said, and turned toward the front door.

"Wait, can I borrow your pen? I need to send some messages."

He fished it out of his pocket. "Pull on the side-thingy to get the screen."

"I am familiar with your advanced technology," I said.

"Right, right." He pointed at me. "Breakfast! What should I buy for breakfast?"

"Just coffee," I said.

Bobby locked the door behind him—trying to protect me. I went to the bedroom door and listened for the hermit roommate, but I heard nothing but a hum that could have been a room fan.

Still, I moved to the far side of the room before I opened the pen's screen. "Message to Rovil Gupta," I said. A stream of faces and contact details scrolled down the screen. Dozens of Rovils, starting with those geographically closest to me. I recognized the one I was looking for, even though it had been ten years since we'd seen each other. He worked for Landon-Rousse, and his title was now VP of Sales—a promotion since the last time I'd checked. Good for you, little Rovil.

I touched the icon of his face and said, "It's me, Lyda." The words appeared under Rovil's face: *It's me, Lyda.* "I thought we should talk." There was too much to say for one message. Hey, so I'm out of the crazy house for the third time, I'm on electrochemical probation, and oh, Edo's cooking our old product.

"Call soon," I said. "It's about . . . spiritual matters." I signed off.

I wasn't sure the message would get through. This phone ID wouldn't be on his white list, and Rovil's spam filters might block me out of hand.

The pen chimed. The screen was still extended, and now Rovil's face—streaming live, no icon—smiled up at me.

Shit. I'd sent the message, but I wasn't prepared to have the conversation *now*. Who immediately calls back like that?

I put on a pleasant expression, then clicked to answer. "How you doing, kid?"

"I can't believe it! Lyda!"

Still the enthusiast. Rovil was our first and only hire at Little Sprout, our designated Rat Boy, though we had stopped calling him that when a visitor thought it sounded racist. He was fresh out of school then, but in no time became Mikala's right hand. The chemistry wizard's apprentice.

"You look like you're doing all right for yourself," I said. "VP now?" Landon-Rousse was one of the Big Four pharmaceutical companies, with headquarters in Belgium but offices everywhere.

He looked bashful. "Everybody's a vice president," he said. "You wouldn't believe the bureaucracy here."

We hadn't spoken since the Greenland Summit, ten years before. That meeting hadn't ended well. I told both Edo and Rovil to fuck off and never talk to me again. Rovil, obedient kid that he was, did as I asked. Even Edo gave up eventually—before disappearing completely.

Every so often over the past few years, usually when I was drunk and feeling maudlin, I'd do a search on my friends from Little Sprout. Gil's status was always the same—still incarcerated. And all the news on Edo Anderssen Vik was either (a) corporate PR-speak from his own company, or (b) speculation on why he'd disappeared from public view. But Rovil seemed to be leading an actual life. I was relieved when he went to grad school, happily surprised when he was hired at Landon-Rousse, then pleased every time his title changed to something more important. I wondered if he'd managed to hide his crazy, or if he was so good that the company kept him on despite it. Maybe Ganesh, the Remover of Obstacles, had cleared the way.

The small talk stuttered to a stop. He had to be wondering why I'd called him after ten years of silence, but he was too polite to ask. Did he know about my stints in rehab, the car crashes, the psych wards?

I said, mock-casually, "So, have you heard from the others? Edo, Gil . . . ?"

He blinked. "Gilbert, no, of course not!" Poor Rovil, walking on eggshells just saying the name in my presence.

"I hear he's allowed to have visitors," I said.

Rovil's eyes widened. "You're not thinking of—?"

"No, no. It's Edo I want."

"Oh," he said. "That may be difficult."

"I tried calling him on an old private number, but it's dead now. Every address I've found online for him is corporate, blocked by either voicemail or receptionists. I've left messages, but he hasn't called me back."

"I know, I know," Rovil said. "A couple times over the years I tried to reach out to him, but he never responds." He grinned. "Like some other people I know."

Wow, little Rovil yanking my chain. "I've had some issues," I said. "But Edo . . . what happened to him?"

"He hasn't been seen in years," Rovil said. "I'm not even sure what country he stays in. He's a, what's the word? Not a hermit . . ."

"A recluse. Growing his fingernails, storing his urine in jars, that kind of thing."

"What have you heard?" Rovil said, shocked. Missing the reference entirely.

"Never mind that," I said. "I have a favor to ask."

Rovil considered this, then with complete earnestness said, "If I can provide it, it's yours."

"Get me Edo's private number."

"I told you, no one knows—"

"He's got to have lawyers, staff, whatever. Get a message through to him. He likes you, Rovil. He'll respond to you. Tell him it's important."

"What is it? What's happened?"

My instinct was to keep him out of it as long as possible. Rovil was the youngest of us at Little Sprout, and not even a partner. He shouldn't have been caught up in what happened at the party. But he had been there, and he'd gone down like all of us. The little Christian boy woke up with a Hindu god in his head. We were part of a very small club.

I asked, "Is this a company line?"

He processed the meaning of the question. "It's my personal device."

That didn't mean that no one was listening. Landon-Rousse might be monitoring its executives' private communications. Plenty of corporations had been caught doing the same. But if Rovil was comfortable, I decided to risk it.

"I met someone who saw God," I said.

Rovil tilted his head, not quite getting it.

"Someone is making Numinous." *That* he got. The word went off like an information grenade, and I watched his face shift through several emotions before he controlled himself and settled on an expression of Polite Doubt.

"You . . . did you have some of One-Ten left over?"

"No. It's new."

"Perhaps it's some other drug. Do you have it with you?"

"Not yet. I'm working on it."

He shook his head. "I don't see how that's possible. Little Sprout shut down before the trial. We all agreed that no one—" His eyes widened. "You think *Edo* is doing this?"

"I didn't say that. I just want to talk to him."

"But he's a . . . spiritual man," Rovil said. "We are all spiritual people now."

"Not all gods are created equal," I said. "Rovil?"

He wasn't looking at the screen. He was imagining our friend Edo breaking the law, and our trust. I'd blown his mind.

"It's probably nothing," I said. "A coincidence."

His eyes slid back to me. "How can I help?"

"Now that you bring it up," I said. "I need to borrow five thousand dollars."

CHAPTER THREE

Oh, we were such geniuses. A company of smarty-pants. Mikala the chemistry wizard, Gil the tech brain, Edo the money man, and me—the neuroscientist with the brilliant idea that we could cure the Afghanistan of mental disorders.

The disease of schizophrenia was a quagmire, swallowing the careers of scientists of all stripes. The definition of what it was and wasn't constantly shifted. Its causes were various and overlapping, with research pointing to everything from genetic mutations to socioeconomic status to amphetamine use . . . or all at the same time.

Whatever the causes, one effect showed up clearly on the MRIs: The brains of actively schizophrenic patients withered with each passing year. Frontal and temporal lobes shrank in volume, and the connections between the lobes became unreliable. The brain literally disintegrated. The illusion of a unified consciousness broke down; now when other parts of the brain spoke, the messages seemed to be coming from outside agents hovering menacingly just out of sight, whispering threats. My mother had fought this civil war for thirty years, and lost.

I'd had the idea for a drug that could trigger new growth in those withering lobes, a little sprout in the dying forest. Mikala was going to make it happen. We were as confident as marines.

But no drug, especially one that crosses the blood-brain barrier, can change just one thing. Unintended secondary effects abound. A drug for hypertension can become a treatment for erectile dysfunction. A hypothermia medicine can find new life in sex parties. And a chemical designed to grow neurons in damaged brains can destroy five lives in a single night.

Edo threw the party at Cité at the Lake Point Tower. A private room big enough for friends and family, surrounded by glass, Chicago lit up around us like an undersea kingdom. Kensington Inc. was buying us out. We were all going to be rich. True, Edo was already a billionaire, and we'd never approach his heights, but we were all going to be so much more wealthy than we'd ever been before. New Molecular Entity 110, the latest NME in a long string of disappointments (a hundred and nine, to be exact), was showing promise, and in the world of bioengineering start-ups, promises were bait, and a big fish had taken the line.

Mikala didn't attend the restaurant, and we were all relieved. She was the only one of the partners who didn't want to sell. Outvoted and angry, she'd told us we weren't just wrong, we were fools. Not just greedy, but evil. She accused me of voting against her out of spite.

The marriage had come apart over the past year. However, until the buyout offer we had never argued, never yelled. We slept in the same bed, ate breakfast across from each other, drove together to the industrial park where Little Sprout's labs were located, and worked in the same room, never more than twenty feet apart. We kept up our routine. Eventually I realized that it was the routine that was keeping us. The marriage had become a set of autonomic responses that let us absent ourselves without having to separate.

I told myself that Mikala exited first. She'd started working later hours, going in to the building without me. She no longer needed me for her work, and maybe, I realized, not at all. She'd always been smarter than I was, but now there was something new in her face, something like pity, as if she understood things I'd never comprehend. What wounded me most was her newfound calm. She was happy. Happier than she'd ever been when we depended on each other. I should have known when she began calling our product Numinous that she'd started using it. She'd found her god, and we mortals had stopped mattering to her.

The party at Cité stretched on, until the friends and spouses and parents went home and the hotel staff kicked us out of the glass room. The four of us—Edo, Gil, Rovil, and me—took the elevator down to the condo Edo had borrowed from equally rich friends. Edo, burly and towering over us all, was so drunk he kept skimming the walls of the corridor. Gil, who was a foot shorter than Edo but at least the same weight, seemed only a few drinks behind him. Rovil and I, the sober sherpas, guided them to the room.

It was sometime past 3 a.m. when Rovil said, "Guess who's here?" Mikala had appeared, carrying a bottle of champagne, already opened. She wasn't intoxicated—not with alcohol, anyway. She was wide awake, vibrating with energy.

Edo threw open his arms and cheered. Too drunk to realize how awkward the moment was. Edo and Rovil the only ones happy to see her.

"I came to apologize," Mikala said.

Gil said, "You sure about that?"

"We made something great," Mikala said. "It's right to celebrate that."

But only Mikala truly understood what we'd created. The rest of us knew only that NME 110 had passed the preclinical tests. The FDA had approved us to go forward with phase I trials, the "first-in-man" trials. Kensington would now finance the human testing, which could cost millions. Only then, we thought, would we find out if we'd created something that could change the lives of people, or only change the behavior of rats. The NME was a lottery ticket that Kensington was willing to pay for, one drug of thousands that went to phase I every year. Only a handful made it to phase II.

Mikala filled our glasses with her champagne. I told her no, I wasn't drinking. Her eyes narrowed. Rovil said, "Well *I* am," and held out his glass.

Edo roared with laughter. "If the Christian boy from India's drinking, we're *all* drinking."

I held out my glass. What could one drink hurt?

I do not remember anything after that moment except fragments. Edo's booming voice. Mikala touching my belly. A light so pure and white that it seemed to bore holes through my eyes to the back of my skull. And a knife.

I remembered staring at the blade. It was a big kitchen knife, and someone was prying my fingers from the handle. I don't remember seeing the face of the person who took it from me. I felt the wood slipping out of my hand, and I did not want to let it go.

I lay in the hospital several days before the doctor told me about the others. Edo was weeping constantly. Gil was raving. Rovil couldn't speak. And Mikala—she was in the morgue.

I wanted to die for my sins, but death was impossible now. I understood that my true self, this consciousness, was not located here, in this body, but woven into the fabric of all things. These lungs could stop breathing, this flesh could fall from my bones, but that had as little to do with me as the erosion of mountain ranges. Which is to say, it had everything to do with me.

I was entangled with all existence, stars and minds and particles all aspects of the same thing. As long as the universe existed, I had no choice but to exist with it. There was no escape, because there was nothing to escape from.

"Don't be afraid," the doctor told me. "I'm here to help you through this." She placed a cool hand on my forehead. "*Gloria in excelsis Deo.*"

· · ·

I'd sent Bobby out for a couple lattes, and by the time he returned he had lost his mind.

"They took me, Lyda!" He slapped the skin just below his neck, where he usually kept his treasure chest. "Just *yanked* me."

"Slow down," I said. It was way too early in the morning, the sun pinging through the slats like a ball-peen hammer. "Did they take your wallet, too?"

"What? No."

"Then you couldn't at least come back with some Goddamned coffee?"

"Be nice," Dr. Gloria said. "The boy's in despair." My body ached from a night on Bobby's couch.

"Okay, okay," I said. "Who took your . . . *you?*"

"Two guys. Mean guys." His hands fluttered like pigeons. "I think they were terrorists."

"Why would terrorists want your treasure chest?"

"I don't know! They said, 'If you want this back, tell Lyda Rose to talk to somebody named Feeza.' Or maybe Fiza."

"Uh-oh," Dr. G said.

I said, "Bobby, think hard. Was the name *Fayza?*"

He pointed at me. "That's it."

Shit.

"What's the matter?" he asked.

"And they mentioned me by *name?*"

"Yes! Now who is this guy?"

"It's not a guy—it's a woman. And she runs the Millies."

"Oh." Even Bobby had heard of the Millies.

. . .

On the way downtown to Millie home territory, Dr. G and I worked it out. Brandy must have passed the word on what we were looking for, and that word made its way up the supply chain to the Millies. I shouldn't have been surprised. The Millies ran a huge slice of the Toronto cannabis trade, and there was no reason they wouldn't have branched into smart drugs. Fayza was one of those hyperentrepreneurs that make even hardcore capitalists nervous.

She and the Millies got their start in 2020 with microloans from a nonprofit that decided that charity begins at home. A dozen Afghan women, riding in on the third wave of immigration from the war zone after the Taliban reclaimed the homeland (again), formed a trust group and were given five hundred bucks apiece. They called themselves the Millionaires Club. The women set up a living room nail salon, a vegetable stand featuring bathtub-grown cardamom and saffron, a postal assistance business, and, in a metamove, a micro-microbank. Ten-buck loans, in a variety of currencies, transferrable to relatives back home.

The bank was Fayza's idea. Utilizing her newly discovered talent for money, she began to convert other women in the neighborhood into business owners and set them up with accounts. She offered seminars on marketing, corporate strategy, and human resources (managing husbands). Then she went back to the women who ran the vegetable stand and the postal service, and explained the word "synergy." Specifically:

Hydroponics + Shipping + Money laundering = Vast cash opportunity.

By 2025, the Millies controlled most of Ontario. They'd allied themselves with the pot farms out in the boondocks and facilitated shipments to the States, but the core of their business remained their locally grown, artisanal, organic weed, each bud glistening with enough THC to flip back your head like a Pez dispenser.

We parked the car on King Street, just inside the Afghan neighborhood. Bobby said, "I can hear them talking. I think they've got me under a blanket."

The sidewalk was wet. The air smelled like an empty tuna can. Overhead, Dr. Gloria kept station between ground and gray sky. Shafts of sunlight perforated the cloud bank, which struck me as very beautiful.

"God is punching air holes," I said.

Bobby looked up at the sky in alarm. *What? Why?*

"Nothing," I said. "Settle."

As soon as we walked onto Tyndall Avenue, the heart of the heart of the Millie empire, a passel of young kids ran past us flicking their pens at each other wand-style, casting spells and deducting hit points . . . and no doubt sending our pictures down the street to their moms and grandmothers. These free-range Harry Potters, I decided, were lookouts for the Millies.

A chubby girl jumped in front of us. "Fling me a dollar? Two dollar I can level up!"

"Kick it, kid."

"Shopping, then? A little something from the grandmothers?"

"I'm good."

The homes on Tyndall were tidy brick affairs, built in the 1970s, with neat lawns and midrange cars at the curb. Dr. Gloria landed gracefully in front of a house in the middle of the block.

Two kids in their twenties sat on the front steps, arguing with each other—in English. The boy in a nylon jacket, the girl wearing tight white jeans and a hot pink hijab.

I said, "I'm looking for Fayza."

"I know," the girl said.

I hid my surprise. First try and we'd found the headquarters? Dr. G said, "Divine providence."

The girl nodded at Bobby. "He stays outside."

"But I'm already in there!" Bobby said. "This is just my body!"

"Be cool, kid," I said. "I'll take care of this."

He slumped to the sidewalk. Dr. Gloria patted me between the shoulder blades. "Here we go. Be polite."

She didn't have to remind me. Running a multimillion-dollar drug business—even a rural one—required a sociopathic outlook and a dick bigger than an ashwagandha tree. People who crossed Fayza and the Millies disappeared into the bay.

I walked up the steps and pushed through the wooden front door. The house was clean but lower middle class: twenty-year-old wallpaper, worn upholstery, pine chairs in the hallway. The air sharp with the smell of spices I couldn't identify. In the living room, five or six old ladies, none of them younger than seventy-five, sat around a low coffee table, most of them holding old-style tablet computers on their laps. They looked like they'd stolen their clothing from a 1980s' hip-hop crew: bright track suits, gold chains, spotless white gym shoes. Only the head scarves marked them as Muslim. They chattered at each other and tapped at the tablet screens. The grandmother closest to me glanced in my direction.

"Fayza?" I asked.

She turned back to her screen. And then I saw what she was looking at: a live picture of my silhouette, in some kind of X-ray mode. The key fob in my right front pocket glowed yellow.

Jesus, they had airport scanners? The damn thing had to be hidden behind the hideous wallpaper. I wasn't sure what these old women would have done if I'd been carrying a weapon—bury me under a five-granny tackle?

The woman flicked her fingers at me in a gesture I took as permission to enter the living room. I skirted the circle of women and headed for the far doorway.

In the kitchen was an old man with a cloud beard, seemingly decades older than the ancients in the living room. He sat unmoving at the breakfast table, holding a fork and staring at a plate of dark meat and browned vegetables. He didn't look up when I entered.

A woman stood at the kitchen sink, gazing out through the window at the backyard. She wore a cobalt blue jacket with a wide black belt, black high-heeled boots, a gauzy black head scarf like an afterthought. The boots alone had to cost five grand.

"I so want those," Dr. Gloria said.

The woman turned toward me. She was holding a cleaver. Dr. Gloria's wings rustled in warning.

"Why don't you have a phone like a normal person?" she asked me angrily.

"I mean to buy one soon," I said—doing my best impersonation of a person who was not talking to a drug lord holding a gigantic blade. She was seventy, maybe seventy-five years old, with pale skin. But her face was made up, and the brown hair under the scarf showed aggressive highlights. "Put together," as my mother used to say. Give me that in thirty years.

"My name's Lyda Rose."

"I know who you are." She turned and put the cleaver on the wire dish rack. "If you don't want me to use junkies to find you, join the twenty-first century."

The old man still hadn't moved, and neither had the plate. A battle of wills.

Fayza walked to the back door and said, "Come this way."

I hesitated. My only backup was a make-believe angel and a brain-damaged kid who believed that his soul lived in a plastic box. I suspected that if I left this house, no one would find me.

Fayza looked back at me. "I want to show you my garden."

"Garden," however, was too gentle a word: It was a horticultural brothel. The yard stretched beyond the boundaries of the lot, creating a lush, shared park that ran the length of the block. Every flower and fern seemed improbably voluptuous, especially for this time of year. Naked and half-dressed statues watched coyly from behind the trees.

"It's a lot to take in," I said.

Fayza led me past a structure that was technically a gazebo, in the same way that a five-layer wedding cake was technically a dessert. She was heading for the back porch of the house across the way. A young Afghan man in a red hoodie held the door open for us.

"I have someone I want you to meet," Fayza said. "They're waiting inside."

I held up a hand. "Fayza, please . . ."

She turned, frowned. "What is the matter with you?"

My brain chattered like a playing card in a bicycle wheel. Had I already pissed off the drug lord? Who was waiting in that house? And would I get out there alive? I had left the House of the Grannies, crossed through the Valley of the Statuary, and was being led into the Tomb of the Unknown Hoodie.

Jesus Christ I wish I'd taken something before coming here. Screw the pellet in my arm.

"You don't need any of that," Gloria said. "You have me."

- - -

The young man on the couch was skinny and black with an Abe Lincoln beard. He was dressed in layers like a street kid, but his clothes were clean and his black trainers were spotless. So, either new to the street, or on his way off it. I bet on the latter.

He nodded at me with great solemnity, and Fayza said, "You know each other?"

"Never seen him before," I said truthfully. We were in a basement rec room outfitted with cheap carpet, Arabic movie posters under glass, and chrome furniture. A terrible place to die, in my opinion. "Who is he?"

"Nobody," the boy said matter-of-factly.

"His name is Luke," Fayza said. "He's an addict."

Gloria bent to look more closely at the man's eyes. "The pupils are slightly dilated," she said. "Though that could be from the excitement of being trapped in a drug lord's basement."

"What's he on?" I asked.

Luke looked surprised. "Nothing."

Fayza said, "A month ago, he was one of my most faithful customers. Not only marijuana, but a variety of pharmaceuticals. Then he stopped cold."

Dr. G said, "Good for you, Luke."

"He wasn't the only one," Fayza said. "Six other customers, some of them his acquaintances, have stopped purchasing from my dealers. Usually that means they're dead or in jail, but these people are still in the city. None of them is buying from me."

"Six people, that's not so bad," I said.

The boy in the hoodie looked at me in alarm.

Fayza said, "Don't tell me my business."

"I would never do that," I said. With sincerity.

"Luke and the others have moved on to another product."

"Which one?"

"I thought you could tell me," Fayza said. "You're the neuroscientist."

I froze for a moment, trying to figure out what Bobby had told her. But of course she didn't need Bobby. Anyone in Fayza's position would have access to hot and cold running infostream.

The basics were free to everyone: my entire résumé from elementary school to PhD, the well-documented debacle at Little Sprout, my arrests.

I'd been told by a certain paranoid inmate of the NAT that with a little cash, my entire online history could be downloaded as well. Fayza probably knew my every credit transaction, social media post, and geolocation ping going back decades. I normally didn't trust paranoids, but I made an exception in Ollie's case.

"What do they call the drug?" I asked.

"They don't call it anything," she said. "They think it's the Holy Spirit."

"If you just open your heart," Luke said, "you'd understand."

I squinted at him. Was he seeing his own angel right now? Or did his God take the form of, say, a blob of light in his peripheral vision?

"You ever hear of the Numinous, Luke?"

He went still, trying to give away nothing, which gave away everything.

"Yee-up," Dr. Gloria said.

"How about Francine Selwig?" I asked.

"Frannie? Is she okay?" Luke said, genuinely worried.

"Who is this Francine person?" Fayza asked.

"Someone else who took a drug like Luke's," I said. "She killed herself."

"What?" Luke said. His surface calm cracked. "I can't believe she'd, she'd . . ."

"She was in withdrawal," I said. "She'd been cut off from whatever she was getting at the church."

Fayza said, "The Hologram Church."

Luke looked hurt. "The Church of the Hologrammatic God is—"

"The stupidest name I've ever heard," I said. "What were they giving you, Luke?"

He shook his head. "It's not a drug. I keep telling you that."

"Then what is it?"

His eyes flicked to the left. Consulting his higher power? Then he looked me in the eye and said, "It's the word of God."

Time for a new tactic. "Tell me about God," I said. "Is he here now?"

He frowned at me. "God is everywhere. That's pretty basic."

"But you can see him. What does he look like?"

That eye flick again. "It's hard to describe," he said. "He's more of a feeling. Watching over me." He brightened. "I built something to portray my feelings for him. If you come to the church—"

"Right, and this feeling—it gets stronger after each church service?"

He hesitated, then said, "Every time."

Dr. Gloria said, "This is like a Turing test for religion. So far, everything he's said would apply to anyone going to a prayer meeting."

Except he'd recognized the word "numinous." I said to Fayza, "We're not going to get anywhere this way."

Fayza nodded. "We've been going around and around for hours," Fayza said. "I can't tell if he's a very good liar or simply an idiot who doesn't know what's happened to him."

"Have you considered that he really did just find God?"

"I might have considered that, before I heard you were looking for a drug with exactly these symptoms. Before I learned that such a drug had already been invented."

The infostream again. No use hiding anything about Little Sprout, or NME 110. "That never left the lab," I said. "It never got to testing, much less market."

"No one's marketing this, either," Fayza said. "As far as I know, they're giving it away for free. You can see how this would greatly fuck with my business model." She stared at me as if it were my fault.

"Look, I'd like to help, but I don't see how I can—"

"Bring me a sample of this drug. Confirm for me what it is. Luke will take you to this church." She nodded to the Afghan kid. "Hootan will go with you."

The kid in the hoodie smiled at me.

"That's okay," I said. I wanted no part in whatever gangland enforcer thing Hootan represented. "I'll do it alone."

Fayza turned to me, her gaze as impersonal as a gun barrel.

"Or he can come," I said. "Either way."

Dr. Gloria rustled her wings, getting my attention, and nodded at Fayza.

"Oh, right," I said. "My friend, Bobby. He was wearing something your men took."

Fayza dipped into the pocket of her jacket, withdrew the plastic treasure chest on its leather thong. She held it in her hand, and for a moment I thought she was going to open it, and Bobby's mind would fly around the room like Tinkerbell.

She handed it to me, as well as a second object—a low-tech flip phone.

"That's okay," I said. "I've got a pen."

"You will call me on this one," she said. "Keep in touch."

· · ·

Hootan led me, Dr. Gloria, and Luke the black Abe Lincoln back to Fayza's house on Tyndall Avenue. Bobby was waiting for us, pacing frantically, while the young Afghan couple ignored him. I tossed the chest toward Bobby. He screeched in panic to see it airborne, then caught it and touched it to his lips. Then he started thanking me, practically pawing me. Crazy people are tedious.

"Go back to the apartment," I told him. "I'll meet you there later, okay?"

"Later, right, yes," Bobby said. Too relieved to be wondering what I was doing with these two new strangers.

Hootan said his car was down the block. He walked ahead of us, and Luke touched my elbow. His lips were pursed, a dam holding back turbulent emotion. "Thank you," he said. "I knew when you walked into the room that we were supposed to meet today."

I doubted that. "So how far away is this church, Luke?"

"It's close," he said. "And you're going to love Pastor Rudy."

CHAPTER FOUR

The call came for the Vincent while Vinnie was branding the spring calves. He was halfway through the shipment of freshly weaned three-month-olds—five bison cows and a bull from the Rakunas, Inc., facility in Santa Monica, California. The cow in his hands bucked and kicked, a real lively one. He ran a thumb along its side to soothe it, took a breath to soothe himself, then pressed the red-hot iron into the animal's fuzzy brown flank. The calf squealed. A thin coil of acrid smoke rose up to the ceiling.

"Sorry, little girl," Vinnie said. Ranching was no business for the sentimental, but the cries of the young ones really got to him. He flipped down the magnifying glass and inspected his mark, a Flying V about two millimeters long. The lines were crisp, and he was satisfied.

He set the cow down on the other side of the foot-high fence that separated the kitchen from the wide-open range of the living room. The calf scampered across the carpet of #10 Giro Home Prairie. The herd (thirty-eight head, counting the six he'd just purchased) had congregated in the shadow of the coffee table. It was midday, and the ceiling's grow lights were turned up strong.

The pen pinged a second time: another message. He would have ignored the device, but this was the

Vincent's pen, the one that hardly ever beeped. Vinnie removed the mag-nifying specs and put the branding iron into its tiny holder. He picked up the pen. The messages were the same, sent only thirty seconds apart: "Please call."

Vinnie would have preferred to do all their business through text, but the employer was an old-fashioned man who wanted to hear a voice. Vin-nie thumbed the connection. After a moment, the call went through, and the employer picked up.

"Is the Vincent available?" the employer said. He knew that the Vincent did not like to be ordered around. He liked to be asked.

Vinnie looked down at the crate of calves. He'd planned on finishing the branding. Then he was going to move the herd to the back bedroom where the carpet was high, so he could use the living room to set up a new breeding area for the two-year-olds. He'd never gotten his herd to breed, despite spending thousands on the highest-rated bulls. It frustrated him to be dependent on lab-grown stock, and upon the money that the Vin-cent's jobs provided. Someday he'd live off his herd, like a true rancher.

"How long is the engagement?" Vinnie asked.

His employer said, "A few days at most. I want him to talk to someone in Toronto." *Talk.* One of those kinds of jobs, then. Most of the time the Vincent *met* people. Sometimes he *saw* them. Talking was a rarity, but it paid the best.

"Okay," Vinnie said. "Send the details. The Vincent can leave tomorrow."

The employer said nothing for an uncomfortable moment. Then he said, "If it's at all possible, I'd like him to be on the ground tonight."

Now it was Vinnie's turn to insert an uncomfortable pause. Buying an international plane ticket at the last minute would raise the Vincent's air travel threat score. Also, would there be enough time for the Vincent's pills to kick in? And what about the calves?

The employer said, "I wouldn't ask if it wasn't of the utmost importance. I'll of course include a bonus for express service."

Vinnie breathed out. "Okay. I'll tell him." By tradition, Vinnie pretended to be the secretary for the Vincent. The name Vinnie was never mentioned by either of them. The conceit was that the Vincent was too badass to ever talk on the phone.

The employer hung up, and Vinnie rested his forehead on the edge of the table and stared at the floor.

One of the miniature calves in the crate bleated. Vinnie wouldn't have time to brand them now, and he wouldn't be around to watch over their integration with the herd. He'd have to release them to the prairie and hope for the best. In a few hours he wouldn't care about such things, but he did now, and he would again when he returned.

He told his pen to search for available flights, then sent an email to his neighbor down the hall. He made sure that the branding iron was turned off and unplugged. What next? The Poomba. He detached the robot from its charger and set it down in the high grass. The little flying-saucer-shaped device did nothing for a moment, but then its sensors caught a whiff of methane, and it swiveled left and rolled slowly forward, the grasses bending before its rubber bumpers. The herd sometimes got spooked by the machine, but what could he do? Without it the whole apartment would fill up with tiny buffalo chips.

He left the apartment, always a nerve-racking experience, and walked two doors down. Al answered wearing only a pair of UNLV basketball shorts, his hairless rounded gut like the dome of a mosque. He was a Hispanic man a foot taller than Vinnie and a hundred pounds heavier, even with the lightweight titanium leg. Like so many men of his age and income bracket, Al had participated in Operation Enduring Freedom, which he'd described as an international limb-exchange program sponsored by the American government.

"I'm going to be gone for a few days," Vinnie said. "I was wondering if . . . well . . ."

"You want me to watch the critters?" Al had served as emergency ranch hand on two occasions. He wasn't Vinnie's first choice for the position, but he had two important qualifications: He was always home, and he always needed money.

"I'd really appreciate it," Vinnie said. "I just emailed you updated instructions. Did you get it?"

"Sure," Al said. "Just came in."

"Great. You can delete the earlier one." It had been several months since Al had watched the herd, so Vinnie unfurled his own pen to go over the major sections of the document: "Water and Lights"; "Veterinarian"; "Pasture Schedule"; "Food Supplements." He apologized for not having time to write up notes on the new stock. "Sometimes the herd rejects the new calves," Vinnie said. "If you see some of them wandering off by themselves, put them in the back forty."

"That's . . ."

"The bedroom with no furniture," Vinnie said.

"Got it," Al said. He shifted his weight to his biological leg. Raised his eyebrows significantly.

"Oh!" Vinnie said. He handed over the envelope that contained the cash. "I wrote the apartment guest code on the envelope. It's a new number. Also, I won't be reachable while I'm traveling, but if you call my home number and leave a message, I should be able to check voicemail at some point."

"Don't worry about a thing," Al said.

Vinnie went back to his apartment. He didn't feel great about leaving Al in charge, but he did know a cure for that feeling. He opened the freezer, pulled out the box of Commander Calhoun Fishstix, and retrieved the bottle of Evanimex that was hidden inside. The pills were provided by the employer as part of his compensation, and arrived at regular intervals by FedEx.

Vinnie preferred to ramp up slowly, taking one pill every two hours, but time was short. He swallowed four. They slid down his throat like lumps of ice, each one (he imagined) ushering his tender heart one step closer into cryogenic storage. For safekeeping.

He stepped over the kitchen fence and walked back to his bedroom via the narrow boardwalk. The wooden structure stood a foot off the ground, and its struts were spaced far enough apart that the bison could migrate without impediment. It also allowed Vinnie to cross the rooms without trampling grass, squashing livestock, or smearing cow patties on his flip-flops.

There was a trick to becoming the Vincent that went beyond chemicals, a ritual that helped realign his headspace. He stripped off his clothes and turned the shower to hot. Afterward he shaved, even though he had shaved just that morning. He unwrapped one of the charcoal suits, as well as a blue shirt and matching tie, and dressed. Then he took down the black Caran d'Ache briefcase and placed in it a second blue shirt, a pair of underwear, and a pair of socks.

Last, as always, the hat. He opened the box and lifted it out, a black 800x Seratelli with a Vaquero brim, one of the finest Western hats ever made. He lightly gripped the crown in three fingers and set it on his head.

That's the ticket. He could feel the Vincent coming on now. Not a different identity, exactly, but a different way of thinking of himself. An alternate approach to the world. The knot of tension he carried in his chest—his worries for the herd, his agoraphobia, his certainty that he was an evil person—began to unwind and fall away.

His plane departed in ninety minutes. By the time it landed in Toronto, he would be at Full Vincent, ready and able to stalk and torture a Canadian.

CHAPTER FIVE

Hootan's car was a tiny biodiesel Honda tricked out with fins and whitewall tires. The kid pressed the remote, and the engine roared like a fighter jet. "Real Engine Sound," he shouted proudly. The recording was ridiculously mismatched for the car. "I can also do Mustang GT and a Ford 150!"

Dr. G and I crawled into the back, with Luke all knees and elbows in the passenger seat. Luke told Hootan the address, and the Afghan kid slipped on a pair of sunglasses and swung into traffic. The speakers under the floor settled into a highway thrum.

"Tell me about this holo church," I said. "Pastor Whatsisface, everything."

Luke twisted to face me, tilting his head to fit under the roof. "Is she really dead?" he asked.

"Francine?" I flashed on her body laid out sideways on the white tile, her arm and belly a coastline for a lake of blood. "I'm sorry. Yeah."

Luke tried to take this in. "It doesn't make sense. She was so much better."

"She was despondent," I said. "She said she had to pay for her sins."

"But she told me she felt forgiven! God had forgiven her."

"Well, evidently he changed his mind. She was

calling for him to come back." I leaned forward. "What did she feel so guilty about?"

"It's private," Luke said. "She confided in me."

"But she was a teenager. It couldn't have been that terrible."

"You're provoking him," Dr. G said. "Why don't you just double-dog dare him to tell you?"

I ignored her. "How bad could it be?" I asked.

"Pretty bad," Luke said. "Not the worst thing I've ever heard. But . . . yeah."

"You won't shock me," I said.

He said nothing for a few moments, then said, "It happened a couple years ago. She was shacking up with this guy, a real asshole. He just wanted someone to live with him and take care of his grandmother. She had some kind of disease where she was getting more and more paralyzed every month, from like the feet up?"

"ALS," I said.

"No, that wasn't it."

"Lou Gehrig's Disease."

"That one," Luke said. Dr. G rolled her eyes. The boy said, "The old woman couldn't walk anymore, and she could barely move her arms, and she had trouble swallowing? Frannie said that it was like feeding a baby—spitting up, choking, a real mess. And then the bathroom stuff! Frannie did all of it, wiped her ass, changed her diapers. She really took care of her."

"What did she get out of it?"

"She got to sleep in a bed. And the old woman's money paid for the drugs. The boyfriend, can't remember his name, was a meth head. And Frannie liked to smoke, too, so it worked out." He took a breath. "So one day the boyfriend has to go out to buy, says his friend has some new stuff, something from the States, and he'll be right back. I'll only be gone for an hour, he says."

"Uh-oh," Dr. Gloria said.

"So she's there for an hour, two hours with the granny. Then it's all afternoon. That night the boyfriend doesn't come back. And by this time Frannie is pissed, because she knows what he's doing; he's getting high without her."

A car horn blared, and Hootan jerked the car to the right. The side of a bus like a silver wall appeared six inches from my face, then swept past.

"Jesus Christ!" I yelled. "Are you blinking while driving? Take off those damn specs!"

Hootan said something in an unknown language that I translated as "Fuck you." The sunglasses stayed on.

Luke said, "So now it's morning, and the old woman is making noises like she has to go to the bathroom. Francine's stuck in the house, and the asshole grandson is out there smoking. She thinks, this isn't even my relative. I am not responsible for this person. So she leaves another message on the boyfriend's phone and says, 'Fuck you, I'm out of here.' And she leaves."

Hootan said, "She did what?"

"She grabbed her stuff and went back to her friends on the street," Luke said. "And a couple days later she hears that the boyfriend got admitted to the hospital. He'd been there for days, an overdose maybe or some bad reaction."

Hootan said, "What happened to the grandmother?"

Luke didn't answer.

"She just *left* her here?" Hootan said. "She left an old woman to choke and die?"

"That's what she told me," Luke said.

"Well, your friend deserved to die."

"*What?*" Luke said. "Fuck you!"

Hootan slammed on the brakes. Behind us tires squealed, horns blared. He yanked off his glasses. "Say that to me again! Say 'fuck you' to me!"

"Shut the fuck up!"

Hootan lurched sideways, trying to get his arm behind him.

"Gun!" Dr. Gloria said.

Hootan's arm came up with a fat black pistol. He pointed it at Luke's head.

"Whoa whoa whoa!" I yelled. Not very helpfully.

"Your friend is evil," Hootan said. "Say it. She is evil and deserved to die."

Luke had pressed himself back against the passenger door, palms raised, but he didn't seem as scared as I would be with a gun to my face. "Yes, she *did* evil," the boy said. "But she isn't—she's not *Sauron*. She just made a bad decision."

"Hootan, you can't shoot him here," I said. "You'll get blood all over the car."

"Yes, she deserved to die," Luke said. "We *all* deserve to die. But God forgives." He looked at me. "God didn't abandon her. If she felt like He was gone, it's because she turned away from *Him*."

"Can we just get to the church?" I asked. "Fayza's waiting for us to get back."

Hootan said something in that unknown language. Then he slipped the gun into the front pouch of his sweatshirt. "God is not as forgiving as you think," he said.

. . .

Pastor Rudy's church was a former auto parts store, the plastic sign above the entrance long gone but the ghost letters still on duty, false shadows on the faded aluminum, their empty screw mounts bleeding rust. In the parking lot a few old vehicles hunkered before the nail salon, the only store in the strip mall that seemed to be open.

Luke unfolded from Hootan's car and loped toward the church, eager as a puppy, which only annoyed Hootan more. The front door chimed as he pushed it open.

The interior was a wide-open space furnished in early AA Meeting: metal folding chairs, a coffee station, earnestness. Along the walls were long tables that held what looked like elementary school art displays.

Luke said, "Oh, let me show you mine!"

He hurried toward one of the tables. "All of us approach God from different angles. We also see a little piece of the whole. But the piece, the shard, is the same as all of God, right?"

"Hologram," I said.

"Right! Pastor Rudy had this idea to get us all to share what we were seeing." Luke proudly showed me a cardboard box. The side facing us was open. On top was a smaller box wrapped in tin foil. The walls inside were bright red and gold, Bollywood colors. A six-inch action figure lay face-down on the floor of the box beneath a much larger yellow umbrella. The edges of the umbrella were singed black.

"Wow," I said. "You made this yourself?"

The boy was immune to sarcasm. "That's me," he said, pointing to the figure. "I can't see God directly, because I'm facing the wrong way, toward Earth. But He's there, protecting me. Look." He reached behind the box, flicked a switch. Inside the tin foil box a light came on, making the umbrella glow.

Dr. G said, "His God is an umbrella."

"Better than a wet blanket," I said aloud.

She walked away from me, flexing her wings. "Here's the guy," she said.

A figure had stepped out of the back, where the storeroom used to be. My first impression was of an Olympic mid-weight wrestler: bullet head, powerful arms that wouldn't hang straight, and a posture that suggested a readiness to shoot the legs. He wore a T-shirt with an unreadable logo, old jeans, brown-and-orange CAT work boots. His skin tone fell in the Mediterranean end of the spectrum.

"Luke. Good to see you," he said. His accent was Mexican. "And your friends." He held out his hand to me, and I noticed a black tattoo lurking under the lip of his sleeve. "I'm Rudy." I shook hands. Hootan didn't lift his hand, but conspicuously put it into the front pouch of his sweatshirt.

Rudy smiled curiously. If he was nervous, I couldn't see it.

I said, "Luke's been telling us about your church, how much it changed his life. We also hunger and thirst after righteousness." I didn't bother to sound sincere.

He looked at Hootan, then back to me. A tilt of the head that said he didn't know what was going on but was willing to play along. I saw another tattoo on his neck: the number "13" in Gothic script. He said, "You must have a lot of questions."

Oh did I. What was going on in the pastor's head right now? Was he taking his own juice, or only passing it on? It was impossible to tell. He seemed as laid back as a Buddhist monk, but that could have been an act, or his natural chemistry. Behind him, Dr. G drifted along the perimeter of the room, taking in the mini-shrines. I got an impression of Aztec gods, clouds of cotton swabs, black-and-white photo collages. It was an Anti-Science Fair.

Pastor Rudy said, "Do you come from a Christian background, or . . ." He nodded to Hootan. "Muslim, maybe?"

Hootan said, "We're here for the drug you gave Luke." Across the room, Dr. G laughed. So much for playing along. Perhaps Hootan was incapable of ironic banter.

Pastor Rudy frowned in confusion, or at least an impersonation of it. "I'm not sure what he told you, but—"

"I told them, there's no drug." Luke said.

Dr. Gloria had reached the doorway at the back of the room. She glanced in, then nodded to me.

"You mind if I look around?" I asked.

Pastor Rudy glanced at Hootan. The kid kept his hand in his front pocket, calling attention to a Bulge of Significance. "I can give you a tour," the pastor said.

"Nah, that's okay," I said. "Why don't you just take a seat out here? That okay with you, Hootan?"

I didn't wait for an answer and walked toward the back doorway that Rudy had stepped out from. Dr. Gloria waited there, wings half-unfurled. The doorway opened to a large space that used to be the store's warehouse. Heavy steel shelving units sat empty except for a few cardboard boxes, a selection of power tools, and building materials: plywood, paint cans, stacks of drywall. Two big doors at the back of the space looked like they led to a loading dock. There were two other smaller doors along a side wall.

"Where do you want to start searching?" Dr. G asked.

"We could split up," I said.

"Very funny." She flipped an imaginary gold coin and caught it in her palm. "Heads, that's the warehouse."

"I'm checking the side rooms," I said.

Dr. G sighed. "You don't have to keep proving you have free will."

One of the small doors opened to an office. The room was empty except for a metal desk and filing cabinet, a futon covered by a bedsheet, a couple folding chairs like those in the front room. Bars guarded the single window. No other exits.

On the walls hung three brightly colored posters under Plexiglas. They looked like extreme close-ups of plants, or machinery: gleaming tubes that could have been roots; wet silvery blobs like mercurial seed pods; broad swathes of orange and red and yellow that suggested the skin of tropical flowers. Where was the "Footprints in the Sand" poster? Hell, even a crucifix?

The only liturgical supplies were crowded together on top of the filing cabinet: a pair of wooden offering plates; a box of white communion wafers; a two-liter bottle of chianti, half gone; and a sleeve of plastic shot cups. I opened the wafer box, crushed one of the squares, and sniffed. Nothing. I popped another of the wafers into my mouth.

"You don't know what's in that," Dr. G said.

"The body of Christ," I said. "As dry as ever." I didn't detect a psychotropic hit. I unscrewed the wine bottle and inhaled. It smelled like . . . cheap wine. I thought about taking a swig, but I knew where that would lead, and did I really want to end my sobriety (and it would end, it always ended) on Costco Kool-Aid?

On the desk lay a ten-inch tablet and a separate keyboard. I swiped the tablet's screen, and it opened to a music player, the cursor paused a couple minutes into something called "Gary Gygax Attax."

"Smell that?" Dr. G asked.

I looked up. Caught a faint tang of ammonia, and then it was gone. "Someone's been printing," I said.

I began opening desk drawers. One was locked, but it was too narrow to hold what I was looking for. I went through each drawer of the filing cabinet, looking for stacks of rice paper, or at least printing supplies. I found nothing but ordinary paper, file folders, tangled computer cables.

Hootan yelled from the front room, "What's taking so long?"

"Shut up," I yelled back.

I walked out of the office. Caught another whiff of amines. I started for the warehouse, then stopped, turned toward the other small door. It was unlocked. I pushed it open and flipped on the light, expecting a scattering of cockroaches. It was a bathroom, newly renovated and sparkling clean: white tile, new toilet, a shower stall guarded by a white rubber curtain. I pulled back the curtain.

"Here we go," Dr. G said, excited.

A new-looking chemjet printer sat on a wire crate positioned in the center of the shower stall. The printer's exhaust fan and runoff port had been covered by an elegant filter and valve system. Plastic tubes snaked down into the shower drain. In the corner of the stall was an open FedEx box agleam with foil c-packs. Many of them were labeled with the hexagonal sperm symbol of phenethylamine, the yeast of artisanal drug manufacturing.

The chemjet wasn't a model I recognized. Most of these machines were made in China or Malaysia and stamped with generic-sounding names like "Print Pro," but this one had no markings that I could see. And those valves were a cut above the usual hobbyist price point.

The printer wasn't turned on, so I thought it safe to pop the lid. It was like opening the hood of a Chrysler K-car and discovering a Ferrari engine. No, an art project. I recognized many of the components—copper tubes, mini-ovens (each costing thousands of dollars apiece), ceramic refrigeration coils, glass reaction chambers—but others were a mystery to me. Tubes and wires crossed and recrossed in a web that reminded me of neurons, or those graphs showing every possible relation in a social network.

This was like no chemjet I'd ever seen. A normal printer was designed to cook multiple recipes within a certain range, like a home bread maker. No reaction chamber connected directly to another, because you might have to plug in other steps—for drying, mixing, or distilling—to make whatever drug you programmed.

But this engine was so convoluted, so complicated, I knew I didn't have the skills to take it apart and put it back together to see how it worked. The best I could hope for was a kind of brain scan: watch it in action and try to figure out what was happening.

"Why does this look familiar?" Dr. G asked.

"No idea," I said. "But this thing makes Numinous, I'm sure of it. We have to take it with us."

"We can't just walk out with it," Dr. G said. "Fayza would never let us keep it."

The angel had a point. I snapped the lid back in place and closed the rubber curtain. I walked out of the bathroom, then back in.

Dr. G said, "We need—"

"A decoy," I said.

I jogged back to the office and grabbed the box of communion wafers.

In the front room, Pastor Rudy and Luke sat on the seats—the pastor relaxed, Luke anxious—while Hootan paced in front of them, still holding his hand in his front pocket.

"Why are you doing that?" I asked him.

"What?" Hootan asked.

"The hand thing. Either show them the gun or not. What's the deal with hiding it, but letting everyone know you're hiding it?"

Hootan resentfully removed his hand from his pouch, sans gun. He looked at the box in my hand. "Did you find it?"

"I have to test it, but I'm ninety percent sure the pastor here is delivering it through these."

"Crackers?"

Oh, right. Muslim. "Communion wafers," I said. "The powder form of the drug mixes easily with unleavened bread."

Luke looked surprised. Pastor Rudy seemed calm. "You're welcome to them," he said to me.

"If you're wrong—," Hootan said.

"Then we come back and bust up the joint. Or whatever it is gangsters do."

"Don't encourage him," Dr. G said.

Luke said to the pastor, "You're not just going to let them walk out of here?"

Rudy patted the man's arm. "Everything works out, Luke." He looked at me. "*Vaya con dios.*"

"Like I have any choice," I said.

. . .

Hootan, his mission accomplished now, dropped me off at Bobby's apartment. It worried me that I didn't have to give him directions.

Before I went in the building, I used the flip phone Fayza had given me to call the hospital. I had to speak my way through half a dozen options until the patient phone rang on the NAT ward. If you're looking for the last pay phones in North America, they're all located in psych wards.

A female voice answered. "Hello?"

"Put Olivia Skarsten on the line, please," I said.

The woman said, "Who?"

I finally recognized the voice as belonging to Alexandra, a Korean college student who'd subsisted for four years on a diet of pita chips and intelligence enhancers, until she began to see Manitous residing in furniture. "I want Ollie, damn it. It's me, Lyda."

"Oh!" Then: "Are you calling from your room?"

"Alexandra, I left three days ago."

"Right." She set down the phone. I could hear the tinny roar of the open line, then Alexandra yelling for Ollie in the distance. Minutes passed while I paced Bobby's tiny apartment. I just hoped Alexandra remembered to lead Ollie to the phone. Separating the wall appliance from wall was an exercise in object differentiation that Ollie was not prepared to execute.

"Hello?" It was Ollie.

"Hey," I said.

"Lyda." She had no problem recognizing voices. "Are you okay?"

"I'm fine," I said.

"So the pellet's working?"

"I'm clean as a whistle. This is something else. I need your help."

"You're in trouble."

"If I'm going to stay out of trouble, I need you."

She knew what that meant. Not the "you" under medication. The old Ollie.

"You want me to ride without a helmet," she said.

"Just for a little while."

The line went silent.

"I'm not going to be very sharp for a while," she said finally. "And then when the meds wear off . . . it's going to be the whole package."

"I figured." With Ollie's particular damage, there was no happy medium for medication. The minimum dose was pretty much the debilitating dose. She was on or decidedly off.

After a moment I said, "So when do you think . . . ?"

I listened to Ollie breathe for thirty seconds, a minute. Mulling it over. Finally she said, "How about tomorrow morning?"

"You can get out by then?"

"It's not Fort Knox."

THE PARABLE OF
the Ticking Clock

In those days, after the fall of the towers and the bombing of the trains and the wars in desert cities, after the chemical attacks of New Delhi and the Arab Spring chilled into the Autumn of the Iron Boot, the woman Olivia Skarsten left her post in the United States Army and became a communications analyst for Calasys, Inc., one of the hundreds of private corporations serving the signals intelligence needs of the American empire. She served her company, and her country, very well, and served them even better when she began using Clarity, a certain designer drug that was all the rage in the spook set. She might have served for longer if it had not been for the Case of the Broken Watch.

One of the subjects on the monitor list that Olivia was responsible for was a Pakistani expatriate living in New York City. The man—let's call him Akbar—had been added to that list because of family relations: Two cousins were known members of the LeT, a Pakistani extremist group that longed to strike a blow against India and its allies. One day Akbar made an internet voice call to his brother-in-law back home in Lahore—let's call him Bashir, for alphabetical simplicity. Akbar in New York mentioned several times that he wanted to buy a luxury wristwatch. Specifically a Maurice Lacroix wristwatch. Could Bashir the brother-in-law help him?

Olivia the Analyst was curious about this exchange. She had been monitoring cell phone calls, VoIP transmissions, and email for over five years,
and she had developed an instinct for the unusual. When she was using
Clarity, her powers of pattern recognition were especially keen, and that
included recognizing items that were *not* part of the pattern. She wondered, why would Akbar go to all this trouble to purchase from a relative
in Pakistan? Akbar could buy any designer watch he wanted online. Or if
he wanted a knockoff, the streets of New York were full of them. Even if
Bashir got some fabulous wholesale discount, Olivia categorized the interaction to be—to use a term of art in her field—"fishy."

She issued a tracking order on Bashir's communications, and learned
that a day after talking to Akbar, Bashir sent an email to an electronics
store and asked about an invoice for a shipment of watches. Olivia noticed that the last three digits of the invoice corresponded to the number
of a Virgin-Atlantic flight from London to Newark.

Yes, she simply noticed. At this point in her career and chemical cycle,
she was firing on all cylinders. The numbers, in a bit of Clarity-induced
synesthesia, rang like chimes. Only a few weeks before, on a different
matter entirely, she had looked through a list of flights to Newark and
New York, and the numbers had stuck in her head.

Olivia, growing nervous now, began to comb through the NSA's data
warehouse for all the signal traffic between Pakistani nationals. She ran
queries on all the cleartext available, be it human-translated, autotrans-
lated, or untranslated. In very little time she turned up forty-two conversations—forty-two!—between Pakistanis that mentioned watches, all in
the last month. Flight numbers kept appearing in the conversations: a
United flight from Pittsburgh, a Lufthansa flight from Munich. Olivia
realized that they were trying to decide on a target.

Time was of the essence. She flagged all the relevant data and wrote an
alert memo, which she sent, per protocol, to her superior. Unfortunately,
this was Memorial Day weekend, and the superior was out of his office,
and Olivia could not get any response from his backup. Olivia was upset.
It was clearly specified in the operations manual that the team coordina-
tor or his backup was to be available 24-7. While she was fuming, a new
cell call popped up from Akbar, her ex-pat Pakistani in NYC, to Bashir in
Lahore. Olivia was listening to it live. Near the end of the call, Bashir read
off the same London invoice number that Olivia had intercepted before.

Olivia knew that flight. She also knew that it was *already in the air*. The plane would touch down in New York at 4:52 a.m. Then Bashir said, "You can expect delivery by morning."

Olivia was not even scheduled to be on duty that night. But she was the only person who could have recognized this pattern.

She tried to call her superior on vacation, but it was 3 a.m. and the call went unanswered. She escalated and called his boss, who curtly told her to file a report for review in the morning. She called the company president and got only so far as his voicemail. Olivia would not quit. She began to call other government offices, ringing pens and cell phones and land-lines all over the District of Columbia and Virginia. Of the people she reached, most had never gotten a direct call from a consultant before and refused to talk to her. She finally reached Willa Frank, the Undersecretary for Political Affairs, number three at the State Department.

Ms. Frank asked Olivia to slow down and repeat the information. Then she asked for Olivia's name again, and what company she worked for. Then Ms. Frank said, "How long have you been awake, Ms. Skarsten?"

Olivia wasn't quite sure. Three days, more or less.

Ms. Frank said, "I'll take care of this."

It was now an hour until the plane landed. Olivia was alone in the building, sitting at her desk with all four computer monitors on. One window showed the Virgin-Atlantic website, a dozen others were open to every TV and web news channel Olivia could think of. She was sick to her stomach. Sweat painted her back. She counted down the minutes to 4:52 a.m. And then, at 4:40, the Virgin-Atlantic website updated. The plane had landed early.

Olivia was shocked, but also relieved. No crash. No bomb. She could not understand what had happened. And then, because she was one of the company's best analysts, she came upon the solution.

Olivia's superior returned early from vacation and found her at her desk, staring at the monitors. Three security officers stood behind him. The boss said, "Ollie, did you call Willa Frank this morning?"

Olivia said, "Nobody else would listen."

He told her to gather her personal belongings, but she had already packed the box. She'd been doing fifty milligrams of Clarity a day, plus another fifty of Adderall, and usually a twelve-pack of Red Bull. She could see, almost literally, what was coming. The writing was on the wall, the floors, and the furniture. Each face like an arrow pointing her toward the exit.

A few years later, when she told the story to Lyda Rose, a fellow resident of the neuro-atypical ward of Guelph Western Hospital, Lyda asked, "What happened to the Pakistani guy in New York?"

Ollie shrugged. "He probably got a new watch."

—G.I.E.D.

CHAPTER SIX

We waited for Ollie at the agreed-upon place, the parking lot of a Tim Hortons three blocks from the hospital. Bobby drumming his fingers on the wheel, Dr. Gloria in the backseat humming Mozart, both of them driving me crazy.

Bobby said, "Are you sure this is a good idea?"

"Is what a good idea?" I asked.

"Helping her . . . escape."

"You think she's dangerous?"

"No, no! I mean, maybe. Didn't she kill a guy?"

"She shot someone. Wounded him. It was a robber who was breaking into her apartment."

"I thought it was her landlord."

"Who told you that?"

Bobby touched the treasure chest at his neck. "Todd."

Fucking Counselor Todd. "Yes," I said, "but she *thought* it was a robber." Actually, she had thought it was an agent sent by her former employers to take her back across the border. Ollie on meds was brain-damaged—couldn't organize her visual field, couldn't separate figure from ground, couldn't recognize her own face in a mirror—but Ollie *off* meds . . .

"She can be a little paranoid," I said.

"She told me that the US has drones the size of house flies, and that they can come in your house and take pictures of you."

"The US government does not want to see you naked, Bobby."

"So it's not true?"

"I didn't say that."

Ollie had worked for six years doing signals intelligence for the US Army, then moved to the private sector to do the same job for three times the money. A contractor, with access to all kinds of classified info, not to mention the government's mil-spec smart drugs. The one Ollie used was a wicked thing, a custom-built enzyme that generated its own battery of agonists for the alpha-2A receptor. They called it Clarity. The drug—or rather, the proteins that the enzyme manufactured—set fire to the forest that was the prefrontal cortex, burned down the trees and encouraged massively interconnected bushes of white matter to grow up in its place. Repeated use at high doses made the new structure permanent.

Nobody used Clarity anymore.

"Besides," I said to Bobby. "You're Canadian. You're perfectly safe."

Dr. G spotted Ollie crouched down between cars, wearing a baseball cap and blue scrubs, not enough clothes for the weather. I got out of the car, and Ollie looked at me without recognition, her face pinched and nervous, ready to run. Then I said her name, and she hopped up, began walking quickly toward us.

Dr. Gloria said, "Bobby's right, we shouldn't be helping her escape. It isn't fair to her. She's better off in the ward."

"She's a grown woman. She can go back whenever she wants, and God knows she can get out whenever she wants."

Ollie touched me on the arm like a runner tagging safe. Neither of us were huggers. She slid into the backseat, and I followed her in.

Bobby said, "Hi, Ollie!" Overdoing the cheerfulness.

She closed her eyes, pressed a hand into her forehead. Still shaky, coming down off the meds.

"Turn up the heat, Bobby," I said. He pulled into the street, and I said to Ollie, "How you doing?"

Her eyes slid across my face, unable to gain traction. "I'll be better when we're away from the hospital."

"So no problems getting out, Doctor . . . Srinigar?"

She touched the badge she wore on a lanyard and allowed herself a half smile. Hospital security had never been a problem for Ollie. She lifted pass cards, security badges, and keys, then kept them hidden in her mattress. We used to go for midnight runs to the kitchen and raid the fridges. She could unlock most doors with the twist of a wire coat hanger, but only with her eyes closed, doing it by feel. My job was to point her at the doors and guide her back to the NAT ward. I had no idea how she'd managed to get out of the building on her own and navigate three blocks, even after twelve hours off the meds. But here she was.

"Did you bring any of your Alisprazole?" I asked.

"About a dozen pills."

Dr. G said, "She should stay on her meds. Going off now—"

"She'll be fine," I told the doctor.

"Lyda . . . ," Dr. G chided.

I breathed in. To Ollie I said, "We don't have to do this. You can stay on them. I can talk to my dealer and get more when we need them."

"I thought you needed me," Ollie said. "Immediately."

"I do."

"So I thought we'd do a jumpstart."

"No!" Dr. G said. "Absolutely not!"

"Unless you've got five or six days to let my system flush out," Ollie said.

"I kind of need you tonight," I said.

The car exploded with subjective light. "I will not participate in this!" Dr. Gloria declared. I heard a shriek of metal, and then a rush of wind. I yelled, thinking, stupidly, that Bobby had also been blinded and crashed the car.

Ollie yelled, "Lyda! What's going on?" Bobby shouted too.

I opened my eyes a sliver. Dr. G's wings were at full extension, and the tips had ripped a ragged hole in the top of the car. The wind roared. The doctor brought her wings down and then shot into the sky.

"Hypocrite," I said. I'd thrown an arm over my eyes, and I was crying from the blast of light. I still felt the wind whipping through the exit hole.

"Are you all right?" Ollie asked. "Was that your—?"

"Give me a second," I said.

There is no wind, I told myself. No hole. No furious angel.

I sat back against the seat, eyes closed. The sound of the wind died down, became the hum of the tires. Bobby, still upset, kept asking me if he should pull over.

"I'm fine," I told him. "Just stay on the road."

After several minutes I said to Ollie, "So. This thing."

She said, "What do you need me to do?"

While we rode into Toronto I told her about Fayza, the storefront church, the printer inside. How Fayza was waiting for me to test the communion wafers. Hootan had insisted on taking half the box to bring to Fayza, and if she decided to check them herself she'd find nothing but water and flour.

"I need that printer," I said. "And the precursor packs."

"That's why you had me get out? To break into a strip mall?"

There was one other thing. But it depended on what happened with the printer.

"I can't do it without you," I said.

I wasn't sure she heard the hesitation before I answered. The old Ollie certainly would have.

After a moment she took a deep breath. "I'm going to need my bag."

Somewhere above us, an angel screamed.

· · ·

Ollie gave Bobby an address on Danforth that turned out to be a two-story building: a Thai restaurant called Bangkok Chop on the first floor, apartments above. Ollie had to ask if this was the place; she still couldn't recognize it. She said, "Tell whoever's working that I sent you, and that you're here to pick up the bag."

"You can't go in?"

She looked up at me. It took her a moment to find my eyes, and then she allowed her desperation to show. Whoever or whatever was inside the restaurant scared the shit out of her.

"Okay, no problem." I said. "I'll be right back."

It was just after eleven in the morning. The place was open, but there was no one at the front counter, no one at the tables. The air was warm, and I could smell noodles cooking. I called out the standard sonar for empty buildings: "Hello," "Excuse me," etc. A dark-haired boy about five years old burst through the kitchen door, saw me, and ran back before I could stop him. A minute later a tiny middle-aged Asian woman came out wiping her hands with a dish towel. "How many?" she asked.

"Ollie sent me," I said.

She frowned.

"Olivia Skarsten? She said to—"

"You know Olivia?" Her voice low and fast, the accent compacting the syllables. I couldn't read her expression.

"Yes. Yes, I do."

"You have seen her lately? In the hospital? She is *well?*" Each question a jab.

"Uh . . ."

"She has *visitors?*" Now the anger was coming through.

I put up my hands. "Listen, I'm just here as a favor. She sent me to pick up her bag."

"Oh, she wants her *things*." The woman started shouting angrily in another language—I assumed Thai. A girl who could have been anywhere from sixteen to twenty-five came running out of the kitchen, and yelled, "Ma! Ma! Settle down!"

The mother kept shouting. The girl's eyes darted from her mother's face to mine, her expression shifting in quantum jumps from confused to concerned to pissed off. Now I had both women to deal with. I said, "If she owes you money—"

The daughter pointed at me. "Stay the fuck there." No trace of an Asian accent—she sounded like an angry Edmonton Oilers fan. I upped her minimum age to eighteen. She shouted something at her mother in Thai and then marched across the dining room, heading toward the restrooms. The mother glared at me, lips pursed, nostrils flaring. Genuine, high-quality seething.

A minute passed, two. I looked back toward the glass door glazed with condensation, hoping that the blurry shape beyond was Bobby's car, ready for my getaway. I felt naked without Dr. Gloria at my back.

The kitchen door bumped open, and a man in an electric wheelchair rolled out. The father, evidently, or maybe the grandfather. He slumped in the chair at an odd angle. His right arm was dead in his lap, but his left hand gripped the armrest controller. The chair coasted to a stop, and his eyes drifted up to mine.

Everything clicked then. The wheelchair, the angry mother, the angrier daughter. Maybe if Dr. G had been there I wouldn't have been so slow to understand.

The daughter reappeared, dragging behind her a wheeled black duffel as big as a body bag. She dropped it between us. The mother burst into tears and spun away from us, slammed her way into the kitchen.

Heat flushed my cheeks. I bent to pick up the duffel, and the daughter said, "Is she still claiming she's insane?"

"I don't think she's claiming anything." The bag was heavier than I expected.

I started toward the door, and the girl said, "Wait. You tell her."

I stopped. "Look, I'm just—"

"Tell her when he was bleeding away on the stairs, waiting for the ambulance, he kept saying, I should have knocked, I should have knocked. He felt *pity* for her. That's the kind of man he is."

I looked at the old man. He said nothing. I said, "I'm sorry for—"

"No more *sorry*," the daughter said. "All those letters she sent—I apologize, I'm so sorry, please forgive me, I wasn't myself. They mean *nothing*. Tell her that my mother wanted to burn that bag. The only reason she didn't is because Dad wouldn't allow it. And because, when that psycho came to pick it up, she'd finally have to face us in person—no hiding behind *letters*." Her smile was a grimace. "I guess we were wrong about that."

I pushed open the door. The girl said, "Tell her she's a coward."

I froze, one hand on the door, one hand on the bag. I turned on her, ready to cut her down: *You fucking bitch, you have no idea how brave she is.* But the old man was looking up at me out of that bent body.

I banged through the door without saying anything. Outside I smacked the trunk of the car, and Bobby popped the lid. I wrestled the duffel inside, then got into the backseat.

"Let's get out of here," I said.

Ollie sat with her arms across her stomach, staring straight ahead. Bobby said, "Did they give you a hard time?"

"No, no. Charming people. I don't think I'd order from there anytime soon, though."

. . .

We carried the bag up to Bobby's apartment and set Ollie up on the couch with the drapes closed and the lights off. She was corkscrewing deeper into the withdrawal, and the headaches and nausea were on their way. We scavenged Bobby's bathroom and came up with some ibuprofen. The roommate's door remained closed—I still hadn't seen him.

I said, "I have to make a call. You two good?"

Ollie waved. Bobby said, "I'll make tea."

I said, "Give me your pen."

Bobby looked hurt as he handed it over. "You should really buy your own." He didn't know about the phone Fayza had given me.

I walked down to the street before I unrolled the screen. I found Brandy's name in the contact list and left the drug dealer a message: "This is Lyda. I'm looking for a custom. Immediately. I'll pay for the rush."

The message wouldn't go directly to whatever burner phone Brandy was using, so it would probably take a while. I started walking. The pen chimed before I'd reached the corner.

The sender's address was an obviously randomized mash of letters and numbers. "Have you found God yet?" Brandy asked, cheerful. The call was voice only; he hadn't turned the video on.

"Still looking," I said. "But thanks for the referral."

A pause as he tried to figure out if I was being sarcastic.

"I warned you, you didn't want to talk to my distributor," he said.

"This isn't about that," I said. "I need something else. Ever hear of a drug called Clarity?"

"Of course. For a while very popular. I can print it up for you, no problem."

"Bullshit. That stuff was enzymatic. You can't print it."

"Did I say print? I will order for you, quick—"

"Nobody makes it anymore, Brandy, not even the Chinese. Too many suicides."

"Don't sound so angry! What I mean is that I can make you something *like* Clarity."

"That's what I'm looking for—something close. There's a drug called Guanfacine that hits some of the same pathways—it's sold under the brand name Tenex. Can you get me that?"

"Students ask for it by name! Why didn't you say so?"

"I need it in an hour."

He gave me the name of an intersection a half mile from me. "There's a threading shop there. You know, Indian ladies doing that thing to eyebrows? Stand in front of that. Or go inside and get some work done."

He laughed. I hung up on him.

"My eyebrows are fine," I said.

The neighborhood grew shabbier the farther I walked. I put out my Don't Fuck With Me Vibe, which deterred the homeless from hitting me up. I put away Bobby's pen and took out Fayza's phone. There were two messages, both from Hootan, asking if the analysis of the wafers was done yet. I'd told him it would be at least forty-eight hours, but here he was harassing me after one day.

Light flashed at the edge of my vision. I glanced up from the pen, expecting to see Dr. Gloria, but there was only a homeless guy, hunched over his black garbage bag. Fine, I thought. Play hard to get.

· · ·

Sometime after dark, after Brandy's custom-printed drug had frolicked for a few hours in her system, Ollie said, "That's a person." I'd just come back from another errand, and she was sitting where I'd left her on the couch, still wearing scrubs, staring at the chair across the room. Bobby was slumped in the chair, asleep. A hole in his jeans showed a white kneecap.

"Wow, look at you, noticing things on things," I said. "You're feeling better?"

"A little, but not too much. The calm before everything starts turning too . . . meaningful." She nodded at Bobby. "He's a sweet kid. He thinks the world of you."

"God knows why."

"I think it was the werewolf."

I laughed. "Jesus, what did he tell you?"

"You saved his life."

"An exaggeration." I sat down beside her. "When Bobby showed up in the ward, he was getting bullied by a thug named Torrence, a huge guy who'd gotten his skull dented in a motorcycle accident and woke up remembering that he'd been a hyena."

"What?"

"Oh yeah, and he could turn back into one at any moment."

"You're shitting me."

"It's called clinical lycanthropy, but the animal can be anything, even a cockroach."

"So how'd you save Bobby? Shoot Torrence with a silver bullet?"

"You're not listening—he was a *hyena*. Totally different."

"Of course. My mistake."

I checked to make sure Bobby was still sleeping. "It wasn't much. I just told Torrence that if he didn't lay off Bobby, I'd tell the doctors about his drawings."

"Drawings?"

"Filthy stuff. I tell you, I'll never think the same way about Lassie again."

Ollie laughed, willing to go along with my bullshit. "So, you ready to talk?" I asked.

She found my face and kissed me hard. "Now I am. Tell me everything you can remember about the church."

I went over the exits I'd seen: the heavy loading dock doors, the reinforced glass front door. I couldn't tell her whether there was an alarm system.

As we talked she tipped over the duffel bag that I'd retrieved from the Thai place. It slammed against the floor and Bobby startled awake. Ollie froze for a moment, staring in his direction. The kid scrunched his face and yawned like a bear.

I said to Ollie, "It's still Bobby."

"Right," she said. She unzipped the bag. There was no lock on the zipper, not even the tiny padlocks they put on cheap luggage. She started pulling out the contents, mostly clothes, and dumped them on the floor.

"Any security cameras at the church?" she asked.

"None that I could see." I picked up one of the articles of clothing, a bulky camouflage jacket. It didn't look like army, but something a hunter would wear. A hunter much bigger than Ollie.

From the bag she lifted out a heavy object that was a bit bigger than a toolbox. It was sealed in opaque plastic wrap. She turned it in her hands, spending a lot of time looking at the zigzag heat seal on the wrap.

"Is there a problem?" I asked.

"Trying to decide if anyone's opened it," she said. "I think we're good."

She tore open the plastic seal. The object was a steel box, with a lid closed by a thick black padlock.

"I hate myself sometimes," she said.

I looked at the lock. It was a mean-looking thing, embossed with the name Medeco. "Do you have the key?"

She rubbed at her forehead. She was sweating, but that was probably a side effect of Brandy's jumpstart. "There is no key," she said.

"You lost it?" Bobby asked, fully awake now.

"I melted it down. That way they couldn't steal it from me, or force me to give it to them."

"*Who?*" Bobby said, alarmed.

She smiled sourly. "You know. *Them*." She hopped to her feet. "Let's see what's in the kitchen."

There was a sharpness to her that I hadn't seen since I first met her, in my early days on the NAT. She'd been palming her meds then, playing a game of chicken with her own crazy. Her paranoia was kicking in. As a newcomer I was of course under suspicion. Lyda Rose, Agent of Them. But I was a testy addict drying out, and of course eager to push anyone's buttons, including those of the tiny chica with the dark eyes. In group, it was her reactions I watched the most. On the floor I could sense her tracking me, monitoring who I talked to. We were wary of each other and tuned in at the same time. The first time we had sex it was like full contact tae kwon do. Eventually I talked her into going back on her prescription, even though—or maybe because—I was in such rough shape myself. The meds soaked into her bloodstream, seemingly having no effect, then *bang*—the paranoia fell away and the agnosia kicked in. She became sweeter, softer, a little out of focus. Easier to love. And a lot less sexy. A flaw in my character, but there it is. I've always been a sucker for the beautiful and the batshit.

Ollie came back to the living room with a collection of junk: wire twist ties, a grocery store bonus card, a paring knife. Bobby said, "Don't you have lock pick tools?"

"They're in the box," she said.

"But why would you—?"

"Shhh." She kneeled next to the duffel. One night on the ward, during one of our after-hours kitchen runs, I'd asked her if picking locks was part of her government training. She laughed, said it was the tweaker itch, one of the side effects of Clarity. A mentor had told her not to fight it. Better to use the itch and get a hobby. So instead of taking apart old vacuum cleaners like a meth head, she attacked locks. Worked her way through the bibles of the field by a guy named Tobias, staying up all night, immersing herself in the craft like parachuting into a foreign country.

Ollie cut the grocery card in two. One half she shaped into a rough key. The other was a narrow strip. She slid the fake key into the lock, then rapped on it with the heel of her shoe. Next she took out the key shape and replaced it with the strip.

She spent the next few minutes poking at the lock's innards with the wire twist ties. A dollop of sweat popped from the end of her nose. Her fingers trembled.

Bobby watched her, nervously gripping his treasure chest. He said, "It's okay if you can't open it."

Ollie's head jerked up. "*What* did you say?"

I said, "Kid, let her work."

"I'm just saying, we could call a locksmith. One time when I was locked out of my car—"

Ollie jerked on the padlock and suddenly it was open. "When you're popping locks, it's not *if* it opens," she said. "It's how fast." She sat back on her haunches, looking worn out. "I'm just not up to speed yet."

"Literally," I said.

She looked up at me and smiled. "I'll do better tonight. How about another fortune cookie?"

I unfolded the paper I'd purchased from Brandy. The page was divided into perforated strips, each strip printed with a sentence. I tore one off. It said, "You will be taking a long trip."

Ollie popped it in her mouth. Bobby nodded at the toolbox and said, "So . . . ?"

Ollie opened the box and began lifting out items: a black velvet bandolier loaded with picks, wrenches, shims, and thin-bladed knives; a top tray full of plastic cases containing electronic components; a lower tray of molded slots for pliers, wire cutters, tiny flashlights, and screwdrivers. Bobby said, "Is that a gun?"

"This?" She picked up a hunk of dark gray plastic with a pistol grip, pointed it at him, and pulled the trigger. Nothing happened. "*This* is a drill," she said. "Which reminds me, I need to charge this thing before our assault on the house of God."

CHAPTER SEVEN

The Reverend Rudy Gallo Velez, naked except for his undershorts, crouched atop a chair in the center of the room in one of the classic stress positions: thighs parallel to the floor, arms tied behind his back, head bowed. A plastic garbage bag, loose at the bottom, covered his head. A figure eight of nylon cord, one loop around his neck, the other around his knees, kept his body in the proper attitude. He'd been in the position, on and off (mostly on), for three hours. He was a strong man, very fit, but sweat gleamed on his skin, and his legs trembled.

The Vincent sat about twenty feet away, his feet propped on the chemjet printer, his hat low across his eyes. A Zane Grey novel was open on his pen. He remained silent, giving Rudy time to think.

The pastor grunted, very quietly. He flexed his bare feet against the seat of the chair. His muscles had to be burning constantly now. Shooting pains would be knifing up his thighs, across his lower back. The discomfort caused by a stress position was psychologically different from that caused directly by the interrogator—say, a punch to the face, or a snapping of a finger bone, both of which the Vincent had inflicted upon Rudy within the first thirty seconds of meeting him—because positional pain seemed to come from within. This predisposed the victim to solicit the torturer's help to end the suffering.

But a predisposition only. The Vincent could tell, even with the hood obscuring the pastor's face, that he was not yet sufficiently distressed. Was he resilient because he was a man of the cloth, a gangbanger, or both? A black hand tattoo covered his left shoulder, and an elaborate "13" decorated the side of his neck, both of which marked him as La eMe—Mexican Mafia. If Pastor Rudy had found religion, it was only after a long allegiance with another hierarchical organization.

A novice interrogator might grow impatient at this point, start beating the man to break him down. That would be a mistake. As the CIA's Human Resource Exploitation Training Manual made clear: Pain was useless. Psychology was everything.

Pain was a tool to get a subject—especially an alpha male like Rudy—into the proper state of mind. Which was why, when the Vincent had surprised the man in the back room of the church, the Vincent had immediately dropped him to the floor with the punch, then bent his finger the wrong way toward his wrist. Swift, unexpected pain hinted at the parameters of the interaction to come, and notified the subject of his change of status, from captain of his fate to passenger on the USS *I Am Fucked*.

For the young man who'd been in the room with Rudy—a gangly African-American who resembled the adopted younger brother of Uncle Sam—that ship had sailed. The black man had tried to run, and the Vincent had collared him like a rodeo calf and slammed him to the cement. The boy was stunned, teetering on unconsciousness, and the Vincent had helped him over that edge.

Despite all the violence and, let's face it, an impressive display of physical prowess, the pastor refused to answer the Vincent's questions. What did you give the red-haired woman, Lyda Rose? Where did you get the chemjet printer? Who gave you the ingredients? The pastor only smiled and said, "She took our communion wafers."

Enhanced coercive interrogation techniques were required. To do the job right, the Vincent needed a private, soundproofed location, preferably one underground with a few metal doors to slam, all the better to convince the victim that he was isolated, helpless, and beyond rescue. Instead he had to improvise with what was available: a plastic bag, a chair, and a windowless warehouse with a cement floor. He'd done more with less.

A few minutes later, Rudy's legs gave out and he tipped sideways. The chair shot out from under him and smacked the floor. The pastor lay on his side, the noose still enforcing a curled position.

The Vincent tipped back his hat but remained seated. "Are you ready to answer my questions, Rudy?" He thought it intellectually honest to call his victims by their names. He would not turn what he did, and who he did it to, into abstractions. That was for people with no control of their emotions.

The pastor breathed hard under his hood, the plastic hugging his mouth, then inflating. The Vincent flicked to a new page on the pen. "My employer would like you to fill out a brief questionnaire. I can read you the questions and record your answers. Ready?"

The hood moved slightly. The Vincent took that as a nod.

"*One*. 'Are you a user of the drug that you've been distributing?'"

The Vincent waited for several seconds. "All righty, then. I'm going to put that down as a yes. *Two*. 'How long have you been taking the drug and in what dosages?'"

Nothing.

"These aren't hard questions, Rudy. For research purposes only, not personal at all. Help me out here."

The Vincent got to his feet. "*Three*. 'Would you say you've been taking the drug for less than a week, a week to one month, or longer than a month?'"

The pastor said, "Are you happy?" His voice was muffled by the hood, but he sounded genuinely curious.

The question surprised the Vincent. Usually at this point, the questions were more along the line of "Why are you doing this?" or "What do you want?" or "Why won't you tell me what to say?"

The Vincent said, "I'm doing well, thanks." It was sometimes a mistake to let the victim drive the interaction, but at least he was talking. And this was the most interesting conversation the Vincent had had in a while.

"I mean happy with your life," Rudy said. "With what you're doing."

Ah. An appeal to his conscience. Talk about a rhetorical cul-de-sac. The Vincent tucked the pen into his jacket pocket.

"I'm happier than anyone else I know," he said. "I'm . . ." What was the word? "Free" was close. "Liberated"? "Unfettered"? "I'm unencumbered."

He moved behind Rudy and pulled him into a sitting position. "I'm like a Goddamn free-range buffalo. Sorry—bison.

"See, you have a god to answer to," the Vincent said, warming to the topic. "Others have society, or Mom, or the gang. Some voice in your head shaming you when you've broken the code. But in my head it's quiet. Peaceful. Up you go."

He helped blind Rudy climb back onto the chair, an awkward series of moves.

"You know in your heart what's right or wrong," the pastor said.

"I know in my *head*," the Vincent said. "And what I've learned is that it's not *knowing* what's right or wrong, it's *caring*. Feeling the wrongness. See, Rudy, when you see someone you love being hurt, you feel an echo of the pain yourself. You only got to imagine it. I can say, 'I kicked your grandfather in the balls,' and you will feel a twinge in your groin. Your morality is not *rational*, or handed down to you on stone tablets by some divine cop, it's wired into your nervous system." He patted the man on his sweat-slick back. "Fortunately, there's a treatment for it."

"But you're alone," Rudy said. "My god is here."

"He doesn't seem to be helping you much." The Vincent leaned close. "Where did the printer come from?"

The man said nothing.

The Vincent said, "I'll track it down eventually, but you could save me a lot of time. Was it the cartel? Have they branched into desktop drugs?"

The Vincent watched the hood for movement. The man seemed strikingly calm. Breathing deeply, but without the ragged gasps of someone under duress.

"Rudy, you've been put in an unfair position. The people who gave you that hardware knew that sooner or later someone like me was going to come around asking questions about it. They knew that you'd tell me eventually."

The Vincent pulled the hood from the pastor's head. Rudy's face was covered in sweat, and he blinked to keep it from running into his eyes.

The Vincent said, "I can tell that you're a good man, trying to do the right thing. But no one but you expects you to keep all this secret."

Rudy looked to his left, as if someone had just stepped into the room. The Vincent couldn't stop himself from glancing in that direction. Of course no one was there.

"I think it's time we move on to the next phase," the Vincent said. He walked to his carry-on bag and unzipped it. He took out a pair of pliers, a serrated knife, a roll of duct tape, a punch awl, a plastic bottle of lighter fluid, and a box of kitchen matches. Set them on the floor in a row. They were all new, picked up from the Walmart soon after he'd landed in Toronto.

He made sure Rudy was watching this presentation of the props. The interrogation was, after all, a theatrical performance. You had to engage the victim in the narrative, a story that followed the classic structure: The hero (our victim), faced with a dire situation, overcomes adversity, and achieves his goals. Well, one goal, really: survival. But it was important that that modest happy ending seemed within reach, right around the corner. The Vincent's job was to inspire not only fear, but hope.

The Vincent picked up the awl. "Rudy, I need you to tell me where you got the printer. It's not like anything I've seen. Was it given to you, or did you buy it? Who did you get it from?"

Rudy shook his head.

"Just one name," the Vincent said reasonably.

"I'm not going to tell you that," Rudy said.

"Why not?"

He opened one eye, squinting. "I'm not going to point you toward another brother or sister."

"So you got it from someone else in the church. One of the members."

"Not this congregation," Rudy said. "Not this building."

"So if I looked for other congregations of—what do you call it? The Church of the Hologrammatic God—I could ask them. Maybe do a few more pastoral visits."

Rudy said nothing.

"I'm going to level with you," the Vincent said. "I'd rather not go to all that trouble. But you're putting me in a corner. If you don't give me some information that I can take to my employer, then I'm going to have to talk to other people in your church, as I'm talking to you now."

Rudy glanced to his left again, a gesture that was getting tiresome. The man just wasn't scared enough. And the Vincent couldn't just start slicing skin and breaking bones. Pain at that level was counterproductive, not only because of the well-documented willingness of prisoners to say anything to stop it, but because of the opposite: Many victims discovered that their tolerance was higher than they expected. And death threats were worse than useless; hold a gun to a victim's head, or a blade to his throat, he might start to think he was going to die no matter whether he submitted or not. The Vincent had seen this happen during an interrogation of a poppy farmer in Afghanistan. The army had botched the job, and the farmer shut down completely. He almost seemed to be at peace. By the time the Vincent had arrived at the scene, there wasn't enough time to win him back. Another human resource, unexploited.

No, it wasn't death threats that motivated his victims to cooperate, or pain, but *fear* of pain. And this man, Pastor Rudy Gallo Velez, seemed to have an extreme deficit of fear.

If he was drugged—and his employer said that he'd be dealing with criminals and users, starting with the addict Lyda Rose—it was no drug the Vincent had seen before. The Vincent had a bad thought: What if his own medication was interfering with the job? Maybe if he had some of the emotional sensitivity that he possessed when he was off duty and off the meds, then he could figure out where Rudy was vulnerable. But off the meds, the Vincent wouldn't have the stomach for the job at all.

It was a conundrum.

Maybe he could grab somebody off the street—an innocent, a little girl, perhaps—and torture her in front of the pastor? But that was crazy. Where was he going to find a little girl at this time of night? The black kid with the beard could have been leverage, but it was too late for that.

The Vincent said, "So what's it going to be, Rudy?"

The man shook his head. "I'm sorry. I just can't." He sounded genuinely apologetic. "I made a vow."

Even on the meds, with his empathy reduced to a trickle, the Vincent could detect the sincerity in the pastor's voice. Rudy was determined to keep his promise.

The Vincent put a hand on the man's neck. Three small dots surrounded the "13" tattoo, representing Prison, Hospital, and Cemetery, the gangster stations of the cross. "Just a first name," he said. Asking, even though it was futile. "Or the initials."

Rudy said, "It's not too late. It's never too late. God can forgive you. Even after you do what you're about to do."

The pastor stared at the floor. He was already gone, gone as that Afghan farmer.

"What are we going to do with you?" the Vincent asked.

CHAPTER EIGHT

Ollie and I rode in the backseat, Bobby alone up front. During the ride to the strip mall she held my hand, running her thumb up and down my wrist. Her fingers were no longer trembling. She directed Bobby to drive around the back.

She pulled my face to hers and kissed me fiercely. "For luck." She jumped out of the car and jogged up the steps beside the loading dock. She looked twice as big in the camo jacket.

I hopped out after her, then leaned back in to the passenger window. "Keep the car running," I told Bobby. I'd always wanted to say that.

Ollie took something out of her jacket pocket and inserted it in the lock of one of the doors. I whispered, "How long will it take to—?"

She pushed the door open and stepped into the dark.

"Okay then," I said.

Ollie turned on a thin flashlight. She played the light around the wall adjacent to the loading dock doors and finally settled on a small white box at eye level. *My* eye level, anyway—the box was positioned just over Ollie's head. The lid hung loose. She reached up and popped it off.

"Huh," she said.

"Problem?" I still had my hand on the door.

"The alarm's already disabled."

I closed the door. Ollie flipped a light switch. I winced against the light, turned to face the room—and my body jerked, then froze—the microseizure of the life-endangered mammal.

In the middle of the warehouse, a figure lay curled on the floor, his back to us. I flashed on the body of Francine, sprawled on the tile of the NAT bathroom, and knew this to be another corpse.

I stepped forward, and Ollie put a hand on my shoulder. "We have to get out," she said. "Now."

I ignored her and walked toward the body. He was naked, or nearly so. His hands were clasped behind him. His neck was straight, supported by something small, so that his head hovered over the floor. Blood had pooled beneath it, then spawned a rivulet that meandered a few feet to a drain.

I moved around his feet to see his face. It was the pastor. His eyes were open, his lips slightly parted. I crouched to see what he was resting on. I touched his shoulder, and he tipped onto his back.

A rounded wooden handle was buried in the side of his neck. The tattoo I'd seen yesterday was obscured by blood.

Ollie said, "Lyda . . ."

I was shaking, and couldn't stop myself. Some neural pathways are so old, the grooves so deep, you're forced to realize that you're an animal first. Reason, choice, self-control? They all showed up late to the evolutionary party.

"The chemjet," I said. "We need the chemjet."

Ollie walked toward the bathroom and I rose to follow her. She pulled open the door. Immediately she put up a hand to have me stay back, but I stepped forward.

Luke, the skinny black kid who'd led us here a day ago, slumped on the toilet. I recognized him despite the plastic garbage bag cinched tight over his face like a superhero mask.

The chemjet was gone. The wire crates still sat on the floor of the shower stall, and a few remnant plastic tubes coiled around the drain, but the printer was gone, along with the boxes of c-packs.

"It's got to be here!" I left the bathroom and slammed open the door to the office, but the printer wasn't there either. I headed for the sanctuary. Ollie grabbed me by the shoulders and spun me around. I was still shaking.

"It's not here," she said. "And we have to *go*."

"Wait. Where are his clothes?"

"The naked guy's?"

I found them in the warehouse: shoes, jeans, and T-shirt folded neatly and stacked on one of the wire shelves. I set aside the shirt and turned out the pants pockets, discovering keys, a smart pen, a wallet. I opened the wallet. Ollie watched me, confused. "What are you looking for?"

In the wallet was the usual: cash, credit cards, receipts. I handed her all the loose paper. "Check for rice paper," I said. "Anything that looks like designer print."

I marched back to the bathroom. I crouched beside Luke, trying not to look up at his face, and pushed a hand into his front pocket. It was empty. I reached across him to the other pocket. He gave off an earthy smell. How long had he been dead: an hour, a day?

There was nothing in the other pocket but some loose change. So, the back pockets, then. I took a breath, held it, then leaned hard into him, shifting him off one butt cheek. I worked a hand into his back pocket, and pulled out a square of stiff plastic like a miniature wallet.

I let go, and Luke slid off the toilet with a sickening thud.

I opened the plastic holder. Inside was a strip of paper with a single word printed on it. "Logos."

Ollie appeared in the doorway. "Got it," I said.

"Good," Ollie said. "Let's go."

She pushed me to the back door, then said, "I'll be right back."

"Where are you going?"

"A little cleanup." She disappeared back into the building.

I stepped outside, and the back parking lot was empty. Where the hell was Bobby? I went down the steps, spun around stupidly. I put the mini-wallet into my pocket and reached for Fayza's flip phone. I was about to dial when a pair of headlights turned the corner.

I backed up to the wall of the store. Bobby's hybrid whined to a halt. "Where the fuck did you go?" I asked him.

"I'm sorry! I'm sorry! You guys were taking so long, then I saw a car and I thought it was the cops, so I—"

"Never mind." I jumped in the back. "Shut off the lights."

"What happened? Where's Ollie? Where's the printer?"

"Somebody got there first," I said.

A minute passed, then two. Finally Ollie appeared. She shut the door behind her and climbed into the car. "Did you have to touch *everything?*" she said. But she was smiling.

"Drive," I told Bobby.

· · ·

"So what does it mean?" Bobby asked. "That word on the paper?"

We were the only three people in the harshly lit dining room of a twenty-four-hour Lebanese restaurant. Ollie sat on my side of the booth, her arm against mine, her hand on my knee. With her free hand she rummaged through a plate of falafel, three different dishes of fried vegetables, and a bowl of hummus. Driving the hospital food out of her system, she said. Bobby was deconstructing his baklava, eating it layer by layer like an archeologist. Me, I was just gripping a coffee, braced for the approach of sirens. I had no appetite. I kept picturing the awl in Pastor Rudy's neck, the bag over Luke's head . . .

"Lyda?" Bobby said. "What logos are they talking about?"

"Log-*ose*," Ollie said. "It's Greek."

"Ding. Two points," I said.

"For Gryffindor!" Bobby said.

"Gryffindor doesn't play basketball," Ollie said.

"The word means 'word.' 'In the beginning was the word, and the word was with God—' "

"And the word *was* God," Ollie said. Her eyes narrowed. "So you *are* religious."

"I was raised by a schizophrenic Southern Baptist," I said. "But it didn't affect me."

"Obviously," she said. She was grinning, almost giddy. Seeing the bodies hadn't seemed to faze her. And now she was flirting with me, leaning into me like an Iowa cheerleader in the front seat of a Ford pickup. Jesus Christ, what had I started?

Bobby asked me, "So are you going to eat it?" Meaning the paper.

"No, of course not." I *would* have torn off a piece and swallowed it, if I'd known which letter had been printed with the drug. Or it could be that the dosage was on every letter, or evenly distributed across the word. I couldn't afford to damage my one sample with a taste test.

"I need access to a lab," I said. "And one special machine."

Ollie squeezed my arm. "Where do we steal it from?" She was wide awake and ready to knock over banks.

"I'm cutting you off," I said. I pulled out the phone and slid out of the booth. "I'll be right back."

Ollie stopped me. "What is that?" Staring at the phone. I heated with embarrassment, which annoyed me, because I didn't think I had anything to be embarrassed about.

"Fayza gave me a phone," I said.

Bobby said, "So how come you're always borrowing mine?"

"She did not give you a phone," Ollie said. "She gave you a tracking device. Give me that."

"You're going to do something to it."

"Yes I am. Give it."

She snapped it in half, then pried off the back and tore out the electrical innards. She picked out the tiny battery and popped it free from the chip, then crushed the chip with the salt shaker.

"Yikes," Bobby said.

Ollie said, "Didn't you wonder why she gave it to you?"

"I thought so she would know the call came from me. Maybe she has a whitelist. Or special encryption . . ."

Ollie was shaking her head before I'd gotten halfway through the sentence. "From now on we use burners. No personal phones."

Bobby made a move to leave. "Bathroom."

"You too, kid," I said.

"But my apps! I have videos!"

Ollie said, "Relax, you can get it all back from your backups."

Bobby morosely took his pen from his pocket and slid it to her. She destroyed it as thoroughly as she had Fayza's device, then withdrew a new pen from the breast pocket of her camo jacket. She played with it for half a minute, activating it, then handed it to me. "Never been used," she said. "We're getting some Wi-Fi here, so I set it to reroute through an anonymizer server, so receivers shouldn't be able to pick up our location. Later I'll set up a hopper network so we can use the cell phone towers."

I didn't understand half of what she was saying. What was a hopper network?

Ollie saw my look and said, "What? This is what you sprung me for, right? These are basic countermeasures."

"I get all hot when you do spy talk," I said.

"Oh jeez," Bobby said. He went to the bathroom, sans pen.

Ollie stopped me before I walked off to make my call. "I know you're upset," she said.

"And you don't seem to be at all."

"I've seen bodies before." She shrugged. "Also, I'm in a weird state, chemically. I'm not sure if I'm reacting appropriately. Like, I can't stop thinking about this falafel—it's fantastic."

"Ha."

She glanced up to make sure Bobby was out of earshot. "We need to figure out who killed them," she said. "Was it the drug dealer?"

"Fayza has no reason to do anything with the pastor, not yet. I haven't given her the results of the test."

"But she thinks it's the Little Sprout drug. So she kills them now, and if it turns out they weren't using that particular drug, she still kills them—because they're competing with her."

"Ollie, come on, Fayza can't be that—" I was about to say "paranoid." But of course she could; she was a drug lord. Paranoia had to be one of the prerequisites for the job. "So this is what? Some low-level drug war?"

"Maybe not low-level," Ollie said. "Your pastor was Mexican Mafia."

"Wait, really?"

"He had the tattoos."

"So he's, what? Mexican cartel?"

"La eMe's primarily a prison gang, but it became attached to the cartels."

"I thought they all wiped each other out in the twenties."

"The old gangs aren't gone, just absorbed when the organizations from Ghana and Nigeria moved in."

"I didn't think he was faking the spirituality," I said. The pastor had seemed so calm and centered. Or maybe he was a user as well as a dealer. So Fayza takes him out, and then—

"I just had a bad thought," I said. "As soon as I give Fayza the results, she has no use for me."

"True," Ollie said.

"Jesus, you're not supposed to just agree with me when I say shit like that! Say something encouraging."

She thought for a moment. "You're not a threat to her," she said. "Not much of one. You're not manufacturing, so you're not a competitor. As a subject-matter expert, you could even be of critical use to her if she wants to manufacture the drug itself."

"I'm not going to let her have the recipe," I said. "That's the whole point of this. *Nobody* gets to make NME One-Ten. Not Fayza, not Edo, not anybody."

"Oh." She put down her fork. "Then she's going to try to kill you."

"Damn it, Ollie." I wasn't mad at her, not really. I was pissed with myself for not taking the printer when I'd had a chance. I hadn't even gotten a picture of it. Dr. G had recognized something about the engine, but then never got around to telling me what it was. And now she was no longer talking to me.

Bobby ambled toward us. He looked worried. "Are you guys fighting?" he said.

"Don't worry, Mommy and Daddy still love you very much," I said. "I need to make a call."

I stepped outside the restaurant. The temperature had dropped to just above freezing, and the cold, wet air first jolted me, then immediately made me more tired than before. I was not used to being out this late while sober. The streets were mostly empty. No flashing lights in the distance, no sirens.

I fumbled with Ollie's pen. The interface was older than I was used to, but I managed to search for Rovil's info and call him. No one picked up. I decided to forgive him because it was the middle of the night. I left a message telling him to call this new number.

Ollie and Bobby came out of the restaurant. I assumed that Ollie had paid. In the car she leaned into me and said, "I can't go back to that tiny apartment."

"Yeah?"

"I've been sleeping on hospital beds for two years," she said. "I want a king-size mattress and you next to me. I want to sleep until noon, have sex without inmates listening to us, and then call room service."

"You're wired," I said. "There's no way you're getting to sleep."

"Okay, sex 'til noon, then room service, then sleep. Do you have a problem with that?"

"Let me just try to call Rovil one more—"

She plucked the pen from my fingers. "Bobby," she said, "drop us at the Marriott."

- - -

Sometime later I woke to bright light. I opened my eyes to slits, expecting a winged messenger of God, but it was only the morning sun firing up the gauzy drapes of the hotel window. The bed was empty. Where was Ollie? Then I heard the shower going.

I found my T-shirt draped over Ollie's big black duffel bag and pulled it on. My shoulder burned from some abrasion. The backs of my thighs ached and my crotch felt sore; the price of sex with a tiny, intense Filipino girl on speed. Ollie had seemed to possess more than one pair of hands, manipulating my body with the fervor and efficiency of an Indy pit crew. Power tools may have played a role. I was already exhausted before we got to the hotel room, so my main responsibility over those two hours was to stay on the bed. I was not entirely successful.

I pushed aside the drapes and squinted at the planet. The room was on the tenth floor, and I looked down on Bay Street at full morning rush. Not a pretty sight. Each lane was a conveyor belt for delivering boxed humans into the mouths of hungry corporations. All those people, thinking that they were unique and special. A million brains throwing off waves of stupidity and pettiness and banality, thinking, *I gotta lose weight, I should have charged my pen, Why didn't I leave that idiot?* The telepaths of the NAT had to be fakes, I thought. Any real mind-readers would have shot themselves at the earliest opportunity.

I managed to find my jeans. The pen Ollie had given me last night was in the back pocket, pulsing with a message alert.

It was Rovil. He'd returned my call an hour ago. I pulled on my clothes, then called him back. He answered in seconds.

"Did you get Edo's address?" I asked.

"I'm sorry," Rovil said. "I'm trying. I've left messages everywhere. I didn't want to be too . . . indiscreet. I've contacted friends in my social network, however, and I'm hoping somebody will have a number."

"Thanks, kid. Keep trying. Now, do you have access to a GC-MS machine?"

"I'm sorry?"

"Come on—gas chromatograph and mass spectrometer. One-stop shopping for all your molecular identification needs."

"I know what one is," he said. "I was just surprised by the question. And the answer is yes, there are several at work."

"I mean private access. Where you could look at something without having it reported."

His eyebrows arched. "You found samples?"

"Just one," I said. "I can FedEx it to you."

"Amazing! Where did you get it?"

"I don't want to talk about it just yet."

He thought for a moment. "If you mail it to my home, I could take it in after hours."

"You rock."

He laughed, and I told him I'd get it to him right away.

Ollie came out of the bathroom while I was pulling on my boots. She wore a white hotel robe. Wet hair shining, skin glowing. She seemed ten years younger than she had in the NAT. She looked me over, taking in the information that I was already dressed. She glanced at the duffel bag, the window, then back to me.

"I thought you were maybe talking to her," she said. "But she's not here, is she?"

"Dr. Gloria? How do you know that?"

"There's a thing you do with your eyes when she's around. You can't look at someone straight on for too long—your pupils jump around, up to the right, then back again."

"I—I didn't know that."

"It's not that noticeable. So where is she?"

"We had a disagreement."

"So that's good, right? No hallucinations?"

"Oh yeah, it's great."

She frowned. "You want her back."

"She's useful," I said. "Sometimes."

"What can an invisible, imaginary angel do for you?"

"You'd be surprised. Have you looked at the news yet?"

Ollie decided to overlook my blatant change of subject. "There's nothing about a double murder," she said. "I don't think the bodies have been discovered."

"Cool." I stood up and grabbed my jacket. "Listen, I have to run an errand."

"I was serious about the room service," she said.

"You order without me. I've got to mail the sample to Rovil. I'll be back in a half hour, hour at the latest."

She regarded me silently. Something had closed down in her face.

I knew this would be a problem. Sex would mean more to her than it would to me. And as soon as I didn't act as she expected, she would look for data to explain that—and we'd be off and running on the Paranoia Express.

I kissed her. "Croissants and a pot of hot coffee," I said. "That's all I want."

. . .

I held the open FedEx envelope in one hand, and the sheet of rice paper in the other. I didn't want to put the paper inside and send away my only connection to Numinous. But what choice did I have? I needed the verification Rovil could provide.

I called up his home address—his apartment building was called "The Ludlow," which sounded tony—waved it onto the package's smart label, then dropped the envelope into the FedEx box.

I walked for fifteen, twenty minutes, looking for a quiet place to sit down. Here in downtown the sidewalks were crowded with young people in an array of skin tones, wearing clothing I could no longer afford. Canada, unlike the United States, was still a predominately white nation, but not in Toronto. You could see the future here. This was the final century for my species, the Pale North American Red-Crested Bitch. Good riddance.

I found a tiny courtyard between two buildings that had the tidy, curated feel of a nationally mandated green space, and sat down on a marble bench. The cold stone immediately numbed my backside. On the next bench sat a homeless man, probably Caucasian, with wild gray hair and a face ruddy from long exposure to sun and wind and snow. He wore several layers of clothing and guarded a black garbage bag of belongings. He was talking to no one I could see, speaking in a low, angry voice. I figured I'd fit right in.

I waited until no one was passing by on the sidewalk, and then I said aloud, "I'm sorry." When Dr. Gloria was being difficult, talking silently in my head was no good. She wanted audible respect. "Did you hear me?" I said, louder. "I'm *sorry*."

The angel did not appear. I hugged myself, the wind tugging at my jacket, as the bench turned my ass into a frozen pork chop.

After a while I said, "I admit it. I'm using her. But I would say in my defense that she's using me, too. She wanted out of that hospital. She wanted me to . . . want her."

I kept my butt planted on the freezing bench. Trying to score points by enduring some discomfort. I said, "I promise that as soon as I can, I'll get her back in the hospital. And if she won't go, then we'll figure out what dosage she should be on, and I'll do it. I just need her sharp enough to help me."

The homeless guy squinted at me. He'd stopped talking to himself. I ignored him.

"I need her right now, okay? You know how important this is. And I need your help, too."

A minute passed. She refused to appear.

"Jesus Christ!" I said to the air. The man shook his bushy gray head at me, looked away. Everybody's a critic.

After a while I reached into my boot and withdrew the green box cutter I'd borrowed from Ollie's duffel bag. I turned it in my hands. "Please," I said. "Don't make me do this."

Dr. G was an Old Testament girl. She knew the story of the binding of Isaac. Abraham climbed the mount with his son, making the kid carry the wood for his own sacrifice, all because his God demanded proof of obedience.

I slid open the catch on the box cutter. The blade, when it touched the skin of my inner arm, made a dimple, then summoned a dot of blood. There were other, older scars in the vicinity. I had done this before, and Dr. G knew I could do it again. She had to.

Abraham's biggest problem was that God was omniscient. Yahweh couldn't be bluffed. There was no way for Abraham to fake his way through the preparations for the sacrifice, counting on a holy interruption, because God could see into his heart each moment and *know* whether he was absolutely ready to kill his own son. I had the same problem. Dr. G lived in my head, and even when she wasn't talking to me, she saw what I saw, heard what I heard. My mind was an open book.

"Hey now," a voice said. It was the homeless man. He was hunched over, looking at me and the knife.

I breathed in. One, I thought. Two.

I opened my eyes. The man was still staring at me with frank interest. But he made no move to stop me. And neither did Dr. G.

I screamed, an extended, primal *"Fu-u-u-ck!"* I jumped up and threw the box cutter behind me.

"Hey now," the man said again. "You can't just leave that there. A little kid could pick that up."

"And fuck you, too," I said. "You were just going to sit there and watch me cut myself?" The bright plastic box cutter was easy to find. I closed the blade and put it in my pocket.

"What kind of sick god would let you murder your own child?" I asked him. "Not one worth worshiping, that's what. It wasn't God testing Abraham, it was Abe testing God. If God let him do that to Isaac, then fuck it, the holy covenant is null and void."

The man did not quite nod.

"That's right," I said. "Ruminate on *that*."

CHAPTER NINE

Later, I started referring to it as the Greenland Summit. I had called the meeting, and I was determined to forge a treaty, or perhaps "covenant" would be a better word, among three clinically insane people—me, Edo, and Rovil—and their gods. It was on a Sunday seven months after the party, on the day before Gil's trial was finally to begin.

My situation dictated the meeting place. Greenland House was a private hospital in the suburbs of Chicago where I'd been staying since the night Mikala died. I chose to use the café. It was midafternoon, between meals, and I had the place to myself except for a nurse who hovered in the hallway. I took a table near the fireplace where I could watch the door. The décor was a cut above any medical building I'd ever been in, and the café was like an upscale restaurant. It had *atmosphere*. Edo was paying for it, of course.

They came in at the same time, as if they'd traveled together. Probably they had. Edo opened his arms, but I was not going to hug him. I stayed behind the table. Edo sat down awkwardly. Rovil, polite as ever, shook my hand before sitting. Dr. Gloria sat to my right. Edo and Rovil's gods did not seem to require their own seats. Only my divine presence was a diva.

"Tell me how you're doing," Edo said.

"I'm fat, sad, and crazy. How 'bout you?"

He laughed, but it wasn't the typical Edo guffaw that he once deployed like a weapon in negotiations. The laugh was a warm, commiserating chuckle. "Are they taking care of you and the—"

"They take care of everybody," I said.

Edo seemed to take up less space than he used to. He was still a physically big man, a giant who overwhelmed the seat like a visiting parent squatting at an elementary school desk. But he was subdued, watchful.

Dr. Gloria said, "Ask them if they want something to drink."

I ignored her. At that moment, I knew she was a hallucination manufactured by fast-growing neurons in my temporal lobe. Other times I was equally sure she was the manifestation of God on this plane, sent to guide me. When this happens to sane people, it's called cognitive dissonance.

We'd all been warned by our lawyers not to talk about the murder. They didn't want us to pollute our testimonies in case we were called to the stand, as if three people with verifiable mental disorders could possibly be trusted to relay facts of the case. I was in the worst shape: clinically depressed and minimally medicated, and the only one of us still in a facility. Edo and Rovil, at least, had managed to impersonate the sane and the unsainted long enough to escape the psych wards.

"You could leave if you wanted to," Dr. Gloria said. "I'll be with you."

Again I ignored her. "Let's talk about the NME," I said.

Edo and Rovil glanced at each other. They didn't know where this was going.

"We bury it," I said. "It can never see the light of day."

Edo frowned. "I don't think . . ."

"The intellectual property stays locked up. We get the lawyers to write something for us. We make sure that Little Sprout never gets re-formed to make the drug, and we don't sell the IP to anyone, for any reason. Promise me."

"Of course," Rovil said. "I would never—"

"I wasn't talking to you," I said.

Edo thought for a long moment. "I know you're hurt," he said. "I can *feel* it. But Numinous is not the problem."

"Jesus Christ, Mikala's dead because of it."

"I can't tell you why Gil—why he did what he did," Edo said. "But that was an overdose; we were all . . . disoriented. Most of us were knocked unconscious. That doesn't mean Numinous can't—"

"*Stop calling it that.*" Numinous was Mikala's name for it. The trial had turned up her computerized log books. She'd been taking the drug, ramping up dosages week by week. Sometime during the experiments she stopped calling it by its number and gave it a name.

"*One-Ten* can still help people," Edo said. "Not in the amounts that we took, of course. Perhaps tiny dosages. Something that would open the door just a little bit."

"What fucking door?"

"To God," Edo said. He was perfectly sincere.

That's when I realized he'd been taken in by the drug. He wasn't even struggling to keep himself sane. He'd given in.

I turned on Rovil. "What about you? Is Numinous a doorway to Jesus?"

Rovil glanced at Edo, then looked at his hands. "I cannot say that, but it has certainly helped me."

"You fuckers."

Edo stared at me. His eyes gleamed.

I pushed back from the table and started to get up. My belly was huge, a thing with its own gravity. Dr. Gloria put out a hand to help me up, but I shoved her away. "After all this," I said to Edo, "you would still put the drug out there. You think people can take just one small dose, then *stop*? What do you think Mikala was doing before she lost herself? She became a fanatic. She made a neurochemical bomb, then she dropped it—on her own child. Why? So we could all see God together."

"Please, sit down . . . ," Edo said.

"Promise me."

"I can't—"

"Swear on your fucking god!"

"I can't do that," he said.

The nurse was hurrying toward me.

"If you ever let it out in the world, I will hunt you down like a fucking dog," I said to him. "And no god will save you."

·   ·   ·

When I returned to the hotel room, Ollie had turned it into a command center. She'd moved the bed and desk to the center of the room, then laid the two chairs on the bed. Dozens of floppy screens had been taped up on three walls. To the left was a rectangular arrangement of screens ten feet wide and five feet tall. Another row of screens were taped end to end, forming a band that ran across the glass balcony door. The right-hand wall was a random selection of single screens.

Ollie stood before one of the singles, flicking through text. She'd showered and changed into a new T-shirt. Without looking away from the screen she said, "You missed breakfast."

She was annoyed with me.

"Missed more than that, looks like," I said. On the screen nearest me was displayed a column of long numbers separated with dots, like foreign telephone numbers. "So what are you up to, Ol? And where did you get all these screens?"

"Have you been in contact with Edo Anderssen Vik?" she asked. Still not looking at me.

"Contact? Not yet."

"Anything—calls, messages . . ."

"Well, I *tried* to get messages through."

She turned to face me. "Have you been crying?"

"I'm fine."

"Lyda, you can tell me if—"

"I'm *fine*. Edo never called me back. Rovil hasn't gotten an answer, either."

"I wish you had told me that," she said. Her gaze shifted from me to some mental screen.

"Why?" I asked.

She walked along the balcony glass, one hand raised, and the text and graphics rippled as she passed, seemingly following her across the room. "You've tipped him off. If you're hunting someone, you don't give them advance notice."

"Is that what you think I'm doing—hunting him?"

"Last night you said you didn't want anyone to get the drug, and you mentioned Edo especially."

"I did?" I did. At the diner, I remembered it now. "Okay, yeah. I'm hunting him."

"Then we're on the same page."

"Uh, you look like you're on fifty pages at once."

"It's been tricky," she said. "Your friend Edo keeps a low profile." She swiped away a graphic, and it was replaced with a picture of a smiling Edo at some business affair, wearing a jacket with no tie. "This is his last public appearance, five years ago." He looked even bigger than in the old days. His eyes gleamed, perhaps from the camera flash. Something about that smile seemed false.

She called up another photo. The man looked like a younger, thinner, and humorless version of Edo. His hair was blond to almost white, and pulled back high on his forehead. The last time I'd seen him had been at the trial, ten years ago. He'd looked less like his father then and more like a shaggy blond hippie.

"Little Edo," I said.

"Don't call him that to his face," Ollie said. "He hates it. Eduard Junior is handling all the business now—he's the public face of the company. He has a beautiful wife, an adopted daughter, and is active in several charities." She flicked through several pictures. Most of them of Eduard Jr., but in several he appeared with his wife Suzette, an ice-blonde Nordic princess in size zero dresses.

Their daughter appeared in only one photo, which seemed to have been taken at an airport. She was eight or nine years old in the picture, with curly hair pulled back in a tight bun. She was looking at something in her hands. Eduard had his arm around her shoulder.

"Are you okay?" Ollie asked. "You're flushed."

"I'm—she's just very pretty."

Ollie's eyes narrowed. "Yes, she is."

I cleared my throat. "So is Edo still calling the shots for the company?"

"Opinion's split," she said. "Nobody can get close enough to ask him."

"So we can't reach him?" I said, frustrated. "Rovil said the same thing. He wasn't even sure what country Edo was in."

"This week he's in his place outside London."

"What?"

She turned back to the screens. "London right now. Before that, he spent fifteen days in the US, most of it on his estate in New Mexico, but he was in New York City for two days. He also has a home in Norway, but he hasn't visited there in years, most likely because of his tax situation."

I was stunned. "You got all that from—" I gestured at the walls. "What? Illegal wiretaps? Your spook friends in the government?"

Ollie shook her head. "They're not allowed to talk to me anymore. If I even reach out, it could cause problems for them. So I don't. This is all from public or semipublic sources. No TSA data, no wiretaps. I've got bots crawling the social web, and a cloud-based analysis engine that's just a generation behind what I used to work with professionally."

"This is what Fayza did to me. She hired a hacker and got all the details on me."

"This isn't hacking, it's data mining." She pointed at the big wall, where dozens of pastel spheres pulsed and shifted. "Everybody leaves a trail. It's almost impossible not to leave footprints all over the online world, and that easily maps to your location in the real world. Unless you're rich—and Edo Vik is very, very rich. He's got a top-notch reputation company scrubbing his tracks. His personal footprint is null, as far as recent data goes. But you can infer a lot from second- and third-degree associates. Like this guy."

She gestured toward one of the smaller circles, and it expanded. "The husband of one of his assistants is a twenty-five-year-old amateur foodie microfamous for his restaurant reviews. He lives in New York, but two nights ago he raved about a meal he'd just had at the 8-Ball, an Uzbek mobile restaurant in Hampstead. That's north London."

"So maybe they're on vacation," I said.

"Maybe. But you have to look at the data in aggregate. I've got the org chart for Edo's whole company, and I can keep track of most of them. The handful of people who assist Edo and Junior are in the UK right now, but they're leaving soon."

I touched one of the spheres, and it shrank. The graphics told me nothing. "Are you telling me you know where Edo will be, and when?"

"I can make a pretty good guess."

I breathed in. "When is he coming back to the US?"

"Next Thursday. Afternoon. New York City."

"Holy shit!" I laughed. "How can you possibly know that?"

"I asked." She allowed herself a smile. "That foodie husband? I friended him and asked him if he was going to be home in time for the Taste of New York festival, and he said he was out of town for the first day, but he'd be back in time for Friday. All the commercial flights are arriving in the afternoon."

Five days.

"I have to be there," I said.

Ollie said, "Where? New York?"

"Yes, New York. I'm hunting him, right?"

"So . . . you want to cross the *border*."

"That's right."

"Lyda, if they catch you on the other side, you could end up in prison—American prison, not some nice Canadian hospital."

"You said people do it all the time. I'll just hop over, then hop back before the devil knows I'm there."

She put out a hand. "I know you don't want anyone to make the drug, but it's not worth doing time for."

"You don't know how dangerous this stuff is," I said.

"Try me."

I took a breath. "Okay. The problem is not that it causes these hallucinations; it's that it's so damn convincing—and you *stay* convinced. Look at Rovil. He knows the chemistry, yet he still thinks that fucking Ganesh is there guiding him. Numinous not only installs a supernatural chaperone, it makes you believe in it."

"Even you?" Ollie asked.

"I *know*, in the deepest recesses of my 'heart,' that Dr. Gloria is real, that she was sent by God to save me from killing myself. *It's a Wonderful Life*, courtesy of an overactive temporal lobe."

"But you're handling it," Ollie said. "You can keep track of what's real."

"Barely," I said. "I know, in an abstract way, that she's a symptom of an overdose, but that doesn't *feel* true. Half the time I can't stop myself from talking back to her. Every day I tell myself, 'Think like a stage magician.'"

"I don't know what that means."

"Know it's a trick and don't forget it's a trick," I said. "The rabbit is already in the hat. Do *not* clap for fucking Tinkerbell. Believe nothing."

"Sounds tiring."

"Exactly. How many people can do that every day? Rovil can't. Gil can't. Not even Mikala. And what about—?" I started to say *What about kids?* "What happens if this spreads? The planet's already too full of fanatics. Numinous could convert millions of people into true believers—each of 'em one hundred percent certain they've been personally handed the fucking stone tablets."

Ollie stared at me. I said, "I'm sorry, was that too ranty?"

"You've been rehearsing this speech," she said.

"What? No. Well, I've been thinking about this a lot. But you get what I'm saying, right?"

"Sure," Ollie said. "You're saving the world."

"It sounds dumb when you say it like that."

She shrugged.

"This really is a dangerous drug," I said.

"I believe that part. I just don't think that's why you're doing all this—breaking out of the hospital, crossing international borders . . ." She shook her head. "Is this about the girl?"

I flinched without moving. Yes, that is possible.

"What girl?" I asked.

"Francine," she said. "The girl who killed herself."

Oh, I thought. Her. "I barely knew her," I said.

Ollie squinted at me. "All right," she said. "But someday you're going to tell me why you're really doing this."

And I thought, No. No I'm not.

"I'm not asking for much," I said. "I have no idea how to get through customs, and I just need you to point me in the right direction. You know what I mean—fake passports, documents . . ."

"Lyda, you have a tracking device installed in your arm. There is no way you're crossing the border with that thing."

"I thought maybe you could help with that, too."

"What makes you think I can do any of this?"

"You told me. You said criminals did it every day."

"I'm not a criminal," Ollie said. She almost managed to say it with a straight face.

Ollie went away to think for a while, by which I mean she sat on the couch and stared at the wall for half an hour. Then she said, "The first thing we have to do is find you a pet."

"What kind of pet?"

.   .   .

"Which one do you like?" the Cat Lady asked.

The house swelled and pulsed with felines. They breathed on the bookshelves, prowled the backs of the couches, swirled in currents around our ankles. The atmosphere was an acrid funk of inadequately suppressed urine and dander. Bobby and I sat on the couch, surrounded. A big orange tabby had jumped onto his lap and was eyeing the treasure chest with a predatory eye. Ollie had refused to come with us, said she had other calls to make, so she gave us directions to this house in Markham and sent us off to choose.

"Does it matter?" I asked.

The Cat Lady scowled. She was a large, dark-skinned woman in her sixties, dressed in a red tank top and purple stretch pants. Her arms were sleeved in densely crowded tattoos that had blurred into paisley. "Fine," she said. "Just grab any old cat, why not."

I pointed to the orange monster on Bobby's lap. "Okay, this one."

"Shandygaff? Don't be ridiculous; he's too old."

"A kitten then."

"*What?*"

"Look, why don't you just pick one out for me?"

She closed her eyes, as if regretting ever letting me in the house. "Fine," she said.

She set down the two cats on her lap and began to look around the room. I could see fifteen, twenty cats, and no telling how many were in the kitchen and bedrooms.

Bobby yelped. He was clutching his treasure chest. "It clawed me!" he said.

"Settle down," I said.

The cat batted at Bobby's closed hands. "Lyda, please, get it off me."

"Let him play with your toy," the Cat Lady said.

"It's not a toy!"

She rolled her eyes. We were scoring no points with the Cat Lady. She put her hands on her hips, looked around at the bookshelves. "Ah! There you are!" She nabbed a black cat and pointed his face at me. He looked morose. "This is Lamont," she said.

"He's perfect," I said. "Where do we do this?"

The Cat Lady led me to the kitchen, a generous space with white cabinets, a center island with bar stools, and old-fashioned white appliances. A plastic trough dotted with cat food lined one wall, where half a dozen cats paced, complaining. "It's not supper time yet," the Cat Lady told them. She shooed a big Persian from the top of the island.

Still holding Lamont in one arm, she opened a cabinet above the stove and began handing me items—a plastic-wrapped towel, a floral-pattern toiletry bag, a device that looked like a battery tester, a white plastic insulin injector—which I placed on the island.

"Unroll the towel on the countertop," she told me. She laid Lamont on the towel and ordered me to pet him while she unpacked the medical supplies from the toiletry bag.

I pointed to a syringe and needle. "What's in that?"

"That's not for you," the Cat Lady said. "Hold him still. There you go . . ." She slid the needle under the fur behind Lamont's neck. The cat didn't seem to notice. "Sleepy times," she said. Then to me, she said, "Now would be a good time to take care of the payment."

I held out the HashCash card, and she produced a slate. "That will be twenty-five hundred," she said.

I pulled back the card before she could touch it. "On the phone you said a thousand."

"A thousand is for the *cat*. Plus five hundred for the cat carrier and the month's supply of food, and a thousand to do the transfer. Unless you want to do that yourself?"

"Lamont better be one fucking great cat for a thousand bucks."

"He has the heart of a champion."

I keyed the card to the amount and let her tap it into her slate.

Lamont lay on his side, breathing deep, completely out. Maybe it was wrong to use an animal like this. But I was sure of one thing: If Dr. Gloria were here, she'd be on the cat's side.

The Cat Lady pulled on a pair of latex gloves. "Let's do you, now."

I stretched my arm across the countertop. She ran a finger along the forearm and tapped the bump. I thought of Ollie, when she'd first touched the pellet. "Looks like you just got this," the Cat Lady said.

"I didn't want to get attached."

She swabbed rubbing alcohol across my inner arm, humming. Then she placed her arm across mine, pinning me to the countertop with her weight. With her free hand she picked up a scalpel. "Look at the ceiling," she said.

The Cat Lady drew a line across my skin. Blood welled in the cut, glossy and bright. I exhaled. "That wasn't so bad," I said.

"Hold still," she said, and pushed into the cut with her finger.

"Jesus Christ!"

She looked me in the eye. "I have to let go of your arm. Can you stay still?"

"Just warn me next time, okay?"

The Cat Lady moved the electrical device between us. She pressed the tip of one wire into the incision, a fresh burn that made me wince. She taped the wire to my skin, then inserted and taped down the other wire.

Her hand reached for the device. "Is this going to hurt?" I asked.

"Does it *matter?*" she asked. Still mad at me about refusing to choose a cat. She pressed a button.

I flinched. But I hadn't felt a thing. Not even a tingle.

"The chip's offline," the Cat Lady said. "An alert will show up in your file, but that's okay—service gets interrupted all the time. They'll think you drove through a tunnel." She unwrapped a soda straw and put it to her lips. Then she poked the other end of the straw into the cut.

"Mother of—!" I yelled.

She capped the top of the straw with a fingertip, then released the pellet into a capful of the rubbing alcohol. "Got it. We just have to pop this into Lamont right away, before it reboots."

She swirled the cap for a moment, washing the pellet. She stripped the paper off another straw and sucked the chip back in to it. She lifted the straw, and something small fell out. "Oopsie."

"Did you just—?"

"Hah. Fell right back in the cap. That was lucky."

She poked inside the cap with the straw, trying to feel for the pellet. "If they hit the floor, they're impossible to find," she said.

"You said, 'right away.' "

"Tiny little bugger. Let me get a spoon."

"The reboot, that's what—thirty seconds?"

"Give or take."

She slid the tip of the spoon into the cap, using tweezers to push the pellet into it.

"Could you hurry?" I asked.

She stopped, looked at me.

I stared back.

Finally I said, "Okay. I'll shut up."

She slowly placed the chip at the top of the insulin injector. "Could you roll Lamont onto his back? There we go."

"I'm dripping," I said. Blood was creeping down to my elbow; I turned my arm so it wouldn't fall on the cat. The Cat Lady rubbed at the underside of Lamont's neck, feeling for a vein. Then rubbed some more. I started to say something, thought better of it. She pressed the white tube into his fur and clicked the button at the top of the tube.

"Is that it?" I asked.

She checked the screen on the device with the wires. "And . . . the signal's back."

"Is it a clean report?"

She looked at me. "How would I know?"

She had a point. The message was private-key encrypted. In the early days of the chips, people built jammers that would suppress the signal, then broadcast a bogus clean report, the whole jamming device no bigger than a wrist watch. It worked great until the medical industry figured out what was going on and started encrypting each report with a date-time stamp hashed into the message. Now there was no way to fake a chip report unless you knew its private key.

However, you *could* move the chip into a new host. And cats' blood, strange-but-true fact, was almost identical to humans'.

Hello Lamont, the Clean and Sober Cat.

CHAPTER TEN

Two nights later Ollie and I were in a marina beer joint half an hour east of Toronto. There were only two other women in the place, including the waitress. The men were blue-collar types in paint-spattered jeans and oil-stained work boots, or else no-collar types in T-shirts and basketball shorts. A room of hefty guts and loud opinions.

"My ginger ale tastes like aluminum," I said.

Ollie grunted. She was on edge, her body still, but her eyes flitting like sparrows. She was watching the windows, which had turned into mirrors of the room. I'd adopted some of her paranoia. The bodies of Pastor Rudy and Luke had been discovered yesterday morning, and the story was all over the Canadian news sites. We moved out of the Marriott and to a cheaper hotel, expecting the cops to come knocking. Ollie was confident that we hadn't been picked up by cameras and that we hadn't left prints at the crime scene, but these days, who knew? A traffic camera could have seen Bobby's car pulling out of that lot. A random bystander could have seen us in the alley.

"That guy's watching you," Ollie said.

"What? Who?"

"The cowboy. No, don't look."

Too late. A man in a black cowboy hat and a white, Western-style shirt sat at the end of the L-shaped bar, kitty-corner from us. He saw me looking at him and tilted back his hat with a knuckle. Then he lifted his shot glass and raised his eyebrows, inviting me over.

"Jesus," I said. "I'm so done with local boys."

Ollie glanced at me, then looked away.

"What?" I asked.

Ollie said, "How done?"

"I don't understand the question."

She grunted, took a sip from her beer.

"Wait," I said, "are we playing the 'who's gayer' game?"

"I'm just curious," Ollie said.

"Just curious? That's a bullshit phrase."

"It's a simple question. How long—"

"No, it's a signal that bullshit is about to follow. It's the hat that bullshit puts on before it goes out to get the paper."

"How long has it been?" she said, refusing to get distracted. "Maybe an experimental phase in college?"

"You can't seriously be doubting what team I'm on," I said. "I was with Mikala for eight years. Five of them married."

"I'm just asking about your life," Ollie said.

"No, this is some weird jealousy thing over a nonexistent person."

She pointed the neck of her beer at me. "And you're not answering the question."

"I will admit to fucking a zucchini when I was in high school. For years I thought I was a vegesexual."

Ollie's not a big laugher, but I caught her as she was drinking, and she had to purse her lips and put down the bottle. For Ollie, that was the equivalent of a spit take.

"How about you?" I asked. "Ever do one?"

She wiped her mouth with the back of her hand. "Boys were never an issue."

"I was talking about vegetables."

She started to answer, then froze, her eyes on a reflection in the window. "Here we go," she said.

This time I resisted the urge to spin around. After an appropriate pause, I glanced casually over my shoulder. Two men had come in, a guy in his sixties with a silver ponytail and a younger man in a Mercury baseball cap. I don't know how Ollie recognized them, because she'd told me that she hadn't met them before. They took a table in the back with no view of the water.

After a few minutes we walked over, carrying our drinks to look natural. They didn't get up. We shook hands, and their palms were dry as burlap. Ollie had said they'd be First Nations people, but if she hadn't told me I would have put down their ethnicity as Weathered. The older one had a face like a crumpled paper bag, and his companion looked out from under his cap with a squint that suggested too many hours out on the water.

We sat down across from them. No one spoke.

These were the second and third drug smugglers I'd ever met, but they supplied a much more dangerous product than Fayza's marijuana: the second-most addictive substance known to man or woman.

I wished Dr. Gloria were there; she could always settle my nerves. After a long while—probably only ten or twenty seconds, but it felt like a minute, all of us staring at each other—I said, "So. You guys smuggle cigarettes."

The men stared at me. Ollie tensed but said nothing.

The man in the ball cap said, "Yah. Pretty much."

Ontario was rife with smoke shacks, most of them on First Nations property, that sold illegal cigarettes smuggled in from the States. Rogue factories on the other side of the border, most of them also on Native American reservations, pumped out millions of cheap, untaxed, generic cigarettes a year. You couldn't blame the Indians. We took their land; they were giving us cancer. Of course, we also gave them alcoholism, poverty, and type II diabetes, so we were still coming out ahead on the deal.

Black-market cigarettes were big business in Canada, had been since the seventies. Oh, there were intermittent crackdowns, and joint task forces of RCMP and FBI and Six Nations police that made big busts on the evening news. But there was no political will for a war on tobacco. The border was just too damn long, and too many people liked their cheap smokes. What politician wanted to shoot their own economy in the foot? Besides, nobody liked to look like the bully when dealing with the indigenous peoples.

Ollie spelled out the logistics of what we needed. The old man said nothing, and the young one said nothing but, "Sure. Yah. No problem."

Ollie said, "I've heard you've had some problems with the rowboats. Interference."

I thought, Rowboats?

"Not ours," the young one said.

My pen chimed. I glanced down at the name scrolling across the narrow body of the pen and said, "I've got to take this."

Ollie said, "Lyda—"

I put up a hand in apology and walked away from them. "Rovil," I said into the pen. "What do you got?"

"I can't believe it," he said.

"You're sure?"

"I can show you the numbers. Can you switch to video?"

I glanced over my shoulder. Grumpy and Son were eyeing me. "Maybe later," I said.

"I'll mail them," Rovil said. "The sample's not pure, and there are other chemicals mixed in it that look biological. But over ninety percent falls within the spectral range. It's ours, Lyda. It's NME One-Ten."

"Shit."

A curse of resignation, not surprise. As soon as I met Francine at the NAT, weeping and tripping on God and talking about "the Numinous," I *knew* it was NME 110 out there. But believing wasn't evidence. The hardware in the chemjet printer told me that the church's drug wasn't just another MDMA or LSD knockoff, but this was the first proof that it was our drug. There was no arguing with a mass spectrometer.

"Where did you find it?" Rovil asked. "Who made it?"

"I found it in a church," I said. "Some brand-new religion. They made it on a custom printer, and we have to assume it's not the only one."

"So this made-up religion—"

"I didn't say made-up. I said brand-new. 'Made-up religion' is redundant."

Rovil laughed, too comfortable to take offense. He knew God was real; he had Ganesh to tell him so. "This *brand-new* church," he said. "They made the printer themselves?"

"I can't see how. Hardware like that takes a load of cash, and these guys were set up in a fucking storefront. So it's either a millionaire or a drug cartel. Or a millionaire running a drug cartel."

"Lyda, drug dealers? You shouldn't be—"

"You wouldn't believe the people I'm hanging out with these days."

Ollie was crossing the room toward me, looking concerned. I covered the phone. "What is it?" I asked her.

Ollie said, "They don't like it when customers hop up and start making calls in the middle of a conversation. Is that Rovil?"

"Yep."

Her eyes widened. She could see the excitement in my face. "So it's for real then."

"*Oh* yeah." I nodded behind her. "So how much do they want?"

"Thirty-five thousand Yuan."

Holy shit. She said it'd be expensive, but I hadn't been thinking *that* much. I wasn't sure what the current Yuan-to-Canadian exchange rate was, but these guys were asking for somewhere around $11,000.

"Apiece," Ollie said.

"Wait, *what?*"

"You have the money, right?"

I'd told her not to worry about the money. Which was not to say that I actually had the money. I said, "That's not what I'm talking about. Eleven K *apiece?*"

"I'm going with you," she said. She looked up at me with those dark eyes, her face set.

"You said you were never going back there. You said it was your own private Mordor."

"We're not arguing about this," she said.

We stared each other down. She didn't flinch. I put a hand to the back of her neck and kissed her, hard.

The kiss surprised her. Me too.

She shook her head in mock dizziness. "Hurry it up," she said, and walked back to our table.

I lifted the pen again. "So! Rovil . . ."

He sensed something in my tone. "No," he said. "No, no, no."

"It's not a lot," I said.

"I can't keep giving you money. You're the rich one!"

"What are you talking about?"

"I know you lost your investment when Little Sprout collapsed," he said. "But after Mikala died, didn't her estate—"

"That money's gone."

"Gone? How?"

"You'd be surprised how much a drink costs in this town." I said it to embarrass him and shut down that line of questioning. Nice people didn't like to hear about an addict's life.

The tactic worked a little too well. The call went silent. "Rovil?"

After a moment, he said, "Lyda, are you using again?"

"What? What the fuck, Rovil. No. That's in the past."

"I want to help you. I do. But if you're spending it on other things—"

"I'm not."

"Then what is it?"

"I can't tell you. Not right now." I glanced back at the Ollie and the smugglers. We could bail out. Find some other, cheaper way, and eventually cross the border.

Except that Edo was landing in New York in three days.

"Fine. Forget the money," I said. "I need something else." I told him what I wanted him to do.

Rovil made sputtering noises. "Lyda, I have a high-level job, I can't just—"

"Sure you can. How many sick days have you taken this year?"

"None! But that's because—"

"Then you're due. Look, you're in this, too. This is the One-Ten. You and I, we agreed to keep it off the market. Don't you want to know who's doing this?"

He took a heavy breath.

"Thanks, kid."

I walked back to the table, and Ollie registered the look on my face. "Everything okay?" she asked.

"No worries," I said. "Are we done here?"

The younger of the cigarette smugglers looked up at me and said, "Half now."

Before I could answer, Ollie said, "Nope."

The two men turned their attention back to her.

"We're not going down like that Pakistani family that got stranded in the middle of the St. Lawrence," she said.

"That wasn't us!" the younger one said.

What Pakistani family? I thought.

"We'll give you ten percent now," Ollie said calmly. "Then forty percent when the rowboat arrives. The rest when we get to the other side." She shrugged. "It's either that, or I go to the Hell's Angels."

I thought, Would she really contact the Hell's Angels? Then: There are still Hell's Angels?

The young one started to speak again. The silver-haired man stopped him and said, "Twenty-five percent now."

Ollie seemed to weigh the offer. Then she reached into her jacket pocket and passed an envelope under the table.

The man in the baseball cap kept it below the rim of the table and peeked inside. "Okay then."

Before the meeting at the marina I'd given Ollie everything I had left in HashCash, less than a thousand bucks. She added everything she'd had hidden in the duffel, for a grand total of $5,500 Canadian. That was before we took the hit on the Yuan conversion. There was no second envelope. She'd just handed them our last dime.

Ollie said to them, "You have some numbers for me, now?"

The older man took out a ballpoint pen and wrote something on the back of a beer coaster. Ollie looked at it, nodded, then put it in her jacket. "See you boys tomorrow."

. . .

Bobby was waiting for us in his Nissan. We'd left him outside like a tied-up dog, figuring a panicky schizo might frighten off the drug smugglers. Or rather, another panicky schizo. "Can we eat now?" he said. "I'm *starving*."

"Get us back into the city first," I said. "This place gives me the willies." Ollie got in the back of the car. Before I climbed in after her, I scanned the parking lot, but there was still no sign of Dr. Gloria. The angel must have been really pissed at me. What happened to "Lo, I will be with you always"?

Once we were rolling I used the burner pen to find a curry restaurant that was still open. I put in our order, then told Bobby to step on it. I was beginning to like having a chauffeur. I should have sworn off driving years ago.

A few minutes into the ride, Ollie said to me quietly, "We don't have the money, do we?"

I could have kissed her again for that "we."

"Not unless there's more in that duffel bag of yours," I said. More than once I'd entertained the fantasy that she was Agent Skarsten, International Spy, with a secret cache of passports and stacks of bills in foreign currencies. But of course that was crazy. If Ollie had had that kind of dough she wouldn't have spent years living above a Thai restaurant, wouldn't have ended up in a public hospital like Guelph Western. And she sure as hell wouldn't be hanging with me.

I'd never been rich. I'd grown up seesawing between middle class and poor, depending on whether my dad had found work or my mom was home from the hospital. But Mikala came from money, and money followed her for the rest of her days. When we were "broke" and I didn't know how we'd afford our first apartment together, a trust fund would mature and a shower of money would descend just in time for the rent. We were invited to parties on yachts—yachts! And when Little Sprout needed an angel investor, a friend of a friend of Mikala's father appeared, and suddenly we were being financed by the loud and large Edo Anderssen Vik.

When Mikala died, her family fought the settlement of the estate. Why give their daughter's money to the white bitch she was going to divorce anyway? (All right, her parents never said "white bitch" to my face, but I liked to imagine they said it amongst themselves, because reverse-racism was the kind of racism my people liked best, and because "white bitch" was infinitely preferable to just plain "bitch," because that would have meant that they hated me because of *me*.) I managed to hold on to the estate, but only because we were still married when she died. In the absence of a will, everything went to the surviving spouse. I gave it all away the same week the check cleared. There were plenty of times I'd wished I'd kept some of it, but this was the first time I'd ever thought so while sober.

Ollie said, "If they'd asked for more than twenty-five down, they would have walked out on us."

"So tomorrow we may be dead, but today we still have a reservation."

Ollie looked at me.

"See what I did there?" I said. "That was an Indian joke."

"Oh, I got it," she said. We were going to meet the smugglers in Cornwall, which was five hours east of Toronto, just across the St. Lawrence River from upstate New York.

I said, "What happens if we don't show up with the money?"

"Best case, they shrug their shoulders and leave," Ollie said. "Worst case is . . . worse."

"I have to get over there," I said.

"We could knock over a bank," Ollie said.

"I am *not* driving the getaway car!" Bobby said. It wasn't clear that he knew Ollie was joking.

We reached the curry place a half hour later. Bobby ran inside to pick up our order.

"He's a good kid," Ollie said.

"For someone who lives inside a Happy Meal toy."

"He's worried about you."

"Bobby?"

"He thinks you're sad. He asked me if I thought you would hurt yourself."

"Holy shit," I said. "How bad is it that somebody at Bobby's level of functioning is worried about *me*?" Ollie didn't answer. I asked, "So what did you tell him?"

"I said you've been sad as long as I've known you."

"Sad? *Sad?* I'm not *weepy*. Jesus Christ."

"I'm sorry," she said.

"I'm just not *happy*. There's a difference."

Bobby came back with three white bags, and the inside of the car blossomed with spicy steam. I hadn't been hungry, but suddenly I was famished. I told him to drive fast. Bobby found a parking spot amazingly close to his apartment, and we practically jogged up the stairs.

Bobby was in front, carrying the bags. The apartment door was ajar, and he nudged it open with his knee. I didn't think anything of the door being unlocked, but Ollie, behind me, grabbed my shoulder. Again I was too slow. The person inside the room saw me.

"Lyda Rose," Hootan said. He sat on the couch. On the floor at his feet, a chubby white boy sat cross-legged, looking worriedly at his toes. He wore nothing but bulky headphones, green sweatpants, and a fluffy white fleece vest.

I couldn't figure out how the white boy fit in with Hootan, and then I realized he was Bobby's roommate. Poor kid. Hootan must have dragged him out of his room and made him a hostage.

Hootan pulled his hand out of sweatshirt pocket. He seemed pleased to be bringing the pistol into the open, and even happier to be aiming it at me.

"Fayza would like to see you," he said.

CHAPTER ELEVEN

We rode in silence. Hootan didn't talk to me, didn't even turn on the Honda's Real Engine Sound™. Every time a light flashed through the rear windshield, I thought: *Gloria*. But no. And no Ollie, either. Back in the apartment, Hootan had pointed to her and Bobby and said, "If you follow, I will shoot her." Ollie *growled*. I'd never heard her make a sound like that, and never seen that kind of hate on her face.

Hootan drove toward the Millie neighborhood. I'd started to sweat. Couldn't help it. The human palm has three thousand sweat glands per square inch, and every one of them has a mind of its own. I'd told Fayza I would have the results by Saturday—two days ago. She'd clearly run out of patience.

A few blocks before Tyndall Avenue, Hootan pulled in at a flat-roofed, one-story building. The wooden sign out front said "Elegant Lady Salon" in pink script. The windows and front door were protected by iron grates.

Hootan drove around back and parked next to a late model Garand S3. "Go in," he said.

His headlights illuminated the back door of the shop. The windows facing the back lot were shuttered.

My body went into Full Norepinephrine Clench: tight chest, closed throat, cinched asshole. I couldn't move.

"Fine," Hootan said. He got out of the car, moved around to my door, and yanked it open.

"Okay, okay," I said. I pulled myself out of his Honda, then made my way up the short steps to the door. My stomach and knees felt like glass. Images flashed in my brain: Pastor Rudy, hogtied on the floor with a metal spike in his neck. Skinny Luke, with a garbage bag over his head.

"For Christ's sake," I said under my breath. "Get your ass over here."

Dr. Gloria, however, refused to appear. I looked back, and Hootan was watching me. He made a shooing gesture.

The door was unlocked. I pushed inside and slammed the door shut behind me. If I couldn't have calm, I thought, at least I could use anger.

The back room was dark and narrow, crowded with dimly seen supplies. A short hallway led to the front of the salon, where the lights were on. I stood for a long moment, listening, but I heard nothing but a faint mechanical sound. I walked forward.

The salon proper looked as garish and migraine-inducing as a Bollywood set: pink swivel chairs, lime green tile floors, neon orange trim. Every stylist station was done up like a Hollywood makeup table, with a big mirror surrounded by lights. Fayza sat in one of the swivel chairs, reading a magazine. Behind her, snipping at the back of Fayza's head with a pair of narrow scissors, was a dark-haired girl who looked to be in her twenties. She wore a beaded emerald dress that looked like traditional Afghan costume, but on her feet were chunky black combat boots. Her glittery head scarf and bangle earrings looked more Gypsy than Muslim to me, but what did I know?

Fayza looked up from her magazine and saw me in the mirror. "Lyda, thank you for meeting me at such a late hour."

I forced a smile that felt like a crack in my skull. "Odd time for a haircut."

"You wouldn't believe my schedule," she said. She turned to face me, and the stylist stepped back. Fayza frowned at me. "I cannot decide if you die."

I opened my mouth, then shut it.

"You have such lovely red hair," she continued. "It looks natural, but you know what tricks women can play."

Oh. *If you dye.* I choked out a reply. "I used to get highlights. Not lately."

She nodded. "When you get older you have to hide the gray with lowlights—a sad reversal. Look at Aaqila's hair. So dark."

The girl, Aaqila, didn't answer. Her head was slightly bowed, and she looked at me through black bangs. She was tall, well over six feet in those boots, with pale skin, full lips, a pointed chin. She was beautiful, but her strong, narrow nose pushed her out of TV-pretty-land into more interesting territory.

"You have too much volume," Fayza said to me. "You look like a wild woman. When was the last time you were in a decent salon?"

It had been years since I'd been in a *decent* salon. I hadn't cut my hair at all since before entering the hospital. "Is it that bad?" I asked.

"Aaqila, do you have time for a walk-in?"

The girl shrugged as if to say, Why not? She gestured toward an alcove where two shampoo stations were set up.

"That's okay," I said. "I'm good."

Aaqila took me by the elbow. When I didn't move, the girl slid her hand down to my wrist and pressed; the pain was sharp, as if small bones were ready to snap, and I dropped to one knee. Good God she was strong. And she still held the scissors in her other hand.

"Please," Fayza said to me. "You need this."

I lowered myself into the shampoo chair. The back reclined so that my head hung over the sink. I was acutely aware of each step of this simple process: the tightness in my hips; the creak of the vinyl padding as my ass settled into the seat; the cold ceramic against my neck. I stared at the ceiling, my throat bared.

The girl did something behind me, then returned with hot towels. "To open the pores," she said. She placed the towels over my face, covering my eyes, nose, and mouth. My heart thumped in panic, but I tried to steady myself.

The sink thrummed loudly as she turned on the water, but the sprayer had not been aimed at me yet.

"You haven't been answering the phone I gave you," Fayza said from somewhere close.

I started to lift my head but Aaqila pushed it back down. "Hold still," she said in a soft voice.

"Yeah, about that . . . ," I said, my voice muffled.

I felt a palm against my forehead. Hot water—very hot water—struck the crown of my head, ran down my hair, the weight tugging me back. I smelled mint shampoo.

"The wafers were just wafers," Fayza said.

"Right," I said. My original plan was to play dumb. *Really, the wafers were substance-free? Huh!* I decided to abandon that scheme.

"Do you have the sample?" Fayza asked.

"No," I said truthfully. I'd *had* the sample—but that was in Rovil's hands now.

The hand on my forehead pressed down, forcing my skull back. The rim of the sink knifed into the back of my neck, directly on the C4 vertebra. I clenched the armrests. If I moved fast I might be able to grab one of the girl's arms, but then what? In an instant she could bring her full weight down on my neck. Maybe it wouldn't kill me. Maybe I'd only be paralyzed from the arms down.

"Please . . . ," I said. I wasn't talking to Aaqila or Fayza.

Fayza said, "Who are you working for, Lyda?"

"What?"

"You heard me."

"I'm not working for anyone," I said. "I swear it."

"You are too convenient," Fayza said. "A week after I discover a new drug in the city, you appear. The creator herself, propositioning one of my employees. I direct you to a location where this drug is sold, and a day later—a *single day*—two men are dead. One of them my *customer*. I think you were trying to plug a leak."

"You didn't kill them?" I asked. I couldn't help myself; I tried to raise my head. Quickly it was shoved back and I cried out.

"Why would *I* kill them?" Fayza asked.

"Competition?"

"How can I compete with these people? I don't even know who they are."

"Mafia," I said. "Mexican Mafia."

A moment of silence. God how I wished I could see her face. Aaqila continued to comb my hair with her fingers.

Fayza asked, "How do you know this?"

"The pastor," I said. "He had gang tattoos."

"I see. And you would have me believe that the La eMe, or their African bosses, are now selling designer drugs in my town. Or, perhaps, someone would like to goad me into believing that. An old-fashioned war that would make room for a third player. Is that who you're working for—a third party?"

"I don't know what you're talking about," I said. "I'm not working for anyone, just—"

I suddenly felt a weight pinning my forearms to the chair. "Who do you work for?" Fayza asked, very close to me now.

"I told you, *no one.*"

Something like a wire tightened around my left forearm, securing my arm to the chair. I yelled, but Fayza's weight was all on my other arm now. A moment later that side was tied down, too. Panic swept through me in a white wave.

"Jesus, no—"

Suddenly hot water filled my nose and entered my mouth. The sprayer had soaked straight through the towel. I clamped my mouth shut, but inside I was screaming.

The spray kept coming. I tried to open my lips a fraction and suck air, but water filled my mouth, entered my lungs. My chest seized because there was no air to push the water out. My back arched, the mammalian drowning response kicking in to force my head above water—but of course there was no surface to break through.

Someone clutched the front of my shirt and jerked me to a sitting position. I retched, coughing and hacking, fighting for air.

The towels had fallen to my lap. Fayza stood in front of me, looking annoyed. "Who are you working for, Lyda? Who are you going to sell it to?"

I used my arm to wipe the moisture from my eyes, a good portion of which were my tears. I couldn't believe how *fast* the drowning had worked. The death-panic was almost immediate.

I would like to say that I was filled with rage, that the torture provoked me into an action hero's steely resolve. But the drowning had broken something in me. I was scared, and aching to get out of that room at all costs.

"Please," I said. "No one. I'm not working for—"

Aaqila pushed me back again and I screamed. The towel covered my face again. I tried to suck in air but the water came too fast. I couldn't breathe.

My mind began to shut down like a city under a blackout, whole neighborhoods going offline. My consciousness coalesced around a single thought: *I am going to die.*

And then, light.

. . .

The towels covering my face burned away like flash paper. Dr. Gloria stood over me, her wings stretched impossibly long, filling the room with coruscating light. In her right hand she held a flaming sword—eight feet long, the flames trembling at the edge of the silver—and in her left she held her clipboard, the text upon it shivering with meaning.

"Thank God," I said.

I could not see Fayza or Aaqila. Her brilliance masked the rest of the room.

"Keep your eyes on me," Dr. Gloria said. Her wings snapped like white sails. I focused on her face, and the flames reflected in the lenses of her eyeglasses. The wings sealed off the world behind a curtain of alabaster.

My chest ached with relief, and shame. Oh, I was crazy. Deep crazy. Dr. Gloria did not exist, but I was so relieved to see her.

"We are *not* reconciled," the angel said. "I still don't approve of the way you're treating Ollie. She's fragile, and you're using her."

"You're right. I know you're right. I promise I'll—"

"Oh please," Dr. G said. "You're in a terrible state yourself. I'm not going to extract promises from you in this situation—that would make me as bad as these waterboarding Afghan bitches." She shook her head. "I blame the Americans for this."

We seemed to be talking in a bubble of frozen time. We weren't. The brain cannot stop the clock, or even slow it. The mind cannot, despite Roger Penrose's cockamamie quantum theories, access a timeless, platonic realm of pure thought. The brain can't even process data faster when under duress. That moment you slipped off the garage roof, and you seemed to hang in the air forever; that first kiss, when the planet shrieked to a halt and your heart composed symphonies between heartbeats; that endless, jellied moment you spent in the glare of the truck lights, your life scrolling past you?

All illusions. We only *remember* some moments as lasting forever, because when we are frightened or thrilled the amygdala stamps every last detail with emotion, marking it as vital, worthy of instant retrieval. Our ancient ancestors could forget a thousand days of gathering berries, but remembering every detail of the saber-tooth's attack was worth its weight in evolutionary gold. Only when we recall that moment (days or even seconds later) does it seem to have happened in slow motion. The huge volume of data messes with the brain's rule of thumb (and when it comes to math, the brain is all thumbs): X Amount of Sensory Memory = Y Amount of Time.

I knew all that. But I also knew that under the shelter of Dr. Gloria's wings, I experienced not just grace but a grace period, and I was thankful for it.

The doctor said to me, "I can get you out of this. But you're going to have to say exactly what I tell you—and with conviction."

"How? What are you going to say?"

"Do you trust me, Lyda?"

Of course I did. More than I trusted myself. "Just stay with me," I said.

"That's the spirit." She tucked the sword away—into whatever nonexistent scabbard holds imaginary swords—and folded her wings around my head. The black was gone now; I saw white and only white. Her feathers were soft and dry.

Aaqila pulled me up again. The room was the same, except that now Dr. Gloria stood at my right side.

I coughed water for almost a minute, my chest heaving. Fayza grew impatient. "Get a hold of yourself," she said.

The angel bent and whispered into my ear. Then I said the words she had given me: "I can get you a sample."

"You said you didn't have one," Fayza said.

Gloria whispered again, and I said, "I don't—but I know where to get it." I coughed again, a grating bark of lungs trying to expel the last of the liquid. Aaqila handed me another towel.

"I know who sold it to the pastor," I said. "And I've set up a deal to get my own."

"Go on," Fayza said.

"After the church—the church I went to with Hootan—I realized that the wafers weren't the delivery system." I coughed into the towel, a distraction that allowed time for Gloria to speak to me. "I didn't have to send them off for testing, because I just swallowed them. I figured I could stand the dose. And they were nothing. No effect."

The lie was delivered with all the physiological sincerity I could muster. Racked by the aftereffects of the drowning, it was easy to let my voice break with emotion, to allow my body to adopt the bent and heaving attitude of the penitent. The rest of the lie depended on Fayza not being the one who killed the pastor and Luke. If she was lying about that, then I was a dead woman.

Gloria nodded approvingly. "Keep going," she said.

"The next night I went back to the church," I said. "I broke in the back door. That's when I discovered that Rudy and Luke had been killed."

Fayza said, "You weren't going to tell me this?"

I looked up at her. I didn't have to force new tears. "I thought you had killed them. And I was sure I was next."

Aaqila said something under her breath. Fayza ignored her and asked, "If they were dead, how did you find out where they got the drug?"

"They had a chemjet printer hidden in the bathroom. All the c-packs had been taken—I assumed you'd gotten your sample. But there was something else in the room I couldn't figure out at first. Cigarettes. Boxes of them. Wrapped in plastic, no cartons."

Dr. G placed a cool hand on my shoulder. "Let her get there."

Fayza frowned. "He was getting it from the Indians."

I nodded, and listened to Gloria. "I have a friend of mine, somebody I met in the hospital, who used to do a lot of business with the Six Nations. She knows the people who run the smoke shacks. She said they smuggled all kinds of things, not just cigarettes. She reached out to them, and we met them tonight to set up a buy."

"For what?" Fayza asked.

"The whole thing. A new chemjet, and a full set of ingredient packs."

"And you are receiving these when?"

"Tomorrow night. In Cornwall."

Dr. Gloria said, "Here is where we make her part of the solution." She told me what to say next, and I almost rebelled. "Trust me," Gloria said.

Fortunately, my hesitation could be interpreted as shame. "There's only one problem," I said. "They want forty-thousand Yuan."

"And you don't have this money?"

I shook my head. It felt so heavy from the water. "Not yet."

Fayza leaned in, squinting, as if she didn't hear me correctly: one of the library of power moves that adults used to signal that other adults were fucking idiots. "You arranged to buy from these people," she said, "and you don't have the money?"

"I was going to call everyone I knew," I said. "Uncles, cousins, old friends. Open credit lines. Go in with loan sharks if I had to."

"Unbelievable," Fayza said. She walked away from me, thinking. After thirty seconds of silence she turned and said, "Hootan and Aaqila will go with you. And if you're lying, they will kill you. You know this to be true, yes?"

Aaqila stared at me. She seemed to be already imagining it.

"I understand," I said. I didn't need any prompting from Gloria.

"Good," Fayza said. "Until we leave, you'll be staying with Aaqila."

"What? No. I'm not—"

"Do not press me, Lyda."

Dr. Gloria bristled. "We are so going to smite her ass," she said. "At the first Goddamn opportunity."

My angel. My protector. Keeper of my rage.

. . .

Aaqila lived in one of the two-story houses on Tyndall Avenue. The drive over in Hootan's car was ridiculously short, like a golf cart ride from green to tee. Hootan didn't have time to ask about my wet hair or what had happened inside the salon. Or maybe he didn't dare; he seemed in awe of Aaqila, or maybe infatuated with her. Aaqila barely acknowledged him.

The house was dark, and Aaqila didn't turn on any lights. In a distant room, someone snored vigorously. I imagined sleeping parents and grandparents, rooms crowded with immigrant cousins. But in the dimness it was difficult to make out any details of the home. Dr. Gloria walked with me, but her artificial glow was no help because we hadn't been in this house before. Fauxtons, I called them; they could not illuminate what I hadn't already seen.

Aaqila led me up to a bedroom, unlocked the door, and woke up a little girl who was sleeping inside. The child was dressed in pink nylon pajamas, and her hair was long and frizzy, almost an afro.

My chest tightened. I stepped back, but Aaqila didn't notice.

"Sleep in my room," Aaqila told the girl. She climbed out of bed without a fuss and walked sleepily past us.

"How old is she?" I asked. "Nine? Ten?"

"None of your business," Aaqila said.

Inside the room, Aaqila patted me down and told me to empty my pockets. I complied as automatically as the little girl, handing over my nylon wallet, a wad of bills, some change. When I touched the pen I hesitated. I needed that to get in touch with Ollie. If we didn't talk before tomorrow night, the plan would fall apart, and they would kill me.

Aaqila took the pen. "Now your boots."

"You're kidding me," Dr. Gloria said.

She wasn't. Aaqila dumped the smaller articles into one of the boots and stepped out of the room with the pair. Then she shut the door and locked it.

I thought, who locks a kids' bedroom door from the outside? What about fires? I went to the single window and opened the drapes. They were blocked by steel bars, like the grates that had sealed off the Elegant Lady salon. So either the parents were afraid of the little girls running away, or were terrified of rapists. Or maybe the Millies required that every house in the neighborhood included a room that could double as a cell.

The girl's taste in décor indicated a future as an Elegant Lady; the walls and the bedclothes all vibrated in the same annoying end of the spectrum as the salon. The covers of the twin bed were pulled back, leaving an empty space where the girl had slept in a nest of stuffed animals.

Dr. G said, "Have you noticed there are no electronics? No screens, no pens. Even the stuffed animals are nonrobotic. And look, books! *Paper* books." She was trying to distract me.

"That little girl," I said. "She was so pretty."

"I didn't notice. Now, about tomorrow—"

"Please, just . . . stop talking." I lay down in the bed. It was still warm.

Dr. Gloria took a seat across the room. My personal night-light. I rolled away from her and pulled one of the pillows to my belly.

THE PARABLE OF

the Million Bad Mothers

There was a woman who gave birth to a beautiful child, and after the nurse washed and bundled the infant in new blankets she came to the mother and said, "Would you like to hold the baby?"

The woman noticed that the nurse did not say *your* baby or *your* daughter. The staff had been informed of the situation, and were careful to avoid possessive nouns.

The woman ached to hold the child. But should she? What cascade of effects would result from that act? This was the first decision she would have to make in the next seventy-two hours, and it paralyzed her.

The fetus had been exposed to a massive amount of NME 110. No one knew what effect the dose had already had on the child's developing brain or what the prognosis would be. The mother knew firsthand what permanent damage the drug could inflict on adult tissue, and neither she nor the doctors had any right to expect a mentally healthy child. Initial tests were inconclusive. The girl had low APGAR scores, but she was also born four weeks premature. Only time would tell.

On the bedside table was a multipage form labeled "Final and Irrevocable Surrenders for Adoption." Not one surrender, the mother thought, but an unknowable number of them, a surrender for every day of the rest of her life.

It would be her decision to sign the form or not. She did not want to make this decision, and was surprised that anyone in her mental condition would be allowed to. She was clearly not sane. On the other hand, the law made it clear that insanity did not automatically render you unfit for parenthood (see: Everyone v. Their Parents).

There were other complicating factors. The mother was a dual citizen of the United States and Canada; the other legal parent, though dead, was survived by a wealthy family who might sue for custody; and the newborn herself was American. Any adoption forced upon the mother by DCFS would be jurisdictionally murky. So: It would be the mother's signature, and hers alone, that would deliver the child unto strangers.

But not yet. The state of Illinois mandated a waiting period after the child's birth, and the mother could not take that final, irrevocable step until the time had elapsed.

Three days. Seventy-two hours. 259,200 seconds.

The woman considered the waiting period to be a punishment. Social services did not realize that being forced to make the decision was itself a life sentence. No, more than that: the sentence of an infinite number of lifetimes. The number of variables she had to consider created not some branching tree, but a node diagram like those models of the human mind created by naïve computer scientists, each node connected to the others by input and output lines, some strong, some weak. The number of paths through those nodes was impossible for her to calculate. Almost any result could come out of a system that complicated.

In some lifetimes, the girl exhibited no effects from the drug. Her IQ was high, her emotions stable, her grasp on reality as firm as any child's.

In other lifetimes, a doctor found a drug to make the mother sane, and she was released from the hospital. The mother, who had refused to sign the adoption papers, was reunited with her daughter before the girl was old enough to remember the absence.

Or, the mother signed and the girl was adopted by a loving family with all the emotional and financial resources to deal with a brain-damaged child.

In other lifetimes, the girl exhibited no symptoms of Numinous until the age of twelve, when she developed early-onset schizophrenia. There were incidents of violence. The adoptive parents—good people, but unprepared for such a destructive child—institutionalized the girl.

In yet other lifetimes the mother refused to give up custody, and so when she failed to get better—in fact, got worse year by year—the daughter was shuffled from one foster home to another, never knowing the love of parents, never knowing a permanent home.

In some lifetimes, the institution the daughter found herself in was full of highly trained, caring people, who knew how to help the girl achieve her potential. She managed her mental disorder and went on to public high school, where she excelled in science and math.

In some lifetimes, the mother insisted upon a closed adoption, and the daughter, confused and terrified by the strange workings of her mind, unable to tell the difference between reality and hallucination, and unable to reach out to her biological mother for explanations, stole a box cutter from her adopted father's toolbox and carved her own kind of sense into her skin. Pain was real. Pain was something she could hold onto.

In the lifetimes in which the mother allowed for an open adoption, the precocious daughter Googled her mother's name and was horrified; the girl's own anxieties, which she had been told were experienced by *lots* of other children, suddenly seemed more sinister, not normal at all, the symptoms of a latent defect that would cause her to live in fear of her own mind for the rest of her life.

And so on. Each node that was touched sent a ripple across the web of possibilities.

The nurse asked a second time, "Would you like to hold her?"

Again the mother could not answer. Her bones felt as fragile as balsa wood. If the nurse placed the baby in her arms, the mother would split and shatter, and if she did not fall apart she would not be able to let the child go.

It was then that an angel of the Lord who had been watching nearby spoke. "You've got to stop this," she said. The mother's mind was filled with nodes and glowing lines, the dreams and nightmares multiplying by the second.

The angel removed her glasses and said, "Listen to me. What the child needs in this moment is to be held."

The mother shouted, "You don't know that! *I* don't know that, so you don't!" She said this aloud. She had not yet learned the skill of talking silently to her angel. Yet immediately she realized the mistake. The nurse stepped back from the bed and turned aside, an unconscious movement to protect the baby. Then she left the room.

"*Goddamn* it!" the mother shouted. She picked up the plastic water bottle and threw it at her angel. The IV tube ripped from her arm. The bottle clattered against the far wall.

The mother put her hand to her bleeding arm. She was dehydrated and did not have tears to waste, but still she wept. She was delusional. She knew that this was the way schizophrenics thought. This was the way her own mother had behaved before they took her away. All her life she'd been on guard, watching for signs of her mind twisting toward its genetic pre-disposition. She'd armed herself with advanced degrees. She was determined that she would not become her mother. And she prayed, as only an atheist can pray, that her own daughter would not inherit the damage.

The angel of the Lord waited for perhaps a minute, then went to the mother's bedside and placed an arm around her shoulders.

"You're imaginary," the mother said.

"It's true," the angel said.

Still, the woman was grateful for that cool touch. Proof, if any more was needed, that she was unfit to be a mother.

"I'm a murderer," she said to the angel.

"You did not kill Mikala," the angel said, but the woman could not trust her. The angel's job, the mother believed, was to comfort her, to tell her things she wanted to hear, and show her what she needed to see.

She decided to sign the form. Her daughter deserved a real mother, a loving mother, who had not committed terrible crimes.

She held fast to that decision for several minutes. Then she thought, But what if . . . ?

There were 71 hours and 30 minutes to go.

—G.I.E.D.

CHAPTER TWELVE

East of the city the 401 rode the lip of Lake Ontario like a dare until it lost courage and angled north into farmland. I'd grown up in a small town an hour north of that highway, and I'd traveled a good chunk of the road from Windsor to Quebec. It was a boring drive, and I was exhausted. Despite the fact that I was traveling against my will with armed gangsters, the trip would be a five-hour exercise in maintaining consciousness.

Throughout the night I'd dreamed of white corridors, then awoke suffocating, unable to catch my breath. For the rest of the day I'd been kept prisoner in the family living room by Aaqila's mother, a woman only a few years older than me who spoke adequate English. I never caught her name. She fed me microwave lasagna and orange soda and forced us to watch a marathon rebroadcast of her favorite reality show, *Beam Me Up!* Each episode, a wealthy first-world family switched places for a month with a third-world one. It was evidently a huge hit. Half the show, the audience could chuckle warm-heartedly at yokels from Darfur oohing and aahing over the Albertson's produce section; the other half they could laugh out loud at white Republicans from Ohio pulling ticks off their asses.

Aaqila came in and out of the living room, but spent most of the time in another part of the house, playing the sulky babysitter. Dr. Gloria and I talked about running away. We were pretty sure I wouldn't get far in this neighborhood. Plus Aaqila still had my boots and other belongings, including the pen. God, I itched for a phone. All I wanted was two minutes with a keypad. If I couldn't reach Ollie, I was never going to get out of Canada, at least not breathing. Fayza would find out soon enough that there was no chemjet coming by boat from America, and I'd find out soon enough what it was like to be dead.

Just before episode nine of *Beam Me Up!*—"The Mackenzies of Colorado are arrested by North Korean police!"—Aaqila's mother paused the screen and went into the kitchen to make us a snack. Something glimmered at the edge of my vision, and Dr. Gloria said, "The writing is on the wall."

Red letters flickered across the striped wallpaper. It said: *Been listening.*

"Are you doing that?" I said to Gloria.

Gloria put up her hands. "Don't look at me."

The words changed—a longer sentence. I jumped from my seat, and my body obstructed some of the message. I turned toward the living room window. There was a two-foot gap between the curtains, and through it I could see a few people on the street. One of them, standing directly across from the window, was a figure in a baseball cap and heavy jacket who could have been a twelve-year-old boy.

I stepped back. The message changed again. Three more sentences written in flickering laser light appeared. Dr. Gloria studied them with me, memorizing them.

Aaqila's mother walked into the room. "Ready?" she asked.

The words were still glowing on the wall. I jumped toward the woman and took the bowl she was carrying. It was full of assorted nuts mixed with a spice that smelled like rosemary.

"Are these an Afghan snack?" I asked, trying to keep her attention on me. "They look delicious."

"I got them at Whole Foods," she said, and reached for the remote.

"Clear," Dr. Gloria said. The words had disappeared.

I tried to look as bored and anxious as I had all day, but inside I was almost collapsing from relief. Ollie had told me that pens were tracking devices, and ever since Hootan had picked me up at Bobby's apartment I'd been praying that she was following me. Now I knew that she'd done more than that: She'd tracked me, listened in, and formed a plan.

Sometime around 5 p.m. Hootan arrived, and we started the long haul to Cornwall. Dr. G sat up front. Aaqila sat beside me in the backseat, looking unhappy. In her lap she held a pink nylon Mr. Squiggly lunchbox. She spent the entire time with her pen open, talking to . . . who? Other emo girls on TalentForTorture.com? The WillingToWaterboard social network?

The sun dropped behind us, filling the car with light for perhaps a half hour before it sank below the horizon. We drove in the dark for another two hours, no one speaking. Hootan wore his glasses, blinking messages or watching a show, an absurdly dangerous thing to do. Aaqila stayed glued to her pen.

I said, "That's the place." A sign announced the Morrisburg Service Center in five kilometers.

"I don't like this," Hootan said.

"Well too bad. They told me to pull over there and wait for further instructions, so that's what we're going to do." Aaqila didn't involve herself in the argument.

Hootan took the exit ramp. The rest area was a vast, empty parking lot somehow made more vast and empty by the three semitrailers parked under the lights. No cars I could see, which worried me. A paved road led off into the trees to the right, toward what I assumed to be a picnic area.

Hootan pulled up to the only building, a brown rectangular shed that had been built by the government but ceded to a "Snoopy's," a convenience store chain I'd never heard of.

"You have the pen?" I asked Aaqila.

"Stop asking me that."

"Is it turned on?"

She scowled. We waited for ten, fifteen minutes. The pen didn't ring. I said, "I gotta pee."

"We wait here," Hootan said.

"Like a fucking racehorse," I said.

Hootan took off his glasses to look at me. "Why do you have to be so crude?"

"You want me to just go all over your upholstery?"

"Aaqila goes with you," he said.

"As long as she lets me go first." I hustled toward the convenience store, and Aaqila was forced to walk quickly to keep up. The clerk, a chubby

blond girl, read my pained expression and pointed me toward the rest-
room.

"Wait," Aaqila said. She put a hand on my shoulder and pushed open the
door with the other. The room was a few days of hard use past clean, with
squares of toilet paper pasted to the grubby linoleum. There were two stalls,
a sink, and a stainless steel mirror. One stall door was ajar, the other closed.

Aaqila knocked on the closed door. "Hello?" She knocked again.

I flashed on a fantasy: *The door bangs open, knocking Aaqila back. Ollie
steps out with a gun. We tie up the girl, duct tape her mouth shut, then . . .* It
got hazy after that. The money was back in the car, in the Mr. Squiggly
box. So we'd have to get the drop on Hootan too.

Aaqila crouched to look under the stall door.

Second fantasy: *I smash Aaqila in the back of the head* (with what?), *drag
her into the stall, and press her face into the toilet.*

"Thoughts like those aren't helpful," Dr. G said.

I disagreed.

Aaqila got to her feet and looked at her palms in disgust. "Nobody
there."

I took the empty stall. I scanned for pens taped to the toilet, messages
scrawled on the toilet paper, words drawn into the grime on the wall . . .
but no. The five sentences that Ollie had beamed onto the wall at Aaqila's
house were all I had to go on:

Been listening
Heard deal for chemjet
All OK
Stop at 401 Morrisburg SC K756
Wait for call from smugglers. XXOO

Historically speaking, phantom messages that appear on walls tend toward the cryptic. I had no Daniel to call on, but I did have an angel on my
shoulder, and while we watched episodes of *Beam Me Up!* Dr. Gloria and I
interpreted the words as follows, adding emotional subtext:

**This is Ollie. I love you and care for you and have been tracking
you through the pen I gave you. I have also, using the same pen**

or perhaps other devices I've placed on your person, overheard the deal you made with Fayza for the chemjet printer. I have a plan that will save us all and get us to America. Just drive toward Cornwall on the 401, and stop at the Morrisburg Service Center located at kilometer marker 756. The smugglers will call with further instructions. Hugs and kisses.

Perhaps, I thought, we'd read too optimistically. Maybe Ollie had no plan at all. Maybe *I* was supposed to come up with the plan.

"Everything will work out," Dr. Gloria said, hovering over the stall. "How could you not trust someone who signs a secret message with those middle school Xs and Os?"

"She was being ironic," I said.

"No, she *said* it ironically, but she was really being sincere. It was both."

"Bi-ronic."

"Bi-rony," Dr. G agreed.

"So what happens when the smugglers call?"

"I have no idea," Dr. Gloria said.

"Then would you let me pee in peace?"

In the next stall, a pen began to chime. I heard Aaqila answer. There was a pause, and then the girl was standing on her toilet and looking over the stall at me. "It's for you."

She handed me the pen. There was no video. A voice said, "Lyda Rose?" It was electronically modified, and sounded like LYda ROZE.

"Speaking."

"I'M SENDing GPS coORDinates. DRIVE THERE."

"Why are they using so much distortion?" Dr. Gloria asked. "There's perfectly good speech modification technology out there."

I ignored her. The voice said, "PARK and turn OFF your LIGHTS."

"They could sound like a British nanny or Samuel L. Jackson, any accent they like, and it would be just as untraceable."

"WAIT for FUR-thur inSTRUC-tions."

"No lights, wait for instructions," I repeated, for Aaqila's benefit. I didn't want to give them the impression that I was making any of this up. "Got it."

The call cut off. A few seconds later I received a text message with a travel link in it. The little map showed our route. I couldn't decide if the call had been from Ollie or from the actual smugglers. Then I couldn't decide if it mattered.

"I suppose they think it makes them sound tough," Dr. G said. "It's like a font for gangsters."

. . .

I took the front seat with Hootan to relay directions. He wanted me to send the map to his glasses, but I refused on the grounds that HUDs were fucking crazy, blindfolds for people with ADD, and Aaqila agreed. The pen directed me, and I directed Hootan. After forty minutes we left the 401 and took 138 south through Cornwall City, which at night looked like every small city at night. We passed an abandoned port-of-entry station, crossed a short bridge, and came down on Cornwall Island.

The island sat in the middle of the St. Lawrence like a mossy stepping stone between nations. It was technically part of Canada, but it was also inside the Akwesasne Reserve, the territory of the Mohawk Nation. The reserve (or "reservation" if you were speaking Anglo-American) included parts of New York, Quebec, and Ontario. The Mohawks had little use for borders. The tribe went to court every time the Americans or the Canadians tried to set up toll stations or immigration controls, taking the position that you could no more divide up their land than you could cut soup. There were homes on the southeast of the reserve where the New York/Quebec border ran straight through the living room. Sometimes the tribe won the case—like the closing of the port-of-entry on the Cornwall City mainland—and sometimes the governments did.

If we stayed on the highway it would turn into the International Seaway Bridge and carry us to America—and straight into the Hogansburg port-of-entry and the arms of the United States Border Patrol. The legal battle over *that* POE was one the tribe had definitely lost.

(I came to know these facts the way we all came to know things in the twenty-first century: My internet told me so. The map on my pen came chock-full of textual tidbits, like this Fun Fact: In winter, smugglers used to cross the frozen St. Lawrence in trucks, but for the past five winters the river has failed to freeze solid. Huh!)

We did not stay on the highway. Well before the Seaway Bridge the pen directed us to turn east. Hootan cruised at unsuspicious speeds through the island's tiny downtown, then into a woodsy residential area. We kept going until we'd almost reached the eastern end of the island, where we were surrounded by a lot more woods than residences. It was still winter here: Snow lined the road and lay thick under the trees.

I pointed to a gap between two large firs. "Pull off the road," I said. "And turn out your lights."

Hootan gave me a look. He didn't like to be ordered around—especially by a woman—but he did as he was told. "Now what?" he asked.

I didn't bother answering. He knew what they'd told me.

There wasn't much traffic on this road, but we tensed up as each pair of headlights passed us. After fifteen minutes Hootan said, "We're going to get stopped by the cops."

"Can you be stopped if you're not moving?" Dr. Gloria asked from the backseat.

"Relax," I said to everyone, including myself.

It was another half hour before the pen chimed. Aaqila had taken it back from me. She held out the device, and all four of us leaned in to hear. "WALK toward the WA-ter," the same electronic voice said. "Bring the MON-ey. Come ALONE."

The call ended. Hootan said, "Screw that."

"Don't be crude," Dr. G said.

"We're going with you," Aaqila said.

"Didn't think I could stop you," I said. To Aaqila I said, "The money?"

She handed me the Mr. Squiggly lunchbox. I thought about opening it to count the cash, but decided I didn't need to antagonize her. Yet.

Dr. Gloria took to the air, and the rest of us entered the trees. I tried to step around the deeper patches, but the snow kept tipping into the tops of my boots. According to the map, the car shouldn't have been more than a hundred meters from the water, but I couldn't see anything through the trees, and I couldn't make out any sound over my huffing and puffing.

Suddenly I stepped out onto a dirt road—really no more than a pair of deeply rutted tire tracks. Dr. Gloria landed in a flurry of wings.

"This wasn't on the map," Hootan said. He sounded hurt.

"I think that's on purpose," I said.

To my right the trail curled into the trees, heading roughly back the way we'd come. To my left it ended in an open area shaped like the head of a sperm. At the edge of the clearing, the land dropped off. Beyond was the moon-flecked river.

A flashlight raked us from the trees at the western edge of the clearing, then focused on my face.

"I told you to come alone!" a female voice yelled.

"At least she's not using distortion," Dr. G said.

I shaded my eyes against the glare. "I have the money," I called back. "You have the printer?"

"Come forward—*just you!*"

I started forward, and Aaqila put a hand on my shoulder. "Don't do anything stupid," she said.

"I think it's too late for that," Dr. G said.

The flashlight moved to cover Aaqila and Hootan, and I walked out into the dark. But not alone; Dr. G of course followed me out. When I was in the middle of the clearing, the voice called, "Stop!" A few feet away stood a mound about two feet high, covered by a tarp; in the dark I'd thought it was a boulder.

I pulled off the plastic. Two cardboard boxes, one big enough to hold a printer. I yelled back to Aaqila and Hootan, "It's here!"

"Throw me the money," the figure behind the flashlight said. She was twenty feet from me.

"No!" Hootan yelled. He marched forward, arm straight in front of him, one-handing the pistol like a Hollywood bad guy. Aaqila followed closely behind him. "Show yourself!" he said.

"What the hell are you doing?" I yelled to them. "Get the fuck back!"

That's when I noticed the man in the cowboy hat. He stepped out of the northern trees halfway between Hootan and me. He was short, maybe only 5'4". I couldn't make out his face under the big brim, but something about the hat and the white shirt and that formal suit jacket looked familiar.

"The bar," Dr. Gloria said. Yes: He was the man at the bar who'd tipped his hat at me.

Before I could answer her, a police siren wailed. Blue-and-red flashing lights lit up the trees. Headlight beams bounced; a police car was coming down that rutted road. In a second it would enter the clearing.

Hootan stopped and whirled toward the lights. Aaqila began to turn too, and then noticed the man in the cowboy hat. For what seemed like a long moment (but was not, the brain grabbing every detail in high def), no one moved.

Then, everyone moved at once. Everyone except me.

The person in the trees behind me with the flashlight said, "Lyda! This way!" Hootan spun toward the printer box. The cowboy raised his arm. Aaqila ran toward the cowboy, arms spread.

And I . . . watched.

The cowboy fired. Aaqila was almost directly in front of the man, but it was Hootan who fell, dropping to the ground as if his knees had been cut out from under him. Then Aaqila smashed into the cowboy and they went down tumbling, a confusion of arms and legs flashing in the glare of the headlights. The strobing blue-and-red lights seemed to sway the trees like a high wind.

Someone seized my arm. "Let's go!" It was Ollie, in twelve-year-old-boy drag: the baseball cap and heavy jacket I'd seen her wearing on the street outside Aaqila's house, plus a backpack I'd never seen before. She yanked me into the trees and we ran, crunching through icy snow, the beam of her flashlight hopscotching ahead of us. I hugged the lunchbox close to my body and followed as best I could.

"Who the fuck *is* that guy?!" I said.

Another gunshot, the sound splintering in the dark. I grabbed Ollie's jacket and jerked her to a halt. We were surrounded by trees. The river should have been nearby, but I couldn't see it.

I grabbed Ollie by the elbow. "Stop, damn it!" I said. "The guy in the hat! Is he a cop?"

"Cops aren't real," Ollie said, and sucked in a breath. "That car—it's Bobby."

"What do you mean it's—?"

"His *car*," Ollie said. "We put a light on it, wired the sound. Distraction. Everybody scatters, you get away."

Dr. G appeared behind me. "You left him back there with those *killers?*"

Fuck.

The doctor unfurled her wings into Maximum Righteousness Mode. The flaming sword was in her hand. She pointed with it like the archangel casting us out of the garden. "Get your ass back there!"

"No," I said aloud. "No no no."

"Come on," Ollie said. "We've got to go—the boat's coming."

I looked back toward the way we came. Ollie said, "Lyda, he's fine, just—"

"Be right back," I said. I shoved the money into her arms and ran. Drifts tugged at my ankles. Hidden roots kicked at my toes, sent me stumbling in the path of trees that seemed to rush at me out of the dark. I burst through curtains of pine branches, scattering snow.

Suddenly I was yanked sideways, and realized it was Ollie; she'd caught up with me and had seized my arm.

"This way," she said. Her flashlight was turned off. "Quiet now."

She led me to my right, around a jumble of boulders. Ahead, the head-lights of the stopped car cut through the branches. I could hear nothing but my own breath and the crunch of the snow, which suddenly seemed obscenely loud. Ollie stopped me with a hand on my chest.

We stood at the edge of the clearing. Fifty feet away, Bobby knelt in the grass, his hands up. He was babbling. I couldn't make out the words, only the panicked somersault rhythm of his voice. The man in the cowboy hat held his pistol to his side, so clearly in control there was no need to aim it at the kid. A few feet from Bobby lay a crumpled form: Hootan. But where was Aaqila?

Dr. Gloria descended in a nimbus of light. She hovered between Bobby and the gunman, her arms extended. *"Now,"* she commanded.

"Stay down," I said to Ollie, then before she could object I called out: "Don't shoot him!"

The cowboy instantly pivoted and brought his gun up, aiming at me. Could he see me in the dark? I couldn't make out his eyes beneath the brim of his hat.

"He's just a kid," I yelled. "He doesn't know anything."

I didn't know anything either. If the man in the hat wasn't a cop, and he wasn't with Fayza, then who the hell was he? One of her competitors?

"Lyda Rose," the cowboy called back. "Why don't you step out and we talk for a spell?" He spoke in a theatrical Western drawl.

No. I did not want to *step out.* I could feel a knot above my sternum like the tip of a bayonet. If I walked forward it would burrow into me.

Dr. Gloria said, "You have no choice."

I stepped into the clearing, palms out—and did not die. Not yet.

Bobby said, "Lyda! I'm so sorry!"

"It's okay," I said to him. Then to the cowboy I said, "Let him go. I'll give you what you want."

"Which would be what, Miss Rose?"

"I have no fucking idea," I said. "But whatever it is, it's yours. Where's Aaqila?"

"The crazy Afghan girl? Run off to die. She was shot up pretty good. And where's your sidekick, the commando girl?"

Commando girl? "Back in the trees," I said.

"Ah." His head didn't move. I still couldn't see his eyes. "I imagine she's a pretty good shot."

"I imagine so." Jesus Christ, he had me talking like him.

He chuckled. "Well, I wasn't going to stick around anyway. I have to ask, though. Is that there an actual printer of Numinous?"

It was a shock to hear the man say its name. After a moment I managed to say, "It's a fake. We don't have the printer, or the ingredients."

He laughed again, louder. "Oh, you're a tricky one," he said. He touched the brim of his hat, just as he had in the bar, and began to back away. "Y'all have a nice night. And say hello to your friend Rovil for me. Tell him, no hard feelings." In a few steps he had backed between two trees and disappeared.

Oh shit. What did he do to Rovil?

Dr. Gloria slid an arm under mine to steady me. "Don't worry about that now."

Bobby jumped up and hugged me. "I'm sorry I'm sorry I'm sorry! I told him everything!"

"You were great," I said. I pulled away from the boy. "You saved my life, okay? Now go. Drive home. Take care of Lamont."

"All right already!" Ollie called from the woods. "Let's *go!*"

Bobby said, "I'll feed him every day."

CHAPTER THIRTEEN

I was a forty-two year old woman. I'd spent the last ten years abusing my body with every illicit drug I could get my hands on, as well as all the good licit ones. Additional pharmaceuticals had been provided over the years by the hospitals I'd attended. A car crash—which one, in which year, I could no longer remember—had left me with a grindingly painful deficit of cartilage in my left knee. I also ate like shit.

All this is by way of saying that I did not have another sprint in me. Ollie, however, forced one out of me. We plunged through the trees, Ollie leading again, now holding both the Mr. Squiggly lunchbox and the flashlight. She seemed to know where she was going. I was blind to everything except the dark in front of my face, my concentration taken up by my burning lungs and the pain spiking up my left leg.

Suddenly the ground turned soft beneath my boots and I stumbled. We were on a dirt path now, a line of dark snaking through the snowy woods. The river appeared on our right, surprisingly close.

"Here," Ollie said. The path bent toward the water, sloping to a landing about six feet wide. We pulled up, and I gulped oxygen. Somewhere out on the dark water lay the invisible dashed line of the US–Canadian border, a ghost-stitch visible only to satellites.

"It's coming," she said. I heard it then: the whine

of an outboard motor. I could see nothing on the river but shadows and an ill-defined mass in the distance. Was that New York? I'd gotten turned around.

The sound of the motor abruptly grew louder. Ollie yelled, "Watch out!" and shoved me aside. A black shape lunged at us up the rocky embankment. It slammed down with a bang, then suddenly the engine cut out. It was a shallow-bottomed bass boat, painted some dark color—and it was full of black garbage bags.

"Unload them," Ollie said. "Quick! It's part of the deal."

"What the fuck happened to the driver?!" For a crazy moment I thought he'd been thrown clear.

"It's a rowboat," she said. She grabbed one of the bags and grunted. It was evidently heavy. She tossed the bag into the bushes. There were more than a dozen of them in the small boat. All the benches except the front one had been removed to make room for the cargo. The craft had been stripped down to a motor, a big gas can, and in the corner a black fishing rod poking up like an antenna.

Dr. Gloria walked across the top of the water toward the rear of the boat. "Get it now?" she said.

Of course. The fishing rod wasn't poking up like an antenna; the antenna was poking up like a fishing rod. The craft was a remote controlled ro-boat.

I started hauling bags, lifting from the bottom because of the weight. I could feel cardboard boxes inside them and hoped that they only contained cigarettes. I wasn't ready to do hard time for smuggling drugs. When the last bag had been tossed into the trees, Ollie threw her own backpack into the boat, where it landed with a clunk.

"Get in," she said.

I climbed over the side and sat down on the bench. Ollie handed me the money box. "Show it to the camera."

"What camera?"

She gestured toward the antenna. I twisted and straddled the bench, then waved the Mr. Squiggly box at the antenna, figuring the camera was somewhere inside it or near it. "We *have* the *money*," I said, trying to enunciate clearly.

The boat lurched—Ollie shoving it a few scraping feet across the rocky bank toward the water. I grabbed the boat's side—the gunwale? whatever they called it—and leaned forward, ready to pull Ollie in when she got us all the way in the water. Behind her, a shadow moved on the path. It was a bent figure, barely visible in the moonlight.

Dr. Gloria said, "Aaqila!" and I shouted something like, "Down!"

Ollie was already in motion. She pushed the boat again—a full-body shove with arms and legs straight—and then let go and dropped below my line of sight with a splash.

Aaqila stumbled forward, her leg dragging behind her. One arm clutched her chest, and the other was straightening to point at me. She screamed a collection of consonants and vowels.

I have two overlapping memories of the next moment. In both, I hear each bang of the pistol—five shots, shockingly loud. But in one memory I am watching the pistol in Aaqila's hand, and see red-orange flames flashing at the mouth of the barrel. In the other memory, I see nothing but Dr. Gloria. The angel is standing on the water between the boat and Aaqila, her wings flaring and trembling as each bullet strikes those pure-white feathers and bursts into light.

The details of both memories are suspect. Did I really see the muzzle flash, or was that something sketched in from countless movies? Alternatively, how does a figment of my imagination stop bullets?

The boat slipped sideways in the river's current. On shore, Aaqila nestled the gun in her bent arm, trying to do something to it with her good hand—reload? Unjam it? Then Ollie rose up off the ground, holding some glossy shape above her head with both hands—a river rock, big as bread loaf. She brought it down on Aaqila's head and the girl collapsed. The sound of the two impacts—the rock hitting her skull, her body hitting the ground—were so faint that I may have filled them in on my own.

"Oh my," Dr. Gloria said.

From behind me came an electrical hum; then the outboard motor belched and fell into a deep rumble. The front of the boat swung toward open water.

I threw up a hand, waving at the antenna, and yelled, "Wait!" The boat continued to turn. I twisted to face the shore. "Ollie! It's going!"

She was bent over Aaqila's unmoving body. I yelled again, and Ollie looked at me over her shoulder, only her nose and mouth visible beneath the cap. Was she grimacing? Saying good-bye? I thought, *Don't you dare abandon me now!*

Ollie abruptly turned and ran, not toward the water, but along the bank to my left. The current was pushing my boat downstream, toward a spit of land, and Ollie was sprinting toward it. She popped open her coat on the run like Clark Kent and tossed it aside, then tore the cap from her head and sent it spinning across the water. She reached the end of the land and leaped, not diving because the water could not have been very deep, and landed with a splash. The water came up to her knees. She took three slogging steps and then launched into a shallow dive. She was eight or ten meters west of the boat, but I was moving away from the shore.

The motor roared and the boat spun hard to my left. I gripped the sides and yelled at the camera, "Goddamn it! Wait!" The bow was aimed at the dark hulk of land less than a kilometer across the water. That was too close for New York; it had to be Île-Saint-Régis, the island on the Quebec side of the border.

The throttle kicked a notch higher. I pushed off the bench and half leaped, half fell toward the motor. The boat bucked and I fell the rest of the way, nearly impaling myself on the tiller. My forearms came down on the fat skull of the outboard cowling. I gripped the sides of the motor and held on as it vibrated beneath me, the entire mount swiveling as if to throw me off. Icy spray struck my face. Gasoline fumes filled my nostrils.

I'd lost track of Ollie.

Dr. Gloria flew overhead, keeping pace easily. "Remain calm," she said.

"Fuck you!" I yelled.

Suddenly Ollie broke the surface of the water, two body lengths away, her arms knifing toward me.

"Come on, baby!" I crouched and reached for her, my thighs jammed against the sides. Too much: My weight tipped the boat and I fell forward. I seized the rim and stopped myself, my face inches from the water. The remote-controlled prop swerved to compensate, and suddenly the boat was almost on top of Ollie. Her eyes shone bright in the moonlight. I thrust out an arm, and she latched on. If I hadn't been wearing a jacket she wouldn't have been able to get a grip.

The throttle kicked into high then. Ollie's weight nearly yanked me out of the boat.

Dr. Gloria landed behind me in the boat. "Pull!" she said.

"You think?" I shouted back.

I got my hips below the rim of the boat, then gripped Ollie with both hands. It took all my strength to hold on; I had nothing remaining to pull her in. The boat slewed left, then right, the drag nearly pulling us apart.

The doctor kneeled behind me and put her arms around my waist. "Ready?" she said into my ear. "One! Two!"

Dr. G yanked me backward. I held on, and Ollie popped half out of the water. Before she slipped back she managed to get an elbow over the side. The wake dragged her feet behind her.

"Almost there," Dr. Gloria said. I reached over Ollie's back to her belt and heaved. She fell heavily into the bottom of the boat.

Ollie coughed water. Soaking wet, hair plastered to her cheeks, she was tiny.

The ro-boat accelerated, the nose lifted, and we charged toward the border. We were home free.

. . .

The engine deafened us with its two-tone whine and rumble; the hull bounced over invisible waves. I sat with Ollie in the bottom of the boat, my arms around her. She was shivering. Her cheek was a slab of cold meat.

After perhaps a minute, Dr. Gloria said, "We have a problem."

"You mean *now* we have one?" I said.

I sat up straighter. The doctor pointed to our left, up the stretch of river that led between l'Île-Saint-Régis and the Quebec mainland. In the distance was a red light crowning a row of white running lights. A big front spotlight raked the water ahead of it. The boat looked to be a long way from us, but distances were tricky at night. "Who the hell?" I said.

"RCMP," Ollie said without lifting her head. She was trembling, and her voice was strained.

"Looks like somebody heard the gunshots," Dr. G said.

"Can we outrun them?" I asked aloud. I didn't know how long it would it take to cross the river, or who was supposed to meet us on the other side. These were only two of the most basic questions I should have asked Ollie back at the marina.

The engine revved, died, then revved again. Dr. Gloria said, "Uh oh."

The tiller swung toward my head. The boat began to turn.

Ollie said, "Drones."

"*What?* The Canadians have drones too?"

"Jamming us."

"Oh come *on*," I said like an angry teenager. I couldn't see anything above us, or hear any noise but our engine. How big were they? How high up? And how the hell were we supposed to get away from them?

Our boat continued to circle, the engine surging and dragging drunkenly. The lights of the RCMP boat bore down on us.

I grabbed the tiller and tried to push it straight, but it resisted me. Fine. I gripped it with both hands and pulled it toward me like a rower. It didn't budge—but then something snapped inside the motor. I fell back, my hands still on the tiller. The boat had turned with me.

"I can steer!" I said.

"Throttle?" Ollie asked.

I twisted the rubber grip of the throttle, and it turned easily—but the engine speed didn't change. Fuck. It was still under remote control.

Ollie pushed herself up onto hands and knees. She reached past me to the antenna, then ran her hand down it until she found something in the dark under the back rim of the boat. She yanked, and the engine died. Her fist held a bundle of wires.

Suddenly I could hear the rumble of the police boat's engines. "Uh, Ollie?"

Dr. Gloria said, "I really don't think they should be allowed to call themselves 'mounted police' when they're on boats, do you?"

Ollie's hands were shaking. She thrust the wires at me and said, "Find two that spark."

"What? Oh Jesus." I let go of the throttle and took them from her.

"STOP YOUR ENGINE!" a voice boomed over the water. "ARRÊTEZ VOTRE BATEAU!"

Jerks. We were already spinning in circles.

I held one wire in my left hand, and touched the copper tips of one of the wires on my right. Nothing. I tried another, then another, while the growl of the RCMP boat grew louder behind us. Suddenly two tips sparked and instantly decorated my vision with spots. The engine coughed.

"Those two!" Ollie said. "Go go go!"

White light hit us, creating an instant tableau: me holding a bouquet of wires, Ollie sprawled at my feet, and Dr. Gloria perched on the bow like an eighteenth-century figurehead. Everything outside the boat became black velvet.

I squinted and pressed the wires together. The boat heaved forward. Ollie reached up and grabbed the tiller to hold us straight.

The policeman behind the bullhorn was not happy with this. "AR-RÊTEZ! STOP!"

The front of the boat rose as we increased speed. Ollie and I were almost on top of each other at the back of the boat, and Dr. Gloria, balancing on the front lip, did nothing to equalize our weight and bring the nose down. We bounced over the water, barely in control. The motion kept knocking my hands apart, and with each gap between the wires the engine stuttered. Binary throttles, I decided, sucked.

The motor was ridiculously overpowered for a bass boat, even one that was usually loaded with cigarettes. But still it was no match for the size of the RCMP cruiser; I could *feel* the cruiser catching up to us. The white light stayed pinned to us like a vaudeville spotlight.

Ollie sat up, looked around in the dark, then pointed a few degrees off to our right. Less than a hundred meters away, barely visible beyond the glare of the RCMP light, lay a hunk of rock and trees.

"The Hen!" she said. "Stay on the gas!" Even shaking with hypothermia, Ollie had a better sense of direction than I did. I'd seen l'Île Hen on the pen map. It was a banana-shaped patch of land only a couple hundred feet long. The US–Canadian border was only about a thousand meters beyond the island, cutting diagonally across the river. But that was still too far; the RCMP boat would be on us in less than thirty seconds.

"We're not going to make it!" I said

"What are they going to do?" Ollie said. "Ram us?" She was grinning. Why was she—*how* was she grinning?

Ollie aimed us toward the Hen. A few dozen feet from it she cut right, skimming the northern tip of the banana, then jammed hard to the left. The spotlight cut out; the island was between us now. We shot along the shore, so close that the trees hid the eastern sky. A rock or submerged log would throw us from the boat. But I held the wires together and we flew at top speed, the sound of the outboard doubly loud this close to the land.

In a handful of seconds we were back in open water. The mainland was half a kilometer or more ahead of us, only visible because of the distant glow of streetlights. As near as I could figure we were heading southeast, paralleling the border. We should have been going due west. I shouted, "What are you doing? That's Quebec!"

"No," she yelled back. "It's Mohawk land."

The white light slid across us again as the RCMP boat made the turn around the Hen, but we had gained some distance. Ollie pointed us at an outcropping. Did she know where to land? Or were we so outside the plan that it was all improvisation now?

Dr. Gloria pointed behind us. "Ladies?"

The police boat seemed to be charging at us at a speed it hadn't displayed before.

"Mohawk Land" seemed to be growing no closer. In moments the RCMP had pulled up along our right side, less than ten yards away, but we could see little beyond the glare of the spotlight. The man behind the bullhorn yelled "CUT YOUR ENGINE!" and then followed up with a barrage of French commands.

Ollie waved.

The police boat surged ahead. "They're going to cut us off," Ollie said.

Their boat was thirty meters ahead of us now, and it suddenly swerved in front of us. Ollie jerked us to the left. We hit the big boat's wake and went airborne.

I reached for the side of the boat, but before I could get a grip we slammed down, and I crashed shoulder first into the wet aluminum floor.

"Throttle!" Ollie yelled. The engine had died; I'd dropped the wires.

I got to my knees. My shoulder felt like it had been whacked by a baseball bat. Ahead of us the RCMP boat made a hard left, the spotlight swiveling to keep us in its glare.

"They got us, Ollie."

"No," she said. She stooped, trying to find the wires dangling from under the engine. "No no no."

The police boat finished its turn. It was heading toward us now, coming at us from our left, but the turn had forced it to slow. Dr. Gloria said, "What's *that?*"

A silver boat smaller than our own zipped out of the dark to our right, engine keening. The aluminum body was narrow as a canoe, with a massive black outboard weighing down the end. It skipped along the top of the waves at tremendous speed, nose high, the prop barely staying in the water. The boat had no lights, but I could make out a figure of a man sitting tall, his hand firmly at the tiller. He was aiming straight for us, racing to beat the police boat to us.

"Ollie!"

She looked up, the wires in her hand. The new boat roared toward us.

There was something wrong with the driver. At first I thought he was wearing a white plastic mask, but then I realized that he wasn't a man at all. His head was a stuffed garbage bag with a face drawn in black marker. His hand was attached to the tiller by a silver mitten of duct tape.

"We're going to be rammed by a scarecrow," Dr. G said.

I'd like to think I yelled "Hold on!" But it may have been only, "Fuck!"

The dummy flashed past us, less than a meter from the front of our boat. It wasn't us that it was aiming for. A dozen meters past us it swerved hard toward the RCMP cruiser. The silver boat hit the hull of the cruiser and flipped up, catapulting the dummy into the air. The body cartwheeled over the deck of the police boat in a convincing impersonation of a drunken boatman flying to his death. The dummy came down somewhere on the other side, out of our line of sight.

The motor behind me shook to life; Ollie had found the right pair of wires. "Aim for the trees!" Ollie said. I didn't move. I couldn't process what I'd just seen.

"*Steer*, please," Ollie said.

The spotlight had swung away from us—probably looking for the madman that had suicided against their boat—and I could see across the water more clearly now. The mainland was only two or three hundred meters away. I pushed the tiller to my left, aiming us away from the RCMP boat and the crash.

"What the hell just happened?" I asked.

"I have no idea," Dr. Gloria said.

Ollie said, "Lyda, just hold on for now, okay?" She pointed toward the outcropping. "There!" A pair of car headlights winked off, then flicked back on. I aimed for them. The police, thank God, had stopped following us.

As we approached the shore, Ollie feathered the throttle wires, slowing us without killing the engine—basically doing a much better job than I had. She directed me to a stretch of grass that sloped up to where we'd seen the headlights. I ran the boat straight into the grass, and Ollie cut the throttle.

A male voice above us said, "Well *that* was a hell of a run." Several other voices broke into uproarious laughter.

I helped Ollie out of the boat. She was still wet, and shivering uncontrollably. Dr. Gloria landed beside us. She flicked her wings, shaking the water from them.

Half a dozen men walked down to us, most of them still cracking up. Hilarious. I couldn't make out their faces in this light, and I couldn't tell whether they were armed. At least two of them held cans of beer. Another of them had a foot-long box hanging from a strap around his neck. As he stepped closer I realized it was a remote control unit, with a viewscreen and multiple game controller pads.

The lead man was round-faced, about sixty years old, with dark hair. Unlike the guys we'd met at the marina, he looked like my idea of an Indian elder. He regarded me without smiling and said, "You got our money?"

The money. A thrill of fear paralyzed me, and for a moment I couldn't think. Ollie looked at me sidelong. *What had I done with the money?* I'd gotten into the boat with the Mr. Squiggly lunchbox, but after all that had happened, I'd completely lost track of it. Was it even still in the boat? We'd been flying at top speed over the river, bouncing all over the place.

"Sure," I said, keeping my voice steady. "Just a sec."

I made sure Ollie could stand upright, then went to the bass boat. I didn't see the box. I climbed over the side, then crouched and looked under the front bench. It wasn't there. I patted the floor under that bench, as if to make sure the bag hadn't turned invisible.

Dr. Gloria said, "Don't panic."

Too late, I thought.

I stood up and duck-walked to the back of the boat. I could picture the green fucking lunchbox flying up into the air when the boat went airborne. It was all too plausible. And without the money, what would these men do to us? We'd sabotaged their boat, and they'd wrecked another one just to distract the police. Ollie was already too cold to run. Even if she could, where would we run *to?*

I knelt down in the back of the boat, and immediately I saw it: The Mr. Squiggly box was jammed in next to the orange gas tank.

"See?" the doctor said.

I climbed out and handed the lead man the bag. He smiled a wide, gap-toothed smile. "Welcome to the Nation."

THE PARABLE OF

the Child Thief

When the girl was six years old, three people came
from afar bearing gifts. The woman who was to be her
new foster mother knelt beside her and nervously presented a doll that was almost as big as the child. The
doll had long dark hair and beautiful, old-fashioned
clothes, and came with a complex historical backstory
that tied into a series of books and videos, live-action
events, and a restaurant chain. The new foster father
crouched on the other side of the girl and showed her
a soft-skinned ball that when spoken to or touched in
the right way could turn into a cube, a pyramid, a
polyhedron. He put it on the floor beside her and told
her (in a forced, cheery voice) that it also could change
colors, sing songs, and play counting games. It had
won several Best Educational Toy awards.

The old man who came with them had also brought
a gift, but he kept it in his pocket, and waited.

The girl sat on a patch of carpet in the classroom,
staring into the middle distance with half-closed eyes,
her head nodding as if she were listening to music.
The doll lay on the floor beside her. The ball rocked
back and forth, eager to play. The girl did not seem to
notice either toy. She had her own possessions. On
her lap lay a raggedy teddy bear with a jaunty pirate
patch over one eye. And in her left hand she held a
deck of playing cards fastened by a rubber band.

The girl's tiny size and skinny limbs were alarming. Developmental difficulties, the file said. But if she was not beautiful now, she promised beauty. Her features were delicate. Her skin was the color of polished oak. Her dark hair, a wild natural afro, burned with red highlights in the sunlight that slanted through the window.

The new foster father spoke to her, but she did not look up. Only her thumb moved, rubbing back and forth over the deck's rubber band as if strumming a guitar string.

The foster father looked up at the Village director and said, "Is this normal?"

"Yes, of course," the director said. Meaning normal for *the girl*. The child never spoke, and often did not interact with children or teachers. If not for the fMRIs that showed a frontal cortex blazing with light when questioned by psychologists, she might have been diagnosed with severe mental retardation. Even her physical capabilities were not well understood. Some days she barely moved. But when a caretaker was distracted, she could disappear in an instant. She'd been known to escape locked rooms. She had stolen, magpie-like, a hundred small and shiny things. Martha, the houseparent who had taken over after Mr. Paniccia decided not to return to the Village, had discovered several of her caches, hidden mounds of safety pins, coins, chrome salt shaker lids, smart pens, syringes.

The foster father could not hide his annoyance. "I mean, has she been *medicated?*"

The foster mother put on an icy smile. "I'm sure they haven't—"

"She receives medication daily," the director said defensively. "We've been very clear about that." The foster father looked up sharply at her tone. These people were not the usual foster parents. They were enormously rich, as well as famous, though the director had never heard of their names before she'd looked up them up online. Everyone in the room, except perhaps the girl, understood that this visit could make the difference not only in the girl's life, but in the lives of all the children who lived here.

Once, decades ago, the Village was a new concept: Not an "orphanage" but a cluster of fourteen homes in suburban Illinois that surrounded a learning center and a small playground. Over seventy-five children had lived here at one time, and many of them came from families or foster homes where they had been physically or sexually abused. A number of them, like the girl, had mental disabilities. Once, decades ago, the Village had been well funded.

The director said, "We'll of course provide you with everything you need for her care for the first month. The prescriptions are good for the next year."

"We'll be seeing our own doctors," the old man said. It was the first time he'd spoken since the visit began.

"Of course," the director said. She seemed disturbed by the old man. Perhaps it was the way his eyes never left the girl, as if he was hungry for her.

"Tell me about the teacher," the old man said. "The one who fell."

"Mr. Paniccia?" the director said. "That was an accident."

"The file says—"

"I don't think we should discuss that here in front of the girl."

The foster mother looked as if she was about to say something, but then quickly rose and clacked away from them on her high heels, clutching her handbag. She was thin and blond, a woman carved from money. The bag cost more than what the director made in month.

The foster father said, "Why don't you wait outside, Dad?"

This was the first of the three visits required before they could bring the girl home. The old man came each time, and spoke little. On the third visit, he helped secure the girl in her car seat (an infant's seat, because she was so tiny), then sat in the backseat beside her. The teddy bear was placed between them. She held on to the deck of cards.

When they were well on their way to the airport, the old man's son caught his eye in the rearview mirror and said, "Happy now?"

The old man didn't answer. But yes, he was very happy.

It was not until later, when the son's concentration was on the road and his daughter-in-law was either asleep or pretending to be behind her sunglasses, that the old man leaned close to the little girl and said quietly, "I have a present for you."

The girl gazed out the car window, refusing to look at him.

He reached into his pocket and brought out a small box. Inside was a gold chain looped around a bronze ring. "This belonged to your mother," he said. "One of them."

He lifted the chain by his fingertips and let the ring dangle before the girl. The first step in building trust, he'd decided, was not dolls or toys. She was too smart for that. He needed to give her something of great personal value. "You see how it has six sides? I can tell you a story about that."

The girl seemed not to hear him. She would not look at the ring.

His son said, "What are you doing now? Can't you wait until we get home?"

The old man apologized. And when he looked back at the girl he realized that the chain had slipped from between his fingers. The girl's gaze was fixed on the traffic outside. The old man scooted sideways, checking the seat, the floor of the car. Then he noticed that the girl's left hand was closed, and peeking from under her fist was a glint of a gold chain.

—G.I.E.D.

CHAPTER FOURTEEN

We lay in the dark, side by side, neither of us moving—yet I knew Ollie was awake. It must have been one of the first skills evolved by mammals, this hyperawareness to our cave-mates sprawled around us in the dark, an instinctive understanding of which movements were the random shufflings of sleep, and which were stirrings of restlessness, fear, or hunger. The rhythm of breath may have been our first language.

Dr. Gloria sat in an armchair near the window, legs crossed, notepad on her lap, writing. She did this all the time, filling page after phantom page. Who would read this invisible book?

Ollie and I were exhausted and should have been able to sleep—even here, in the heart of the Mohawk Nation, in the house that untaxed tobacco had built. The home of Roy Smoke. When he told us his name I thought he was fucking with us, but he assured us that Smokes had lived here for generations. He loaded us into a gleaming pickup that probably cost a fortune to keep in gasoline, then drove us three minutes down the road. Somewhere in the dark we crossed over from Quebec to New York. There was no port-of-entry on the Akwesasne Reserve, not even a border marker that I could see.

Roy's house was a sprawling two-story McMansion with ten bedrooms and kids' toys strewn across the carpet. "Oh those grandkids," he told us, pushing a plastic trike out of the way.

Everyone was asleep, but his wife Linnie woke up to greet Roy, and didn't blink when Roy said we'd be spending the night. She was a heavy-set, apple-cheeked woman with stiff black hair and an easy way about her. She made a fuss over Ollie, who was still wet and shaking with cold, and gave her a fleece hoodie and sweatpants to wear. (Whatever was in Ollie's backpack, it wasn't clothes, and I didn't dare ask her to open it in front of the smugglers.) The sweats were several sizes too big, but everything was too big for Ollie.

They sat us down in the kitchen and started hauling out chicken-fried steak, gravy, corn, mashed potatoes, and cornbread, plus a loaf of white Wonder bread and a bucket of real butter.

"They're beigetarians," Dr. Gloria said.

I wasn't about to complain. Comfort food was exactly what we needed. Or what *I* needed. Ollie barely ate, and spoke even less. At first I chalked it up to the cold, but even after her chills had died down she seemed to be somewhere else, her gaze fixed on the middle of the table.

It didn't seem to bother Roy or Linnie. Roy talked as I ate, explaining at length the justness of his tobacco business. I thought of Christian soup kitchens where the price of the meal was a sermon, and like other home-less people, I took the deal. Roy let me know that the tobacco trade was absolutely legal and, more than that, integral to their tribal independence. Canada, he said, had no right to place taxes on products that the tribe produced, on their own land. Tobacco had transformed the Akwesasne Reserve from a third-world nation to a first-world one. If Canada would stop illegally seizing their product, they wouldn't have to run it over the water in boats.

I didn't ask him what smuggling *people* across the border had to do with tribal self-determination; this person shut up and ate, pausing only to nod in agreement.

Afterward Linnie showed us to a guest bedroom, gave us towels, and pointed out the bathroom. Finally we were alone. But still Ollie looked grim.

"What's going on?" I asked her.

"We shouldn't be here," she said.

"In this bedroom?"

"In this house. These people are criminals, and they're being kind to us for *no reason whatsoever.* They've been paid. We should be driving the hell out of here, now."

I didn't need to remind her that we had no car, and our ride wouldn't be here until the morning. "If they were going to axe-murder us they would have done it by now," I said. Then: "No, you're right. Axe murderers always try to kill you *after* you've gone to bed, when you're having sex."

Ollie was not amused. She pulled off the pile of decorative pillows covering the queen-size bed and crawled in, still wearing the fleece suit. I stripped off to my underwear and got in beside her . . . where we lay, wide awake, listening to each other breathe.

"He knew about Rovil," I said. "How the hell does he know?"

"He could have tapped Bobby's phone before I made you stop using it. He could have followed you when you mailed the FedEx package. Were you followed?" She sounded angry.

"No, I wasn't—fuck, I don't know," I said. "How would I know?"

"And we don't know if Rovil's still coming."

"He'll come if he can," I said.

Ollie didn't answer.

"Are you okay?" I asked.

Dr. Gloria looked up from her notepad. "You have to consider what she's gone through."

What *she* went through? I thought we'd both had it pretty rough.

"Think, Lyda," the angel said. "What happened back there? Tonight."

Well, a shit-load happened back there. The fake drug exchange, the man in the black hat, Hootan getting shot. Then the run to the boat, and Aaqila . . .

Oh.

Ollie was facing away from me, her head tucked into her chest. I could picture Ollie, the rock raised above her head. The way she looked down at Aaqila's body. She'd killed someone for me. I put an arm over her stomach and pressed my forehead into her back. "I'm so sorry," I said.

Ollie didn't move. Then she said, "For what?"

"For Aaqila. The Afghan girl."

"She was shooting at you. I hit her in the head." She said this calmly.

"I know, I know. But I put you in a position where you had to do that."

"Don't worry about it."

I sat up so I could see her face. "Ollie, I never wanted you to kill for me."

Ollie blinked up at me. "She's not dead. At least not when I left her. She was still breathing; I checked."

"Oh. Thank God." Maybe, I thought, Fayza wouldn't hunt us down now.

"But I would have if I needed to," she said.

Not for the first time I wondered what Ollie had done before she'd been an analyst. She said she'd been in the army, but she refused to talk about where she'd been deployed, or what she had done. I'd never pressed her. It wasn't that kind of relationship.

"Keep telling yourself that," Dr. Gloria said under her breath.

"I never should have put you in that position," I said.

"You didn't put me in that position," Ollie said. "*I* put me in that position. It was my plan."

"Because I forced you to break out of Guelph Western. I made you go off your meds, then—"

Ollie sat up. "Are you that egotistical?"

That stopped me. Ollie got out of bed looking like a child wearing her mom's clothes. "You didn't force me to do anything," she said. She dropped her voice. "You didn't make me go off my meds, or trick me into helping you. I *chose* to help you. So did Bobby. You think you're so damn smart that you can manipulate everybody into doing what you want?"

"Of course not," I said.

"Of course she does," Dr. Gloria said.

"I'm the one who fucked up," Ollie said. She started pacing. "I should have known that the cowboy would still be tracking you."

"How could you possibly—"

"Not the cowboy exactly, though I should have realized back at the marina that he was watching us too carefully. But somebody. Someone went to the church after you did, then killed those people and took the printer." She was trying to keep her voice down, but she was talking fast, growing more agitated. "He *had* to have followed you. But who is he working for? We know now that he's not working for the Millies."

"Not after he shot them," I said.

"So he's working parallel to us, trying to shut the church down. His accent was American. Does that mean anything?"

"It sounded fake to me," I said. "A little too John Wayne. He could be anyone who watched a lot of movies."

"But American beneath that," she said. "Midwestern."

"Okay." I wasn't going to argue with a woman who used to monitor phone calls for a living. "So a drug agent then. DEA."

She fanned the idea away. "No, not a cop—he wouldn't be working alone. Maybe an ex-officer." She spun suddenly, looking at nothing. "What if he's working *for* the church? Plugging leaks? He follows you, sees you talk to Luke and Pastor Rudy, then kills them. He gets to Rovil somehow. Then he follows you to the beauty salon, then to Cornwall—I should have spotted him!"

"Easy, easy," I said. "Edo's a billionaire; he can afford to hire good people."

"You're sure it's Edo, then."

"Pretty fucking sure."

She said nothing for a moment, then: "If you find him, will you kill him?"

I laughed nervously. "Jesus, Ollie!"

She crouched down in front of me. "You can trust me. If there's something you're going to do, or something you've done . . ."

"I haven't—"

"You can know that whatever it is, I've done worse."

"You want me to confess my sins?" I tried to make it into a joke, but my heart was beating fast.

When I was a girl, before my mother's disease made it impossible, we went to church three times a week, and every night during revival week. It was at a revival service when I was twelve years old that I first felt God working on my heart. As I sat there in the pew during the altar call, I suddenly understood that if I didn't surrender to Him I would go to Hell when I died. It wasn't Hell itself that scared me—or not *just* Hell. It was the idea that my mother was going to Heaven without me.

I began to shake in the pew. I wanted to go up and be saved, but I was afraid to move. In my church we called that "being under conviction." And then my mother touched me on the shoulder, and it was like a boulder tipping off the edge of a cliff. I plummeted, into the arms of a loving God.

"What is it?" Ollie asked.

My eyes had filled with tears. When—how—did that happen?

"You can tell her," Dr. Gloria said.

"I've never told anyone," I said to both of them.

Ollie put a hand on the back of my arm.

"I remember a knife," I said.

. . .

I told her everything I could remember, which was hardly anything at all. I'd woken up on the floor of Edo's apartment suite, blinded by a white light. In my hands I felt the wooden handle of a knife—and then someone took it from my hands.

"But Gilbert confessed to killing her," Ollie said.

"Yes, he did."

"So it couldn't have been you."

"Unless he was lying."

"Why would he do that?" she asked. "Do you remember stabbing Mikala? Striking her at all?"

"No."

"Then you don't know," Ollie said. "What does your angel say?"

"My angel tells me what I want to hear," I said.

"I will ignore that," the doctor said. "Aren't you glad you told her?"

'Glad' was the wrong word. I felt like I'd stripped naked in the middle of the street. The fact that Ollie had not shut down, that she'd opened her arms to me—I just couldn't fathom that.

Ollie and I talked for another hour. I was aching to fall asleep, but she was growing more excited by the moment, churning through all this new information.

I took a breath and said to Ollie, "Do you have that bottle of Alisprazole?" The antianxiety meds she'd stolen before leaving the hospital.

"They're in my clothes," Ollie said warily. She'd draped her wet things on doorknobs and across the room's furniture. "But I'm not taking them."

She was going for maximum cognitive sharpness, even if that meant flirting with paranoia. Off meds, her Clarity-wired brain was in charge. On them, she was that slave to agnosia she'd been back in the NAT, unable to connect the dots. No doctor had been able to find a chemical balance between the two extremes. My job was to decide when the paranoia was becoming too dangerous and force her back on the Alisprazole.

"Not for you," I said. "I figure a couple for me."

"You told me you were staying clean."

"But we also need to sleep tonight. I'm keyed up, you're keyed up . . ."

"I'm not taking those pills, and neither are you."

After another minute of silence I turned toward her. "I suppose we could try more natural remedies."

"Natural remedies," Ollie said skeptically. I touched her chin. She said, "Like what?"

I slid my thumb across her jaw, then down her neck to the valley of her clavicle. Her skin was no longer cold; she felt hot, almost feverish.

I said, "I think we need a little dose of sexytocin."

She laughed. "What about the axe-murderers?"

"Fuck 'em." I ran my palm along her shoulder, pushing aside the neck of the fleece shirt until it dropped over her shoulder. Then I bent and kissed the side of her neck. In the hospital I'd fallen in love with the taste of her skin.

She said, "I feel like we're making out in my parents' bedroom."

"That's so hot," I said, and she laughed again.

I pushed the fleece from her other shoulder, then let my hand glide down, hovering a hair's breadth above her breast, not touching except for tiny incidental touches, moth wing touches that raised goose flesh across her skin. Her nipple hardened and brushed my palm. I circled there, the point of contact between us so tiny, so intermittent, like neurons firing to each other.

"Hmm," Dr. Gloria said. She jotted something on her notepad.

"You can get the hell out of here," I said.

"Don't mind me," she said.

"Out!"

She put away her notepad, rather sulkily I thought, then with two beats of her wings vanished through the ceiling.

Ollie touched my neck. "Hey. Where'd you go?"

"I'm right here," I said. I moved my hand down, firmer now, one facet of my ring tracing a path along her ribs, across the ridge of her hip, then under the waistband of the absurd fuzzy pants, then down, my ring finger dragging across her cleft. She arched her back, and her hands gripped the carpet. "Right . . . here," I said.

· · ·

Love at first sight is a myth.

I was twenty-five, two years into my PhD program and already tired of my fellow grad students, when I got roped into going to a party in an apartment on Door Street. The place was packed, doors and windows open to the humid night air, the typical low-rent shoutfest fueled by cheap beer, grocery store cheese, and Ke$ha pounding on the speakers. I was drinking my first and last beer of the party and plotting my exit when I noticed the tall black woman with the plaited hair.

She stood in front of a pair of windows, towering over a white boy, explaining how he was wrong—about the Greenland ice sheet, or fracking, or the Supreme Court, or Radiohead, or any one of the hot topics on her agenda in those days—simply *wrong*, and we'd better all get our heads out of the fucking sand *now*. She was over six feet tall in flats, slender and muscular as an Olympic volleyball player, and wore a purple maxi-dress with a slit that ran the length of her thigh.

My body reacted on its own. Dopamine, norepinephrine, and serotonin— the whole damn monoamine family—kicked in like a band of mustangs.

Love at first sight is a myth, but thundering sexual attraction at first sight is hard science. The limbic system knows what it wants and does everything possible to keep the prefrontal cortex, that yammering, censorious maiden aunt, from shutting down the party. My genes clanged their tin cups across the bars of their jail cells and shouted to fulfill their evolutionary mandate: Rep-li-cate! Rep-li-cate! Not all of them had gotten the news about my sexual orientation. Genes are notoriously indifferent to details.

So with their chemical commandments pounding in my bloodstream, I pushed through the crowd toward her and the white boy. He might have been my age or older, but his mall-issue cargo shorts and American Eagle T-shirt placed him fully in Boy Territory. I eased up between them until my right shoulder was just in front of the boy's left, setting the pick. He still hadn't noticed this; his attention, predictably enough, was on the black woman's braless tits and their friendly, attentive nipples. Perhaps I noticed them myself.

She reached for her wineglass, and I saw the small tattoo on the inside of her arm, a circle nested in a hexagon. I was no chemist but I'd taken enough hours to recognize what it stood for: six linked carbon atoms, each one attached to a hydrogen atom.

I stepped in front of the boy and said to the woman, "So, you're toxic?"

She glanced at her arm, then turned her attention to me. The boy said something like "Excuse me?" but I cut him off.

"Get the lady a drink," I said. Her wineglass was half-full, but being an optimist for my own chances I decided it was half-empty. Mikala seemed amused by my cheek, which was what I was going for. She looked me up and down, barely moving her eyes.

"So," I said. "Benzene."

"The mother of all hydrocarbons," she said. "It's crucial in everything from plastics to . . . opiates."

"And it's also really flammable," I said.

She smiled. "The best things are, honey."

Maybe she didn't say "honey." But that's how I remembered it.

When after three years of living together we decided to marry, we of course—Mikala being who she was, and me being who I was—set about defining, redefining, contextualizing, and negotiating everything about what our marriage would mean, and what the ceremony would communicate about that meaning, down to venue, flowers, wardrobe, and the most important props of all: the rings. What to do about the rings? We were not chattel. Traditional symbols held no weight for us, but the hex and circle was something we could get behind. The benzene ring, we decided, would represent stability and creativity, but also danger: the rings would remind us to be careful with each other.

When we told the Sprouts what we were looking for, Rovil nodded as if this made perfect sense, Edo laughed his Santa Claus laugh (a back-of-the-throat chortle he deployed at every opportunity—as greeting, as filler, as disarmament tactic in business negotiations), and Gil shook his head at us. "Nerds," he said. This from a man who spent $2,000 for a Joss Whedon T-shirt. Not a shirt with a *picture* of Joss Whedon, mind you, but a shirt that had been worn by him. (It was blue.) Gil was five-two, over two hundred pounds, and flew into rages when Stupid Humans fucked up his equipment. Not even Mikala would cross him when he was in a mood. So we were shocked when a few days later he presented us with two petri dishes, and in each rested a hand-forged brass ring. It was the most touching thing anyone had done for us.

Years later, at the trial, Gil would tell the jury that he was jealous of our relationship. He was in love with Mikala, but Mikala wouldn't leave me.

That's why, he said, when the dosage took hold in that suite at the top of the Lake Point Tower, he stabbed my wife to death.

· · ·

Dr. Gloria was not in the bedroom when I awoke the next morning. But Ollie was. She woke as soon as I slipped off the bed.

"Thank you," she said.

"Yeah, that was pretty good," I said.

"No," she said. "For trusting me."

I didn't know what to say to that. Part of me wanted to take it all back, untell the story of my crime. Go back to where we were before. "I smell breakfast," I said.

It was seven in the morning and the house was jumping: Linnie and two women who might have been her daughters packed lunch bags in the kitchen; older kids helped younger kids pull on shoes; teenagers appeared, ate cereal standing up, then left without saying good-bye. At least three TVs yammered away. The dining room table had been turned into a buffet, loaded with loaves of white bread, Pop-Tarts burning in the toaster, a Crock-Pot of steaming oatmeal, and jugs of juice and milk. Roy sat at the end of the table reading from a real newspaper, undisturbed by the noise and chaos.

A girl who was perhaps three years old ran toward us and happily slammed into Ollie. Ollie looked at me in alarm. The toddler glanced up, realized that these legs did not belong to the mother/cousin/grandmother she thought they did, and ran into the kitchen.

"I'll be outside," Ollie said. She shouldered her backpack, grabbed a Pop-Tart, and headed for the front door. We had finally been able to fall asleep last night—thank you, oxytocin and prolactin, you were great—but the anxiousness had returned. Her mind was back to writing worst-case scenarios, and she wanted to be out of there.

I took the seat beside Roy and made small talk about children, a topic I knew nothing about. The oatmeal was too salty for my taste, but I was happy for more hot food.

Linnie gave me a pair of plastic travel mugs filled with coffee, and I took them out to Ollie. It was there I noticed a shimmer of pure white hovering above the trees.

"Hark," she said. "Your ride approacheth."

A black sedan with tinted windows pulled into the driveway. I checked my pen: 8 a.m. on the dot. "That's my boy," I said.

Roy and Linnie came out to say good-bye. Linnie said, "Are you going to be okay? We can lend you clothes."

"You've already done too much," I said. I shook Roy's hand. "Sorry again about the boat—and the dummy."

He laughed. "My son Jimmy already uploaded the video," Roy said. "That was worth it."

"We aren't visible on that, are we?" Ollie asked sharply.

Roy frowned.

I said, "Of course not; that would be crazy."

The car pulled to a stop. A brown-skinned man stepped out, looking dapper in a blue dress shirt and charcoal wool pants. And then I noticed the bruises on his face, and that several fingers of his left hand were wrapped in bandages.

"Oh Jesus, Rovil!"

Despite his injuries, he still smiled at me and held out his arms. I was surprised; in the old days Rovil was uncomfortable with physical contact. We exchanged a quick hug. His haircut looked expensive. In person he was a little fuller through the torso than I expected, but not fat. Our Rovil had been working out. And he smelled like aftershave, like a man.

"Are you okay?" I asked. His left eye was bloodshot, the cheek puffy and yellow. It looked painful.

"I'm fine."

"I can't believe you came. This is Ollie."

"Pleased to meet you," he said to Ollie, and held out his unbandaged hand. She nodded without shaking and climbed into the backseat.

Rovil seemed to take this in stride. "No luggage?"

"Just Ollie's backpack," I said. "It was kind of a quick exit." I got in the front seat. As we started to roll away I lowered the window. "Watch out for the tax man, Roy."

The couple watched us go, standing side by side in the sunlight: American Indian Gothic.

It took only a few minutes to leave the Smokes' neighborhood and turn onto Highway 37. The car accelerated smoothly, and I settled back into leather seats that already seemed more comfortable than the mattress we'd slept on last night.

"Holy shit, Rovil, I do believe you could get laid in this car."

He laughed. "I may have tried once or twice."

Rovil, kidding about sex! A breakthrough. After another mile I said, "So, what happened?"

He glanced down at his damaged hand. "I . . . I don't want to alarm you."

"It's a little late for that," I said. "I know about the cowboy."

He looked surprised, then nodded. "He knew about you. He wanted the sample you sent. He wanted to know everything I knew about the making of Numinous. Which was very little, though he did not believe that at first."

"Oh Christ. What did he do to you?"

"Nothing I can't recover from," he said. "Ganesh was with me, and I was not afraid."

"But he let you live," Ollie said. "And he let you live, too, Lyda."

"Because he thought you were covering him with a fucking sniper rifle or something."

"Or maybe he had orders not to touch you," she said.

"Excuse me," Rovil said. "You have met him? What happened?"

"It's a long story," I said.

He glanced at the navigation screen. "We have seven hours."

Seven hours? That would exceed our Total Lifetime Talk Minutes by at least six hours. At Little Sprout I'd never broken through his force field of shyness; it was Mikala who knew him best. But I'd dragged him into this, and put his life in danger. He deserved to know what was going on.

I didn't tell him everything. I left out the fact that we'd broken into the church and made it sound like we'd just walked into the building and found the bodies. I also neglected to mention that Ollie may have killed a girl. But I laid out everything else, including our theories about Numinous, the Church of the Hologrammatic God, and those custom, highly expensive chemjets.

"I can't believe Edo would do this, not without talking to us," he said.

"You promised never to touch the stuff," I said. "And he knew I'd never go along with it."

He nodded. "So we have to find him."

"All right," I said. "Tomorrow afternoon, at the Peninsula Hotel in Manhattan, I'm going to march into Edo's room, hold a gun to his head, and make him confess to organizing the murder of a couple of dopeheads, as well as illegally manufacturing NME One-Ten."

"What?!"

"A metaphorical gun," I said. "But still."

Dr. Gloria, if she were in the car, would have scowled at me for being so blunt. But I couldn't help it; even after ten years, I still enjoyed shocking the Rat Boy.

THE PARABLE OF
the Man Who Sacrificed Rats

Once there was a shy young man who needed a job. He was twenty-one years old, and among his few possessions were a smile that a classmate once called disarming, a mountain of debt, and a freshly minted yet completely unmarketable bachelor's degree in neuropathology. A BS in any neuroscience without a master's or PhD was a three-legged dog of a degree: pitiable, kind of adorable, and capable of inspiring applause when it did anything for you at all. When the two women who ran the biotech startup chose him to become their unpaid intern, he told them he felt very lucky, and tried not to think of the monthly payments on his educational loan.

Every lab needs a rat wrangler; that is what the young man became. Though unsalaried, he took his job seriously. He ordered the rats online, unpacked them when they arrived, and set them in their plastic cages along the metal racks. He fed and watered them and monitored them for seizures, blindness, difficulty in walking, or any other signs of neurological damage. And every day at 2 p.m. he selected one rat and killed it.

Lab people use the term "sacrifice," which appealed to the Wrangler. Was not the rat giving his life in the name of science, humanity, and an eventual patent? One of these animals would make them all rich.

He was as meticulous in administering death as he was at maintaining life. He gently placed the rat's head inside the clear plastic funnel and waited patiently for the CO2 to do its work. Once the rat had stopped breathing, he placed its body into the stereotaxic frame, a metal contraption that would have looked at home in any woodshop. The rat's chin and nose went into the little stirrup, and two rods extended to press against the bones just in front of the rat's ear, holding its skull in place. The Rat Brain Atlas lay open on the table, with its many pages of diagrams, each important location annotated with its three-axis coordinates. Soon he barely consulted the atlas, having come to know the tiny lobes and crevasses of the rat's brain as if they were the streets of his home neighborhood. Rovil was on patrol, alert for aneurysms, stroke effects, and tumors. He filed careful reports assessing the damage.

He came to know the humans at the company with more difficulty, but he attacked the problem scientifically. As was his habit since he was a boy, the Wrangler assigned the humans scores in three categories:

	Physical attractiveness	Kindness	Intelligence
Gil	1	2	5
Mikala	8	5	9
Lyda	7	3	7

The system, he realized now, was a three-coordinate matrix much like the stereotaxic coordinates in the Rat Brain Atlas. Rat brains, however, were easier to understand than human ones. Why did Lyda, the red-headed woman who seemed too fond of low-cut tops, always bring up sex? She talked constantly about who was getting fucked, whether Mikala was going to fuck her, and whether Rovil—for that was the Wrangler's name—would ever get fucked if he didn't stop dressing that way. *Fuck fuck fuck fuck fuck.* No one else seemed to take offense, and Gil especially seemed to find Lyda hilarious. He was a nearly spherical man who, the Wrangler guessed, did not get fucked very often. Perhaps that was why he so often lost his temper: He behaved as if every piece of equipment in the lab belonged to him personally, and when someone did not clean an instrument to his standards or failed to return it to its Gil-designated space, he would shout like a madman. In the first two months his target was most often the Wrangler, but the young man took some comfort when Gil occasionally yelled at Lyda or Mikala.

It was Mikala who showed him the most kindness. Yes, she was intellectually intimidating, and could ask him questions that could freeze his tongue, but she often defended him when Lyda embarrassed him or Gil yelled at him. And it was Mikala who came to him after he'd been on the job for six months to tell him that he'd been doing a great job, and they'd like to keep him on. The Little Sprout partners hired him as an actual employee with a salary of $24,000 a year, which in the year 2015 allowed him enough money for a grubby apartment on the south side of Chicago, as long as he shared it with two other people.

The fourth partner was Edo Anderssen Vik (PA 5, K 5, I 4). Vik dropped in every couple weeks to check on his investment, and when he arrived he seemed to take up all the space in the building. He liked to put an arm over the Wrangler's shoulders and shake him like a dog. Rovil would laugh good-naturedly and then escape to the rat room. He suspected that Edo did not enjoy people as much as he appeared, but that would not change his score: The matrix only assessed *perceived* attributes. Kindness was as much an act of presentation as physical beauty. Even intelligence could be faked, for a time.

The Wrangler's goal was to raise his own scores as perceived by his co-workers. He could do little about his attractiveness (though with more money he might someday be able to correct some of his flaws, such as his spotty skin and his crooked right canine tooth), but at every opportunity he tried to demonstrate that he was a caring person who could also contribute ideas. He took on more responsibilities, especially the onerous ones, such as cleaning the bioreactor, a large stainless steel vat on wheels that Gil called "the Dalek."

The Dalek grew tumors. Rat tumors, to be precise, steaming batches of pheochromocytoma, whose cells Mikala then injected with genetically modified plasmids, which in turn prompted the cells to generate an array of neurotrophins, which, when injected into the rats, spurred their brains to grow new neurons . . . and occasionally, when things went wrong, new tumors.

"The circle of death," Mikala told him.

It was Mikala that the Wrangler most wanted to impress; she was clearly the brightest person in the company. She had designed the genetically engineered plasmids herself, using open-source molecular CAD software. True, Gil had rewritten the software almost from scratch, which caused Rovil to raise the man's intelligence score by a point. And Lyda was the schizophrenia expert who had come up with the idea that led to the creation of Little Sprout. But it was Mikala who would make the idea work, down among the amino acids.

The Wrangler made it his mission to become a better chemist, and he studied the New Molecular Entities that Mikala had created, even going so far as to copy Gil's CAD program so he could run it at home. More than anything the young man wanted to contribute his ideas to Little Sprout, and his opportunity came at a time when he was feeling the most stupid and the most helpless.

His rats were dying. Something in NME 109, the latest batch, was causing them to drastically lose weight. After a few days the animals stopped drinking water, stopped eating, and retreated to the corners of their cages, where eventually they died. A dozen brain examinations revealed nothing: no tumors, no strokes. Then, even though he had not been told to do so, he began working overtime to do full dissections. He examined each organ, comparing it to the healthy rats still in his population. He found nothing.

He began reading more and more online, and took home books from Mikala's shelf. He studied all the neurotrophins that Mikala's modified cells produced—BDNF, VGF, NGF, CREB—an alphabet of proteins that kept neurons growing and dividing and forming new connections. Schizophrenics didn't develop all the connections that normal children did, and even as adults their blood contained smaller amounts of neurotrophins. Lyda's original idea, and Little Sprout's goal, was to find a way to boost levels of neurotrophins and make the brain plastic again.

The Wrangler found a clue in one of Lyda's own research articles. A footnote about BDNF—Brain-Derived Neurotrophic Factor—gave him an idea. He went back to the dissections, this time diving deep into the rat brains. It took him two weeks to be sure enough of the idea to share it.

Mikala and Lyda were in the lab, working at separate computers. Some days they barely spoke to each other, yet they were rarely apart. The Wrangler stood in the middle of the room, equidistant from them. He held his lab reports in one hand, and his laptop in the other.

"The rats are depressed," he said.

"You don't say," Mikala said without looking up.

"I went back and extracted each hippocampus," he said. "They're twenty to thirty percent smaller than they ought to be."

He carried the reports to Mikala's workstation, and she leaned forward to study them. Her neck was very beautiful, a strong contributing factor to her high physical score. Her hair smelled of citrus. He had never accounted for scent on his score card, but he wondered if he should start tracking that as well; research suggested that scent played a strong role in mate choice.

"Damn it, you're right," Mikala said. "Lyda, take a look at this. The poor little guys are clinically depressed." Both women laughed, and he laughed with them, though he didn't quite understand why it was funny. He was flush with the heat of their regard.

"This is great news," Lyda said. She walked up behind Mikala. "We can market it as pest control. All you need is a bunch of really tiny nooses."

Mikala laughed again. "The rats just kill themselves!"

"The tough part is teaching them to write the suicide notes," Lyda said.

The Wrangler watched their faces—especially Mikala's. He had never seen her laugh this hard. He'd hardly seen her laugh at all, lately.

When they settled down, he said, "I do have a suggestion for the next batch, however."

"You do, huh?" Lyda said. Still grinning.

He said, "Is it possible—and I'm not sure it is—to increase the transcription rate of BDNF? I was looking at the CAD program—" He saw the two women exchange a look of surprise and said, "I'm sorry, was that not appropriate?"

"No, no," Lyda said, still amused.

"We're just impressed," Mikala said. "Continue."

He opened his laptop and showed them the change in the tumor cells that he thought might work. The women looked thoughtful, and finally Mikala said, "It's worth a shot."

They were taking him seriously! He could practically see them updating his scorecard.

In the end Mikala could not implement the exact change he suggested, but the idea led her in another direction. A month after he had brought her his diagnosis, she handed him the first batch of NME 110.

"I think the rats will be happier with this," she said. "Thanks for your help on this, Rovil."

At last he was being recognized. The Wrangler was dead. What would he become next?

—*G.I.E.D.*

CHAPTER FIFTEEN

"Holy shit," I said to Rovil. Ollie and I stood side by side in his foyer, surveying his apartment. "This is like a fucking Sims house."

He smiled hesitantly, not getting the reference.

"The Sims," I said. "Computer game when I was a kid." Supposedly the point was to guide your virtual self into getting a job and falling in love and starting a family, but I spent all my time using cheat codes to get virtual dollars which I then used to build the *coolest* house and fill it with the *coolest* gadgets and furniture.

Rovil was playing it in real life. The apartment was overcrowded with trendy objects: white leather couches, a La Cornue gas range, white walls that became video screens and video screens that acted as walls, a sleek steel dining room table that appeared to hover over the floor, a glass-encased samurai sword . . . Each item was tremendously expensive, and each looked like it belonged in a different house.

Just like the twelve-year-old me, Rovil had no taste.

"How much is Landon-Rousse paying you?" I asked.

"It's only two bedrooms," Rovil said.

"It's two bedrooms on the Lower East Side with *that* fucking view," I said. The floor-to-ceiling windows were the classiest things about the apartment. We were on the twentieth floor, looking across the sparkling night city toward the Williamsburg Bridge, which glowed and pulsed with the lights of traffic. If it were me, I would have emptied the apartment except for a single couch and then set it in front of the window.

"I'll be back in a bit," Dr. Gloria said. "I need to see the city." She slid through the window and flapped into the night.

Rovil said, "LR does compensate me a little better than Little Sprout did."

"What do you do for them?" Ollie said. She was scanning the room as if it were a vault to unlock. She'd barely spoken during the ride south, and I was growing nervous about her mental state.

"I'm a product owner," Rovil said.

"Which means . . . ?" she asked.

"I'm responsible for overseeing everything to do with a product during its entire life cycle, from R&D to testing to marketing."

"What product is that?"

"Ollie, leave him alone," I said.

Rovil smiled, embarrassed. "It's not out yet. I would have to have you sign a nondisclosure agreement."

Ollie bristled. "After all we've shared, you're going to ask us to sign an *NDA?*"

"I'm sorry," Rovil said, truly apologetic. "I didn't mean—"

I stepped between them. "It doesn't matter. Let's get settled. I need a shower, and then Rovil's going to take us out for dinner, right, Rovil?"

I hadn't mentioned this to him, but he grinned. "Yes, of course."

"Great," I said. "Now show us where we're bunking."

Ollie and I carried our shopping bags into the second bedroom, which Rovil didn't seem to use. There were cardboard boxes stacked in the corner, a small desk, and a futon. He found us towels and bed linens, and then showed us the guest bathroom.

I took the first turn in the shower. When I got back, Ollie was crouched over one of the boxes.

"What are you doing?" I said, whispering and laughing at the same time.

She showed me the open box, which was lined with several white plastic bottles. "Rovil brings his work home with him," she said.

"Are those drugs?" I kept my voice low. "What kind?"

"The bottles aren't marked," she said. "But the boxes are all Landon-Rousse."

"Well put 'em back. Most of what they make are cancer drugs. The side effects are killer."

"What's he doing with them?" she asked.

"I dunno. Factory seconds?" I opened the shopping bag full of clothes that Rovil had bought for us. I'd made him stop at a mall on the way home. "I can't see Rovil as a drug dealer. Though, hey, he *is* loaded." I lifted out a pair of new black jeans and a gray sweater.

"You shouldn't have told him all that stuff," Ollie said. She closed up the box. "He can testify against us now."

"Nobody's testifying against anybody. He's in the same boat as us, now." I pulled the sweater down over my head. "Besides, Rovil's god wouldn't let him harm us."

She leaned against the desk, her arms wrapped about herself as if she were cold, and stared at the Persian rug (a beautiful piece, with the price tag still attached by a string to one corner). Her eyes flicked across its surface as if reading fast-moving messages. "Now that we're in the US, we're vulnerable. He lured us—"

"*I* called *him*," I said. "I dragged him into this."

"But still—"

"You're doing it again, Ollie. This is exactly how you felt at the Smokes' house. You didn't trust them; you didn't know why they'd help us. But that worked out, didn't it?"

"This is different."

"Honey, it's time."

She looked up, squinting. "No. Not yet."

"You did your job; you got us across the border. You need to start getting these meds into your system."

"We still haven't gotten to Edo," she said. "Until that happens, you do *not* want me off my game."

"I'm just saying, you need to start loading up. There's no jumpstart for going the other way."

"What about you? Are you going to take *your* meds?"

"I don't take any meds," I said. My heart rate had revved like the throttle on that fucking ro-boat.

"The antiepileptics you were taking in the NAT," she said. "The ones to keep your hallucinations in check."

"Those don't work. I lied to Counselor Todd about 'em."

"You never took them—you palmed them and threw them in the toilet. So how do you know they don't work?"

Fuck. I didn't know that Ollie had sussed that out.

"This isn't about me," I said, doing my best impersonation of a calm person. "You're deflecting."

"*I'm* deflecting?" Ollie said. "You are bullshitting me, right now, to my face."

"Ollie, please . . ."

"It's not your job to *manage* me," Ollie said.

I sat down on the futon and tried to steady my breathing. Right about now Dr. G would have made some comment about the likelihood of two brain-damaged patients holding it together during the world's craziest road trip. We both needed professional supervision.

"Okay," I said. "We just both need to keep our shit together for a little while longer."

. . .

I hadn't been in New York for over a decade, so I asked Rovil to pick a place we could walk to. He chose an Egyptian restaurant that he said had the highest aggregate score across the major social networks of any establishment that was (a) in SoHo, and (b) did not require reservations. "Have you ever been there?" I asked him.

"Oh yes."

"Did *you* like it?"

"I'm not a good enough judge of food to disagree with the scores."

Dr. Gloria was waiting for us at a street corner, looking happy after a couple hours of sightseeing. "Have you noticed how *clean* the city is?" she asked me.

It was true. The sidewalks were swept, and I didn't spot a single homeless person on the three-block walk to the restaurant. Was it just Rovil's neighborhood, or the entire city? Times Square had already been Disneyfied by the time I first visited as a teenager, back in the 2000s. Perhaps they'd been pushing the circle of cleanliness wider and wider, an event horizon of money that made ordinary reality disappear. The economic collapse that had knocked my father out of the workforce for half a decade was long forgotten. The new boom had made Manhattan into an island of millionaires.

My mood improved as soon as we walked into the restaurant. The dining room was crowded and noisy. I got the hostess to seat us at a sheltered spot in the corner where we could talk more easily. We sat at a low table on padded stools, and soon I was scooping piles of unidentified vegetables and beans onto the wide, floppy Egyptian bread. I said to Rovil, "Do you want me to rate it dish by dish, or only when we're done?"

"When we're done is fine," he said.

. . .

A while later I asked him, "How'd you do it, Rovil? The car, the job, the apartment . . ."

"I try to work hard."

"Do your bosses know about your condition?"

"I told them it was a bicycle accident."

I laughed. "Not the bruises. I meant your other condition."

"Oh! Yes, of course." He looked embarrassed. "But not exactly. They think I am cured."

"But you're not, are you?" Ollie asked.

"Oh no," he said, not taking offense.

"Because I don't see your eyes jumping around," she said.

"Pardon?"

"When Lyda talks to her angel, she can't help but look at it," Ollie said. Rovil glanced at me, surprised.

Dr. Gloria said, "I hadn't noticed that."

"See?" Ollie said to me. "You just did it." To Rovil she said, "But you, you're steady, all the time. You're not distracted by it?"

"Ah," Rovil said. He wiped his mouth and sat back. "My god and I have . . . I guess you would call it an agreement. It was important to me that no one suspect that I was different. People would not understand. So, my god stays out of sight unless I desire him to appear."

"I wish mine would do that," I said.

"Ahem," Dr. Gloria said.

Rovil smiled. "I *feel* Ganesh with me all the time. But only rarely does he speak in words."

"Again, jealous."

Ollie said to Rovil, "It doesn't bother you that he came to you only after you overdosed on a drug?"

"It's a fair question," Rovil said. "I of course understand your skepticism. It's logical to think that I'm experiencing a hallucination. But the overdose *awakened* me; it didn't put me to sleep. I believe that this sensitivity to the godhead, this facility, exists in all humans, but we cannot access it on demand. The higher power is waiting there for us to reach out to it. The drug simply tore down all those defenses, all the walls that kept God out."

"But your god has an elephant head," Ollie said. "Hers is an angel. Gilbert sees some kind of organic, plant-like structure, and Edo—"

"I need to stop being impressed every time you know something about my life that I haven't told you," I said to Ollie.

"The trial was covered in the news," she said. "The transcripts are all online. I read them the day you came to the hospital." She shrugged. "Don't take it personally. I did a backgrounder on everyone back then." *Then* meaning in the hospital, when she was off the meds, paranoid and determined enough to run a search despite being allowed no access to pens or the internet. She said, "From what I read, all of you were exposed to the drug, but you all had different experiences."

"It's true," Rovil said. "God appears differently for each believer. He—or She, this higher power—takes whatever form that the believer can understand. It's always been this way, which I admit has caused some problems. Hindus, Christians, Muslims, Buddhists—they perceive Him differently, but it's all the same God."

"Amen," the doctor said.

"The Divine Asshole hypothesis," I said. "God's fucking with us, putting on masks, changing His name, hiding dinosaur bones in rocks—just to test our faith."

Rovil laughed. "You are as profane as always. Our misunderstanding of God is not His fault. Our job is to seek Him out."

"He's sure not making it easy," I said. "At this point there must be *some* evidence for the existence of God. But where's the proof?"

"This isn't about proof," he said. "It's about faith. Science and religion do not have anything to say—"

"Spare me the NOMA bullshit. God *is* a testable hypothesis."

He smiled. "You're quoting Victor Stenger."

Ollie frowned, not following us.

"A physicist," I said. "One of the old New Atheists, like Dawkins and Hitchens."

"They're in Hell now," Dr. Gloria said.

"And NOMA?" Ollie asked.

"Nonoverlapping magisteria," I said. "Stephen Jay Gould's phrase, which was just him trying to pussy out of the argument and declare a truce. But he was wrong. If God created the universe, then He ought to at least be *detectable*. Even if He's some deist god who set the clockwork in motion and then left the scene, never to interfere again, we ought to be able to see a few of His fingerprints on the Big Bang. But no, not even there. And don't get me started on the anthropic principle or Intelligent Design."

"I will not defend ID," Rovil said.

"How about prayer, then?"

"You want me to defend prayer?" he asked.

"You believe in it, don't you?"

"Of course. I commune with God every day, even if not in words. Don't you?"

"I'm talking intercessory prayer. People all over the world pray for God to heal their loved ones. They've been doing that for thousands of years—millions and millions of prayers. Surely *one* of them had to be answered in a verifiable way. Just give me one double-blind, placebo-controlled trial where those prayers healed a sick person, and we're done here."

"Please don't bring up amputees again," Dr. Gloria said.

"Oh, and amputees!" I said. "Why does God hate them? He's hell on curing cancer, but if you happen to be a vet with your leg blown off, you're shit out of luck, no matter how hard you pray. How do people still believe in this shit?"

Rovil said, "You can't just dismiss—"

"Let me finish. The only thing that gives me hope is that the fundamentalists are on the ropes here. When I was a kid, they were this scary political force. Remember the Tea Party? Right-wing, Christian, and white. But then gays started marrying, minorities started outvoting them, the climate kept throwing hurricanes and floods at us. Their agenda fell apart, mostly because no young person could buy into their narrow-mindedness."

"There's still a right wing," Rovil said.

"But now they're way out on the fringe, and they've turned feral. They eat their young. Yeah, they're still vicious, but now they're a little ridiculous, like coyotes poaching the occasional poodle."

"You can be religious without being narrow-minded," Ollie said.

"The open-mindedness is almost worse," I said. "All this vague, wishy-washy spiritualism. People going to church just to *feel* better. You ask them what god they worship and they don't even know. They're morons."

Rovil glanced at Ollie, then frowned. I followed his gaze. Ollie was staring at her hands, her lips tight.

"Oh, Lyda," Dr. G said. "Have you ever asked Ollie if she believes in God?"

Fuck.

"I didn't mean *you* were a moron," I said.

She pushed back from the table, started to turn away, then said, "You don't have to be so . . . so . . ." She raised a hand, then walked away, toward the restrooms.

I thought about following her, then decided to give her some space. "Speaking of morons," I said.

Rovil nodded, not objecting.

I said, "I keep forgetting that people take this God stuff personally."

"This is why people don't like atheists," he said. He raised his bandaged hand to signal for the check. "The rudeness."

"It's the stress of being outnumbered even though we're right."

"That's what I don't understand," Rovil said. "You're not an atheist, though you pretend to be one. You *know* the truth as well as I do."

"Sorry, no."

"You're a smart *gal*," he said, failing to keep the smile from his face. "You've been trained as a scientist. Why do you ignore the evidence of your own experience?"

The Rat Boy, busting on me. I liked it.

"Because personal experience is the crappiest evidence of all, kid. If there's one thing I've learned, the brain is one lying son of a bitch."

When Ollie returned I tried to apologize, but she brushed it aside. Her face was composed. "Let's talk about how we're going to reach Edo," she said.

CHAPTER SIXTEEN

The Peninsula Hotel spoke to me, and what it said was, Welcome to a 1920s Broadway musical. The bellhops wore white pillbox caps and crisp white uniforms with double-breasted brass buttons. The doormen were dressed as generals of obscure European countries. The lobby, visible through the glass doors, resembled an itinerant worker's dream of Heaven. I hadn't even stepped inside, and I already knew that I would never be able to impersonate a plausible customer of the place.

"*This* is where Edo likes to stay?" I asked. The Edo I'd known disliked pretense, drank cheap American beer, and ate from street stalls. This didn't seem like his kind of place at all. Then again, the Edo I'd known didn't exist anymore.

We were in Rovil's car, across the street from the hotel. Vehicle access in this part of Manhattan was restricted, but Rovil had purchased the necessary permit. Ollie had sent me to the backseat and ordered me to slouch, staying out of sight of the windows—even though they were tinted almost black. As if that wasn't enough, she'd also insisted I wear the fedora we'd bought on the way down from Canada. Why? "Cameras," she said. The hat did not make me feel like a spy. It made me feel like a ridiculous person pretending to be a spy.

Ollie wore a knit cap and dark sunglasses, and she'd done something weird to her face. Before we'd left Rovil's apartment she'd applied a strip of clear tape to each cheek, giving her an instant facelift. "Fucks with the facial recognition software," she said.

She was keyed up, intently watching the hotel entrance and the surrounding sidewalks. It was a beautiful day, cold but clear and sunny. Dr. Gloria was somewhere above us, flying with the city's red-tailed hawks or communing with urban deities—whatever it was that angels did on vacation. We shouldn't have long to wait. Edo and Eduard's jet had landed an hour ago, and we'd rolled up to the hotel ten minutes later. There was no way they could have beaten us here.

Rovil said, "I should be at work."

"Come on, we're on a stakeout," I said. "How often do you get to do a stakeout?"

Ollie said, "Here we go." A team of doormen and bellhops began to assemble outside the hotel. They seemed to be under the command of a man in a dark suit who wore a proud, jet-black pompadour. A few seconds later, a pair of sleek black BMWs pulled up to the curb.

"Those are the hotel cars," Ollie said. "Keep your head down."

I ignored her and tried to get a glimpse of Edo. Four or five people exited the cars—none leaving by the doors facing the street—and were immediately surrounded by hotel staff, then ushered inside. It was over in seconds. I'd seen only the backs of the passengers, but several of them were tall and blond and male. At least four Edo candidates.

I said, "Tell me one of those guys was Edo."

"I told you to keep your head down," Ollie said. "Edo was the one on the right. Eduard Jr. was to his left. The other three were assistants. Are you ready to go in?"

"What about cameras?" I asked.

"Just keep your hat on, and walk fast."

"There's no way I can pass for a customer," I said. "This dress is about two thousand dollars too cheap. And this haircut—"

"Your husband is the customer," Ollie said. "You're just the suburban housewife."

"That's sexist," I said. "And how is it that my husband is so much younger than I am?"

"You put him through grad school," Ollie said.

"Thank you for that," Rovil said.

"You're welcome," I said. "But if you trade me for a trophy wife now that you're finally successful I'll cut off your balls. And I'm keeping the house."

The plan was for Rovil and I to rent a room on the highest floor we could manage. Edo and company would be staying in the Peninsula Suite at the top of the building. Our room keys wouldn't convince the elevator to take us to that floor, but Ollie said staff badges could override that. Where, exactly, Ollie was going to get a staff badge she refused to say. She promised to meet us in our room, and then we'd zip up to chat with Edo.

"Let's give them a few more minutes to check in," Ollie said. "Then we can—oh shit."

The man in the black pompadour was walking across the street toward us. Ollie twisted around to look past me out the rear window and said, "Rovil. Drive. Now."

I looked out the back. A tall, blond man, one of Edo's staff that I'd seen going into the building with him, strode toward us. Rovil pressed the start button, put the car in gear—and then said, "Ollie?"

The blond man had reached Rovil's window. He twirled a finger, the universal symbol for Roll Down Your Windows—universal despite the fact that no one had manually rolled down a window in twenty years.

"Damn it," Ollie said quietly. Then to Rovil, "Might as well."

Rovil pressed a button, and the glass slid down.

"Good afternoon, Mr. Gupta," the man said. He leaned in so he could make eye contact with me in the backseat. No: so his eye contacts could make eye contact. His eyes gleamed with the false wet of data overlays. Was Edo watching this video feed?

"Ms. Rose," the man said. "Mr. Vik would like to talk to you."

Ollie stared at the man. She seemed to vibrate with barely suppressed anger. Whether she was mad at the blond man, herself, or me I couldn't tell. She'd told me to keep my head down, but did I listen?

"Your friends can wait here with the car," the man said. "We wouldn't want it to get towed."

I started to object, but Ollie said in a clipped voice, "We'll be fine."

Yes, but would I?

·   ·   ·

The lobby was grander and more beautiful than the online photos suggested. I'd noticed this effect before, the first time I'd visited Mikala's family and stepped into rooms I'd only seen as background in her family photos: There was a resolution limit in capturing really expensive objects. Money radiated in a spectrum that was impossible to record.

The clerk with the black pompadour didn't lead us to the elevators, as I expected, but toward another set of doors off the lobby. The blond man gestured for us to enter.

I hesitated, conscious of the smart pen in my purse. Ollie had better be listening in.

It was a conference room, with a glossy cherrywood table in the shape of a surfboard. The room was empty except for Dr. Gloria, who sat at the head of the table, writing on her notepad. It was pathetic how relieved I was to see her.

"Nice of you to show up," I said in my tough voice. I was, after all, wearing a fedora.

She looked up, then removed her glasses. "I thought you might need someone to hold you down. Do you think you can get through this?"

"Of course," I said. "All Edo has to do is confess everything."

The blond man closed the door and asked, "Are you carrying?"

"You mean like a weapon?"

He looked me up and down with those gleaming eyes. He blinked entirely too much. "Raise your arms, please? Thank you." He moved his right palm along my arm, hovering a few inches above it. Then he floated down over my ribs and hip, and quickly repeated the moves over the other side of my body. I had no idea where the scanner was. A ring? His watch? I'd already decided that if he went for the cavity search I was going break his fingers.

He removed a small black bag from an inside pocket of his jacket and nodded toward the purse, which I'd put on the table. "May I?" Without waiting for a response, he slipped my purse into the bag. He cinched it closed and left it sitting on the table. I had a feeling that if Ollie had been listening, she wasn't anymore.

The bodyguard stepped back to the door, blinking again. A few seconds later the door opened.

It was not Edo, but a younger version of him. Just as tall, pale, and fair-headed as his father, but a hundred pounds lighter and more finely boned, a greyhound to Edo's bulldog.

"Little Edo," I said. "All grown up."

He smiled tightly. "I prefer—"

"Oh, I know. But *Eduard* seems so stiff. Doesn't seem to fit the wild kid who got kicked out of two prep schools."

"You won't get far by trying to insult him," Dr. Gloria said.

I thought, *We'll see.* Eduard was trying to power-play me. That nonsense with the bodyguard? The body scan? Well, that shit went both ways.

"Where's your dad?" I asked.

"He's in his room. He won't be coming down."

"Call him and tell him to get his fat ass down here."

"Please," Eduard said. "Sit down." He was holding himself very still.

"You're making him angry," Dr. Gloria said.

"Good," I said to her. Then to Eduard: "He has to answer to me, in person."

"I'm not sure why you've roped Rovil Gupta into our personal business. We've received a dozen calls and messages from him in the past two weeks. There is not going to be a . . . Little Sprout reunion, or whatever you think this is. My father is not a well man. There are very few people he is allowed to speak to."

"Allowed? You're *controlling* him?"

"Barely," Eduard said. He sounded tired. "If you want to send him a message or paint him a picture—you people seem to like that kind of thing—I'll consider delivering it, as long as it won't affect his mental health. If you have something to say now, you have two minutes, and then this conversation is over."

"Fuck you."

"All right, let me do this for you: Sasha is doing very well. She's healthy, she's happy, and she's making excellent progress. She's getting the best care—"

"Who the hell is Sasha?"

He blinked at me. "Your daughter."

Dr. Gloria reached out to steady me. For a moment I couldn't speak. "How—what do you . . . ?"

"All these calls," Eduard said. "I always assumed that you'd find out about the adoption eventually."

"Edo *adopted* her?"

"No," Eduard said. "I did."

I must have made a motion; the bodyguard shifted his weight but did not move from the door.

Dr. Gloria said, "Sit down. Breathe. You won't do any good if you faint."

I sat in one of the chairs and rubbed my hand over the leather armrest. I pictured the girl I'd seen on Ollie's screens at the Marriott, a pretty black girl with red highlights in her hair.

"My wife and I adopted Sasha four years ago. As I said, she's doing well despite her disabilities."

"Disabilities?" I was amazed that I was not screaming at him.

"She's mute," he said. "And in the past she's experienced hallucinations, though her doctors think that's under control now. She's intelligent, though, and she has other gifts."

He reached into his jacket pocket and withdrew a piece of smartpaper. He ran his thumb over it a few times, then set it on the table and pushed it toward me.

I looked at it without picking it up. It was a charcoal drawing, or rather, a picture of a charcoal drawing. On it, a grizzly bear stood on its hind legs, its mouth open in a roar. It was beautifully done, full of mass and movement, and very realistic, except for the fact that the bear was thrusting a curved sword into the air, and wore a black eye patch.

"Like the rest of you, she's artistically gifted," Eduard said.

I stared at the picture. *Like the rest of you.* What he was *not* saying filled the room like a shout.

"Call your father," I said to Eduard. "Right fucking now."

Eduard regarded me with an expression like pity. "She's better off with us. Until she's of age, you won't be permitted contact with her. You're obviously . . ."

"What?"

"*Unfit,*" Eduard said. "Multiple suicide attempts. Multiple drug charges, two DUIs, too many hospitalizations to count. My staff tell me that you're not even here, because you're in Toronto under house arrest, serving time for a car accident that injured several people." He stood up. "I will not allow you to harm my family. If I ever see you again—if I *sense* you within a mile of me, my father, or Sasha—I'll have the police haul you back to Canada before you know what hit you."

He walked toward the door. The bodyguard followed, but kept his body between me and his boss.

Eduard paused at the door, then looked back at me. "Get help, Lyda. I mean that sincerely."

CHAPTER SEVENTEEN

"Think about it," I told the girl. "*The end of religion.*" I say "girl" but she was in her mid-twenties, a sleek brunette in black tights and Marc Caisan shoes. Her pupils were the size of dimes. She worked with Rovil at Landon-Rousse, or perhaps worked *for* him—I was not in a state to catch details. Half the people in the bar seemed to be employees of Big Pharm. Pharm Boys and Pharm Girls.

"If you had your own god," I said. "If She was right there with you, what would you need church for?" My voice had gone gravelly from shouting above the music. "You wouldn't need to *seek* God. You wouldn't need to learn about Her. You sure as hell wouldn't need to learn the *rules* of your religion—She's right there! Ask Her!"

The girl nodded as I talked, her fingers automatically unfolding a white piece of paper.

Dr. Gloria said, "You're making a fool of yourself." She was perched on the back of the loveseat just behind me.

"Church isn't for people who already *have* God," I said. "It's where they go when they're looking for God's last known address."

"Here," the girl said, and handed me the paper. "You need this." On its face was a cartoon duck holding a red-and-blue beach ball.

"Absolutely not," Dr. Gloria said. "You have no idea what that—Lyda!"

The paper dissolved in my mouth. "What is it?" I asked. I'd taken a lot of paper tonight. Also a lot of scotch. It turns out that Rovil's coworkers liked the old-fashioned drugs as well as the new ones. I admired the closed-loop economics of their field: Make the drugs, sell the drugs, use the money to buy the drugs. But where *was* Rovil? And where was Ollie? Oh right—she was back at Rovil's apartment. She'd refused to come with us, and gotten angry with me that I was leaving the apartment at all.

Well, that high horse don't ride itself. I reached for my scotch glass just as the paper went off in my brain. COLOR BOMB! Maroon and aquamarine light exploded behind my eyes with a thunderclap. Dr. Gloria tumbled off the back of the couch and hit the ground with a thud that shook the building.

"Paintball," the girl said.

I blinked hard. Coral and turquoise smeared across my vision. "I like it," I said.

Dr. G pulled herself to her feet, looking bedraggled. She shook out her wings, and loose feathers drifted down. "What was *that?*"

"You seem sad," the girl said. "What do you take?" I gave her a blank look, and she said, "Let me guess—Paxil. I can always tell. You seem like a Paxil person."

"Lately I've been taking it straight," I said. "Sorrow, no ice."

"Not tonight you aren't," Dr. G said. She put out a hand to steady herself.

"I'm on Nardil and Oleptro," the girl said. Her skin had turned gecko green. "But not for long, right?" She laughed like I was in on the joke, and I laughed with her.

"Everyone develops a tolerance to happiness," I said.

"Rovil *has* told you about Stepladder. I knew it. He's so paranoid about the NDA, but he can't stop bragging about those mice. As soon as he kicks the tolerance problem, we're golden."

Stepladder? "He does love his mice."

"We've got some *very* happy mice. LR is going to sweep the competition with this. Forget Paxil and Marvoset and Nardil. We will *own* this space." The girl leaned forward and lowered her voice. "He told you to buy stock, didn't he? Everyone's buying stock."

Whump. A flash of scarlet and turquoise, and Dr. G stumbled sideways, flapping to keep her balance. I stood, a little shakily. "I need to find Rovil."

The girl put a hand on my arm. "Wait." She wasn't making a pass at me. Her expression was 80 percent pity, 20 percent high as a kite. "Be careful."

"I'm fine."

"Yes, he's going to make a lot of people rich," she said. "But he's a soulless prick."

Rovil? "Yes, well, thank you for the . . ." I pushed off through air rippling with parti-color currents. The bar was crowded and loud, and the synesthesia was kicking in hard now, neon sounds ricocheting off the walls.

I found Rovil at the bar, talking with a handsome young Pharm Boy in a tight-fitting suit. Rovil broke off the conversation when I approached. "How are you doing?" he asked chartreusely.

Like I've eaten an entire box of sixty-four crayons, I thought. But I said, "That girl thinks you'll make her rich."

The guy in the tight suit raised his glass. "Truth."

"She also said you're a prick," I said.

"Also truth," the young man said, and laughed. The noise zigzagged across the color spectrum, ROY to the G to the BIV.

Rovil frowned and looked past me. "I'm sorry about that. Ilsa and I once . . . never mind. Are you ready to leave?"

"I'm drunk, I'm in New York, and it's three a.m.," I said. "I need a fucking *slice*."

. . .

We walked three blocks, following the map on Rovil's pen. I was growing hungrier by the minute. "I don't want you to get the wrong idea," he said. "What exactly did Ilsa say?"

"She said you're soulless."

A car horn sent up a misty pastel plume, but the effects of Paintball were fading in the cool air. New York was returning to its proper level of grayscale grittiness: black sky, buildings the color of headstones, bone-white sidewalks.

Rovil shook his head unhappily. "I'm not very good at breaking up. When I realized I could not be with her, I stopped talking to her, stopped taking her messages. She was not happy."

"Because you were being an asshole. Is this it?"

On the map our blue dot had arrived at the pizza shop, but we had not:

The place was closed. *Long* closed, the front crawling with graffiti, the windows shellacked with paper notices of rock bands and lost kittens.

"This is unacceptable," I said. I turned in a circle, desperate.

High overhead, Dr. Gloria said, "Food truck!" and flew off.

"That way," I said, pointing after her.

Rovil hurried to catch up. "I suppose it was because I did not know what to say, and I wanted to stop thinking about what to say."

"I get it, kid. I spend most of my energy trying to not think."

It was not a food truck but an aluminum trailer, a single guy working a propane grill. Pictures of each food item were tiled across the top and sides, a necessary feature when serving the drunk community. I pointed at a faded picture of a gyro and said, "That. In my belly. Now."

Rovil ordered a water. While we waited for my food he said, "Did she talk about our new product?"

I decided not to get her in trouble. "What product?"

"Because we have a strict policy at LR. I could be in trouble if one of my staff violated the NDA."

"Relax, kid. Your ex-girlfriend is fine."

The cart man wrapped up my pita and set it on the counter. Rovil waved his pen at the man.

"Wait," I said. "I've got the tip." I dug in my purse. And what a miracle it was that I still had a purse! I never carried the damn things. I found the bronze coin I was looking for and slammed it down on the counter. The gyro guy took one look at it and shook his head.

"What? Bad juju?" I asked. "One ju? You got something against jus?" At that moment, I believed this to be the most hilarious thing I had ever said.

Rovil picked up the coin, my six-month AA chip. He obviously didn't recognize what it was. He read aloud the words on the face: "Unity . . . Service . . . Recovery . . ."

"Back in the U-S-R," I said. "Rhymes with User."

I saw his expression change as he understood. "Lyda, I'm so sorry. This is why Ollie didn't want you to go out."

I thought, Have you not read my history? I started walking back to the club and Rovil's car. The gyro tasted wonderful. O steaming slabs of processed lamb! O Tzatziki sauce!

Dr. G looked at me over the top of her glasses. She was not amused by my little joke with the AA chip. I knew what she was thinking. Day one of sobriety starts now.

"Well it ain't dawn yet," I said.

"Pardon?" Rovil asked.

"The women in my life are overprotective." I wiped sauce from my lips. "There's nothing you could have done about it—I was going out with or without you. Sometimes my brain needs a little hammering to get it to shut up."

"You're worried about your daughter."

I stopped short. "I don't have a—wait. I've been talking about her, haven't I?"

"A lot," he said. "And not just to me."

I flashed on a memory of telling the brunette at the bar about Sasha. And someone else as well—a tall man with a chinstrap beard. And someone else . . .

I tossed the remainder of the gyro into a doorway. Rovil looked at me in surprise. I'd only taken a few bites.

"What was I thinking, buying the street shit?" I said. I started walking again. "All I wanted was a fucking slice. Take me home, Rovil."

"Please, one more thing." He touched my elbow to stop me. "Are we friends?"

"Of course."

"Then please trust me when I ask this of you."

"Yeah?"

"Stop fighting your god. You will be happier."

"Amen, brother," Dr. Gloria said.

"If you do that, I believe you will not need all the other . . . substances."

"Oh, Rovil," I said. "You better hope the other Pharm Boys don't hear you say that."

.   .   .

By the time we returned to Rovil's place, dawn was muscling its way past the skyscrapers. Ollie was asleep on the living room couch, fully clothed. She jerked awake when Rovil shut the door behind us.

"Don't get up," I said, and headed for the guest room.

"Where have you been?" Ollie said.

"Later," I said. I left the living room before she could turn those Analyst Eyes on me or smell my breath.

CHAPTER EIGHTEEN

On the edge of the desert there was a very large house where a girl named Sasha lived with a great number of people, some of whom lived there all the time, like Sasha and the maid Esperanza; and some, like the Gardeners Three, who did not live in the house but worked there almost every day; or the Mexican cleaning ladies who came on Mondays and Fridays. Others appeared only when Sasha drew them from the IF Deck, and still others arrived and departed unpredictably, like Grandpop, who lived in the house almost all of the time until he suddenly had to go on a trip, and Eduard and Suzette, who were hardly there at all but could show up on any given day.

This was one of the rare Full House days. Eduard, Suzette, and Grandpop were all returning to the house together. That morning, Esperanza began frantically picking up all of Sasha's art supplies and toys and clothes and carrying them to Sasha's bedroom. Later the maid cut short Sasha's latest project, forced her to change into a clean outfit (she'd dribbled green paint on her white shirt), and confined her to her room before she could do more damage.

This was not exactly a punishment. Sasha preferred her room to any other place in the house, and Esperanza knew this. Sasha spent hours there reading, or watching crime dramas that Grandpop would not have approved of, or using the house to spy on the adults. But there was no time for that today: Sasha had to call out the Deck Council.

Bucko the Pirate Bear sat on the bed, propped up between two pillows. He was her oldest friend, with fur rubbed thin in patches, and a wobbly eye that Esperanza had stitched back into place more than once. (He could not afford to lose another one.) He considered it a point of distinction that he was not confined to the Deck like her other friends.

Sasha closed the door, and Bucko hopped up. "So I was thinking," he said. "Me, in the middle of a pack of zombies. I'm fighting 'em off with a cutlass in one hand, and in the other I've got my flintlock, right? And I'm shooting it right into the face of a zombie."

"Sorry," she said. "Emergency council meeting."

"Oh jeez. You're not bringing out Zebo, are you? He's a pompous ass."

"I'll bring out whoever I need." She climbed over the bed and dropped down into the space between the bed and the wall. The blue drinking straw still lay across the floor vent. Good—Esperanza hadn't been cleaning back here. Sasha popped the floor vent from the carpet. A thin cord was tied to the underside of the vent. She pulled up the cord and retrieved a black bag that had been hanging down into the ductwork. The bag was something she'd found in Eduard's office. The little tag on it said it was a "Portable Black Hole," made by Sony. She'd looked up the product online. It blocked all electromagnetic fields, which was exactly the kind of thing you needed if you were trying to prevent people from geolocating their misplaced data devices.

She opened the bag. Inside were seven smart pens, two data fobs, a set of electronic keys that opened the high-security doors in the house and most of the cars, a tangle of data cables and adapters, and a deck of playing cards secured by a thick rubber band wrapped twice around: the IF Deck.

She rolled the rubber band from the deck and fanned through the cards. Most of them were ordinary playing cards, useful as decoys. But in the middle of the deck were eleven special cards that had been decorated and colored in, the newest in permanent marker, the oldest in crayon. But which did she need now?

Mother Maybelle, definitely. Her card was the eight of hearts, the two red circles of the number fattened with red crayon, the topmost circle sprouting two chubby arms. Then Zebo, the jack of diamonds, heavily redrawn with black marker. And of course Tinker, the three of clubs, to serve as secretary.

Her fingers hovered over a fourth card, the seven of spades. He was an old card, but she'd rubbed out the black crayon outline she'd scrawled when she was five, and had redrawn him as accurately as she could in black Sharpie, no colors. The 7 was the spine of a thin man in a black coat, leaning back against a wall, his wide hat covering his eyes. The card had been torn in half, width-wise, and taped back together. The Scotch tape blurred his face.

The Wander Man. She tilted the card, and he seemed to shift and nod. *Howdy, Miss Sasha.*

She quickly pushed his card back into the deck. She may not have been able to get rid of him, but she did not have to bring him out.

The remaining three cards she turned faceup and tapped them: *One, two, three.* Immediately she smelled cigar smoke.

"My oh my," said a deep voice. "I sense that we are on the cusp of a momentous decision."

Sasha raised her head over the top of the bed. Zebo the Zalligator reclined in a chair that had not been there before, one hand tucked into the pocket of his red, diamond-pattern vest, the other nonchalantly holding a cigar to the side of his long, toothy mouth. He chuckled dryly. "A 'damned if you do, damned if you don't' type situation."

"Pay no mind to the carnivore, sweetness," Mother Maybelle said. She glided across the room in a cloud of petticoats, her golden curls swaying and bouncing. Sasha's friends never appeared in a puff of smoke or a flash of light. She simply noticed them, already in place like actors on a dim stage, waiting for the spotlight of her attention. And when it was time for them to go, she merely had to glance away and they'd slip into the shadows.

Mother Maybelle said, "There is always a right decision, and we will make it."

Tinker the Robot Boy trundled forward and clanged in agreement.

Sasha climbed back onto the bed next to Bucko. The bear said, "You don't even know what the question is, damn it. Let her talk."

"We know what the question is, bear," Zebo said. "It's all she's been thinking about. Does she, or does she not, tell ol' Grandpop that his son is pulling the wool over his eyes, and darn near covering his entire head?"

Mother Maybelle said, "Are we talking about the secret messages, again?"

"Yes, it's the secret messages," Sasha said. Months ago she'd discovered that Eduard was not delivering messages to Grandpop, even though they were explicitly addressed to Edo Anderssen Vik. They were text messages, emails, phone messages—scores and scores of them. Grandpop's account, by contrast, received only messages from Eduard. Sasha had called a Deck Council to decide what to do. The council had advised to table the issue until more data could be collected. Sasha had set to work. In this house, there was no room and no account she couldn't get into. And it had become clear that Eduard was continuing to keep others from contacting his father.

Bucko had the same opinion as last time: "Eduard's a grog-sucking weasel."

"Young man! That's Sasha's father you're talking about," Mother Maybelle said.

"*Adoptive* father," Bucko said. "Junior's trying to steal Grandpop's money and take over the business. I say we expose the rat and let the bodies fall where they may."

Mother Maybelle said, "We still do not know if this is something sons regularly do for their fathers."

"Then I hope to never have sons," Zebo said. "However, let us not lose sight of the possibility that Edo *told* Eduard not to give him the messages. A firewall, if you will, protecting him from the tawdry world of business."

"*Well,*" Mother Maybelle said, puffing the syllable full of air. "When it comes to the world of business and the world of adults in general there is too much that we do *not* understand."

"If Grandpop is okay with this, then he won't mind when we tell him," Sasha said.

"But Eduard will," Zebo said. "If you demonstrate that you've been snooping through his personals, he will come down on you like a mighty rain. There will be no more access to electronics. You will be a prisoner."

"Then you got to make it count," Bucko said. "Eddie Junior's been away for weeks. Get the latest messages off his pen and show 'em to Grandpop. Leave no room for Eddie to bitch out of this."

Sasha frowned. Even with a roomful of IFs, deciding was so hard. "Okay," she said. "I'll get the latest messages tonight. If Eduard's still hiding things, then I'll tell Grandpop tomorrow morning. Did you get all that, Tinker?"

The robot boy dinged twice. Of course he'd gotten it; Tinker forgot nothing.

"All right then," Sasha said. "Back in the deck."

CHAPTER NINETEEN

Somehow, impossibly, Rovil got up and went to work the next morning. I ate a rock star breakfast: dry toast at noon.

Ollie watched me eat. She said, "You want to tell me what that was about?" "That" meaning several things: the freak-out after seeing Eduard, the night with Rovil, my decision to flood my bloodstream with toxins.

"Not really," I said.

"You're not solving anything by not talking to her," Gloria said. She sat in the living room, and if I didn't know better I would have thought she was nursing her own hangover.

"I know about Sasha," Ollie said.

"You *know*?"

"That day in the Marriott. I looked at your face, and I looked at hers. She has your cheekbones. Your eyes."

"You're fucking with me."

"I should have put it together earlier, but I wasn't on my game. I knew you'd had a child. And four years ago, Eduard and his wife Suzette became foster parents for a mentally handicapped girl from a group home in Lockport, Illinois. They adopted her a few months later. She was mixed-race, and six years old. The same age as your biological daughter."

"Is this what you've been doing? Digging through my life? Can you even help yourself?"

"You know I can't."

"Jesus Christ."

"Obviously Edo was behind the adoption," she said. "I have a theory on why he'd do it."

"Of course you do," I said.

"It's a legal maneuver," Ollie said. "Vik can't make Numinous legally because he doesn't own the intellectual property outright. You could sue him. He owns only forty percent of the company and its IP. Gil owns ten, and you and Mikala split the rest, with two percent for Rovil."

"How the hell do you know all this?"

She blinked. "I read the corporate filings."

"Ollie, people don't . . . nobody does that."

"They should."

"Rovil's percentage came out of Mikala's share," I said. "He wasn't a founder, and we hadn't promised him anything, but she said he ought to get something when we were bought out."

"That was generous of her."

"She was probably already on Numinous when she decided that."

"Where are you going?" she asked.

"Out."

"Out? Where?"

"Just—" I raised a hand. "Give me some fucking space, okay?"

She followed me to the front closet, where Rovil had put my coat. "Mikala's shares went to you when she died, but you officially transferred them to a trust. For your daughter?"

"Get to the point," I said.

"When she comes of age, that trust can only be hers if she's mentally competent. Otherwise the guardian gets control."

I opened the front door. "I can't believe you knew about her."

"I was waiting for you to tell me," she said.

- - -

An addict off the wagon is a fundamentally boring creature, an animal with one dietary requirement, one habitat, and one schedule. It's a fucking koala bear, minus all cuteness.

For the next four days I clung to my barstool as if it were a eucalyptus tree. When the bars closed I made my way home down spotless streets to Rovil's apartment, slept hard, and got out of there before he returned from work. Ollie of course knew what I was doing; there was no fooling her brain. My strategy for dealing with this was to see as little of Rovil and Ollie as possible. I wanted to ditch Dr. Gloria as well, but I wasn't able to do that until the second night.

We were in a faux-Czech bar that served tall pilsners and short vodkas. "This is just cowardice," the angel said. She sat on the empty stool to my left, sipping water as if she were the designated flyer for the evening.

I said to the guy to my right, "A horse walks into a bar—"

"Good one," he said. He was in his mid-fifties, and he'd been trying to look down my top for the past two hours.

"Wait for it, damn it!"

"If you want your daughter back, go see her," Dr. Gloria said.

"So the bartender says, 'Hey buddy, why the long face?' And the horse says, 'My wife just died.'"

He smiled uncertainly.

"Fuck you," I said. "That is an *excellent* joke."

"Sitting here self-medicating is not going to accomplish anything," Dr. G said.

"Physician, heal thyself," I said.

The man next to me said, "Pardon?"

"It's funny," I said, "because the horse is clinically depressed."

"Ollie knows where he lives," the doctor said. "Rovil can drive us."

I wheeled on her. "You think we can just roll in to Little Edo's estate? Did you see those fucking bodyguards? He'll have us fucking arrested!"

The bartender appeared in front of me. "Okay, I warned you once. Get out."

Shit. I'd been talking out loud again. "It was a joke," I said. "These two guys with multiple personality disorder walk into a bar, and the fourth one says—"

"Let's go, or I'm calling the cops," the bartender said.

"Do as he says," Dr. G said.

"*Goddamn* it!" I yanked the stool out from under her, but she recovered gracefully. "You think this is making anything better? Do you? You think you can *nag* me into doing what you want? Get the fuck away from me."

Dr. Gloria's expression had turned stony.

My departure was assisted by the bartender and one waitress. They did not toss me into a back alley like a 1930s' drunk, but the exit was just as firm. It was three in the morning, and the sidewalk was empty, not an angel in sight. I was free.

For the next two days, the space in my head was cavernous, an empty warehouse in which I heard only my own footsteps, my own voice. Paradoxically, I had to work twice as hard to muffle those few remaining thoughts. But I was ready; I had trained for this moment for ten years. Yes, I'd dabbled with many substances over the past decade, but booze was the mortar of my addiction, making all other abuses possible. I knew how to build that wall. My body, like a good horse, had learned the way home to Rovil's place, and whatever crime-stopping fairy circle was in effect continued to protect me. On none of those early-morning trail rides home did I run into anyone who made me nervous, much less made me fear for my wallet. When I passed a figure sleeping in a doorway it was almost a relief.

I started to point him out to Dr. Gloria, but of course she was long gone, missing for days. I walked on, then stopped. There was something odd about that homeless person, and I walked back to him.

He lay on his side upon a cardboard box, one arm under his head, his face toward the street. A black garbage bag was wedged into the space behind him. Most of his face was in shadow, but I could see that his eyes were closed. His hair was a wild expanse of gray.

No, I thought. Information that is too strange to process is literally too strange to process. The mind's first defense is to recoil, retreat, deny. My body, responding to that mental whiplash, jerked back. I told myself, *It's not him.*

Then he opened his eyes, instantly focusing on me. "Hey now," he said.

It was the homeless man from the park in Toronto. The man who'd watched me try to summon Dr. Gloria with a box cutter.

I backed away from him, then stumbled as I stepped off the curb. I crossed to the other side of the street, already trying to shove down the memory of what I'd seen, my head roaring like an ocean.

· · ·

"I need to show you something," Ollie said.

It was daytime, though I wasn't sure of much more than that. I tried to roll back over, but she dragged me out of bed. "It's important."

The living room was lit up like Times Square, every wall screen vibrating with color. I winced and said, "Why would you do this to me?"

"I've got a surprise for you," she said.

The images kept changing. Each one was a digital re-creation of an abstract oil painting, and each done in fireball colors of yellow, red, and orange. There were dozens of them, varying in size from a few feet square to rectangles three meters long. They faded in and out on the walls according to the apartment's slideshow program, so there was no telling how many paintings were in the collection. But it was clear that they were all by the same school, if not the same artist.

"I've seen these," I said. "Or something like them."

"You said that Eduard Jr. told you that if you sent Edo a picture he'd pass it on. That seemed like an odd thing to say. So I started looking at Edo's art collection."

"He posts his entire collection online?" I said. "People do that?"

"These are special," she said. "They weren't on Edo's personal site, or his corporation's. They're on a government site, for artwork created by federal prisoners in a rehabilitation program."

"Edo funds it or something?"

"Through the Vik Group. There are thousands of pieces, almost all of them crap. But these are the paintings that are highlighted in the collection. They're the only ones available in archival-quality hi-res files. And they're the only ones that the Vik Group bought outright."

"So where are they now?"

Ollie looked smug. "Edo's private residence."

"All of these? They went directly to Edo?"

"One a week, for months."

I looked up to see a four-foot by four-foot painting start to fade, and I jumped up. "Bring that one back."

Ollie touched it to make it stay. "This one was hanging in the pastor's office," I told her.

"We didn't go in the pastor's office," Ollie said.

"I did, the first time I was in the church. There were two other posters just like it on the wall."

"All these are a series," Ollie said. "They're numbered with major and minor version numbers, like software: one point one, one point two, two-oh. The major numbers get more and more dense, like sketches getting filled in. The minor versions seem to be alternates of the same picture."

"There's something else," I said. "They remind me of something, not just the church posters . . . shit."

I sat down on the couch, trying to concentrate, but I couldn't put my finger on where else I'd seen them. My brain felt . . . dull. It wasn't just the alcohol, though there was enough in my system that any traffic cop would qualify me as drunk. No, my body could handle that. It was that I was trying to function without Dr. Gloria.

We shared the same memories because we shared a brain, but *having* memories meant nothing if you couldn't access them. Access depended on associations, one neuron tripping another, and her initial set of associations was different from mine. We had two different maps to the territory, and some locations weren't on my map at all.

"Fuck," I said. "I need Gloria."

"Why?" Ollie asked. "What for?"

"It's hard to explain."

"Try me."

I told her about associations and maps, about the chain of firings that led to this thing in the prefrontal cortex called "recognition."

"Okay then," Ollie said. "Why don't you pretend to be Dr. Gloria?"

"Uh . . ."

"Look, I used to talk to people all the time, try to help them remember details. It was one of my jobs. Pretending can help. Just treat it like a game. Maybe it leads somewhere, maybe it doesn't."

All I wanted to do was go back to sleep. "Okay, what do you want me to do?"

"You're feeling like Dr. Gloria has something to do with this memory, and you remember seeing the posters in the church. She was with you when you were there, right? So start there. What else did she see?"

"We started in the sanctuary," I said.

"Walk around as Gloria," Ollie said. "What does she see? Where does she go?"

I pictured myself as the doctor, walking around the edge of the sanctuary as I—as Lyda—talked to the pastor and Luke. There were dioramas and art projects, all depicting the members' gods. None of them rang a bell. After that, I waved Lyda into the back rooms: the warehouse, the pastor's office, the bathroom. The smell of amines was in the air. Then Lyda pulled back the rubber curtain to reveal the printer. She lifted off the lid—

"That's a painting of the chemjet engine," I said. I said the words, knowing I was right, but without knowing why I was right.

I looked up at the picture, trying to reconcile the shapes in that image with my memory of the internals of the chemjet. The intense colors of the painting made this difficult, because the machine was all silver and black inside. Also, the orientation was wrong.

"Flip the painting," I said. "Can you do that?"

Ollie grabbed the edge of the current image and turned it.

"No, the other way," I said. "Ninety degrees."

And then the two images—one in front of me now, the other hovering before my internal eye, but both firing the same neurons—seemed to snap into place.

Ollie saw the change in my face. "What is it?" she asked.

"This isn't just a painting," I said. "It's a blueprint."

Ollie thought for a moment. "That kind of makes sense."

"Tell me who painted them," I said, though I could already guess the answer.

"That was my big surprise," she said. "These were all painted by Gil Kapernicke."

· · ·

Rovil sat on the couch facing the wall and the camera. His palms lay on his knees, the two fingers of his left hand still taped together. He wore a business suit, and his face was locked into a pleasant expression. He was on hold.

Ollie and I stood in the kitchen, out of sight of the camera. Ollie had connected her pen to a receiver Rovil wore in his right ear, and she'd synched the display with the wall screen so that we could see what he was seeing. Right now, that was a commercial for the Delwood Detention Facility, a private prison in Ohio that offered excellent outsourcing options for overcrowded state and federal prisons. The minute-long commercial had already looped a dozen times.

"Just hang in there, Rovil," I whispered into the pen. He nodded, very slightly.

We'd applied for the visit three days ago, and it had taken that long to get approval from the Delwood. Ollie told us that the odds of being granted a visitation were not good; Rovil was not a relative, and his status as a witness in the murder trial had probably flagged him as an Inappropriate

Contact. But the paintings told us that Edo, another witness, had been allowed to have contact with Gil. Of course, that could have been because he was a billionaire who'd donated millions to Delwood.

The final step of the approval was Gil Kapernicke himself. If the prisoner didn't want the visit, he couldn't be forced. So when the approval came through, we knew that Gil was interested in talking to his old intern from Little Sprout.

"Are you okay?" Ollie whispered.

"I'm not going to fall apart when Gil pops on screen," I said.

"You shouldn't even be in the room," she said. "Let Rovil handle this."

"I'm fine."

This was a lie. Ever since the day Ollie showed me the pictures, I woke up every morning asking myself the question, Are you going to drink today? My alcohol-starved brain was still cramping from my cruel trick. Over the four-day bender I'd given it a good long gulp of what it most craved—and then I'd yanked away the cup.

Ollie had asked the question too, but not aloud. I felt her tense every time I went out alone, then assessing me when I returned, that analyst's brain checking for signs and symptoms. Each morning I had no idea if I was going to make it through the day without a drink. And so far, for three days at least, I'd arrived back at home each night, achingly sober.

And I'd done this every day without Dr. Gloria. The angel was still angry with me.

The wall screen flipped on to show a man's face. It wasn't pale, fat Gil, but a Hispanic-looking guard. He adjusted something at the top of the screen, then stepped out of the way. The camera was sitting on a table, pointed at an empty chair.

"Hello?" Rovil said.

No one answered. A minute later there was movement at the edge of the frame, and a prisoner in an orange jumpsuit appeared. He was fifty-five or sixty years old, white hair shaved down to bristles. He was very thin, with ropy arms.

He sat down in the chair and rested his arms on the table. "Rovil," he said, his voice radiating pleasure. "I know that Gil is so pleased to see you."

Rovil glanced over at me, his eyes wide. He turned back to the camera and said, "I think there's been a mistake. I'm to speak with Gilbert Kapernicke."

The man laughed, and it wasn't until then that I could see that he was Gil. He'd lost at least 150 pounds. He looked simultaneously more healthy than the Gil I'd known and much older than he should have been.

"Gil is here," Gil said. "Anything you say, he'll hear."

Rovil blinked at the screen.

I took the pen from Ollie. "Ask him if he's Gil's god."

"Are you Gil's god?"

"Not just Gil's," he answered. "But yes, I speak, and Gil repeats what I say. Years ago he decided not to fight me, but to get out of the way. He has surrendered his life to me. I decide everything—what he eats, when he should exercise, what he should do for recreation, and . . ." He nodded at the screen. "Who he should talk to."

"That's awful," I said.

"That's . . . fascinating," Rovil said.

Gil shrugged. "It's Gil's choice. He chooses, every day and each moment, to let me guide his life. He could stop listening to me at any moment."

"But he doesn't?" Rovil asked. "Not ever?"

"Gil would be the first to say that he was not doing a very good job of managing himself. Surely you could understand that better than anyone, Rovil. Don't you think your life would be better if you gave it all to me?"

"To *you*?" Rovil asked.

Gil tilted his head. "There's only one god. Even if I take a different form for each person."

I said into the pen, "Ask him to tell you something that only you would know."

Rovil glanced at me, frowning.

"Jesus Christ," I said into the pen. "Why'd we give you the earpiece if you're going to keep looking at me?"

"Breathe," Dr. Gloria said.

Gil said, "Rovil, put Lyda on the line."

"I'm sorry," Rovil said, "I don't know what—"

"It's all right," Gil said. "The guards don't pay any attention to these calls. We have been such a good prisoner, for so long, that they let us talk to whomever we want."

I covered the pen and looked at Ollie questioningly.

She shrugged. "Your choice."

I handed Ollie the pen and walked into the living room. I didn't sit down. My heart was racing, and I felt a rush of heat across my chest. The wall screen was gigantic, and Gil's face was as big as the Great and Terrible Oz. In the corner was a small mirror window that contained a miniature version of me and Rovil.

I sucked in a breath. "How you doing, Gilbert?"

The giant face smiled slightly. "I've been expecting you to call. Gil had hoped you'd visit in person before his parole, but this will have to do."

"You think you're going to get out on parole?"

That head tilt again. I could remember the old Gil doing that. "We'll be out in a year."

It was a shock, but I absorbed it. "That's . . . good," I said.

"Gil is in no hurry to leave," he said. "We teach art here. We counsel troubled inmates. It's been a rewarding period. But he accepts that it's time for us to move on."

I said, "And what did *Gil* want to talk about before you moved on?"

"He wanted to ask your forgiveness."

I wasn't ready for that. The emotion hit in a rush, the gates of the limbic system thrown wide open. I didn't know what I was feeling—rage? confusion? sorrow? The flood washed everything downstream and knocked me to hell.

At the trial Gil had said that he had only fragmentary memories of killing Mikala. He testified that his first fully conscious thought came as he stood over her body with the knife in his hand and he realized what he'd done. He confessed immediately. He told the police he'd become obsessed with Mikala. It was absurd, an obese white man falling in love with a beautiful black lesbian, but that was why, he said, he'd never admitted it before, not even to himself. In the frenzy of the overdose, his jealousy had taken over. He cried several times during the trial.

It was a performance. Gil didn't kill Mikala. And we both knew it.

"Yeah, well . . ." My voice was shaky. I cleared my throat. "You can shove your apology up your ass."

"Lyda, please . . ."

"Tell me about the paintings, Gil. The ones you gave to Edo."

Gil sat back. His hands dropped to his side.

I said, "I know he's been talking to you. Did he ask you to build a machine, Gil?"

"We only paint," Gil said. "We don't build machines anymore."

"Fine. Did he ask you to *paint* a fucking machine?"

He tilted his head. "Have you seen our paintings? I know that you have. If you've seen them, then you know."

"Are there more, Gil? Are you still painting them?"

He smiled, but didn't answer.

I leaned against the wall with both hands leaned close to that smug face. "Give Edo a message, Gil. Can you at least do that?"

"What would you like to say to him?" Gil asked.

"Tell him to call me—now—or I will tell the world about his printers. And you and your god will never get out of jail."

. . .

Within twenty-four hours, a message appeared on my pen:

> 1 White Mesa Drive, Los Lunas, New Mexico. Gate code: 7221.
> Do not come until after Saturday.—Your old friend, E.

CHAPTER TWENTY

Since the time she was very small, on the days that Grandpop was coming home she would wait in the hallway, out of sight, listening for the sound of the door. (If it was only Eduard and Suzette returning, she would stay in her room with her music on loud and pretend to hear nothing.) Grandpop would step inside and yell, "Where's that little girl who lives here?" Sasha would launch herself across the room and crash into his legs. This giant man would stumble back in a show of how strong and fast she was, and then scoop her into his arms. She would direct him around the house, pointing out all the things she'd painted and made while he was gone.

She was older now, and too big for Hello Tackles. She waited with Esperanza in the foyer, and when the maid opened the door Grandpop looked at Sasha in mock confusion. "I'm sorry. Where's that little girl who used to live here?"

She could not help herself; she threw herself into him and hugged him tight. He laughed and said, "Ah! There she is."

Eduard and Suzette stepped around them. Suzette handed her coat to Esperanza, and Eduard gave her his briefcase. Sasha released her grandfather and presented herself to her parents. Eduard said, "Hello,

Sasha." Suzette patted her on the back as if she'd seen this greeting behavior on a nature documentary.

Sasha knew that she was adopted, and she knew that it was Edo who wanted her, who loved her. Eduard and Suzette did not have to say a word; they deferred to Grandpop for all decisions about her. It didn't occur to her that this was unusual; stories were full of children who were unloved by their False Parents, and had to search for their True ones. She felt lucky that the search had ended before it had begun. She had Grandpop, and she didn't need anyone else.

He was tired tonight, but still glad to be home. They ate together in the big dining room, and Grandpop cried only once, when Suzette mentioned seeing homeless people in Chicago, but quickly recovered. Afterward, Eduard went upstairs to his office. Later Sasha heard him yelling at someone over the phone.

Suzette, as usual, went out to the patio. Sasha did not know what her mother did by the pool at night; she didn't swim, didn't look at any of the screens, and didn't even look at the stars. The few times Sasha had interrupted her mother out there she found her staring at the water with a tablet of paper on her lap. The top page of the tablet was always blank, but with some portion of it torn away, as if she'd written something there and then destroyed it. Sasha imagined that Suzette was writing an invisible diary; each day, once recorded, could be disposed of. No one could ever steal her thoughts.

Even though he was tired, Grandpop made sure to tuck Sasha in. The tutors were coming in the morning, he said, and she needed to be in bed on time. He sat down on the floor beside her bed and made up stories about haunted hotels and terrible room service. "I ordered breakfast in London and they brought me antlers. They did! I opened the silver lid and there was nothing on the plate but reindeer antlers. And a bottle of hot sauce."

She knew it was an effort for him to make up funny stories, and not just tonight. Eduard said Grandpop "carried the weight of the world." Sasha knew it was the weight of his god. Every day, he'd told her, God reminded him that most people in the world were suffering terribly.

"It's a wicked world out there," he said to her as he tucked her in. "We all have to do our part to make it better. But what? That's the question."

She didn't answer. But when he left her room, she sent a text to his bedroom wall that said, *We'll figure something out, GP! Love you.*

A minute later (Grandpop was slow at working the house interface) he sent back: *I know we will. Now go to sleep!*

. . .

Two hours after midnight, Bucko shook her awake. "Time to get our raid on." Sasha retrieved a few items from her black bag, and then the bear climbed onto her back.

Eduard's office was on the second floor. To get there they had to walk past the master bedroom. "They're probably having sex," Bucko said into her ear. "You know they do it all the time." She did not want to think about what Eduard and Suzette did in their bedroom. She'd seen enough sex online to know that she didn't want to see it in person, especially not between her parents.

The office door sensed the key fob in her pocket and unlocked itself before she touched the knob. She closed the door behind her but did not turn on the light. She did not know this room as well as she knew the other rooms in the house—Eduard did not like her in here, and it was one of the few rooms that the house did not let her see—but the gap in the drapes allowed enough moonlight to make out the desk, the armchair, the bookcases. Leaning against one of the walls was a stack of paintings wrapped in brown paper, each one much taller than Sasha and wider than she could span with her hands outstretched.

"Blimey, more paintings?" Bucko asked. "Since when does Eduard like art? He sure doesn't like yours."

She'd discovered the first painting on a raid months ago. And now there were four, no, five paintings. Eduard hadn't unwrapped any of them.

"Forget that," Sasha said. "It's the briefcase we're after."

"I'm on it," Bucko said. He hopped down from her back and ran over to the desk, where the briefcase lay. "Let's pop the lock on this dead man's chest."

Sasha climbed onto the chair beside the bear. She ran her hands over the lock like a safecracker. She'd found the combination two years ago, written on a piece of paper in Eduard's desk, and Tinker had memorized it for her. Eduard had never bothered to change it. She worked the wheels, and it popped open.

"Avast!" Bucko said.

Inside the briefcase, the slate was in its usual holder. She turned it on and unlocked it with the same four-digit code he used on all his devices. Why was he so lazy about security?

The messages she wanted to look at were in the Vik Group network storage. She didn't have the latest password for that, because it was the one password Eduard was forced to change regularly—and that's why she needed his slate. Eduard never logged off the device.

She searched for all messages addressed to Edo Anderssen Vik, or that mentioned him in the body. There were thousands. Many messages she'd seen before, but there were hundreds of new ones since the last time she'd broken into his slate. She transferred them all to her own storage on the house's network. Then she put everything back where it belonged, and Bucko remembered to give the slate a wipe with his furry paw to erase any of her fingerprints.

She wondered, not for the first time, if she was a bad person. There seemed to be something in her that wanted to sneak and steal. It was this bad thing, she was sure, that had caused her real parents to leave her at the orphanage. It was this bad thing that had made her listen to the Wander Man. And it was this bad thing that had made her try to kill Mr. Paniccia when she was five years old.

She wasn't like Grandpop. He was a good person, and his IF was God himself. Sasha's friends, on the other hand, could be so . . . immature.

"Let's roll," Bucko said. "Mission fucking accomplished."

"Wait." There was something new on the floor near the desk, a package about two feet square. Did Eduard bring that into the house with the latest paintings?

The box was marked up with shipping stickers, and the flaps had been opened. Sasha squinted to make out the label in the dim light. It was addressed to Grandpop. The "from" address was a series of numbers. She should have brought Tinker with her to remember it for her.

Bucko was opening the flaps. Inside was a cube of pale plastic. It was too big for her to lift out.

"Just so we're keeping track," Bucko said, "Eddie's now intercepting mail, art, and office equipment."

She had no idea what the object was, or why her father was keeping so many things from Grandpop. Adults were crazy.

. . .

She could not sleep until she'd read the new messages. She knew the IFs would be curious, so she called up Mother Maybelle, Zebo, and Tinker, and together they went through the files.

A number of them had already been flagged by Eduard as important. A dozen were from someone named Rovil Gupta, and several more were from Lyda Rose. Both of them mentioned "Little Sprout." She knew that name.

"Hey Tinker," she said. "Do you remember that photo? The real one, on paper?"

Of course he did. They'd found it in Grandpop's desk drawers once. The next time she'd looked for it the photo was gone, but fortunately Tinker had been with her the first time.

The robot boy whirred, and a length of paper unrolled from the slot in his chest. Mother Maybelle leaned down, fabric crinkling, and tore off the strip.

"Hmm," she said.

She handed the paper to Sasha. In the photo, four people stood facing the camera, holding glasses. A toast, just like in a wedding movie.

Grandpop looked about the same as he did now. Next to him was a hugely fat white man with brown hair and a sour look on his face. Beside the fat man was a pale redheaded woman, her head thrown back, laughing at some joke. And beside her was a tall woman with skin darker than Sasha's. She was smiling too.

Tinker had also remembered the words that had been written on the back of the photograph: "NME 50! Little Sprout 3/5/17."

Sasha had no idea who these people were, or what most of the words meant. But she could find out.

Mother Maybelle saw what Sasha was thinking. "You are not staying up all night hunting around on the internet," the woman said. "You have school tomorrow!"

"Just let me finish," Sasha said. She turned back to the message list, and on impulse she searched for "Little Sprout." One of the messages had come in just a few hours ago, from someone named Gilbert Kapernicke. It wasn't addressed to Edo, but to Eduard. Zebo read it aloud:

> Dear Eduard,
>   Rovil Gupta, whom you may remember from Little Sprout, visited us today by phone. We talked about Lyda, so much so it was

like having her in the room. She is hurting, and she would very much like to speak with your father. We would be pleased for you to arrange this, but of course that is your choice to make.

"Who the hell is this Gilbert nitwad?" Bucko asked.

"Please," Sasha said. "Just let me think a minute." She had to figure out so many things. Who were these people? What did they want from Grandpop? And how was she going to tell him without Eduard ruining her life?

"I think we're going to need the entire—" She was going to say the entire IF Deck. But there was one card she was definitely not going to bring out. "I think we're going to need more imaginary friends."

CHAPTER TWENTY-ONE

Rovil said he didn't want to drive us across the country, but he put up only token resistance. "You want to get to the bottom of this, don't you?" I asked. "Don't you want to find the fucker that broke your fingers?"

"I want to think that someone besides Edo is doing this," he said.

"Keep trying," I said. "Meanwhile, Ollie and I need you. We can't rent a car, since we're both supposed to be incarcerated in Toronto."

"If you can get us in to see him, I don't see how I have any choice."

"That's right," I said. "Free will is an illusion anyway."

- - -

The drive was making Ollie's symptoms worse. The confinement, and the inability to take action, was taking its toll. She spent most of the time on her pen, but by Illinois she was twitchy and cranky. By Kansas she was picking fights.

"You really think we have no free will?"

This seemed to come out of nowhere. We were south of Wichita, Rovil chauffeuring us across miles and miles of sun-blasted land.

"Have you been stewing about this since New York?" I asked.

"Ever since Gilbert said his god was in control," she said. "So answer the question."

"We do not have free will," I said formally. "At least, not the way you're thinking of it."

"How do you know how I'm thinking of it?" she said.

"Like how everybody thinks of it. That there's a 'you' weighing several alternatives, then choosing one of them. But there's no choosing. That's an illusion created by the mind to make you feel like you're in control."

"I'm pretty sure I'm choosing right now not to throw you of the car."

The Midwest was in another drought, and everything outside the windows was winter brown. I kept expecting a flash of wings, hoping Gloria was pacing us like an albatross, but she was nowhere in sight.

I said, "Let's say we run a wire into your brain."

"Let's pick Rovil's instead."

"Hey!" he said. I hadn't realized he'd been listening.

"Okay, a doctor runs a wire into his brain, and every time the doctor presses a button, a certain neuron gets fired. And every time it fires, Rovil turns left."

"The opsin experiments," Rovil said. He glanced up in the rearview mirror and said to Ollie, "It was actually a fiber-optic cable channeling colored light to genetically modified neurons."

"Oh, of course," Ollie said. "That old thing."

I laughed, and Ollie said, "So he hits the button, and Rovil goes left. Remote control."

"It doesn't feel like remote control to him," I said. "Rovil's walking naturally, and then he turns, and it feels completely natural. Except there's no choice involved—well, except for the doctor choosing when to hit the button."

"Wait, how does that feel natural?"

"The urge is subconscious. It's like you've got an itch on your nose, and you reach up to scratch without thinking about it."

"I feel like there's a catch coming somewhere," she said. "But go on."

"Now let's say there's another area of your brain where Free Will lives," I said. "Call him Free Willy. He's just like the doctor. He decides when to trigger that neuron and make you turn left."

"How did this stop being about Rovil?" she asked.

"Here's the problem: Free Willy is made up of nothing but more neurons. So in order for the decision to occur, a *bunch* of neurons have to fire. That means one of those neurons has to be the first neuron. But who makes that one fire? If it's yet another neuron, then you're just running in circles."

"That's my point," Ollie said. "You can't get something out of nothing."

"But it's not coming from nothing, 'cause the brain's not a closed loop," I said. "There's input constantly coming into it, from all over the body, all those physical senses." I took her hand in mine. "But there's also input coming from other parts of the brain."

"The subconscious," she said.

"Sure. *Most* of the brain is subconscious, and there's neurons firing all over the place, constantly processing. And I know what you're thinking—"

"Here we go again," she said.

"You're thinking, hey, that's fine for low-level actions, like moving a body part. But how about higher-level decisions? One little wire can't make me, say, decide to follow a crazy woman across the country, can it?"

"No way," Ollie said. "That would be ridiculous."

"So maybe there's *another* free will node that handles higher-level thought."

"Free Willy Two," Ollie said.

"The sequel," I said. "So now we have Free Willy Two, but he's made out of neurons too. Maybe he needs many, many neurons to form a complex thought, maybe they even have to fire in a certain order, or a certain frequency. But it's all just neurons, and when it comes down to it, everything depends on *one* of those neurons being fired first. Every neuron's connected to surrounding neurons, and charges travel by known rules. Their action is absolutely mechanical. Thoughts, decisions . . . they just happen."

"Mechanically," Ollie said. "Like a gun going off."

"Yup. Except there's no one to pull the trigger."

"When *I* pull the trigger, it sure feels like I'm the one doing it."

"Exactly—it's a *feeling*," I said. "It happens after the brain's gone off. You think you're in control, but that's just the warm fuzzy of false confidence."

"But if there's no free will," Ollie said, looking up at me, "then there's no such thing as sin." I was surprised by how steady her voice was. "If no one's responsible, then there's no morality."

"You cannot prosecute a gun for murder," Rovil said.

"You can if the gun's complex enough," I said. "Look, you can't think of a person like it's one thing, one 'I' that decides everything. The brain is a collective, a huge number of all these thinking modules. It doesn't *make* a decision, it *arrives* at one."

"Words," Ollie said. "*Something's* got to be responsible."

I thought for a minute, trying to figure out how to explain this. "When the brain starts working on a problem, all those parts of the brain start working, using all the data they've got—personal experience, cultural rules, moral impulses . . . all those things go into the hopper," I said. "The brain parts solve the equation of what to do—that's what we *call* a decision, but it's really just an answer. And each answer is input to the next equation. In fact, each answer changes the brain itself in minute ways, strengthening some connections, weakening others. That's why people who think of the mind as software and the brain as hardware have it wrong—there's nothing but hardware, jolts of electricity running down the wires, building up a charge, waiting for that emotional trigger to be pulled. The gun fires itself."

"When you load it properly," Rovil said.

"This is madness," Ollie said. "We can't have people murdering each other and then say, too bad, can't do anything about it, no one fired the gun."

"I never said that. We punish the gun."

"What?"

"The gun is collectively responsible," I said. "It's like Congress, or a corporation. And when the gun breaks the rules, society punishes it."

"But that's not fair," Ollie said. "The gun's just doing what it was primed to do."

"Maybe we've gone off track with the gun analogy," I said.

"No, stick with it. *Bang.* The gun fires, and kills someone."

"Okay, yes."

"And then we put it in the electric chair," she said.

"Yes," I said.

"How is that fair?! We don't execute mentally retarded people."

"Except in Georgia," Rovil said.

"Those are retarded guns," I said. "We're talking about fully functioning, complex guns that have the power to process all the information available. That includes the rules of society. That information about what's 'good' and 'bad' is data the brain needs to make its decision. The next gun that comes along might think differently."

"I can't agree with this," Ollie said. "You may be right about how the brain works, but I don't want to live in a world where no one's responsible."

"I keep saying, we *are* responsible, just not in the way—"

"Stop," Ollie said. "Please stop." She took her hand from mine and looked out the passenger window.

I noticed Rovil looking at me in the rearview mirror, his eyebrows raised questioningly. I shook my head. I'd thought I was distracting her, relieving the tension, but I'd only packed the powder a little tighter.

- - -

We pulled off the interstate at Amarillo, short of the New Mexico border, an hour before sundown. It was Saturday night, and the instructions had been to wait until at least Sunday. I wanted to do the last leg of the trip so that we arrived at Edo's place in daylight.

We found a motel a quarter mile from the interstate. When we stepped out of the refrigerated capsule of the car, the heat slammed us. We'd left spring up north; Texas was well into summer.

Rovil bought his dinner from a vending machine and said he wanted to hole up in his room and do work, leaving Ollie and me to find supper on our own. We started walking toward the nearest restaurant on our maps, and immediately began to sweat. In two blocks we reached La Cantina, a rundown brick building squatting between a Discount Gas & Liquor Drive Thru and a shop with a sign that said simply INCOME TAX.

Ollie thought the place looked sketchy, but I argued that it was impossible to get bad Mexican in Amarillo. And yet: enchiladas microwaved to hell, salsa from a can, Velveeta cheese coating everything. Only tequila could have saved the meal. Ollie, however, seemed to barely notice the food; her eyes were tracking the restaurant staff and the handful of other customers. She would not be surprised by the cowboy again.

She stayed on guard after we returned to the motel. She sat on the bed, turned sideways so she could watch the door, her pen screen unfurled across her lap. I was on my own pen, watching a free version of *Pride and Prejudice*. I flashed on a memory of Mikala and me lying beside each other like this, our minds somewhere else, our bodies touching, while we wondered whether certain cells were dividing and growing inside my body.

I said to Ollie, "I'm going to check on Rovil."

She started to get up, and I said, "Please. Stay here. I'll be back in a few minutes."

Her eyes narrowed.

"Don't let the Clarity get the best of you," I said.

She didn't like this, but she let me go. Outside I half expected Dr. Gloria to be waiting for me with a disapproving frown on her face, but no.

Rovil's room was to the left. I turned right, toward town. It was 9:40. I had twenty minutes to make it. It should be plenty of time, but I walked fast just in case. The night was still alarmingly muggy, and by the time I reached the Discount Gas & Liquor, sweat was rolling down my ribs.

The sign on the door said 10AM-10PM MON-SAT. I was there with minutes to spare.

I walked the aisles, considering the rows of glass bottles. Not a big bottle, I decided. Just enough to get me through the night. I circled back to the front of the store. The pocket sizes were on the shelf behind the cash register. The clerk was an old Latino with wild tufts of gray hair. His eyes tracked me from beneath the shelter of an imposing monobrow.

After a minute he said, "We are closing."

"I know, I know."

"Are you buying or not?"

"Just relax, okay? I'm deciding."

He stared at me.

"Smirnoff is on sale," he said.

"I fucking hate Smirnoff's."

Another minute passed.

"Wild Turkey?" he asked.

"Jesus fucking Christ!" I said.

I stalked out. The skies were as empty as my hands.

. . .

The human egg is a Mrs. Bennet, desperate to marry off her daughters. She starts life with as many chromosomes as any other cell in the body, but when hormones sound the alert she divides herself, making poor little daughter cells, impoverished things with only one set of chromosomes, each in great need of a long-tailed prince to make her whole. The male germline cells were just as desperate. It is a truth universally acknowledged that a sperm must be in want of a matching strand of DNA.

Well, fuck Mr. Darcy, and his sperm too. A couple of eggs could do the job on their own, thanks to modern science.

Mikala and I decided to make a child out of only ourselves, pairing up two half sets of chromosomes. The process was a few years old, created by a (female) scientist in Melbourne, Australia. It could create only daughters—and debt. The $85,000 bill was not covered by any insurance and was definitely not something Mikala could ask her family for. We emptied our savings and cashed in our 401ks, gambling on a long shot. The success rate was somewhere below thirty percent. But we were optimists.

Both of us became pre-pregnant together. We gave each other shots of Follistim to stimulate our follicles and Cetrotide to stem the tide of ovulation. And when it came time to mix our eggs, we flew to Australia, and in a hotel room loaded up the so-called "trigger shot" of chemicals extracted from the urine of pregnant women. We giggled and made jokes about pissed-off fat ladies. Then we counted to three and pulled the trigger together.

They put us under during the egg extraction. By the time we awoke in adjoining recovery rooms, our sides aching from the puncture wounds of long needles, the lab techs were already at work, trying to get our girls to pair up: one set of chromosomes from Mikala's eggs, one set from mine. Twenty-nine of these hybrid eggs fertilized. The doctors chose the dozen best prospects and put the second-stringers in the freezer. Then, on the third day, a catheter slid into my vagina and shot the lucky eggs into my uterus. The catheter, satisfied, immediately dozed off.

We flew home. For the next two weeks Mikala and I waited for an egg to implant and start growing into our girl. We were so nervous. We'd traveled so far, and sacrificed so much, that we could not admit that we'd made a terrible mistake.

I don't know now whether Mikala even wanted children. She told me she did, but it was clear to both of us that my desire for a child far outstripped hers. I was older, and my longing bordered on a biological imperative. For a long time I thought that she went through the process with me—shot by shot, appointment by appointment, over the course of a year—to make me happy. But that wasn't it, exactly. She wanted to *prove* she could make me happy. Mikala did not permit herself to fail at anything.

As for me, I powered forward on the plan with the certainty that a child would be the final catalyst to bind us together permanently, the last link in the benzene ring. Those two weeks after the implantation were the happiest I'd experienced in a long time, and the most nerve-racking. On several nights, Mikala and I fell asleep holding hands.

Then, nothing happened.

All but one of the eggs failed to implant, and that sole survivor clung to the placental wall for days before, inexplicably, letting go. They'd warned us that pregnancy was unlikely. We were scientists, and understood statistics. But the loss struck me like a judgment, like its own proof.

I went into mourning, but I didn't recognize it as that. I took a job as a fixed-term instructor at Loyola and stopped coming to Little Sprout. The lab didn't need me, and neither did Mikala. She'd become consumed by NME 110.

This latest iteration was performing amazingly well in animal tests. The rats refused to die or develop tumors, and in fact were prospering. They were happy, energetic, and smart. Memory tasks, especially visual memory, became trivial for them. They navigated mazes as if someone were whispering in their ear.

Months after, when it was too late, I realized that Mikala had been in mourning too. I understood why, when she saw those happy rats, she tried the drug, and why, after she had tasted it, she decided to use it again. Just a little touch of the God. A glow that told you that you weren't alone, that you were connected with all living things. And once that door to Heaven opened a crack, who could blame her for pushing it wide?

It was in February that I went out to dinner with Edo—without Mikala or Gil. Edo was excited about the progress with NME and wanted to sell; he'd already entered talks with Landon-Rousse and Kensington, Inc. Gil was ready to cash out, but Mikala and I had always said that we would remain in control of the intellectual property. We'd lease development and manufacturing rights, but the IP remained with us—even if it cost us millions in lost revenue. When we first enlisted Edo he'd said he was fine with this, but that was when our chance of success had been minuscule. I think he always assumed that if Little Sprout produced something viable, he could talk us into selling.

And he was right.

"The marriage is over," I told him.

Edo expressed shock, then sympathy. He was always good at social niceties. But he was a businessman first, and immediately understood what this meant for him. He tried hard to tamp down his excitement. "Of course you must take care of yourself," he said. "Do you think this would change Mikala's mind—make her vote with us?"

"Never."

Edo nodded. He had expected this answer. It did not change his plans, however; with my vote we did not need Mikala's.

"I need a favor," I said.

"Of course," Edo said. He knew I'd demand something for my agreement, because that's what he would have done. I told him the amount I needed to borrow from him, and that I needed it now.

"May I ask what for?" he said.

"Ransom money," I said. He laughed, thinking I was joking.

Edo sent me the paperwork the next day. He was too much of a shark to trust our deal to a handshake. In return for the loan, I gave him the right to vote as my proxy, without relinquishing any IP rights. The money immediately transferred to my account. Two days after that I paid for the release of seventeen frozen eggs.

· · ·

I woke to a hand shaking me. "Trouble," a voice said.

"Gloria?" The room was dark, but the angel glowed with artificial light. "You came back." It was embarrassing how happy I was to see her.

"It's Ollie," she said, and pointed toward the bathroom. A sliver of light shone at the bottom of the door.

I sat up, pawed for the clock, finally lifted it in both hands: 2:45 a.m.

"Ollie?" I called. I pulled myself out of bed and made my way to the bathroom door. "You all right?"

Ollie said something I couldn't catch. The door was unlocked. I pushed it open and squinted against the light.

She sat on the edge of the tub, arms on her bare legs, staring hard at the floor. She'd laid out scraps of toilet paper. No, not scraps, *shapes*: stars, squares, triangles, cigar rolls. She'd arranged them on the tile in the small space according to a scheme I didn't understand.

"Whatcha doing, sweetie?" I asked gently. It was the voice you'd use on a growling dog as you reached for the door.

"I'm your gun," she said without looking up.

"What?"

"You brought me here to kill Edo."

"What? No!"

She looked me in the eye. "Of course you did. You got me out of the hospital and brought me here and loaded me up with *clues*—and now you're going to aim me at him. Bang. You get the girl, and I go to jail. But no one can put this on you, because I *chose* to shoot."

"That's crazy."

"Then what's the plan?" Ollie asked. "What are you going to do when you meet him? What are you going to do with the girl?"

"I don't know! There *is* no plan."

"You're lying. You know what I used to do. You brought me here to do it again."

"I don't know what you used to do—you never told me."

She squinted at me. She opened her backpack and brought out a silver pistol with a black grip.

"Jesus, what are you—?"

"This is a Sig Sauer P226 with an E-squared grip. It's my favorite side-arm. I've had it since Toronto."

I didn't know what was more alarming, that she had a gun, or a favorite.

"It's that she's got a gun," Dr. Gloria said.

"I don't blame you for bringing me," Ollie said. "You were probably afraid that you wouldn't have the strength to do it when the time came." She smiled tightly. "I can be your strength."

"Look, sweetie . . . no." I leaned toward her. "That's not what I—"

Ollie put her hand on the gun. I sat back on my heels.

"You're scaring me," I said.

"I don't mean to."

"Have you taken your meds?"

"Don't condescend to me."

"I think it's time to take those pills."

"That's not an option right now," Ollie said. "It's too dangerous. The cowboy is still out there. Edo has your daughter. Rovil could be working with Edo, or with Gil. The text message could be a trap. They could be trying to get you out there in the desert and—"

"Hon, please . . ." I held out my hands, palms up. Nothing to fear from me. "I need you to stay here tomorrow."

She looked shocked. "I'm not leaving you."

You're already gone, I thought.

I couldn't call the police or we all went home. I couldn't call 9-1-1 to have her committed, because *they* would call the police. But if she got in that car tomorrow, someone would die. I just wasn't sure who.

I covered my face with my hands. I might have been praying.

"Give me the words," I said to Dr. Gloria.

"There's got to be another way," the angel said. "If you do this to her—"

"I'll make it up to her later."

"There may not be a later. If she loses trust in you, then she's got no one."

"Give me the words."

Dr. Gloria removed her glasses. I'd never seen her tear up before. She cleared her throat and said, "I don't love you."

"What else?" I asked the doctor.

"I will never love you."

I began to speak. I laid out the words the doctor had given me like scalpels. I convinced Ollie that she'd been lying to herself, that I found it kind of *sad* that she thought just because we had sex and shared a few late-night conversations, that I'd told her things I'd never told anyone else—that somehow that *meant* something. Her damaged brain had taken a few bits of data and strung them into the story she wanted to hear—a fairy tale.

It was not as hard to convince her as I would have thought. Ollie already suspected that I did not love her. She'd invented a dozen conspiracies to explain why I came for her, why I stayed with her. After only thirty minutes of tears and yelling and icy insults, she threw on her clothes and slammed the motel door behind her.

I'd won.

I'd won.

CHAPTER TWENTY-TWO

The two men kneeling in the cornfield weren't scared, despite the hoods and the plasticuffs and the near certainty that they were about to die. The Vincent had gotten used to this stoicism by now. He'd been on the trail for two weeks and had interrogated so many of these pastors and deacons of the Church of the Hologrammatic God, each one calmer and more pain-resistant than the last, that he was getting bored. It was a necessary job, like branding cattle, but it wasn't exactly rocket science.

The original assignment had been to follow Lyda Rose and engage in heavy conversation with whomever gave her the drug. That had led him to the first church and that Mexican pastor, then into the woods of Cornwall Island for the most confusing dead end of his career: fake cops, fake smugglers, and two teenage Afghan gangsters. A circus.

He'd been worried about Lyda's ex-Special Forces, ex-SIGINT sidekick. He'd known a lot of those folks back when he worked with the government, and some of them were Goddamn nuts. He didn't recognize the name or face of the woman—Olivia Skarsten was probably as fake as his own new name—but they'd probably known some of the same people. Those social circles weren't all that damn big.

If he'd had his druthers he would have shot Rose

and Skarsten both, just because they'd seen his face, but the employer had given him clear orders on how to handle them. He was forced to let them escape.

He had his own trail to follow. He found the second church in Toronto just by asking around. It wasn't that hard; the thing about evangelicals is that they really wanted you to come to church. He also changed his interrogation method. He didn't have to spend all night coercing some martyr who believed Jesus was perched on his shoulder. He just had to spend one hour coercing *two* guys.

That led him, eventually, to Detroit, the kookiest damn city he'd ever visited. It was the first time he'd seen abandoned homes and decrepit skyscrapers alongside acres of fresh farmland, all part of some inner-city rejuvenation project to turn the industrial revolution inside out. Hell, maybe even white people would come back to the city. That would take some doing, but it would happen. The government was broke, and there was plenty more cheap land to buy. A man could raise cattle out here. Of course that man would have to get over his agoraphobia and panic attacks, and maybe buy the upgraded bison that were as big as Saint Bernards, but it was doable. Perhaps even Vinnie and the Vincent could work together. Rancher and Gunslinger, working side by side.

The pair of true believers he was currently in dialog with were cut from the same cloth as the others he'd talked to. The senior pastor was another hardcore gangbanger with a long record. The Vincent bet that if he looked into it, the pastors had probably served time together. This one had gotten out of the federal prison only last year and moved to the Motor City. The sidekick was a local with tracks on his arm. That pattern held up, church to church. Ex-gangleaders in charge, with a congregation of junkies, prostitutes, bums, and lowlifes. It made a certain kind of sense; religion was most needed by the most desperate, and these folks were on the lowest rung of society, what his grandmother used to call "the least of these."

Except that's not what the Vincent's employer expected. Someone, somewhere, was supposed to have a connection to a pharmaceutical company.

"You're the one, aren't you?" the senior pastor said. No trace of anger or fear. His name was Arun, and according to his prison records his religion was Nation of Islam. That file, obviously, was out of date. "You're behind the disappearances."

Rumors are spreading, the Vincent thought. He said, "Aw, you don't want to know me, Arun. I take off them hoods then you know what I got to do."

Both of them assured him that they would tell him nothing, regardless. Then the Vincent looped a cord around the young one's neck and let the pastor listen to him gargle for a while. He released his grip before the boy expired.

This was his new method. These Holo-Jesus freaks were tough as nails alone, but they had an overreactive sense of empathy. Just crumbled when someone else was in pain. So you nabbed two of them and started slapping around the least knowledgeable one.

Right on cue, the pastor said, "Please, he doesn't know anything."

"But you do," the Vincent said.

In a matter of minutes—and a few more strangulations—Arun was spilling details. That empathy is a bitch, the Vincent thought. Like a puppet show—put your hand on one, and the other one talks. The Vincent made him answer all the questions in his employer's questionnaire, then they moved on to the important topics, like who was providing them with precursor packs and hardware.

The Vincent's pen buzzed. He flicked it open. "Hey there, boss."

His employer was not happy. The Vincent was taking too long, and he still hadn't found out where the chemjets were being made, and what pharmaceutical company was supplying them.

"I've got some good news and bad news on that front," the Vincent said. "I'm staring at a couple of guys who were building a printer." In the basement of the church the Vincent had found not one printer, but three of them, and the second two only partly assembled. There were stacks of new machine parts still in their packing, and tools and soldering irons on the workbench. "They had enough to build four, maybe five of them.

"The bad news is that there's no way they could be building all of 'em, not even all the ones I've found. Strictly a small-scale operation. So that means other people are making them, too."

His employer wanted to know whether he'd found the assembly instructions, and the Vincent said they were on the pastor's phone. "I'm working on tracking down where that came from, too. But like I told you, these guys are organized like terrorists cells—they don't know much but the one or two fellas they talk to in the other churches. I think we got to consider the possibility that there ain't no factory, and there ain't no central leadership. I just don't think there's a Big Pharm company pulling the strings."

The employer started yelling then, and the Vincent pulled the pen away from his ear. When his tone finally changed the Vincent said, "Sorry, what were you saying?"

More yelling. The Vincent didn't let it bother him. Finally the employer settled down and gave him an address. The Vincent thought, New Mexico?

The rest of the instructions were explicit. "Just to be clear," the Vincent said. "No restrictions on Rose and Skarsten?" He was surprised at the change, but relieved. He wouldn't have to go behind his employer's back to get rid of witnesses.

"One more thing," the Vincent said. "I'm running a mite low." He did not have to say its name aloud; the employer understood that when the Vincent brought up amounts he was talking about not cash but Evanimex. There were several knockoff street drugs—Brick, Darwin, HooDoo— that purported to provide the same effect and that he could have purchased himself. But he'd tried all those, and there was no comparison; Evanimex, the pure pharmaceutical product, was the only guaranteed solution. He'd first tried it several years ago when the government treated him for PTSD. It had worked well—so well that he never wanted to go back to his old self.

The problem, of course, was tolerance. Take the drug too often and it wouldn't have any effect at all. So, he rationed. He used it for work first and daily phobia-management second. The rest of the time he tried to distract himself with his hobby.

His employer told him that he'd already shipped the latest package of pills.

"That doesn't do me much good out here on the road," the Vincent said. "I've got enough for about a week, then—"

The employer told him he'd be done in a week, and hung up.

The Vincent stared at the pen for a moment, imagining a few things he would like to do to his employer.

"I'd like you to consider something," Arun said. Again, calm as a houseplant. He was a smart guy; he knew that now that he'd heard the Vincent's conversation, and heard those names, there was no way he was living through the next fifteen minutes. Still he didn't lose his composure.

"And what would that be?" the Vincent asked. He reached into his pocket for another set of plasticuffs.

"You have our printers; you have our paper," the pastor said. "After you're done here, find a quiet place, and just try one of the Logos pages."

"I will give it to you boys," the Vincent said. "Every one of ya's tried to witness to me."

"Just consider it," the pastor said. "You'll thank me for it."

"I sure do appreciate your concern, Arun," the Vincent said. He looped the cuff around the man's neck and cinched it tight. Arun fell onto his stomach and began to flop around. The sidekick heard all this and started crying. "Arun? Arun?" The Vincent lassoed him too and put him down.

No restrictions, the Vincent thought. Maybe he really would be home in a week. It sure would be good to get out of all these shitty hotel rooms. And Vinnie would be happy to get another turn at the wheel. Jesus, he loved those stinking little buffalos.

CHAPTER TWENTY-THREE

The sun hammered the freeway, turning the air above it to jelly. Still we three pushed on—Rovil, Dr. Gloria, and I—Tint Shields on full, air-conditioning turned up to eleven. Rovil tried to chat, but I had become hazardous cargo, silent and toxic. Ollie had vanished. That morning I'd tried to call her pen, but she didn't answer, and the desk clerk claimed to have no idea who I was talking about.

I felt like shit.

Rovil couldn't believe we were leaving without her, but I told him to keep out of it, letting him think Ollie and I had split over some female relationship thing he'd never understand. "She's just cooling off. She'll be fine. Ollie's, like, hypercompetent."

He looked worriedly out at the motel parking lot and said, "I suppose."

"You're still my pal, right, Rovil? You're still with me on this?"

Rovil breathed out. "Sometimes I think you don't need a friend so much as chauffeur."

"A chauffeur would quit."

That got a smile out of him. "Look, I know I'm an asshole," I said. "But we're almost there, kid—a few hours from Emerald City. Just take me the rest of the way."

He relented, and after a couple of hours on the

road he'd dropped the worried pout. He listened to his music, a grating form of Indonesian pop, and when we crossed the border into New Mexico he set the car to auto and let go of the steering wheel, excited to finally be in a state that allowed autonomous cars—proof that there was as much joy in surrendering free will as exercising it.

Sometime after 2 p.m. we left the interstate, and Rovil took the wheel again. Los Lunas was a surprisingly green town on the Rio Grande, with lawns and trees living the high life off the river. The car's GPS led us confidently out of town along Highway 6, west into the desert, through brown, rolling hills. Then we left the highway for a smaller road, then exited that one as well. Each turn seemed to lead us onto narrower, sketchier roads until finally a white cement drive appeared on our right. A black steel gate blocked it, and bleached stone fences curved away in both directions.

Rovil stopped the car. "Are you okay?" he asked.

"Fine." I was sweating in the cold air-conditioning, every pore open. I tried to think of something to say. "Hell of a driveway."

The road ran for five miles and ended in a cul-de-sac. According to the satellite pictures there was a cluster of buildings at the end of the road, but their details were obscured in a cloud of fuzzy pixels; the rich could afford privacy agreements.

"He owns everything within ten miles of the compound," Rovil said. He rolled up to the gate and the entry panel.

Dr. Gloria said to me, "Put your head down."

"What?" I couldn't concentrate.

"Cameras," she said, and nodded toward the gates. "It's what Ollie would have had you do."

"Jesus, how could cameras make a difference? Edo knows we're coming. He *invited* us."

Rovil had rolled down the window. I started to tell him the gate code that had been in the text message, but he said "I remember" and typed it in.

The gates slid open. We rolled through, started to pick up speed, and I said, "Wait. Pull over. *Now.*"

He stopped the car and I jumped out. I marched across the pebbled ground toward a set of boulders, toward a clump of gnarled bushes, toward . . . fuck. Nowhere. Into the heat. Sweat poured from my face and dried almost instantly.

I stopped in front of a large juniper bush. Its limbs were gray as old bones. The plants around it were equally dead and strange, a cohort of parched alien bodies buried standing up. Humans didn't belong out here.

Dr. Gloria descended from the sky and landed upon an Old Testament-quality boulder.

"You have absolutely no idea what's going on in your own brain, do you?"

"Not now, Gloria."

"Would you like me to explain?"

"I would like you to *explain* what the hell Edo's doing out here in the middle of nowhere."

"I like the desert," she said.

"It's the fucking waiting room of the apocalypse. In a hundred years half the planet's going to look like this. So, what, he just had to get a preview?'

"You could have stayed with her," Dr. Gloria said. "Called off this trip until she could come with you."

"What do you do if you want to run out for milk?" I said. "How long do you have to wait for a fucking ambulance out here?"

"I'm concerned that you're thinking of ambulances," she said.

"I'm concerned that I have not punched you in the fucking throat."

"You love her," Dr. Gloria said. "Maybe you should admit that."

"Why, exactly, did I want you to come back?" I turned back toward the car and was surprised to see that it was more than a football field away, American *or* Canadian rules. Rovil leaned against the fender, gazing out at the landscape, watching me but pretending not to. When I started walking back he casually got back inside the car.

Minutes later I dropped into the front passenger seat. "Sorry," I said to him. "Mexican food." He nodded as if he believed me and handed me a bottle of water. I drank half of it in two long swallows.

We zipped along the white road for several minutes. The air-conditioning triggered something in my body, and another tide of sweat swept out of me. I felt like I was being wrung out: cell walls rupturing, epidural levees crumbling, veins—

"Now you're being melodramatic," Dr. Gloria said.

A figure appeared ahead of the car, walking toward us in the middle of the road. It was a man, wearing shorts but naked from the waist up, tall and broad with a big gut. A floppy hat obscured his face.

Rovil slowed the car. We stopped when the man was perhaps thirty yards from us. He stopped walking and peered at the darkened windshield.

Rovil glanced at me.

"Yeah," I said. "It's him."

I got out of the car again. Dr. Gloria alighted by the side of the road.

"Edo," I said.

Edo Anderssen Vik stood up straighter. "*Lyda?*" He took off his hat. "Lyda Rose!"

I walked toward him. Behind me, Rovil got out of the car.

"And *Rovil?*" Edo said. Again completely surprised. "This is amazing!" A bad thought occurred to me: Edo was not only God-drunk, he was afflicted with Alzheimer's.

He stepped toward me, arms wide for a hug, and I stepped back. Edo dropped his arms, confused, the hat forgotten in his hand. His round gut looked permanently red; his chest was covered by a mat of white hair.

Rovil moved up and shook Edo's free hand. "How are you doing, Mr. Vik?"

"Rovil, please, you're not an intern anymore. Call me Edo." He looked from Rovil to me, still grinning. "What are you doing here?"

"We got your text," I said.

He frowned, not understanding. Then he glanced up. He listened for a moment, then nodded. Someone was speaking to him from the sky.

"Ah," he said. "Of course." He looked back the way he'd come, then said, "The house is just down the road. Lyda, will you walk with me? It's less than a mile."

I said to Rovil, "I promise to be good."

"I'll follow in the car," he said.

"Closely," Dr. Gloria told him, but of course he couldn't hear her.

· · ·

We walked for a while, Dr. Gloria trailing me like my maid of honor, the car creeping along behind her.

"You're a hard man to find," I said.

Edo laughed. "I suppose so."

"We've been trying for weeks," I said. "We even tried to see you in Chicago, but Eduard cut us off."

"He did?" Edo looked upset. "But of course. I suppose he'd be very upset if he found out you were here."

"So he's not home."

"Oh no. He and his wife left last night for Amsterdam." He smiled. "Nick of time, eh? Otherwise . . . whoosh. He'd run you off."

"What's he so afraid of?"

He thought for a moment and said, "A few years ago I was in my car, and I saw a man by the side of the road. It was very cold out. He was holding a cardboard sign that said HUNGRY. Just that one word." He shook his head as if seeing it for the first time.

"I felt that hunger myself, Lyda. I felt like I was starving, that I was going to die. Is it like that for you? I could feel his weakness, how cold he was. I told the driver to stop. I gave the man my jacket. I took off my shoes. Then I gave him my wallet, and a smartcard that had access to my accounts. I even tried to give him the car!"

He chuckled. "My driver tried to stop me, but what could he do? I was his boss. In any case the man was too frightened by me to accept the car, or my clothing. He took my card, though." He laughed again.

"My son heard what happened. The driver told him. Eduard took away my access—to my money first, then my company, then to anyone I used to work with. I kept trying to help people, give them what they needed. I couldn't be trusted, he said. If I fought him, he would have me committed." Edo shrugged. "Given my history, I knew this was no idle threat, eh? And I couldn't afford to let that happen. So we moved out here. Oh, I travel when necessary. But Eduard only lets me see a few members of the board, and key customers who insist on meeting me, and I *must* follow the script. Because if I don't—"

He stopped suddenly and put a hand to his face. He was overcome with some intense emotion: sadness, grief? I couldn't tell. Something in the Numinous had made Edo into an empathic wreck. No wonder his son had isolated him.

I said, " 'Give everything to the poor and you will have treasure in Heaven.' "

"I'm sorry?" Edo said. His cheeks were wet with tears.

"The Bible story," I said. "Rich man, the eye of the needle . . . ?"

He still didn't know what I was talking about. What kind of know-nothing god possessed him? "The rich man goes away sad," I said. "He loves money too much to get into Heaven."

Edo nodded. "Sounds like my son."

The sun beat down. I could barely breathe, but Edo seemed to soak it in. During the trial he'd described his god as a great pulsing ball of light and heat, a flame that surrounded him but did not burn him. He was his own burning bush.

We eventually reached the compound. There were three buildings: a sprawling, two-story Spanish-style house; a four-bay garage; and, farther back, another adobe-walled building that could have been a guest house or offices. Rovil parked the car in the circle drive.

Edo stepped up to the front door, then realized I wasn't following.

"I should have told you," he said. "I was afraid."

"You were afraid? Of me?"

"I was afraid you'd take her away."

He opened the door. After a moment I followed him in. The foyer felt like an icebox. A dark-haired woman appeared from a far doorway and stopped, startled to see someone with Edo. She was even more surprised when Rovil stepped into the doorway. "Mr. Vik, how did—?"

"These are friends of mine," Edo said. "Esperanza, this is Lyda Rose and Rovil Gupta." Somewhere in the distance was a bass beat of music, and I was ninety percent sure that I wasn't imagining it.

Esperanza nodded at us, then handed Edo a white towel and a sport shirt. "Sasha's still in her room?" Edo asked her.

Dr. Gloria put a hand on my elbow. I became aware of the tightness in my chest, my tripping heartbeat.

Edo tugged the shirt down over his gut. "This way." He led us into a vast, airy room. The ceiling slanted up to a peak thirty feet above us. A huge stone fireplace filled one wall, and a staircase led up to a railed balcony and the second-floor rooms. The sturdy furniture, I was pretty sure, had been constructed from the hulls of eighteenth-century battleships, then upholstered in buttery, deep-brown leather that could only be obtained from cows fattened on foie gras.

"Tell Rovil," Dr. Gloria said. "*This* is how you decorate a house."

Edo led us through an archway to a long corridor. The door at the end of the hall was ajar. The music blared from there, a heavy funk beat under a massive horn section. It sounded like a New Orleans marching band that had added a rank of synthesizers.

"Ten years old, and already a teenager," Edo said, grinning. I could barely hear him. My eyes were fixed on the wedge of sunlight spilling from that door. A shadow flickered there, and I sucked in my breath.

Edo reached the door and pushed it open. The room was large and bright with windows on two sides, the desert sunlight blasting in. A skinny girl with a wild nimbus of red-brown hair danced in the corner of the room where the windows met, her back to us. She wore a lime-green T-shirt, multicolored tights, and a Hawaiian grass skirt. In front of her stood a large easel with a rectangle of white paper bigger than she was, three feet wide and four tall. The easel's tray was full of liquid paints in shallow plastic cups. She held a paintbrush in each hand like drumsticks, dancing and painting at the same time, her little booty shaking that skirt, hands swiping and stabbing at the paper, throwing down colors.

She spun around, skirt fanning, droplets of paint flying—and stopped cold. She was a cartoon of shock: mouth agape, eyes wide, arms outstretched. No one moved for a long second.

Then something broke inside me. A bark escaped my body, a wild laugh, and then the laughter kept coming, tumbling out of me. My knees weakened and I nearly lost my balance. The dancing, the grass skirt, those *paintbrushes*!

I couldn't stop laughing. Tears filled my eyes. The girl looked stricken, which only made the moment more hilarious. I didn't know what was happening to me. My stomach began to cramp.

The girl looked up at Edo, then back to me. I kept thinking, She dances. My daughter dances!

I was past hilarity now and deep into some unlabeled emotional state, something roaring and chaotic. How does a wave feel when it crashes into the beach?

The girl (*my daughter, my daughter who dances*) stared up at me. She smiled tentatively, set the wet brushes on the floor, and touched my elbow. Dr. Gloria stood behind her, hands on her hips, waiting patiently for me to recover. Edo walked to the wall and did something that silenced the music.

I wiped at my eyes. "Whoa," I said. I smiled to reassure the girl.

Rovil stared at me. "Are you okay?"

I had no idea *what* I was. Edo, though, seemed unperturbed. "Sasha," he said, "this is Lyda Rose."

She held out her hand. So polite. I took a stuttering breath, then took her hand in both of mine. I pumped officiously. "Pleased to meet you, Sasha."

She nodded, equally mock-formal, in on the joke.

Edo said to Sasha, "Do you know who this is?"

She was staring at my hand. My left hand. Then she pirouetted away from me. The room was huge, much larger than the bedroom I'd grown up in. The queen-size bed was unmade, the bedclothes a riot of pinks and greens. Every wall that wasn't a window was covered with her paintings and drawings. There were charcoal pieces like the one Eduard Jr. had shown me in Chicago, and pieces done in marker, but most were paintings on pages the size of the one on the easel, singing with color. The paintings looked like random swirls and stripes, but I began to see figures in them: an alligator in a red-checked suit; a fat woman holding a pink parasol; a parrot wearing a top hat, hiding in a tree. The pirate bear was a frequent subject—and there was the toy itself, a stuffed bear half buried in the sheets and blankets.

Sasha crouched and reached under the bed. She brought out a rolled-up page, then looked over her shoulder at me. I went to her and helped her unroll it.

In the center were two figures, holding hands. One woman was tall and thin with an imperious afro; the other shorter but with wild red hair that spiked in all directions like flames. Their outside hands were waving at us. The paint was bright, the paper unwrinkled. I thought it must be a recent piece.

Sasha reached for my left hand. She lifted it up so she could touch the ring there. Then she reached inside the neck of her shirt and drew out a necklace. Dangling from the end of it was a benzene ring—Mikala's ring.

"I think she knows," Dr. Gloria said.

· · ·

Sasha took us on a tour first of her room, showing us her artwork and toys, then of the entire house, then outside to the pool and the rock garden and the sprawling vegetable garden, where three Hispanic men in long-sleeved shirts were assembling aluminum sprinkler frames. They greeted her in Spanish, and she made Edo introduce me and Rovil. Then it was into the huge garage, where Sasha demonstrated her skill with a device that looked like a cross between a skateboard and a teeter-totter. I could not even stand up on the thing. Sasha kept trying to coach me, putting her hands on my shins and ankles, but I was hopeless. Finally she flicked open a digital fan and shook it at me until I understood that she wanted me to take out my pen.

I produced mine and she tapped it, not with her fan, but with her finger. A message appeared: *Stand on the dots!*

Ah: the two orange circles on the toy's deck. I put one foot on one dot, stepped up—and the device shot out from under me. Edo caught me before I hit the ground. Sasha shook her head in mock disappointment.

My pen kept filling with messages from her. I couldn't see how she was typing—the fan wasn't even in her hand anymore. It was the closest thing to telepathy I'd ever seen. The fake mind readers in the NAT ward would have been so jealous.

We walked back to the house down a path made of pink gravel. Sasha was at my side, chattering away electronically. Rovil and Edo were up ahead, talking pharmaceutical biz.

"You sent that message to me, right?" I asked Sasha quietly. "The one telling me to come here?"

My pen flickered with a new message: *Are you mad?*

"No, I'm not mad," I said.

"Not in the way she meant, anyway," Dr. Gloria said. She was walking a few feet behind us, her hands clasped behind her back. She'd stayed within a dozen feet of me since we'd come through the gate, ready to swoop in as soon as I fell apart.

"Bug off," I told her.

You've got a friend. Like Grandpop.

I stopped. "You noticed that?" I asked Sasha.

I do too. Lots of them.

The pen slipped from my hand. Sasha crouched and picked it up. She opened the screen wide and held it up to me. The letters were blurry. I blinked until they came into focus.

That's okay. GP cries all the time too.

I said to Sasha, "I don't usually . . ." I cleared my throat. "I mean, twice in one day? I think it's the heat."

She nodded as if this made any kind of sense and pulled me toward the house. The rest of the group had gone inside and gathered in the enclosed sun porch. The room was positioned at the back of the house, facing the expanse of desert. Floor-to-ceiling windows let in maximum sunlight while the house's air-conditioning delivered maximum cold, a textbook example of the kind of have-your-cake-and-burn-it-too attitude that the über-rich specialized in. Fuck you, Mother Nature. I thought about saying something, and then Esperanza came into the room with cookies and lemonade. It's hard to be a militant liberal when you're being served kindergarten snacks.

My pen pinged. *We grow our own lemons!*

"They're great," I told Sasha.

Rovil had noticed this latest exchange. He leaned over and said to Sasha, "How long did it take you to train the network?"

The girl shrugged. I pushed my pen to him. It said, *It's still learning.*

"What's this networking thing?" I asked.

Edo nodded toward the ceiling. "The house is watching her. Fingers, gestures. Some of it's virtual keyboard, but some of it's body language. She's got her own dialect." He sounded proud.

Sasha nodded. The pen said, *Macros!!!*

Rovil said, "Why don't you just talk?"

Edo frowned. After a moment I said, "Rovil, Jesus . . ."

"What?" Rovil asked. Embarrassment has a frequency, like a dog whistle. Only some people can hear it.

The pen said, *Why should I?*

"Good point," I told Sasha.

Of course I was dying to know why she didn't speak. Eduard had said she was smart and artistic. Was the muteness congenital? Had the Numinous done this to her?

I said to her, "I need to talk to your . . . to Edo now. Adult talk."

Sasha looked offended. She flicked her eyes to the side, then up to Edo.

"Just for a little while," Edo said. "Go with Esperanza and pick out the best of your drawings. We can do an art show later."

Esperanza had appeared on cue. "Up you go," she said. Sasha grabbed two cookies and hopped from her chair.

"I hope you'll stay the night," Edo said.

"I don't think so," I said.

He frowned. "You should get to know her. She's a wonderful person."

"How impaired is she, Edo?"

"The speech issue? We're working on it. You have to believe me, we've consulted all the top specialists."

"That's what Eduard said. Great doctors. The best money could buy."

"It's true. But she is also *fine*." He leaned forward. "She's so smart, and funny, and gifted."

"She's not speaking, Edo. Do these *specialists* know why that is?"

He shook his head. "Her vocal cords work—I've heard her make sounds in her sleep. And it's obviously not comprehension—look at how she writes! But the MRIs show that her visual centers are hyperactive, firing all the time, as if she's constantly being bombarded with images."

"So something deep in the wiring," I said. "Something Numinous did to her."

Edo shook his head again. "You don't know that."

"Oh come on, Edo. Do you think that stuff is harmless?"

"I'm not saying that, but there may be . . . other reasons."

"Like what?" I said testily.

"I think there was a trauma at the foster home, before we adopted her."

He didn't speak for a moment. "What happened at the foster home, Edo?" My voice was flat.

"There was an accident," he said. "A houseparent fell down the stairs, ended up with a fractured disk. He blamed Sasha."

"A six-year-old girl," I said.

"She tripped him, he said."

"What did he do to her?"

He seemed not to understand me.

"She must have had a reason. Did he abuse her?"

His eyes widened. "No one suggested anything like that."

"It's a pretty common profile. A man—and they're almost all men—gets himself access to vulnerable children. Grooms them with gifts. Makes them dependent on him. He may even adopt them."

Edo looked at Rovil, then back to me, blinking hard. "That's not—you can't think—"

"What the fuck are you doing with my daughter, Edo?"

His eyes filled with tears. "No," I said. "No fucking tears."

Dr. Gloria said, "Keep your voice down."

I leaned across the table. "Why did you take her? What the fuck are you up to?"

Oh the tears, the tears, they were a-rolling down the motherfucker's face.

"I made a mistake," he said. "I thought she was *safe*, Lyda! The foster home was one of the best, very high-rated." He wiped tears from his cheeks. "Sasha had not yet been adopted, but that wasn't their fault. I swear that I thought she was in the best possible place."

"Except you were wrong."

"After the accident with that volunteer I realized that it would be better to get her out of there," Edo said. "I didn't think I would be approved as a parent, so . . ."

"You got Eduard and his wife to sign the papers."

"I was very insistent. I told him I would go to the press, even wreck the company if he didn't do this for me. I had to help her. He knew I was serious in this."

"So you hid her out here, away from the world, away from any other kids."

"That's because I live here, not because I'm hiding her. I told you, I made sure that she saw specialists—"

"She told me she has 'friends,' Edo."

He blinked. "Oh." He nodded. "You noticed the pictures in her room."

"Those are her gods?"

"Many of them," he said. "She has a whole pantheon."

"How many?" Rovil asked.

"We don't know," Edo said. "About a dozen. But she's stopped talking about them with the therapists."

"She's practically Hindu," Rovil said.

I silenced him with a look, then turned back to Edo. "Tell me what you did to her."

"I haven't done anything!" he cried.

"*Lyda*," Dr. Gloria said. "Not now."

I became aware of Sasha's quick footsteps, coming toward us. The girl popped into the room, a worried look on her face. She looked at me, then at Edo. She saw my anger, Edo's tears. Then she walked to Edo and leaned against him.

"It's okay," he told her. "You know how I get."

And I thought, She chose him.

. . .

Sasha pleaded with "Grandpop" to let us stay for supper, and if we were staying for supper, then to stay overnight. I was tempted to leave and come back in the morning, but I wasn't done with Edo yet. I didn't want to return to find the gate code changed and a cop waiting to hand me a restraining order.

We retrieved our bags from the car, and the maid led Dr. Gloria and me to a room done up in Mandatory Southwestern: wall-mounted cow skull, turquoise lamps, Navajo blankets. The doctor fell back onto the queen-size bed. "Authentic's the wrong word," she said. "Authentish?"

"Authentique," I said.

"Made in China," she said in a TV voice. "But with real American small-pox."

I unzipped my bag, looking for clothes fresh enough to change into. The doctor raised her head and said, "Ahem."

I turned. The maid still stood in the doorway. "I would like to know your intentions," she said.

"Excuse me?"

"Mr. Vik is a good man," she said. Her voice was clipped. "He loves the girl and has never done any harm to her. I am sure of it."

"Esperanza, don't get me wrong, but—"

She bristled. "I've taken care of Sasha since she entered this house. If you try to take her from here, you will destroy her."

"Notice she said 'from here' instead of 'from him,'" Dr. Gloria said.

"Okay then," I said to the maid. "I will be sure to keep that in mind."

Esperanza stood in the frame of the door, studying me coldly. Finally she turned and left.

I sat down on the edge of the bed. "Woof."

"She doesn't just take care *of* Sasha," Dr. Gloria said. "She cares *for* her."

"I know, I know," I said.

Dr. Gloria exhaled sleepily. After a while she said, "She's so pretty."

"I know."

I could see so much Mikala in her. Those cheekbones, those long limbs.

"But she has your nose," Dr. G said. "Your way of laughing."

"She doesn't make a noise," I said.

"You know what I mean," the angel said. "The way you throw your head back."

"I do no such thing." I looked around at the walls. Aloud, I said, "So where are the paintings?"

"Hmmm?" Dr. Gloria's eyes were closed.

"The paintings from Gil. Big paintings with bright orange colors, the ones that looked like plants. And machines. Ollie said they'd be in the house. We've been in all the *public rooms*, but we haven't seen them."

Dr. Gloria sat up on her elbows. "What are you doing? Why are you talking to me like that?"

"Just wondering aloud," I said.

CHAPTER TWENTY-FOUR

Who owns a house? The banks have one answer, the mortgage payers another. It's the houses, though, who decide who they're loyal to. Sometimes it's the carpenter who hoisted the walls and laid the beams, forever marking the house as his no matter who moves in after. Sometimes the house pledges fealty to the cleaning lady who each week carefully mops the floors and wipes the banisters. Some houses realize, not unhappily, that they belong to the termites who burrow into the walls and carry out their enthusiastic renovations. A house, after all, wants nothing more than to be lived in.

The big house in the desert had its own answer.

Sasha was seven years old when she began to talk to her house and teach it tricks. At first they were small stunts, like turning on lights when she flicked her fingers. But soon, after she discovered the network that controlled the wall screens and their built-in cameras and microphones and motion sensors, she taught it to wake up for her, and listen for her, and speak for her. Once she mastered the entertainment system, it was one small step to the thermostats and appliances and door locks, which greatly expanded the number of tricks the house could play *on* the people who lived with her.

But most of all, the house spied for her.

At bedtime on the night that Lyda Rose and Rovil Gupta came to visit, the house alerted her that Grandpop was heading toward her room. Sasha quickly hid the IF Deck beneath the bedcovers and picked up a book. Bucko the Pirate Bear sat beside her, mouthing the words.

Grandpop knocked and pushed open the door. "Ready for bed?"

She pretended to be engrossed in the book. Grandpop sat beside her, squashing Bucko between them, and peeked over her shoulder. "Ah, *The Phantom Tollbooth*. I should have guessed."

She read much more difficult books than this now, but it was *Tollbooth* that she kept always by her bed. It was one of the rare books that got funnier the more she read it.

"So," Grandpop said. "How long have you known about your mother?"

Sasha threw her words onto the wall: *Not long.* Then: *Are you angry with me?*

He laughed. "You should be angry at *me*. I planned to tell you. I didn't know when you'd be old enough to—no, that's not true."

Sasha flipped one palm. The wall said, *What?*

"I was going to say that I was waiting for you to be old enough to understand, but I think you've been ready for a long time."

But YOU weren't ready.

He laughed again. "So smart." She leaned against him. Bucko swore and made a strangled noise.

Grandpop said, "I suppose you know how your other mother died."

She nodded. *Looked it up.*

Grandpop's eyes turned shiny with new tears. Oops! She quickly fingertyped, *It's not a big deal!*

That was a lie. It was a very big deal. She'd found hundreds of articles about Little Sprout and what had happened in Chicago before she was born. Bucko thought it was the greatest story ever. Murder! Money! Madness! An R-rated thriller, with special appearance by Sasha Vik as the Fetus.

Grandpop was weeping openly now. "You must have lots of questions."

A couple.

Thousands, actually, but which ones could she ask? Most of what she knew she'd learned by eavesdropping and snooping. Why didn't Grandpop tell Lyda about adopting her? Why didn't Eduard want Grandpop talking to Lyda and Rovil? What was Eduard hiding in his study? And why was the man who murdered her mother sending friendly emails to Grand-pop?

I need some time to think, the wall said.

"You know you can talk to me any time," he said.

He tucked her in, then told her not to read too late, and carefully closed the door.

"*Finally,*" Bucko said. "That man's gotta lose some weight." Sasha fluffed up the bear and straightened him. He said, "Now?"

"Wait," she said. She pretended to read for exactly four minutes, then threw back the covers and slid into the nook between bed and wall, Bucko right behind her. With her finger she drew a circle on the wall and—abracadabra!—a magic mirror appeared there. She swiped and poked until she'd called up one of the views into the guest bedrooms.

Rovil Gupta, the Indian man, sat on his bed, still wearing all his clothes and even his shoes. He tapped at a slate whose screen Sasha could not quite make out from this angle. He was using the house's network to communicate, but all the data traffic was encrypted, so she had no idea what he was doing. After a minute he stood up, looked out the window, then sat down again.

"Booooring," Bucko said. "Let's see some boobies."

"That's my mother you're talking about," Sasha said. "Show some respect."

"Bio mom," Bucko said dismissively.

Sasha flipped the mirror to show the other guest room. Lyda Rose lay in the bed, the covers up to her neck, staring at the ceiling. The room was dark except for a bedside lamp that turned half her face to shadow. On her stomach was a page of white paper. Something was written on it in big block letters.

"Ooh, zoom in!" Bucko said.

The wall's cameras were pretty clumsy, and the light was not good, but she got a view of the page. On it were written the words, "WHERE ARE THE PAINTINGS FROM GILBERT KAPERNICKE?"

"What the fuck?" Bucko said.

Sasha quickly wiped away the mirror. "She knows we're spying! That message was to me!"

The bear burst into laughter. "Serves you right."

Sasha opened the mirror again, but only a few inches. Lyda Rose still lay on the bed, and the page hadn't moved. Could she see Sasha, too? No, if she'd hacked the house network, she wouldn't have needed a paper; she would have just sent the message to Sasha's room.

"She's talking about the paintings in Eduard's office," Sasha said.

"I figured that out, yeah," Bucko said. "I suppose this means . . ."

"That's right," Sasha said. "Emergency council meeting!"

· · ·

A little bit after three in the morning, the wall in the guest bedroom began to glow. When that failed to wake the woman in the bed, the house sounded a gentle *boop boop boop.* Too loud and others would hear; too soft and she'd sleep right through it.

Lyda Rose sat up suddenly. She looked first at a spot beside the bed and said, "What?" Then she noticed the wall and the flashing neon-green arrow pointing at the door. She laughed, a low chuckle.

"All righty then," she said, and moved to the door.

Back in her room, Sasha and Bucko exchanged a high five.

The rest of the IFs murmured or cheered or dinged according to their nature. Sasha had allowed nearly everyone out for the occasion: Mother Maybelle, Tinker, and Zebo, HalfnHalf and Elk Heart, the Snoring Man and MothCatcher and the rest, all of them huddled around the bed, while Squidly floated above them all, bobbing against the ceiling like a balloon. Only the Wander Man remained in the deck. He was buffered top and bottom by mundane cards, but Sasha could still feel his lean black presence, monitoring the proceedings, waiting for her to mess up.

"She's into the hallway," Bucko said.

Sasha lit up the next arrow, about five feet down the corridor. *This way, this way!* Lyda Rose shook her head in what looked like amusement or exasperation, but she followed the flashing symbols down the hallway, then to the great room. It was surprisingly well lit there. Moonlight poured through the big two-story windows, with extra illumination provided by the neon arrow prompting her to continue up the stairs. Lyda Rose looked down the hallway that led to Sasha's room, and for a tense moment Sasha thought she was going to march down that way . . . but then Lyda turned toward the arrow and went up the steps to the second-floor balcony.

At the top of the stairs Lyda stopped. There were two doors to her left and two to her right. The next arrow pointed left, but Lyda seemed unsure. Sasha flashed it more brightly. There were fewer wall screens up there, just a few patches here and there to host photographs and a virtual inter-com. The doors couldn't display anything at all. All she could do was keep strobing that one arrow, which Lyda seemed to ignore.

"What's Bio Mom doing *now?*" Bucko said.

Lyda went right. The first door was the guest bathroom, used by no one. She peeked inside and moved on. Then she came to the double doors that led to Eduard and Suzette's bedroom. She put her hand on the doorknob, but it was locked.

Lyda looked up at the ceiling, palms out: *Well?*

Sasha was not about to unlock the door. Lyda tried the door again.

"There's nothing in there," Bucko said. "Get her to turn around."

"How?" Sasha asked.

Fortunately, Lyda changed her mind. She spun about and walked back to the left . . . and passed the office door. She was headed straight for Grandpop's bedroom!

"Oh my stars and garters!" Mother Maybelle exclaimed.

Sasha quickly opened a new set of controls and typed *STOP!* The word appeared on the wall between the office door and Grandpop's room.

Lyda looked straight at the wall—which gave the illusion that she could see Sasha and was looking into her eyes. The woman's eyebrows were raised, and she wore a slight smile. Sasha suddenly realized that Lyda knew exactly what was happening and who was doing what.

"She's jerking you around!" Bucko said.

"Ah think it's Miss Rose who does not appreciate being 'jerked around,' " Zebo said in his deep alligator voice.

Sasha typed: *The office is open.* She'd unlocked it before she woke up Lyda for this treasure hunt. *I won't be able to see or hear you in there.* Sasha cleared the screen and typed a new line. *The paintings are leaning against the wall.*

Lyda saluted. Then she slipped into the office and closed the door.

"I hope I'm doing the right thing," Sasha said.

"It wasn't the most *straightforward* way to proceed," Zebo said. "But ah approve of any tactic which keeps you at arm's length from Eduard."

None of the Imaginary Friends were fans of her parents, though a few of them pitied Suzette. Their opinion on this newly discovered bio parent was divided. Could Lyda Rose be trusted? If she cared for Sasha, why hadn't she shown up before now?

One fact trumped everything: Lyda had her own IF. She was like Sasha, and Grandpop. That meant she already understood her in a way that Eduard and Suzette never could. Lyda would get to the bottom of what Eduard was up to, and Sasha would stay safely on the sidelines.

Ever since she'd discovered who Lyda Rose was, Sasha had nurtured a secret wish, a daydream really, which she so far had managed to keep from the IFs. That was no easy trick; they were an intuitive bunch, and Mother Maybelle especially was attuned to what Sasha was feeling. But Sasha held the dream inside her, and when no one was looking she lifted the lid to check on it:

Tomorrow, or the day after, Lyda moved into the big house in the desert, and there she lived with Sasha and Grandpop and Esperanza. Eduard and Suzette vanished off to London or New York or wherever it was that they *really* wanted to live, and Sasha was finally able to bring the IF Deck out into the open and talk to her friends whenever she wanted. Because Lyda wasn't just her birth mother, she was like Sasha and Grandpop, what he called "God-blessed." The three of them understood each other in a way that outsiders, alone in their heads with only their own voice to keep them company, never ever would. Oh, Esperanza *said* she knew exactly what was going on in Sasha's head, but she didn't, not really. Everything would finally be—

"Mother*fucker!*"

The shout came from the wall, which was still tuned in to the hallway outside Eduard's office, but it also traveled through real space and down the hallway to Sasha's room. In the magic mirror, Lyda Rose had stepped onto the balcony, holding a big beige cube. It was the thing from the package Sasha had found a few days ago in Eduard's office, the one that had been too heavy for her to lift. It looked like a printer/copier.

"*Edo!*" Lyda yelled. "Get the fuck out here!"

She threw the cube off the balcony. A moment later Sasha heard the crash. Sasha quickly flicked through the various screens until she got a shot of the great room. The cube had hit the big granite coffee table and exploded. Pieces were everywhere.

"*That,*" Bucko said, "was the coolest thing I've ever seen."

Sasha flicked her hands at the wall, making the sign for mosaic, and two dozen mirrors opened at once, showing almost every room in the house and a few views of the outside. She watched Esperanza throw open the door of her room, pulling on her robe with fire-drill urgency. Rovil, still wearing all his clothes, stood in the middle of his room, looking at the door as if deciding whether to come out. And Grandpop, poor tired old man, was the last to appear, wearing nothing but boxer shorts. By the time he stepped onto the balcony, Lyda was already below, pulling at pieces of machinery.

"What have I done?" Sasha cried. "Why is she so *mad?*"

Elk Heart's knuckles tightened on his spear, but the chief said nothing. Squidly drifted down to place a tendril on her shoulder. Tinker watched her with his headlight eyes.

"Maybe we should turn off these windows," Mother Maybelle said.

"Screw that," Bucko said.

Lyda and Grandpop were fighting now, or rather, Lyda was yelling at Grandpop and he was trying to get her to calm down. Then Esperanza turned on the lights to the room, which startled them both and interrupted Lyda's shouting—but only for a moment.

"Should I go out there?" Sasha asked.

"Ah advise against it," Zebo said. "For now." HalfnHalf nodded his two heads in agreement.

Tinker pinged significantly, and Sasha noticed something strange in one of the far windows. Somebody was moving out by the garage. She zoomed in, and saw that it was a man in a black cowboy hat, a white man she'd never seen before. An electrical box attached to the garage was open. He reached inside it—

The wall blanked. The mirrors were gone, and with it all light in the room. Sasha flicked her hands, but the house, her faithful house, refused to respond.

"Uh-oh," Bucko said.

A tiny flame flared in the corner of the room. Sasha stood up.

He leaned against the wall, the brim of his hat pulled low over his eyes. He touched the match to his cigarette, puffed once, then dropped the match to the floor.

Bucko said, "How the hell did he get out of—?"

Sasha held out her hand. The bear shut up.

The Wander Man ground out the match with the toe of one black boot. "You know who that man is out there, right?"

Sasha nodded. "He's you."

"Close enough, Miss Sasha. Close enough." He looked up and smiled. None of the IFs moved. They were all, even Elk Heart, terrified of him, and he knew it.

"You listen carefully," he said. "And do exactly what I say."

CHAPTER TWENTY-FIVE

"You crazy motherfucker." I threatened him with a fragment from the broken machine, a length of flat steel that ended in a sharp tip. "You're building them."

Edo blinked at me as if the light was too bright. Esperanza and Dr. Gloria hovered in the corner of the huge living room, like seconds ready to step between the combatants. Well, good luck with that.

"I don't know what you're talking about," he said. "I've never seen—whatever that is."

"The paintings are upstairs, Edo. The fucking blueprints. You got Gilbert to design it for you, and you fucking made it, then you've got one sitting in your fucking *house*."

"Please, Lyda, I—"

"How many did you make, Edo? Where's the factory putting them together? How many churches do you have out there?"

He stared at the coffee table and the remains of the printer. Most of the machine was intact, but shards of plastic and bright pieces of stainless steel were scattered over the wooden floors. "Did this—did you get it from Eduard's office?"

"Do *not* try to blame this on him," I said. "You're the evangelist, Edo. I never thought you'd actually try to do it, but then I saw the first one in Toronto—a chemjet to print One-Ten."

"I swear to you—"

"Stop lying. I know about the churches. I know about 'Logos.' Just tell me what you've done to Sasha. Are you giving her Numinous?"

"What?" He gave a very good impression of being shocked. "Of course not!"

Dr. Gloria said, "You don't believe that."

"Why not?" I said to Edo. "You told me you thought everybody should be on it."

"Yes, but a small amount. Not like *us*. God is . . . too strong in us. I would never do that to a child." He stepped toward me, and I swiped at him with my improvised blade. He stopped and raised his hands. "Lyda, she's been like us since the beginning. You have to believe me."

"How about everybody else, Edo?" I asked. "How about dosing the world?"

The room went dark. Even the hallway lights winked out. I jumped back from Edo, keeping him and Esperanza in front of me. But they seemed just as surprised as I was.

Only Dr. Gloria's figure was clear to me in the dark. Her appearance required only fauxtons. "What's going on, Doc?"

Before she could answer, someone darted into the room: Sasha. She ran to Edo and threw her arms around his waist.

"It's okay," Edo said to her. "Nothing to be afraid of."

The girl gestured frantically toward the kitchen. "It's just a power failure," he said. Her hands fluttered in exasperation, but of course with the power out, the walls were silent.

Esperanza moved toward the kitchen. "I'll get the flashlights," she said. Sasha threw up her hands, a clear *No!* But the maid did not see her and stepped through the arch.

Sasha was frantic now, pulling at Edo, and he tried to soothe her. From the kitchen I heard a thump, then a crash of metal, as if Esperanza had knocked over a rack of skillets.

"Esperanza?" Edo called. He moved toward the kitchen. Sasha seized his arm, trying to keep him from moving. "Please, Sasha—stay with Lyda."

A silhouette appeared in the archway. "Howdy, folks," the voice said.

It was the cowboy. He tilted back his hat and said, "Good to see you again, Lyda. And you must be Mr. Vik."

Dr. Gloria stepped in front of me. Her wings snapped open in a blaze of white. "Don't move," she told me, "until I tell you to move."

Edo had stopped in the middle of the room. "I'm sorry," he said to the cowboy. "Who are you?"

The cowboy lifted his hand. Moonlight glinted on the barrel of the pistol. "Have the little girl take two steps away from you."

Edo stepped to place himself in front of Sasha. "No," he said.

"I'm going to count to three," the cowboy said.

Sasha looked to her left, into the dark at the edge of the room. Then she looked back at the cowboy. She didn't move from Edo.

"I'm a traditionalist," the cowboy said. "And it's customary to spare the child. But I *will* do what's necessary."

Sasha looked up at Edo. She gripped his hand in both of hers, and seemed to squeeze it.

"I love you, too, sweetie," Edo said. "Now go on. Don't worry about me."

She let go of him and stepped away, moving not toward me, or even toward her bedroom, but toward the corner of the room where she'd been looking a moment before.

Edo raised his arms. "If you harm anyone else in this room, God's judgment will be upon you."

Sasha stopped, and picked up something from the floor. A length of metal, just like mine.

The cowboy hadn't seen this—his eyes were on Edo. "Aw," he said. "I thought you believed in a god of infinite love." He fired: two loud bangs. Edo jerked and fell forward. His huge body crashed into one of the chairs, then slid sideways. The cowboy swung his pistol toward me.

Dr. Gloria shoved me backward. The fiery sword appeared in her hand. She raised it and rushed forward like a whirlwind of flame. The pistol fired twice more. I was jerked backward by some force, and then suddenly my legs tangled and I fell to the floor.

The cowboy screamed and fell to his knees before the angel reached him. "No more," she said, and plunged the sword into his gut.

The cowboy looked down in amazement. The weapon was sunk to the hilt in his stomach; I could see its fiery blade on the far side of his body. After a moment he tilted sideways and collapsed to the floor.

The angel stepped back, withdrawing the blade as she moved. She seemed to be made of brilliant, rippling flame. She turned to me, and I could barely look at her.

"Do not be afraid," she said. "Everything is going to be all right."

The dark contracted around us, until I could see nothing but her light, feel nothing but her heat.

CHAPTER TWENTY-SIX

Someone was holding my hand. And as soon I understood that, I recognized the cool, otherworldly touch
of Dr. Gloria. I couldn't move and didn't want to;
neither was I particularly interested in opening my
eyes. But I could feel the doctor's fingers around my
own, and I thought, So. I'm dead.

I didn't feel any anger about this, or disappointment.
Only relief.

A decade ago I'd woken up in a hospital with Dr.
Gloria sitting beside me, her hand in mine as it was
now. My mind had been hammered flat by three
facts: There was a Higher Power; It loved me; and
there was no escaping It.

In the years that followed, I desperately tried to forget this revelation. Write it off. Discredit it with everything I knew about the untrustworthy brain, how
NME 110 rewired it even further. *Know it's a trick, and
don't forget it's a trick.*

But I wanted to be wrong. I wanted that ol' white
magic. For a brief time, a decade ago, I'd become convinced that there was nothing to be afraid of. I had
known that the universe was a living thing, and that
it cared for me. But the moment had passed, and I'd
become convinced that it was all a sham.

Now, finally, that certainty had returned. I could
stop struggling now. Give up this body. Surrender.

"Not just yet," Dr. Gloria whispered. I could feel her lips close to my ear. "Shhhh."

. . .

I heard the roar of water. No, *air.* Air hissing into me, out of me.

I did not open my eyes, but the doctor became visible nonetheless. She sat beside me, her left arm in my right, but I could barely feel her. Her touch was light as mist.

I tried to speak, but my throat wouldn't move, and suddenly I was choking. The doctor touched my forehead. "Easy, easy. It's just the trach tube. Don't try to talk out loud."

And then I thought, Fuck. I'm alive.

"You're in the ICU of St. Vincent's, in Sante Fe," Dr. Gloria said. "You're going to be fine."

Oh, I was pretty sure I was *not* going to be fine. Moments ago I was free, a liberated soul. Now I was caged inside a body, a body which itself was strapped to a bed with a length of plastic jammed down its throat.

"So close," I said to her. I did not have to move my lips to speak with her.

"I'm sorry to do this to you," the doctor said. "But that's the way it has to be."

"Let me go."

"Stop it," Dr. Gloria said. "We have no time for self-pity. There are others you should be concerned with."

Others? Oh God.

"Sasha is fine," Dr. Gloria said. "Untouched. She was the one who called nine-one-one. Rovil and Esperanza kept you from bleeding out until the ambulance arrived."

I had faint memories of that: Esperanza pressing a towel into my shoulder; Rovil frowning, so scared he looked almost angry.

"And Edo?"

"You already know."

It was true. I'd seen the spray of blood as the bullets left his body, the way his big body fell, slowly, like a century oak crashing to the ground.

"And me? What about me?"

"You were shot through the chest," she said. "Your right lung collapsed. The bullet did a lot of damage as it tumbled around your chest cavity. You're fighting an infection now."

"So pretty good, then."

She laughed. "You are not allowed to die, do you understand? Not for quite some time. And the man who is responsible for this will not bother you again."

"You saved me."

"That's my job."

"Your job is to tell me what I need to hear. I didn't think you'd come out and stab someone through the chest."

She shrugged. "It was time for me to reveal myself."

"Waited fucking long enough."

She laughed again. "I work in mysterious ways. Doubt is all well and good, but now it's time, again, to trust me completely."

"One more time," I said.

. . .

I slept for what felt like a long time, until gradually I became aware of a splotchy light against my eyelids. News of my body returned to me in stages, like distant armies reporting in: my throat (burning); my left arm (aching); my ribs (whinging like a rusty machine). No word yet from my legs. Pain massed at the border, ready to rush in if I let down my guard.

Somewhere two women were speaking, though I couldn't make out their words. I didn't need to open my eyes to know where I was. Hospitals have a scent as complex as any perfume: The sickly sweet tang of Pine-Sol, the floral bombast of antibacterial foam coating a nurse's hands, the pervasive undercoat of bleach like a constant high whine. Baked into the walls and ceilings are lingering notes of institutional food—Salisbury steak, chicken broth, burnt coffee—and the effluvia of human bodies. Mop and wipe all you want, but that will only whisk molecules of shit and blood and urine and pus into the air, where they will soak into the paint and infiltrate the acoustic tiles. Connoisseurs of medical establishments— and I consider myself an expert—can detect even the most subtle aromas: the milky odor of drug-resistant bacteria replicating on an IV tube; the fustiness of an old man's flannel shirt hanging in a cabinet two rooms away that will never be worn again; the tears of parents in the pediatric cancer ward.

A voice said, "Lyda?"

I opened my eyes, but the glare was too much. I closed them against the light.

"It's me," the voice said. "Rovil."

Oh, the damaged little shepherd boy. Faithfully standing watch. Was he afraid I'd slip out of reach?

I allowed my eyelids to raise a fraction, a tiny twist of a venetian blind. He sat in a chair beside my bed. Dr. Gloria stood behind him, leaning against the window, scrawling something on her clipboard. What was she always writing on that thing?

Rovil leaned close, his voice low. "I told them I was your boyfriend. It was the only way they'd let me stay in the room. I hope you don't mind." He seemed pleased with himself. "Can I get you anything? Water? Some ice chips?"

I shook my head. Or tried to.

"The surgery went well," Rovil said. "The doctor says you're recovering better than he expected. They've got you on antibiotics, and pain medication of course, and the antiepileptics indicated in your file."

Antiepileptics?

"Hmm," Dr. Gloria said. "We'll consider this a kind of test." There was something off about her. Her lab coat had become the same pale green as the wall, so that she seemed to be disappearing into it.

"Ollie," I said. My voice was a croak.

"I'm sorry, what?" Rovil asked.

I gathered my breath and said it again, and again, until he suddenly understood. "She's in town," he said quietly. "She heard about Edo and . . . we've been in touch." He nodded toward the door. "She can't come in to the hospital, though. The police."

Of course. We were wanted felons.

"They've been here several times. Do you remember? There's an officer outside the door now, making sure no reporters get in. The media is camped out in the lobby."

Billionaire white man shot in his own home, I thought. Big news, if it was a slow news day.

"Well, the detectives will be back, now that you're awake. They've questioned me several times, and when I go back to New York tomorrow I have to check in there."

Tomorrow, I thought. Maybe the shepherd was not so faithful after all.

He looked uncomfortable, and leaned forward, hands clasped. "I'd like to ask a favor." His voice was very low; I could barely hear him over the sound of the machines in my room. "I told them that I didn't know that you and Ollie were here illegally. Do you understand? I told them we were just visiting an old coworker. Can you go along with that?"

The room began to swim. I closed my eyes. "Ollie," I said. "Please."

I think I said this aloud. I'm almost sure of it.

· · ·

"Lyda. Wake up."

The room was dark. It was sometime in the thin hours between midnight and dawn. My skin felt hot. Rovil slumped in the guest chair, dead asleep. I should wake him, tell him the fever is cooking, and that I needed meds. I should call the nurse. I should . . .

"It's getting close to my time to leave."

I looked to the right. A few feet away, light and shadows formed the shape of an angel. Her face was the orb of a street lamp glowing through the window; her wings, spread against the wall, were made from the light spilling through the open door.

"You're fading," I said.

"It's the meds," she said. "They're making it hard to get through." Someone passed outside my door, and her wings seemed to flutter. "You could have silenced me a long time ago. All those prescriptions from doctors of the NAT ward? But you kept palming those pills, hiding them under the tongue. Strange behavior from a nonbeliever."

"Guardrails," I said. I had wanted to give her up, but I was afraid that without her I'd be dead. And now, finally, the automated delivery system of the IV drip proved to have more willpower than I did.

"You'll need to be stronger than Francine," Dr. Gloria said. "It's the withdrawal that killed her—not the judgment of God, but My absence."

"Not making any promises," I said.

"I want to tell you: Do not mistake the messenger for the message. Just because you won't be able to hear me soon, don't imagine that I'm gone."

I almost laughed. Oh, the double-talk of a feverish brain yammering to itself.

"I was with you in the beginning," she said. "And I'll be with you always."

In the beginning.

"Tell me," I said.

I didn't remember much from the night of the party. But I remembered the feel of the knife in my hand. And I remembered Gil taking it from me. Which was true?

"Please."

"You did not kill Mikala," the angel said. "And neither did I."

Her head seemed to tilt toward me. "Oh, Lyda. Did you really think that you were the kind of person who could murder your own true love?"

For the sake of our child? I thought. I didn't know. I was afraid that I could, and afraid that I couldn't.

"It's time to abandon your confidence in your own guilt," she said. "Your self-loathing is beginning to look self-serving. For the sake of the child, you've got to protect yourself."

"What are you talking about?"

A figure stepped into the room, blocking the light from the hallway. The movement broke Dr. Gloria into pieces. Where she'd stood had become nothing but patches of light and shadow, and I couldn't make out her pattern for the noise.

"Lyda." The angel's voice whispered like the hiss of an air vent, like the static of a radio. "You have been betrayed."

And then even her voice was lost to me.

· · ·

A figure in scrubs bent over me. A woman. She touched my cheek. "You're burning up."

"Ollie?"

"I can't stay long," she said.

So clever. Dressing up as a nurse. The old tricks are the best tricks.

"I'm so sorry," she said. "I shouldn't have walked out on you. If I'd been with you—"

"If," I said. "Dead." I meant to say, *If you'd come you'd have been killed.* The cowboy had been hired to kill us all. Or most of us. I finally understood why.

"Has her fever been this high before?" Ollie asked. She was talking to Rovil. He hovered behind her, a worried look on his face.

"She was like this after surgery," he said. "They thought she wouldn't make it, and then her fever suddenly dropped. A little miracle. I was glad to be there when she woke up."

I tried to speak, and Ollie asked, "What is it, Lyda? What do you need?"

"Ganesh," I said. "Where is he?"

"I don't understand," Rovil said.

"It's the fever talking," Ollie said. She straightened, but her eyes held mine. Oh, she was so quick. All she needed was the smallest nod to point her in the right direction.

"Call the nurse," she said to him. "I can't be here. I'll see you outside in a couple hours."

CHAPTER TWENTY-SEVEN

The parking lot of the CHRISTUS St. Vincent Medical Center was a black page, the cars set upon it like characters from a metal alphabet. Empty spaces separated the characters into words, and each row formed a sentence. Hospital staff and media people and ordinary visitors had cooperated with the parking lot in the writing of it, and they rewrote it over the course of the day, adding and removing vehicles, adjusting by make and model, by color and year, until finally, just before dawn, the editing subsided and the final message of the night could be read. The sadness of the world's parking lots was that no one was ever there to decipher it.

Almost never.

Olivia Skarsten leaned against the hood of a black sedan parked at the edge of the lot and considered the pattern laid out before her under the dim lights. The message came to her just as Rovil Gupta stepped out of the hospital's sliding doors. He saw her standing by his car and began to walk toward her.

" 'The skin of the ground is cold,'" Ollie said. " 'But the sun is coming.'"

"Pardon?" Rovil said.

"Nothing," she said. "Just something somebody told me. How's Lyda doing?"

"They gave her meds to bring down the fever, and something else to let her sleep," Rovil said.

They got into the car. "I'm staying in an out-of-the-way place," Ollie said. "If you could drop me there I'd appreciate it."

"Of course," he said. He asked for an address to punch in to the GPS, but she said she'd just direct him. They left the hospital parking lot and turned south.

"I'm going to go back to my hotel and sleep for a few hours, then start the drive home," he said. "I hate to leave Lyda, but I've been away too long."

"You've done enough," Ollie said. "Turn left at the light." Eventually they got onto Central Avenue and followed that under the interstate. The sky began to lighten above them. "You and I never got the chance to talk much," Ollie said.

He smiled. "I just assumed you didn't like me."

"I get that a lot," she said. "I don't have a spiritual advisor to remind me when I'm being too harsh."

"It *is* a great help," he said.

"Maybe we'd all be better off with a touch of the Numinous," she said. "Maybe not so much as you and Lyda."

"I wouldn't recommend that," Rovil said. "Then again, most substances turn toxic at extreme levels."

"Water, for example."

"I'm sorry?"

"Turn up here."

"Of course," he said. "Is your hotel nearby? It seems pretty residential."

The houses along the street were one-story brown boxes like miniature prisons. The front yards were desert rock and clumps of parched plant life.

"It was cheaper to get a house for a week," she said. "More like house-sitting. I found it online. Slow down . . . okay, this one."

It was another rectangular brown home with a one-car garage and a few clumps of trees to provide some privacy. It had gotten terrible reviews online and was in no danger of being rented soon. An hour ago she'd disabled the amateurish alarm system and moved in. Rovil didn't think to ask how she'd gotten from the house to the hospital. The silver pickup she'd stolen was sitting in row three, one letter in the parking lot's little prayer.

Rovil put the car in park. "I'm sure I'll see you again," Rovil said. "I hope—" He noticed the pistol in her hands and raised his eyebrows.

The garage door began to open.

"Pull in," Ollie said.

"What are you doing? Where did you get that gun?"

"We'll talk more inside," she said.

She had him turn off the car and give her the keys. The garage door slid down behind them. Then she escorted him into the house and down uncarpeted stairs to the basement. It was dim down there, but not dark: Earlier she'd covered the three narrow windows with cardboard and put fresh mini-fluorescent bulbs in the ceiling lights. The space was unfinished, with a cement floor and walls bare to the studs. Most of the room was taken up with junk: boxes of dishes and plastic ice trays, an old-fashioned plasma TV, a stained loveseat, a toddler-sized carousel with three plastic horses upon a cracked base. Things you didn't bother to take with you. Ollie had decided that the family that had lived here had planned to make the basement into a rec room, but then the young father lost his job, the marriage hit the rocks, and the woman and her child moved back east.

Ollie made Rovil face the wall, then crouched and quickly tied his ankles together with zip ties. He yelped and nearly lost his balance. She emptied his pockets, then helped him shuffle to the loveseat and drop into it. The gun was in her jacket pocket now.

"This is insane," Rovil said.

"It's pretty standard, actually. Hands together." She cinched his wrists. "One time in Syria I let the guy stay in bed. Figured, we're going to be here a while, might as well be comfortable."

"You're not going to torture me?"

Ollie grinned. "See, I knew you'd looked up my résumé." She shook her head. "No, we're just going to talk."

"Then why are you tying me down?" He delivered this with a well-modulated tremor of desperation, not too over-the-top.

"Because you're a guy. You'd be tempted to try to overpower me or do something stupid, like yell for help. By the way, the house next door is empty, and the one on the other side is too far away to hear you. But if you do scream, I will gag you, and if you fight me I will have to hurt you. I don't want that. I'm not like the man you hired. He's got an antiquated way of dealing with people—Guantanamo Classic."

"I'm sorry, I don't know who—"

"The cowboy, Rovil."

"The cowboy? But you can't think that I—?"

"Breaking your own fingers was a nice touch. Not that many people would have the commitment to the gag. But you were right to do it—just bandaging up your hand wouldn't have sold it."

"I don't know what you're talking about!"

"It's okay, Rovil. I know you feel the need to keep up the performance. But we'll all go home a lot faster if we can get past that."

He kept professing his ignorance, pretending shock and confusion. While he talked, Ollie arranged the space. She placed a wooden chair a few feet in front of the loveseat. Beside it she set a small pile of rags, including a couple of pillowcases and bath towels that she'd cut into more manageable strips. Nearby was her black backpack, as well as a plastic bucket, a case of bottled water, a jug of Lysol, and a radio. Rovil didn't ask about any of the items—he just kept talking, reasoning with her.

She sat down in the chair and waited for him to stop babbling. "Can I ask a question?" she asked at last.

Rovil sat back. He breathed deep, then exhaled, performing his exasperation. "Sure."

"What do you like on your pizza? For later, I mean. I'd like to plan the menu."

· · ·

"Why are you asking me questions if you're not even listening to the answers?"

"Oh, I'm listening," Ollie said without looking up. It was late afternoon. They'd been in the basement for ten hours. She'd emptied the piss bucket for him twice. So far he'd resisted the urge to shit—he did not want to do that in front of her—but sooner or later it would have to happen.

And sooner or later she'd have to decide what to do with Rovil. They could not stay down here forever. If he did not talk soon, then she had only one other option. She'd been trying to decide if what she was contemplating was a sin.

She did not always believe in sin, or in God. For most of her adult life she'd considered faith to be something she'd left behind in her childhood with her high school track suit. Then, on a cold February day about a month after she lost her job as an intelligence analyst, she was surprised to find herself walking through the big wooden door of St. Patrick's Cathedral. A midday service was in progress. Ollie took a seat in a middle pew.

She hadn't been thinking of God, or religion, or the church—especially not the Catholic church. She was raised Lutheran, for goodness' sake. About the only thing she'd given serious thought to lately was suicide. Late at night, and often in the morning, and sometimes in the afternoon as well, she'd lie in bed, turning the idea over in her mind like a black opal. Admiring the way it gleamed. Lusting after it, like a woman saving up her money.

She stayed through the service to the end. Then she went back the next day, and the day after that.

She went only on weekdays, to the 12:10 service. Less than a dozen people would show up, old women mostly, a few tourists. (And Ollie thought of herself as a different kind of tourist.) They would settle into the pews one by one like lumps of cold dough, leaving plenty of space between them. The air inside seemed only a bit less cold than the street. Before the service began, Ollie would stare at the votive candles flickering at the Virgin Mary's feet like spiritual pilot lights. Then the voice of the priest would call out and the voices of the old women would murmur in response, stirring the air. They would rise to sing, and the organ, a fortress of silver pipes, would bellow and thrum, vibrating her chest. Then she would kneel, resting her forearms on the back of the pew, and the old polished wood under her would seem to radiate like a lodestone charged from a hundred years of prayers. And sometimes (not every time, but often enough, barely often enough) something in her that had been numb and silent would slowly unclench, unfold, and fall away from her.

For a day. Sometimes only for a couple hours. But it was enough to get her through the winter.

"I've told you everything I can think of," Rovil said sometime later. "And you've got all my devices. What more can I give you?"

She was looking at his corporate slate at that moment. She also had his wallet and personal pen. Electronically speaking, she had become him. It had taken her less than fifteen minutes to get access to every bank account, mail service, and online drive he owned. The rest of the day she'd spent browsing, reading, and copying files. She found her own name in his personal contacts list. He'd discovered her last name, and had pasted in links to the few pages on the internet where her biographical information popped up.

More interesting were the custom fields next to her name, and the names of dozens of other people. He'd created over twenty attributes such as Loyalty and Intelligence, with scores for each. He'd reduced everyone to a character sheet from a role-playing game. Ollie had scored three or below on most categories.

"Only a one on *scent?*" she asked. "That's hurtful."

"I'm sorry," he said. "I never meant for anyone to see those."

"You've got Lyda and Mikala in here—everyone from Little Sprout—from when you used to take care of the rats."

"I did a lot more than that. I was a trained neuroscientist. In fact, I was the one who steered them toward the change that made One-Ten possible."

She looked up from the screen. *Finally,* she thought, a little ego. She'd been waiting for the real Rovil to show up. With very little prompting she got him to tell her the story of how he came to work for them, and how he almost-singlehandedly saved the company.

"And you only got five percent of the stock?" she asked, her tone sympathetic.

"Two percent."

"Ouch. You must have been pissed."

He opened his mouth, then shut it. "I've made peace with it. My god has helped me—"

"Ganesh. Right." She flipped to a new page on the pen. "Hey, Landon-Rousse's stock price is up," she said.

"You don't say," he said flatly. He didn't like being interrupted.

"You have over five thousand shares in your ESOP," she said. "You should be happier." She'd been able to go surprisingly far into Landon-Rousse's network with Rovil's permission set. Most of the files were in plain text, but the encrypted ones with interesting names she'd outsourced to cracker services—paid for with Rovil's credit. Some of those decrypted files were already back in her inbox.

"Of course, a lot depends on the new product you're in charge of," she said. " 'NME: Stepladder.' I like the code name rather than numbers."

"Please! This is all proprietary information!"

"I know, I know," she said. "Didn't sign the NDA. Did *you* come up with the name?"

He took a breath, then decided to answer. "I did, actually."

"Why not, it's your baby. That's got to be a lot of pressure, though, everybody depending on you to keep that stock price going up. No wonder the church scared you—they were going to give your drug away for free. Hard to compete with that."

"What do you mean, competing? They have nothing to do with each other."

She ignored the fake ignorance. "Stepladder, the Logos paper, Numinous . . ." She opened the backpack. "It's all NME One-Ten." She took out a large, white plastic bottle.

"Where did you get that?"

"Stole it from your apartment. You had boxes of them. I didn't think you'd miss one." She opened the bottle, shook one of the capsules into her hand, and showed it to him. It was robin's egg blue. "I've had people look at them," she said patiently. "You're not the only guy with access to a mass-spec machine."

He stared at the pill. "The substances are different," he said, angry now. "In key respects. Yes, there are some molecular similarities, but years of development went into Stepladder to make it marketable."

Ding, Ollie thought. Two points. She hadn't been a hundred percent sure that the pills in his apartment were for the drug he'd been working on. Also, the bit about the mass spectrometer was a complete lie.

"It takes six billion dollars to bring a drug to market," Rovil said. "Six billion on *average*. You know how much initial R&D costs, that first little idea? It's a tiny slice. It's all in testing, figuring out the right dosage—"

"Sure," she said. "You can't have it going off like a bomb like it did at the Little Sprout party."

"We've done extensive testing," Rovil said. "Our drug is completely safe when taken at the recommended dosages."

Ollie liked that "we." The ego was percolating at full strength now. For the first time since she'd known him he seemed to be fully in his body, fully *alive*.

"Can't have a drug that makes everyone schizo," she said. "Look at Lyda and Gil—completely insane."

"Exactly."

"But not you. I mean, not crazy in the same way," she said. "You're just a run-of-the-mill sociopath."

"I'm done with this," he said, and got to his feet.

"Sit," she said.

"Untie me, *now*. This has gone on—"

"Si-i-i-it," she said, and thumped a palm into his chest. He tipped backward into the loveseat. "Take a breath. Lyda figured it out, Rovil—you don't have your own personal Jiminy Cricket. Where's Ganesh? Nowhere. You've been faking it." Her hand was in the pocket of her jacket, reminding him of the pistol.

"Tell me what happened in Chicago," she said.

He shook his head. "There is no way for me to win, Ollie. In your state, anything I say will be taken as a lie. But if I try to guess what you want to hear, that will be taken as a lie as well."

"Just talk. I'll be the judge."

"You're in no *condition* to judge!"

"You were angry that they'd cheated you," she said. "So you decided that no one would get the buyout money. An overdose would queer the whole deal. Kind of shortsighted of you, though. Two percent is better than nothing."

"This is what you do," he said. "You take fragments and guesses and unrelated details, and you make up stories. This is your mania for pattern recognition talking."

"Sometimes when the crazy talks, you got to listen."

"That sounds like something Lyda would say."

"It does, doesn't it? But here's the thing. When there's a real conspiracy, I am indeed hell on wheels."

He groaned.

"You're a bright person, Rovil. I'd rate you a three on Intelligence, maybe even a three point five."

He blinked. "You're trying to insult me."

She showed him the pen. "You rated yourself a five. *Really?* That in itself is a sign of diminished intelligence."

"If you let me go now," Rovil said. "I promise not to tell anyone about this. You're not thinking clearly, and you need help. Look around—we're in a basement in the suburbs of Santa Fe. You're not a secret agent anymore. You're not NSA, or Special Forces. You're a patient who is off her meds."

Ollie breathed out. "So you're not confessing then?"

"I can't confess to something that isn't—"

"I'll take that as a no."

She made her decision. Or rather, if Lyda was right, her brain decided for her. She also hoped that Lyda was right that there was no God to punish her.

From the backpack she took out a box of latex gloves and withdrew a pair.

"What are you doing?" he asked. His voice wavered—and not just for show. He was truly nervous now.

She wriggled into one glove, then the other. "Let me ask you a different question." She picked up the bottle again. "As a professional in the pharmaceutical industry, and the *product owner* of Stepladder . . ." She shook a dozen pills into her hand. "What's the dosage equivalent of what Lyda took in Chicago? Ten pills? Twenty? A hundred?"

His eyes widened.

"How many steps on the Stepladder?" she asked.

"You can't do this."

She placed an empty water bottle between her knees, then unscrewed one of the blue capsules and let the white grains drop into the bottle. "Forget the question—you'll only lie. I need to talk to someone who has a conscience."

He watched her as she emptied six, then ten, then fifteen capsules into the bottle. She found herself humming "Stairway to Heaven."

"What do you want to know?" he asked.

"The name of the cowboy. All contact info, too."

"I don't know this cowboy. I swear."

"See? Lying." She unscrewed another capsule. "I figure a hundred ought to do it."

"You'll kill me!"

"Nah," she said. "You may go insane, but Landon-Rousse's own studies put the fatal dose at well over a hundred pills. Or so I read this afternoon."

Rovil lunged forward. The water bottle was between her legs, and both her hands were occupied with the current capsule. His own hands, bound at the wrist, reached for her. She brought up her knees, but he threw himself over them and seized her throat. The chair tipped backward, and she slammed into the floor with Rovil on top of her.

She'd been expecting this move for some time; the only surprise was in how long he'd taken to try it. She made sure he'd committed to the throat; then she seized both thumbs, and twisted.

He screamed, tried to get off her. She opened her knees and circled her legs around his waist, holding him to her. He was tilted at an angle, head down, feet in the air, his thighs pressed to the lip of the chair. The ties around his ankles made it impossible for him to get leverage, and his tethered wrists made it impossible to attack her.

She twisted her hips and rolled him off the chair and onto his back. She squatted above him, still holding the good thumb. The Sig Sauer was now pressed to his forehead.

"I told you I would have to hurt you," she said.

"Please," Rovil said. "Don't turn me into one of them."

"The cowboy," she said.

He gulped air. "I don't know who you're talking about."

"Okay then," she said. "It's time to meet your god."

THE PARABLE OF
the Man Who Sacrificed Himself

Once, in a city by a lake, at the top of a high tower, a rich man held a party. Unbeknownst to him, one of the guests had invited God. The deity was smuggled into the party inside a champagne bottle.

Gilbert, IT expert and the fattest guest at the party, was the first to drink. He hoisted the bottle and took two great swigs before passing it to the rich man, whose name was Edo. Edo drank a long pull, then passed it to the neuroscientist, Lyda. She sipped it once before offering it to Rovil, the former rat wrangler. Rovil only pretended to drink, pressing the mouth of the bottle to his closed lips. He quickly wiped his mouth with his sleeve and smiled broadly. He thought he felt the tingle of the psychotropic on his skin, but told himself not to worry. Such brief skin contact, he knew from helping Mikala with her experiments, should affect him only mildly. "You too," he said to Mikala, and gave the bottle to her. She drank deeply and handed it back to him.

A moment later Gil stumbled backward, into the coffee table. His eyes had rolled back, and he began to speak in an unknown language. Mikala called out his name in alarm. He crashed to the floor, his arms and legs shaking as if electrified.

Edo gripped his head as if he'd been struck by a migraine. He dropped to his knees and looked up at the ceiling, moaning. Lyda was on her back, convulsing, her face making ugly grimaces.

Only Mikala and Rovil were still upright. She looked dazed. Slowly she realized that Rovil was watching her. "What did you do?" she asked him.

Oh, but she already knew. Even freshly dosed with the NME, she was the brightest of them.

She had trusted Rovil. He'd become her confidant, and when he accidently discovered her self-administering NME 110, he became the observer for her experiments, the keeper of the records. She'd asked him not to tell Lyda or the others, and he had obeyed her wishes. He was too interested in the outcome not to. She never permitted him to try the drug; the risk was to be hers alone. She began with a dose of 25 micrograms, far less than a grain of sand. Over the course of six weeks she ramped up to 50 micrograms, then 100, about the same as an average LSD blot.

He'd asked her to describe the effects for their records. "It feels like . . . the numinous," she said. And that became its name in the notebooks.

It eventually became obvious to him that her interest had moved beyond the scientific. She was becoming an addict. Her personality was changing, the effects of the drug persisting well beyond what either of them predicted.

Still she wanted more, and more frequently. In those final weeks, they would spread out a yoga mat, and she would drink a vial of 100 milliliters of distilled water mixed with 300 micrograms of NME 110. He held her down while she bucked and kicked in epileptic ecstasy. The hallucinations became permanent. God, she said, was watching over her.

Sometime in those weeks Edo announced that he'd struck a deal to sell Little Sprout, and that Gil and Lyda had voted with him against Mikala. Rovil, with his paltry two-percent share of the company, was not even asked his opinion. He was nothing to them. Even Mikala, with her new god, was too enraptured with her own anger and sorrow to see that he was the one who'd been wronged. They were about to become millionaires, and he'd be left with perhaps enough to buy a new car. He pretended to be happy for them.

The night of the party, he had called Mikala from the restaurant and begged her to come to the afterparty in Edo's suite. It's over, he told her. You should forgive them. He came down and met her in the lobby of the Lake Point Tower and shepherded her into the elevator. Before the doors opened he handed her the bottle of very expensive champagne he had purchased. "We should celebrate together," he said.

The dosage had been tricky to figure out. There were so many variables he had to consider. The bottle was 750 milliliters. Alcohol tended to break down the structure of the NME over time, so he had to consider how long would pass between injecting the substance into the bottle and when it would be opened. Some would undoubtedly bubble out with the foam when they popped the cork, perhaps quite a lot. Then there was the possibility that not everyone would drink, or drink only a small amount.

In the end he figured he had better be safe than sorry. He loaded the syringe with a full gram dissolved in distilled water, the equivalent of about five thousand hits of LSD, and about three thousand times the maximum amount Mikala had taken at one time.

After they had all drunk, the bottle was still half-full and heavy in his hand, but everyone was reeling from the effects.

Everyone except Mikala. He should have accounted for her tolerance. A sudden dose would not put her down like the others; God had already burned into her brain, rewired it for His presence.

She stalked toward him, and he backed away. "Mikala, what's going on? What's happening? I feel so strange. We've got to call an ambulance."

"You will be judged for this," she said.

She went to Lyda and crouched by her side. Her wife was thrashing and babbling, speaking in tongues. "Don't be afraid," she said, and placed a hand on her forehead. "I'm here to help you through this." With her other hand she flicked on her phone, and tapped the digits with her thumb.

"Hello? Yes. My name is Mikala Lamonier. I'm in Lake Point Tower. There's been an—"

He didn't know what she was going to say next. An accident? An attack? He struck her across the temple with the bottle, and she slumped onto the floor next to Lyda. He was surprised that the bottle had not broken.

He kneeled down and clicked off the phone. Mikala was still breathing, but shallowly. The blow had reshaped her face into something strange and leering.

He forced himself to do nothing for a full minute, until he knew exactly what to do. Then he went into the kitchen and retrieved a large, hefty knife. He would have to make this look like a crime of passion, a crazy, unthinking attack. But what about the blood splatters? He removed

Lyda's short jacket, slipped it over one arm, and set to work on Mikala's body. When he was done he wiped the knife handle with the sleeve of the jacket and placed the weapon in her hand. Then he took the smallest of sips from what remained in the champagne bottle and set it on its side between Lyda and Mikala.

Last, he lay down to wait for the police. Would they believe that Lyda had murdered her wife? Had he left behind some obvious bit of evidence that could implicate him? The minutes dragged on. He kept his eyes open to slits, watching the others moan and thrash, until finally they subsided. The room became quiet.

Gradually Rovil became aware of another presence in the room, standing just to the edge of his peripheral vision. He thought at first that it was a waiter, because he was dressed in bright red pants and vest. But then the figure turned, and he could see that the man's head was huge, and his nose was absurdly long. An elephant's trunk! He almost laughed. Ganesh was here. Deva of intellect. Remover of Obstacles.

Across the room, Gilbert pushed his fat body up. He looked around at the room, blinking in surprise. Then he saw Mikala, and the knife in Lyda's hand. He knelt down beside them, and began to weep, great aching sobs like a schoolboy who'd lost his dog. It was ridiculous, Rovil thought. The apartment intercom began to chime. Gilbert pushed himself up and waddled toward the door, out of Rovil's line of sight. The desk clerk on the other end of the intercom sounded quite worried. Gilbert answered his questions in a low voice, and then said, "Please come up. Someone's been murdered."

Gilbert walked back into the living room. Then something amazing happened. Later (when the drug wore off, and he "came to his senses"), Rovil would change his mind about this, but at the moment, in the sway of the drug, he was sure that Ganesh had made this happen. The god had removed the final obstacle to Rovil's plan.

Gilbert took the knife from Lyda's hand. He wrapped his hand around it, then pressed it into Mikala's bloody chest. Blood smeared Gilbert's sleeve. Then he stood, the knife still in his hand, and waited for the police to arrive.

Rovil, the shy young man who'd sacrificed so many animals, could not understand why this fat man would offer himself in place of Lyda. It was the most selfless act he'd ever seen, and the most senseless.

CHAPTER TWENTY-EIGHT

"For years I could not understand why he did that," Rovil told Ollie. "I thought the drug had made him crazy." His voice was raspy. He'd been lying on the basement floor, talking and weeping for hours. "Why would Gilbert do that? He wasn't the father of the child. What did he care?"

"Why does anyone get up on a cross?" Ollie said.

"Yes," Rovil said. "I understand that now. Finally." He began to cry again. He'd been crying a great deal since Ollie had administered the dosage. After the convulsions and glossolalia, after the wailing and laughing and calling out to unseen powers, Rovil had finally remembered where he was, and what he had done. The avalanche of remorse nearly buried him.

Ollie was getting tired of it. She tried to get him to focus, to answer her questions. At first he only wanted to tell her the Good News that had been revealed to him by Numinous: They were loved; every human was connected to everyone and everything else; they were all part of one organism; and on and on.

"Okay, I got it," she said. "But you have to tell me what you've done."

"Confess my sins," he said. He sat slumped in the loveseat, still tied at the wrists and ankles. His clothes were plastered to him with sweat. "There are just . . . so many."

He began to speak. He told her not only about Mikala's murder, and the poisoning of everyone at Little Sprout, but all the transgressions he had committed before—and so many after. Over a decade at Landon-Rousse he had crafted a trail of evidence that allowed him to pass off NME 110 as his own work. It wouldn't stand up under investigation, but no one at the company was motivated to look their gift horse in its molecular structure.

"Then Lyda called," he said.

Somehow, impossibly, the drug was on the street. The lab analysis of the Logos sheet had removed all doubt. He suspected a leak inside Landon-Rousse. He'd made enemies within the company, he told her. The old Rovil of course suspected that his coworkers would steal from him.

"That's when you hired the cowboy?" Ollie asked.

"Oh no," he said. "I'd hired him long before that, for other work at LR. This was just the latest assignment."

"*What the fuck do you do for Landon-Rousse?*"

He blinked at her through his tears. "Terrible things."

"Jesus Christ," she said. "You've out-conspiracy'd my own brain."

Rovil's theory about a leak at LR disappeared, he said, when Lyda told him about the church. No one with access to ready-made pills would do something so indirect as try to form a church and build printers. Lyda was right—it had to be Edo. But Rovil, even with his resources, could not get close to the man.

"I had no choice but to follow where you two led," Rovil said. "I needed to shut down the church, shut down Edo. No one could know the drug came from Little Sprout. It would ruin me." He winced and smiled. "I didn't care about the company, you see, just my position. My power."

He shook his head. "I don't even understand that person now. There was something wrong with me. I couldn't see it before, but now—now I'm a new person. I feel reborn." He took a breath. "I'm ready to make amends."

"See, that's the thing," Ollie said. "I don't want you to be redeemed." She took the pistol from her pocket. "I find it offensive that someone who's done so much evil should be chemically converted into a saint. I believe—and maybe this is old-fashioned of me, Lyda would think so—I believe that there is a *you* who is responsible. Not a corporation. Not a machine. One person. A soul."

"I agree with you," he said earnestly. "I know now that there's something bigger than this life. Something . . . after."

"I do too," she said.

"If you believe in Hell," he said, "and even if you don't—don't do this. For your sake, don't do something that you'll regret."

"We're almost done," Ollie said. She thumbed the hammer, cocking the gun. "You know what I need to hear."

He nodded. "His name is Vincent."

CHAPTER TWENTY-NINE

I woke in a different room, a smaller space but some-how less crowded. Fewer machines, I realized. So, out of the ICU, then? Rovil wasn't there, no nurses were in sight, and Dr. Gloria . . .

A chill of panic moved through me. I was alone. For the first time in years, truly alone.

I could feel the emptiness where the doctor used to reside. Even when she was angry with me, staying out of sight, I had never felt this absence. I remembered talking to her during the height of the fever, the way she seemed to be slipping away into shadows, the way she leaned over me that final time.

You have been betrayed.

I tried to sit up, but a stab of pain in my shoulder brought me up short. The left side of my body was wrapped in an elaborate sling. I pulled aside the sheet. My right ankle was in an oversized handcuff (footcuff?), which was secured to the bed by a steel chain. What the hell?

I lay back down. My body was heavy with fatigue, and my brain felt sandbagged with painkillers and an-tiepileptics and whatever else they'd pumped into my veins. But the fever was gone. I was fully awake for the first time since the shooting. And all I could think about was Ollie.

Eventually a nurse—a skinny kid who looked, despite

his muttonchops, to be sixteen years old—arrived with a breakfast tray. I pointed to a bouquet of white and red flowers that sat on the windowsill. "Who are those from?" I asked. My voice came out as a croak.

He found the tag. "'Get well soon,'" he read. "'The Millionaires Club.'" He smiled. "Hey, that's nice."

Fuck. Fayza and the Millies had found me.

Hootan was dead, Aaqila was dead or injured . . . and I was alive. Fayza had to assume that I was associated with the cowboy and had set up her people. Could she have sent someone across the border to kill me? Was someone in the hospital right now?

When the police arrived I was almost glad to see them. They were three detectives from the New Mexico State Police. They told me they'd been here twice before, but I'd been too out of it to answer their questions. "How about now?" they asked.

They spoke to me as if I were a criminal. Understandable, I suppose; they knew how egregiously I'd violated my parole. One of them even checked my arm for the missing pellet. It was also clear that they had already talked to Rovil, and there was no telling how much he'd told them.

"Start again from the beginning," one of the other detectives said.

The beginning? I didn't know when that was. Francine? The night Mikala died? Or before that, on the night I first saw her, standing in a crowded room, a wineglass in her hand? And then where to stop—with Dr. Gloria's flaming sword?

I was exhausted and angel-less. There was no narrative line I could skate, no combination of facts and lies I could imagine that would make my position any better. Worse, any details could be used against Ollie and Bobby . . . and Edo. If I incriminated Edo, I would only hurt Sasha.

I said the only thing I could think of: nothing.

My silence made them angry, and they did not give up so easily. At some point one of them said something that got me to react: "You don't have to be afraid of him. We can protect you."

"Afraid of who?" Then I got it. "Wait, he's *alive?*"

"We found blood, and a bloody handprint as he left the house."

The cowboy was alive! I'd been sure he'd been mortally wounded by the doctor's sword. During the fever, that had made perfect sense. I'd even bought her reassurance: *The man who is responsible for this will not bother you again.*

"That lying bitch," I said under my breath.

"Pardon?"

"I thought he was dead," I said.

"Just tell us what you saw," the lead detective said. I shook my head and ignored him. "Okay," he said. "How about Rovil Gupta? Have you heard from him?"

"Rovil? Why?"

"He last checked in with us two days ago. He said he was driving home to New York, but he hasn't arrived at work, and no one has heard from him." He made his voice sound reasonable. "If he attacked the shooter, he's not going to be in trouble. It was clearly self-defense."

"I haven't heard from him since he left me in the ICU."

"Then you wouldn't mind if we looked at your pen?"

"I don't have a pen."

"It's in with your clothes." One of the detectives reached into the cabinet and withdrew a large, clear plastic bag. Inside were smaller bags containing my shirt, my jeans, my shoes. They all looked bloody. "We would like to look at your local or externally stored messages, as well as related files and internet history." He'd said this sentence many times before. The southland was way behind Canada when it came to electronic privacy, but the Supreme Court had set *some* limits.

"Fuck no," I said. "I want my lawyer."

"You don't have a lawyer," he said.

An idea came to me. "Sure I do," I said. "It's the same guy who represents Eduard Vik, Junior."

The detectives looked at each other.

I stopped speaking, which made the interrogation more difficult for them but almost enjoyable for me. They grew more frustrated and I grew more tired, nearly falling asleep between their sentences. Eventually a doctor came in and said I should be resting. The detectives reminded me that I was under arrest and implied that unless I cooperated, they would need to keep me in the US—and not in some cushy hospital. This smelled of bullshit. I was a Canadian citizen, here illegally but only a witness to a crime, not a suspect. Jurisdictionally I was as complicated as an Akwesasne cigarette smuggler. But I didn't have the energy to spar with them.

"One more thing," the lead detective said. "Olivia Skarsten." I didn't bother to open my eyes. He said, "Your hospital said she skipped out the same time as you, and Rovil said she traveled with you as far as Amarillo. I don't suppose you've seen *her*?"

I said nothing.

When they finally left I asked the doctor for a favor. "Jeans, back pocket," I said.

She fished out the pen, then wiped it down with an antiseptic.

Turns out, I had a few messages. The first three were from Ollie.

· · ·

The fever had screwed with my biological clock. For the rest of the week I could not stay awake during the day, but nights I spent staring at the TV or the pen. Mornings crashed through the window like the grille of a Mack truck. Of course that's when the cops liked to time their visits. The detectives came twice more, the second time to tell me that the US Marshal Service would be escorting me back to Canada. Their case was going nowhere. Rovil still hadn't shown up in New York. The descriptions of the cowboy—Esperanza, Sasha, and I largely agreed on what he looked like—hadn't led to anyone.

Every time I wanted to move off the bed, my RN had to find the head nurse to get the key to the leg irons. My skinny, sideburned, day-shift nurse—his name was Dan, but by the time I'd learned that I'd already nicknamed him Baby Chop—helped me hobble back and forth to the bathroom and instructed me on how to shower without soaking my bandages. After five days my body still felt as sturdy as a corn husk, but I was deemed ready to travel. Suddenly I could no longer put off a particularly onerous task.

· · ·

"I got your flowers," I said.

The woman on the other end of the line said, "I'm so glad. We were worried about you." There was no video on the call. An additional restriction was that neither of us knew who else might be listening in.

She said, "I was surprised to hear that you were so far south."

"Yeah, that kind of surprised me myself."

"But you're coming back north soon, I hear."

"Any day now," I said. "They say I'm doing much better."

"I wish I could say the same for others."

"Is, uh, your hairdresser okay?" I asked.

"I wouldn't say 'okay.' Someday, perhaps, but not anytime soon."

"Fuck. I'm sorry to hear that."

"Yes. Well."

"The reason I called . . ."

"I was wondering about that."

"I feel bad about what happened," I said. "To the hairdresser, but also . . . the one who drove your hairdresser."

"I'll pass on your condolences to his family."

"I was hoping to do more than that."

"Really."

"The man who is responsible for the driver is the same man who put me here in the hospital."

"I find that hard to believe."

"He was never on my side. I want you to know that. What happened . . . out east. That was a third party."

"What you want me to know, and what I believe, are miles apart."

"I'm not asking you to take this on faith."

"I'm not sure what you're asking me at all."

"I'm asking for a chance to make amends."

"Amends?"

"Amends," I said.

"What can you possibly offer?"

"A name. And soon, I'll have more than that."

"Go on."

. . .

The morning of my deportation, Baby Chop unchained me and helped me into my new clothes. The hospital—or maybe the police—had provided me with a pair of jeans with an elastic waistband, a floral shirt that must have been popular with the geriatric crowd, and a pair of cheap cotton loafers. The marshals were due any minute. Baby Chop locked me back up just the same.

"You could leave the key," I told him. He laughed good-naturedly and went to his next patient.

I was sitting on the edge of the bed, reading my pen, when the knock came.

"Just a sec," I said. I typed another sentence and the door started to open. "Jesus, hold on!" I closed the pen, then turned awkwardly to see who'd come in.

Eduard looked years older than he had in Chicago. His suit was just as beautiful, but he was missing his tie, and the top two buttons had come undone. He glanced at me, then looked away, fixing his gaze on other objects in the room: the window, the plastic water jug, the black slab of the unpowered TV screen.

"I thought you might stop by," I said.

"The police think my lawyers are representing you," he said. "I told them you were lying."

"Maybe you should rethink that," I said.

He looked at me then. His face was haggard, days away from sleep.

"We're on the same side," I said. "I didn't tell the cops that the chemjet was in your office. Or that you've got blueprints for making more of those machines."

"What are you talking about?" He seemed genuinely confused.

"The paintings from Gilbert Kapernicke. They're instructions. Anybody who looks into it will know he's talked to you—and that you've got the money to manufacture all the NME One-Ten that you want."

"You're out of your mind. You think I want more of you people? You think I want *anyone* to—"

He seemed to realize he was shouting. He glanced at the door, then put his hands on the rail of my bed. "You think I want anyone to be like *Sasha*? Like you?"

"I believe you," I said. And I did. Eduard Jr. wasn't the one who started a new religion to distribute Numinous. And he wasn't the guy who made a deal with Big Pharm to manufacture it. Eduard, like his father, had been used.

Finally I said, "How is she?"

He said nothing for a time. "She's fine." Then he shook his head. "No. That's not true. She's a wreck. After what she saw . . . She loved my father very much."

"I know you'll take care of her," I said.

This seemed to make him angry. "You'll have nothing to do with her," he said. "I'll make sure that Sasha never sees you again."

"Don't do that. You shouldn't punish her like that. If she wants to talk to me, at least let her—"

"You're poison," he said. "You brought death to our house."

That was true. I had led death straight to their door. Straight to Sasha.

"I *am* unfit," I said. "I know that. I don't want to be her parent; I just want to be . . . I don't know, *there*. To answer her questions."

He shook his head. "You'll never have the opportunity to hurt her again."

My bearded and baby-faced nurse entered the room, looking concerned. Eduard said, "I was just leaving."

"Wait," I said. "At least do this for her. Keep Esperanza."

"What?"

"Don't fire her. Sasha needs her."

"I'll decide what she needs and what she doesn't," he said. "I'm her father." He pushed past the nurse and walked out.

I flipped the pen back open. On the screen it said, *Is he there?*

Just left, I typed. *Thanks for the warning.*

No prob.

My nurse said, "It's time to go, Lyda. Do you need any help with your things?"

"I'm good." I typed, *Are you okay? How was the therapist?*

Talkety talkety talk.

Was she nice?

I guess. Ed and Suz keep asking me how I'm doing. Weird.

Two cops, a man and a woman, entered the room. I didn't recognize the uniforms, but I assumed these were the US marshals. I pretended I didn't see them and kept typing.

Last message for a while. Taking me to airport now.

Then prison?

Yup.

!!!! Aren't you scared?

I wondered, should I tell her that this wouldn't be the first time? Surely a ten-year-old didn't need to know that her mother was a hardened criminal. *I'll be fine,* I typed.

TWO YEARS!!!!!

Maybe less. Depends.

One of the marshals said, "Let's go."

Tell your angel to watch over you, she typed.

. . .

I was evidently too dangerous to be held by mere leg irons. The marshals manacled both ankles, then circled me with a waist chain. My damaged arm couldn't be moved to the sling, so they handcuffed my remaining arm to the chain. Then they took my pen and placed it in a bag with the other surviving personal items: a HashCash card; a smartpaper sketch of a pirate bear; my brass wedding ring. I signed a paper that consigned them to the care of the US government.

At least I didn't have to shuffle through the whole hospital. Baby Chop brought a wheelchair and thoughtfully covered my new hardware with a blanket.

Outside, the sky was a clear, cloudless blue. It was before 10 a.m., but already the day was heating up. The marshals helped me out of the chair and led me to a white van. The male marshal opened the side door and helped me into the bench seat. He even buckled my seat belt for me.

A movement outside caught my attention. Past the marshal, standing at the edge of the parking lot, stood a small person in a big jacket, wearing a baseball cap pulled low. Her hand lifted a second time, at waist height. Her fingers slowly opened.

I opened my fingers in answer. The van door slid closed, and a minute later we were rolling north, dragging my heart behind me like an anchor.

CHAPTER THIRTY

Vinnie woke up with a shout, the image of a gleaming metal blade blazing before his eyes. Then he realized that he was behind the wheel of a moving car, and he shouted again.

The rear end of a vehicle was in the lane ahead of him, and he was rushing toward it. He slammed on the brakes, and a jolt of pain shot up his leg, tore at his gut. He felt like his stomach had been torn in half.

The pain made him drop his foot from the pedal. The car swerved, and he corrected, but each movement sent another wrenching pain through him. He was wide awake now, and terrified. He moved his left foot to cover the brake, and eased to the side of the road. He was on the interstate. Thank God no one had been right behind him.

He was dressed in a suit, though his shirt was open. Bloody bandages wrapped his abdomen. The inside of the car was a mess. Crumpled bags from fast food chains, plastic bottles of Black Lightning energy drink, a wad of bloody gauze bandages. He'd thrown up somewhere in the car, and the stench was terrible. Most shocking was the condition of the Seratelli; the black hat had fallen onto the floor of the passenger side with the rest of the trash. Foul, bloody napkins and bandages were piled inside it.

What had happened? If he had time to concentrate, he could recall those memories. After all, everything that happened to the Vincent also happened to him. The calm, confident veneer that *made* him the Vincent was gone, evaporated between moments while he was hurtling down the highway at sixty-five miles per hour.

This had never happened before.

All other times when he'd worked as the Vincent, he had returned home with plenty of Evanimex in his system. Over the course of a few days he came down, returning to his old personality like a glider returning to earth. But this time the drug had worn off—and suddenly, in a rush of terror.

On the seat beside him, mixed in with the garbage, were a pistol and two pill bottles. The one that used to contain Evanimex was empty. The Vicodin bottle, thank God, was half-full. He found a bit of liquid at the bottom of a Black Lightning bottle and swallowed half a dozen of the pills. He was soaked in sweat, and every movement sent pain racketing through his body. He wanted to lie down, but he knew that falling asleep in the car was inviting the police to investigate. He had to keep moving.

Tears rolled from his eyes. *This wasn't fair!*

He started the car again. The GPS told him he was thirteen hours from home.

· · ·

The apartment was dark, and strangely silent. The air smelled of death. He flipped on a light and moaned.

In the center of the kitchen floor, a bison cow, barely three inches long, lay on its side, dead. How had it gotten in here? It shouldn't have been able to get through the barrier. The air stank of grease and methane. On the counter was a cutting board, and beside it a small pile of fur and bones.

Al, he thought. Al, the neighbor he'd trusted, had been eating the herd.

He hobbled to the living room, trying to keep his weight on his left leg. The grow lights were off, even though it was daytime. The living prairie grass had turned brown, and was dying in vast patches. He could not see any of his bison. Where was the herd?

He made his way back to the bedroom. There he found the Poomba, inert, in the middle of the carpet. The little robot was dead, not even an indicator light. The herd was nowhere in sight.

Then he heard a faint chirp, the high-pitched grunt of the micro bison. He braced himself against the bed and dropped to one knee, grimacing from the pain. If not for the Vicodin he would have passed out. Slowly he lay down on the dry, sickly grass. There under the bed was a pair of cows.

Two, out of thirty-eight.

Al would pay for this. A man's herd was sacred. Vinnie would become the Vincent, get his gun, and take that walk down that hallway. . . .

He passed out dreaming of frontier justice.

. . .

Someone was knocking at his door. Banging, really. He wasn't sure how long the noise had been going on, but soon enough it stopped. He was drifting between sleep and wakefulness on a raft made of pain.

He heard a deep voice. *Al.* Coming to poach the last of his cattle. He struggled to open his eyes. He needed the Vincent's gun. Where was the gun?

"You can go," another voice said. This one was female. "I'm his sister."

"What's the matter with him?"

"Accident," she said. "I'll take it from here."

"Just tell him it wasn't my fault," Al said. "He was supposed to come back in a couple days! The critters just started dying. What was I supposed to do?"

"Don't worry about it."

Some time passed. Lights came on, and he shut his eyes.

"Do you know who I am?" the female voice said.

He tried to guess. The Vincent's memories were hard to sort through. Was it the red-haired one? Or the tiny one? If it was the tiny one . . . that would be bad. The Vincent had been afraid of what she could do.

"You shot my girlfriend," she said.

"It wasn't me," he said.

"I'm getting tired of hearing that."

She crouched next to him. He heard a click, and then the woman was talking to someone else on the phone.

"I'm here," she said. There was a pause. "Right. Is Aaqila ready for the video?"

The woman touched Vinnie on the face. "Open your eyes, Vincent.

That's it." He was looking at the pinhole camera of a pen. Then the woman said, "See? It's him. I'm sending the address now."

Another silence, and then the woman said, "So we're good?"

A moment later the woman clicked off the pen. She seemed very satisfied. "We've got some time," she said. "Tell me all about yourself."

CHAPTER THIRTY-ONE

My father used to say that every evil in Canada could be found within a mile of the 401, and he would have included the Elgin-Middlesex Detention Centre. The EMDC was an overcrowded, aging prison campus a couple hours southwest of Toronto, in London. After six months I'd had enough of the place. Unfortunately they made me stay another year and a half.

Bobby had been pacing the waiting room, and when I finally appeared he galloped to me and crushed me in a hug. The treasure chest still hung from his neck, though now it hung from a metal chain.

"How you doing, kid?" I asked him. "Still hanging in there?" He didn't get the joke.

Toronto was no place for me—I still didn't quite trust Fayza to abide by our deal—so instead we drove north, toward Lake Huron. The trees were ablaze with color. I'd missed a few seasons while inside, and I was glad to get out before the snow came down.

Our destination was over three hours away, but Bobby seemed prepared to deliver a monologue that lasted the entire trip. He had a new roommate who had a set of weird habits completely different from the weird habits of all previous roommates. He'd gotten a new job, working in a distribution center for a big on-line site. He'd stayed off drugs like I'd asked.

"How's Lamont?"

"Oh," he said. "I had to give him up. No cats allowed in the new place."

He wanted stories from prison. "Like what?" I asked. "Showers? Pillow fights? Nazi lesbian guards?"

"No! I mean . . . no! I was talking about, I don't know, escape attempts?"

"No escapes, kid. It was actually weirdly calm."

"Oh." He sounded disappointed.

We stopped for supper at an Italian place that promised Killer Kalzones. I went into the bathroom and opened the little plastic bag given to me by the helpful doctors of the Ministry of Public Safety and Security. Inside was a bottle of 120 pills of phenacemide, the antiepileptic I'd been taking while in their care. Best to take with food. I looked myself in the mirror as I swallowed two pills. The only person looking back was me.

It was well past dark when we arrived in Meaford, a little town on the shore. My mother had grown up there. The car directed Bobby west of town. Bobby pulled in the driveway and cut the lights. The windows of the farmhouse were dark.

"This is it, right?" Bobby asked.

"Yeah, I just thought . . . Well. You want to come in? It's too far to drive back to Toronto tonight."

"Are you sure?"

"You like sleepovers, don't you?"

We went up the steps. The email I'd gotten said the key would be under a ceramic pot, which I hoped I could find in the dark. Before I could look down, the door opened and the lights flicked on.

Ollie. Her expression was worried. She looked at my face, but her eyes weren't quite tracking mine.

"It's me," I said.

Her face lit up. The visual was hard for her when she was on her meds, but voices always broke through.

She pulled my face down to hers and kissed me fiercely. We stood like that for a long time, unwilling to let each other go.

Something brushed past my ankles. I broke the kiss and looked down. "Is that *Lamont?*"

"Still clean and sober," Ollie said.

"Poor bastard."

. . .

Ollie had made a cake, but wouldn't let us eat it.

"What are we waiting for?" I asked.

She wouldn't answer. Playing coy.

Bobby lay on the floor, trying to get Lamont interested in a catnip-filled mouse, but the cat was taking a hard-line antidrug approach. Ollie and I sat on the couch, leaning into each other, holding hands like teenagers. We didn't need to talk; we'd done nothing but talk for twenty-four months. In prison, no cell phones, pens, or internet-capable devices were allowed, but it was impossible to keep them out; just about everything these days was an internet-capable device. My second day at the EMDC I traded my dessert for a piece of smartpaper with a Wi-Fi connection. On our first call, Ollie walked me through installing what she called "real" encryption software. Every night we talked about the past—including everything she'd learned from Rovil and his sociopath-for-hire—and about the future. We burned up the airwaves with our words.

While we waited for the proper, secret time to have cake, Ollie showed me the latest news on one of our most frequent topics. Numinous was spreading through the States and Canada's biggest cities. The Landon-Rousse scandal, and Rovil Gupta's video confession, recorded just before he disappeared, had only accelerated curiosity about the drug. Stepladder was dead, but NME 110 was alive and well. It had spread beyond the walls of the Church of the Hologrammatic God. The chemjet blueprints were all over the internet. Numinous was a recreational drug now, with all that entailed: theme parties, overdoses, suicides, novelty T-shirts.

"I didn't think it would happen so fast," I said.

"We've never had something like this before."

"Sure we have," I said. "It was called the Great Awakening. But this time the crash is going to be bad."

The message icon on the screen blinked on, and Ollie flicked her hand at it. The screen changed to show a hand-lettered sign that said WELCOME HOME!

The sign dropped away. Sasha, looking sophisticated in a pale green dress, opened her arms in a ta-da.

She had only a few minutes until Eduard and Suzette checked on her, so we ate quickly. On her side of the screen Sasha bounced on the edge of her bed while eating one of Esperanza's cookies.

I leaned over to Ollie and whispered, "She has little girl boobies."

"I know," she whispered back.

"Should we tell her about bras?"

"Not in front of Bobby we don't," Ollie said.

The eating didn't interrupt Sasha's texting; the words scrolled across the bottom of the screen almost too fast to read. *It seems like we should have a chair for Dr. Gloria,* she said.

"That party's over," I said. "She's long gone."

YOU CAN'T JUST THROW HER AWAY!!

"Kid, there's nothing to throw away."

Just 'cause she's imaginary, doesn't mean she's not real, Sasha said. *You can't throw away yourSELF.*

. . .

Meaford was a small town, but even here there were cameras in the stores. Our faces would eventually pop up in some database, and anyone with enough money and energy would be able to find us. Fayza, for example. We'd have to keep moving, even if it meant breaking my parole.

But there was one person I wanted to find me. It took a few days, but I finally was able to get a message through to him. The call came on what felt like the last day of fall, a cold wind whipping off the lake, picking off the last of the leaves from their limbs.

"Hey, Gil. Thank you for calling me."

"Gil is pleased to see you," the god said. His face was still thin and bony, with the strong cheekbones of a prophet.

"I'd rather we talked in person, but . . ."

He nodded. We were both convicted felons. He could never cross over to Canada, and I'd never set foot in the States again. Legally, at least.

"I never thanked you," I said. "For what you did."

"Thanks aren't necessary. We did it not only for you, but for the child. And we knew that Gil needed to be in prison, among those people, to start the ministry."

Sure, I thought. That's always the way with divine plans. No such thing as an accident.

"Can I tell you a story?" I said. "About three months into my sentence I got cornered. A couple of women I'd pissed off—it's too complicated to explain. They caught me in a bathroom. One of them had a knife. I should have died.

"But here's the crazy thing. Four other women I'd never met burst in and saved me. I didn't get a scratch. Afterward, they gave me a slip of paper. You know what it said?"

He smiled.

"Half of EMDC is on Numinous," I said. "The male units, the female unit I was in—paper is flowing through there every day. Some of the guards are converts. They think it's their duty to spread the word. I wouldn't be surprised if one of your chemjets was running in a back room."

"It's been known to happen," Gil said.

"The first time I ever saw one of them was in a church in Toronto. I thought, Edo built this. I thought only a rich man could afford to make it."

"Churches raise money," Gil said. "That's what they do. Even peasants can build a cathedral."

"But you're losing control," I said. "Numinous may have started in the prisons with you, but it's out there on its own now. It's a party drug. Frat boys are getting religion."

"We never wanted *control*," Gil said.

"What *do* you want?"

He smiled deprecatingly. "For people to know me," he said. "That's why I sent the printer and pictures to Edo, so that he would see what I was doing, and share. I wanted him to know me. And you as well, Lyda."

"I know you," I said. "You're not a god; you're a symptom. Now that people can get the drug outside of your church, it'll lose its mystique. Once people understand how NME affects the brain—"

"It won't make any difference," Gil said. "The more people hear of it, the more people will try it—and then they'll never go back."

"Unless they overdose or die," I said. "Numinous can't escape the physics of tolerance. People will stop being able to feel God's love as intensely as before, and they'll have to ramp up the dosage. It's already happening."

"Then we'll print more," Gil said.

"Jesus, Gil, you want more overdoses? Freaks like us? And what about the people who can't get the drug after they've used it? Emergency rooms are already filling with Francines, looking for a shortcut to the afterlife."

"Francines?"

"A girl. She was the first person I met from your church. She killed herself after she went into withdrawal."

"Was she so happy before she came to the church?"

I didn't want to answer that.

"People *need* the divine in their lives," Gil said. "Science is a pale, unconvincing story compared to faith. You offer nothing—a mind that dies with the body. Numinous offers a living god. A god of love."

"You're an obese IT geek who overdosed on an experiment."

He laughed hard. "Formerly obese," he said after he'd recovered. "But yes, that's true." He wiped away a tear of laughter. "Nobody jokes with me anymore. Too awestruck."

"I knew you when," I said. "If you're God, we're all screwed."

Gil caught his breath. "Don't be afraid of what's coming," he said. "Everything's going to be all right. Think of those prisoners who saved you. Think of the old Gil, the old Edo and Lyda—even Rovil. Even if it's just a drug, and I am lying to you now about being a deity—aren't we better people than we were before?"

THE PARABLE OF
the Faithful Atheist

There was a scientist who did not believe in gods or fairies or supernatural creatures of any sort. But she had once known an angel, and had talked to her every day. Mostly they argued, often about whether or not the angel existed. The scientist finally won the argument by trapping the angel inside a prescription bottle.

One day, two years after the angel had been captured, the scientist grew curious and decided to look inside the bottle. She opened the lid and peeked inside. She saw nothing but pills. Then she tossed out the pills. But still the angel was nowhere to be found.

This confused the scientist, and also saddened her.

Sometime later, in the middle of winter, she went walking in the woods, and came upon a man sitting on a rock. The snow was piled all around him, and he looked like he'd been there for some time. He was a white man with ruddy skin and a great halo of gray hair.

The scientist stopped, and was very afraid. She had seen this man twice before, once in a city in the north, and once in another city hundreds of miles away to the southeast, and now here, in the northern woods. He did not look like the kind of man who could afford airplane tickets. He was dressed in many layers of clothing. The outmost coat was crusted with snow and dirt. Below were jackets, fleeces, sweaters, dress shirts, and T-shirts, each layer older than the one above it, like geological strata. At the man's feet, resting against the base of the rock he sat upon, was a bulging black garbage bag that the scientist assumed contained all the man's worldly possessions.

The scientist overcame her fear and marched up to the man. "What the fuck are you doing here?" she said.

The man said nothing. He sat on the rock, looking down at his black bag.

"You think this is funny?" the scientist said. "This magical hobo shit? My god, why didn't you make yourself black, too? I mean, Jesus, what's the point?"

The man became very still. His skin grew pale as porcelain. Hairline fractures appeared, and then began to split wide. Light burned through the seams, and the scientist fell back, holding up a hand against the light. With a sound like a crack of thunder, the man's outer shell shattered and fell away, clothing and skin and hair crackling like glass, until the angel was revealed.

"Behold," Dr. Gloria said. For that was the angel's name.

"You are such a fucking drama queen," the scientist said.

"I told you I would be with you always," Dr. Gloria said. She stepped down from the rock and flexed her wings. In her hand was a notepad bursting with hundreds of pages.

"That trick at Edo's," the scientist said. "That thing with the sword? I know why you did it."

"What trick?" the angel said innocently. She blew some snow from the top page on the pad.

"What do you have there?" the scientist asked.

"Oh," the angel said. "I've been working on a book of parables."

—G.I.E.D.

ACKNOWLEDGMENTS

I would like to acknowledge that I am a lucky man.

For example, I have in my corner the agent Martha Millard, whose enthusiasm for this book when it was nothing but a synopsis got me fired up to write it.

I am extremely fortunate to have David Hartwell as my editor. He was an early supporter of my short stories, and then insisted that I send him the early chapters of this book. Somehow he saw some potential for a novel despite their disheveled state. He introduced me to the fine people at Tor, including Alex Cameron and Marco Palmieri, who helped put this book together.

The right books fell into my hands when I needed them. I'm indebted to the work of the neuroscientists Antonio Damasio, V. S. Ramachandran, and Oliver Sacks, as well as to that of the philosophers and scientists Richard Dawkins, Daniel Dennett, Christopher Hitchens, and Daniel Wegner.

This book wouldn't have been completed without three retreats that came along at the best possible time, in the company of the right people, in three inspiring locations. The book was begun on a beach on the Atlantic, with C. C. Finlay and the Blue Heaven crew. The final sprint on the first draft took place in a cabin in the Poconos, alongside Matt Sturges and Dave Justus. The second draft was completed within spitting distance of the Pacific, at Patrick Swenson's fabulous Rainforest Writers Retreat.

But I am especially lucky to have such great friends and family who read this book in draft form and offered advice. My thanks to these readers, in geographical order from east to west: Kathy Bieschke, who lives right here in our home; Gary Delafield, Elizabeth Delafield, and Mary

"Gold Star" McClanahan in State College, Pennsylvania; Kevin McCullough Wabaunsee of Chicago, who shared his experiences working in a neuroscience lab, including the secrets of rat sacrifice; Kurt Dinan in Hamilton, Ohio; Dave Justus and Matt Sturges in Austin; and Nancy Kress and Jack Skillingstead in Seattle. Adam Rakunas, in far-off Santa Monica, not only read the book, he allowed me to rustle the miniature bison from his story "Oh Give Me a Home" and shrink them to apartment-sized critters.

In a surprise twist, the best copy editor on the planet, Deanna Hoak, moved to my little town so we could go over the manuscript in person.

Finally, Kathy, Ian, and Emma put up with me when I was distracted and missed me when I was gone.

See? Damn lucky.